# Ravens
# Raid

## Sojourner 5

*Catherine Gruben Smith*

*Illustrated by*
*Emilie Gruben*

*Sola Deo Gloria*

*Scan for a curated playlist of mood music!*

*"And hope maketh not ashamed; because the love of God is shed abroad in our hearts by the Holy Ghost which is given unto us."*
*- Romans 5:5*

*To My Anna: Remember you have an influence on everyone around you, and it can flow through generations. Use your strength and wisdom wisely, my girl.*

*Note to Readers:*

*Sign language is another language, not just a form of English. A signer thinks in pictures, they sign what they see, not full sentences. I translate Joe's dialogue as I would any language; making it smooth and sensible in English, just as someone would do in their mind when watching a signer.*

# Contents

# Introduction

The rubber ball bounced against the corner of the wall and back up to Will. His massive fist closed on it and sent it back in the same second. The sound of rubber hitting wood floors, bricks, and human flesh came again, and again, and again. Jill closed her eyes and pinched the bridge of her nose.

"Are we close to time?" Bill asked. Huskiness clung to his voice from the strain of waiting as he paced over the wooden floor. The boards squeaked with each step. Jill's eyes flitted to the clock on the wall behind him.

"Wolf said six," she answered. The perfect rhythm of the rubber ball, "thump, thump, thump," underlaid everything like a madman's song. "It's thirty seconds short."

The small house on the outskirts of Paradise, capital city of the People's Kingdom, held only one large central room. Will's hair brushed the ceiling when he stood. The furnishings were simple and practical. But it boasted fresh paint, solid walls, and none of the stinking mud that clung to everything out here in the summer months. For Paradise that made it almost opulent.

Jill's lips began to move, silently counting out the seconds. She found herself counting to the rhythm of the ball's incessant bouncing.

A bright light burst in the room and the ball melted into a puddle of bubbling plastic.

"Honestly, how long were you going to stand that?" Wolf's voice broke from the top of the room. The trio spun, pulses racing. Their security measures stayed on, untouched, untripped. But in the single gray chair by the burning fireplace a figure slowly lay a hot Ruby pistol on his leg. A retractable metal military helmet hid his face. It distorted the voice, making it muffled and metallic enough to avoid any recognition. For an instant Jill felt immensely relieved an actual human sat in front of them. Then a chill ran through her and she almost wished the Wolf was something different, something not-so-human. His actions proved him too much of a monster to be comforted by a human form. "I thought I would go insane with that noise that just went on and on."

"Get me a new ball," Will demanded in his deep gravelly voice, his huge hands closing into fists. Bill spoke over him, drowning out Will's words with what came out as a high-pitched squeak.

"How long have you been sitting there?"

"Too long to ignore the 'thump, thump, thump,' how are you still sane? Never mind, you're rational enough to work this job." The Wolf gained his feet in a smooth quick move, his bearing excited. Another chill went down Jill as she stared at the bug-like compound eyes on the helmet and wondered what expression went on underneath it. "Tonight, minions. You three will clear the way and I will take the *Communist Manifesto* from the perfect little red room where it's waiting for us. Given the nature of the country, we will have to wait a few months for the payoff. Or bring disintegration and take what we want during the chaos. Either option will bring large dividends, and it will be all ours. This is nearly our last heist, and we will fall back, enjoy our spoils, and wait. In another few months we will take Story Land's book, and that will truly be our last. All of the major kingdoms will then have been spoiled by my brilliance, and know their own vulnerability!"

Bill cleared his throat nervously, then stopped, shifting from one foot to the other. Jill jabbed him in the ribs impatiently. The Wolf's head lifted, his hands going to his hips, and Jill could tell underneath all that metal protective shielding, his eyes rolled heavenward in exasperation.

"Look Wolf," she burst out, "we were just wondering what happens after you retire. Powerful people don't like having their vulnerabilities pointed out, and there's going to be a world-wide hunt for the book thieves. It's not going to be much fun enjoying the spoils if we have to keep watching over our shoulder all the time. Have you given any thought to..." Her courage faltered when she came right to it, and Jill's throat closed, hot and thick with her own fear. The metal mask turned

and the huge bug-like eyes stared at her.

"I'm not planning on making you the fall guys," Wolf said. Contempt and amusement rode the tone. But relief filled the Trio too strongly to take offense. "I have a much better one than you." Hatred crept into the voice, making it thicker and deeper. "Who is it the Raven protects with all his little being? Who is it the whole world already wants to eliminate and destroy?"

"Can't fix it on two people," Will growled, his big brow furrowing in confusion.

"The Way," Jill and Bill both chorused, and Will's forehead cleared. The metal mask gave a single nod.

"I have evidence ready to plant in the major kingdoms, pointing out the IDP[1] as the perpetrators of the book thefts. Details and facts only the thieves themselves could know, all obviously gathered by someone inside the IDP, things no one can argue," the Wolf said, smug and happy. A laugh spilled from Bill.

"That's a work of brilliance," he said. "The whole world already hates the Christians, you've found a uniting point for the hunt. Nothing can withstand that kind of a chase, it will be a massacre! And the Raven will be in the front lines of every attack, trying to keep the tide of death from happening. He will be one of the first to go."

"I'd rather he's the last, after he watches the rest of his precious people slaughtered around him," the Wolf stated. "But we don't really have to worry about him. He's a GI, how much do we have to fear from a creature like that?"

"What?!" the Trio burst out, every spine straightening.

"A little shocking, sure, to find out the one who managed to set us twice is actually a GI beasty, I know," Wolf said, waving a hand airily. "But we grew careless. We thought no one knew we were out there. Now we know better, and no one will know our

---

[1] The International Discipleship Program, the name of the Christian underground running through most kingdoms. Because being a Christian is dangerous in most places, the IDP use a necklace for identifying brethren. Each person chooses their own personal symbol to mask the identifier, but when activated, the metal rearranges to become the universal IDP cross.

plans till it is too late. What, Jill?" Wolf barked, and Jill leapt a foot, cursing herself for having let her hesitation show on her face.

"I just thought," she stammered, "I mean, he may be a GI, but he has set us twice now, and I...if you know so much about him, why not just kill him now?"

"I want what he knows," the Wolf growled, the hatred deep and strong and almost vibrating out of him. "I want to watch him dance for me, and tell me about this treasure he's hiding."

"He's hiding the treasure you've been chasing?" Jill asked, trying to make it neutral. Her doubt and surprise still came through.

"He's the one who sent you after those journal pages, and he can get more, I'm certain of it! Somewhere in those pages is the key I'm missing. *And* he knows where Ariel is. Because of that she-wolf, I'm still having to play the game under the radar to keep out of her claws, and I tire of it. The Raven is hiding facts from me. A few more months, and I'll have him dancing to my tune. When he no longer amuses me, then we kill him." Wolf's hands clapped together with a sound like a pistol shot and rubbed enthusiastically. "Now, tonight, minions! Tonight we move in on the *Manifesto* and bring home one of our largest takes." The Wolf reached into his gray, fur-lined coat and flung a large paper flat on the table with a flourish.

"The Brotherhood's House. Most secure and well patrolled place in the People's Kingdom. A hundred soldiers comb through the halls each day, most of them fresh and eager and ready to notice anything out of the ordinary. But we will waltz in tonight and take that book without a trace. We're keeping it simple; too many details leave too many things to go wrong. We all get to do what we do best. You three come in from the roof with your gliders. Keep your interference running strong, and make it local. We want a bubble around the three of you as you move, showing your path."

"You want them to see our path?" Jill said doubtfully.

"Shut up and listen," Wolf snapped. "Keep exactly to the

timing I have written down. If you miss it by a minute it could
ruin it all. This is your entry point, make it fast. Slide inside and
go to the book room. Don't let anyone give the alarm on your
route. Will, a few dead bodies found after you leave would add
to the chaos, but only if you happen to pass someone on the
way. Get to the book room. Then set off the alarm." A strangled
noise came from Jill and Bill but the Wolf's hand rose in a sharp
order to stop complaining and listen. "Don't go in the room.
Your exit point is right above you. Blow a hole in the ceiling,
hop to the next level, blow a hole on to the roof, scoot out, grab
your gliders and go. You'll have plenty of time to get out before
anyone arrives on the scene. Then chaos erupts behind you.
And in the midst of it, I stroll in, tuck the book in my pocket,
leave a blank substitute, and stroll out again." The Wolf's hand
came off the paper as he straightened, his bearing triumphant.
The Trio stared at the notes scrawled over the blueprint, studying the angles. "Do your part and we have easy access to our
next book."

Across the town of Paradise inside the Brotherhood's House
rests a five-by-five square affectionately known as the Listening Room. The soldiers of the People's Kingdom use it to monitor the citizen's loyalty to the state. Most businesses and homes
have a government planted listening device, and the soldiers
cycle through them randomly, on the alert for any suspicious
activity.

The Wolf knows the Listening Room, of course, and blocked
the government signals on his entry into the small house on the
outskirts of town.

But it only takes one person to change a country, and even
the Wolf can't know all things.

A knothole in the wooden floor underneath the gray chair
boasted a tiny protuberance on its side. Neil Hanson, citizen

contractor to the People's Kingdom, quietly reached for his pen and pad of paper as he sat in the Listening Room that gray morning, the headphones over his ears. The soldiers on duty grimaced, assuming he would be making tune-ups for the rest of the day, and they would have a whole new set of protocols to learn. But they were too well trained to comment. His pen began to scratch at a quick pace, his face concentrated as he listened.

The UPC[2] would be very pleased with his work today. A smile twitched over his face as he heard the perfect clarity of his own Hanson 200 drifting through the headphones. The voices came in flawless precision, and obviously it had escaped detection.

Today, his new device might save a whole kingdom.

---

[2] United Peoples Commission, a secularist group running under most kingdoms in the Book Base Age employing handpicked, specially trained agents to help shape the world according to their ideas and protect those they deem need it. The UPC do not approve of Christians.

# Chapter One: A Morning in Paradise

*"For, brethren, ye have been called unto liberty; only use not liberty for an occasion to the flesh, but by love serve one another." Galatians 5:13*

Joe spun and danced on his rhythm makers. His hair whipped into his face, tickling till he wanted to sneeze and laugh. A reel zinged around the square in Anna's superb voice. She laughed as she sang, her own enjoyment streaming out to invade the audience. Nehemiah sat the guitar back on its stand and Joe swirled to the next rhythm set. As their final encore (Joe drew the line at three), Anna and Nehemiah both joined the mute. Nehi leapt into the rhythm makers, catching the beat and creating new ones. Joe spun out to snatch his whistles, and spun back in again with a grin. Anna leapt in at his heels and the three moved around each other in perfect timing and harmony. Joe set whistles to his lips and sent the reel dancing around the square with the astounding rhythm setting it off. It rebounded around the gray square on the outskirts of town, bouncing off the sagging tenement houses and the broken gray fountain. But Joe didn't notice the soldiers who had wandered in to listen, or the dirty townspeople gaping at the spectacle, or even the dilapidated town around him. The music claimed him.

It was perfect. Every beat spun. Every note danced in the right way. The world felt right when the music danced in perfection. Joe wished he could stay here for the rest of his life, with Anna and Nehemiah beside him, creating perfect music to the honor of God. For a moment he longed for it with such strength his heart physically ached. But all things must come to an end. And the longer he let it lag, the better chance at a mistake, such as a bruised knee or stomach from a foot flying the wrong direction. Joe began to slow the reel down. Anna twirled out of the rhythm makers and started to sing again, a little breathlessly, just enough to make her voice laughing. Joe spun out, harmonizing on his whistles, and Nehemiah slowed the rhythm down to match the change in music. They came to the last phrase, Nehemiah dropped out, Anna stopped, and Joe let the last note hang, a solitary, clear, haunting note. He drew his whistles away.

Silence.

The mute closed his eyes and a smile flitted over his face; a look of peace, of perfect joy and exultation, beautified his scarred face. That lovely, perfect silence after a perfect song. The audience taking a breath of awe before it erupted. A tingling thrill of wonder, excitement, and human harmony, all in that single instant. To Joe it was God's applause for a job well done.

The concrete square erupted with noise. The ragged townspeople yelled and whistled, most of them too tightly packed to free their arms for applause. People leaned out from the ramshackle houses of hewn wood and plaster that had long ago begun to rot and peel, adding the applause. The noise merged into an enormous roar of enthusiasm. Joe bowed with Anna and Nehemiah once, turned, and began to reattach the rhythm makers to the wagon. The reaction felt so normal by now even the twins hardly noticed the wild fervor of the crowd.

"I'm surprised to see how many people showed up for a concert at eight in the morning! We made a good first performance here," Anna said as she helped pack up.

"Perfect," Joe signed with a smile, keeping the sign small as he faced the wagon. *We're in the Boarding Quarter and caught the factories' night shift just as they got back to their rooms, of course we had a good crowd,* Joe thought. But he didn't sign it. Too many people might notice it out here. But Anna took his single word, grinned at him, and shook her finger.

"Next time, don't put a perfect performance over people, and I won't lecture you about wearing out your musicians with over-practice."

Joe quickly put his hand on his hip and leaned forward, shaking his finger and looking sideways at the beautiful young

woman. It was such a perfect imitation of Anna in lecture mode that Nehemiah burst out laughing. Joe went back to putting away the instruments as Anna grinned at him and spun away to gather the violin. It felt nice to be able to tease someone. Poor old Glue always took it literally. The instruments swiftly went in place, and Daniel strolled back from his last collection. Not much, but then Joe hadn't expected much. Not here. They hardly had enough to buy food here. He carried a full hat, though. Not bad for the People's Kingdom. Daniel handed the hat to Anna; their official bookkeeper since she had the best head for figures. Joe watched out of the corner of his eyes as he worked quickly with the instruments. It would have been nice to have that money with him today...but he could do fine without it.

"Now, what's for breakfast for the late risers?" Daniel asked. His sister laughed.

"You keep lying huddled in your blanket until after I have it all cleared away," she said. "Go find something yourself, lazybones." Daniel started muttering complaints about the insult, but Anna turned to Joe, ignoring her brother. "We have a check-in with Paul in ten minutes, remember? He said Peter and Elizabeth won't be there, but he wasn't allowed to tell us why because they wanted to do it when they have the chance. I'm hoping they're off wedding planning and I can cajole a date out of Paul." Joe nodded, idly wondering what it was like to attend a wedding.

"I think you're just mean to clean it all up before I get to eat," Daniel butted in. Anna made a face at him and they ducked inside to work on dividing and hunt for food, still bickering good naturedly. Joe started Prissy back toward their little meadow outside of town. The wagon hissed and shifted back and forth as it hovered over the muddy road, wet from the foul bogs they had splashed through to get here. Joe turned toward the back of the seat to hide his signs from the curious glances of the people they passed on the street.

"Hooray for a pig who does not mind muds, think of the

trouble and how big the suds!" he signed to the wood, his green eyes twinkling at Nehemiah. His gloves spit it back out again in their computerized way, so Nehi didn't have to turn around and stare to catch it.

"Bathing Prissy in this country so boggy, would be a fool's errand and really quite soggy," Nehi grinned, shifting the pig's steering stick to guide her around a young man standing in the middle of the potholed street, staring around him like a haunted, lost soul. "What's with all the vagrants in this place? Half the populace looks like out of work beggars." Joe's eyes lost their smile.

"They have wandered from the Traitor's Quarter," Joe signed. Nehemiah quickly started asking what that meant, but Joe ignored him. He checked a sigh as he realized Nehemiah could handle the wagon just fine and there was no excuse for him to stay longer. The mute turned back to the wooden seat again, pretending to hunt for something as a cover for his signs. "I have some errands to run, Knee-High. Think you can make it back to the meadow and keep yourselves safe?" Nehemiah's smile faded. His thoughtful gaze turned on Joe, studying the mute. Joe kept his expression unreadable.

"Yes," Nehemiah sighed. "I wish you would let me come along. I don't like you wandering around on your own here, and don't care what errands you're running. If you would just open up a little, and let us help..." Inside, Joe winced and curled around himself, looking again for a way out. He finally had a friend who cared about him, and he kept having to shove him out at arm's length. It hurt to do it again. But the mute just shrugged on the outside.

"I will be fine. Tell Beauty I will not be back for supper," Joe signed.

"When should we start worrying about you?" Nehemiah asked.

"How about when mushrooms grow upside down?" Joe signed with an impish grin.

"Joe..."

"I should be back at least by morning. Tell Glue hello for me, and take a pair of bruised ribs from his reply." Joe winked. He flipped his scrambler out of his pocket and toward his friend. Nehi caught it and slid it into his own pocket, but it didn't change his frown as he watched his little friend. Joe slid his gloves off since Nehi stared at him anyway and stuffed them in his bag.

"Tell P-a-u-l hello. I'll leave it up to you when to shut down the conversation," Joe signed. "I'd prefer no three hour channel open though. I guess you have to tell them everything?"

"Any reason not to?" Nehi asked. Joe shrugged.

"Telling everyone your location and business is just...risky."

"Paul is hardly everyone," Nehi commented. Joe shrugged again, and his eyes turned away. He grabbed the hoverboard he had placed beside the seat, slid his shoulder bag's strap on, and dropped off the wagon onto his board. He waved at Nehemiah as he flipped it on, leaned forward, and shot off into the town of Paradise.

He didn't have to hurry if things stayed as he planned them today. But something always happened. Joe threaded his way through the traffic and pedestrians, his eyes never still. People didn't throng the streets, but there was always someone out in Paradise. Sightseers, displaced workers hoping for better jobs, soldiers on patrol, hundreds just wandering with nothing better to do as they waited for the government to "process" their work visas. Joe wove in and out, eyeing the faces to try and keep away from those willing to murder for a board. He headed into the heart of the city, the rotted and crumbling heart, the type of places he didn't bring Anna and Nehemiah. Anything could happen in the back streets. Especially to two wide-eyed, handsome youngsters who talked to everyone.

The buildings dilapidated and sagged harder, and Joe smiled to think how surprised Nehi would have been that the town could get worse. The people changed too. Faces hardened, eyes grew sunken and darted in desperation, gaunt fear and worn despair showed everywhere he looked. Joe's face began to harden too, and his gaze shifted to rest straight ahead of his feet. He had learned to ignore the desperate faces. But it still wasn't easy. People called this the Traitor's Quarter. Those the Brotherhood deemed unfit to renew their work visas ended up here. Those who had said a loose word against the State, or showed signs of disloyal activity. Those with no chance left to earn a living. No clearance to use the State bread lines. No way to sneak onto the transports and get out of the country. Those wasting with no hope.

His board slowed, and his lowered eyes darted to a doorway. A woman sat on the stoop, her dress so threadbare holes showed through it. The material sagged around her form. Two bone-thin hands swiftly braided the black hair of a little girl, sitting on the step in front of the woman. The child's face was pinched and pale, her eyes listless as she sang a little nonsense song and held a worn, filthy teddy bear. A man crouched on the other side of the woman, his eyes fevered, darting everywhere, haunted despair in every line on his wasted face. It was rare to see a child in Paradise, the boarding schools were mostly in the agricultural district. Whatever this man did must have sent the girl home so he could watch her die slowly of hunger.

Perhaps her parents had dared to try to keep her home.

Joe kicked his board off and the nose shot into the air as his black boots plunked into the street. He pulled the orange and cheese block he had brought for his lunch from his pocket and handed it to the little girl. She looked up at him, wide, dark eyes unnaturally large in her shriveled face. He flashed her a smile and trotted off before they could say anything, clicking his board in its sling. At least he had given them a smile. *I wish I could tell them there really is a God and life really does matter,* Joe thought. He sighed and rubbed his neck where the GI mark seemed to burn, hidden by his turtleneck, high leather jacket collar, and shaggy blond hair. *But if there's anything you've learned in life Joe, it's that God always knows what He's doing.*

He turned a corner, then dived back again to press himself against the termite ridden timbers of the apartment building,

his heart thundering. *Stop it Joe, just a reaction! The blue wagons aren't coming for you. Not this time.* He leaned around the corner again, his heartbeat slowing a little as he took in the scene. A blue government wagon stood parked at a local grocer and a blue uniformed officer rifled through the store's stock. Joe's green eyes caught the stick-thin grocer's desperate ones, and his own grew hard. It would be nice to be able to tell them that stealing was wrong, too. Especially stealing by the State. But not now, he had things to do. And besides, he had a price on his head as an incomplete in this country.

Three men stared at him from the alley across from his. Their eyes fastened hungrily on his hoverboard.

Joe leapt straight up, kicked off the side of the building, caught the roof with the edge of his fingers, and drew himself smoothly up. He ducked down and moved along the rooftops. If he traveled soft and quick and stayed hunched over, no one noticed him on a rooftop walk. And it was a very good thing to go unnoticed. Joe moved deeper into the huge, sprawling town. This city seemed like a small kingdom, filled with close packed houses and starkly distinct districts. And filled with discontentment and hunger for more than the hard bread and gruel of the State food lines. The feeling ran through the ordinary citizen's quarters; the few middle-class areas clinging to their places with a desperate fawning on the Brotherhood, and the thousands of factory workers in the Boarding Quarter. Meanwhile starvation ran rampant among the Traitor's slums and the death cart caried dozens of people out every day.

The bog-tinted fog oozed along the ground and covered it all. The brown fog slid its icy stench under worm-holed doors in the winter, but in the summertime it changed to a disease spreader that left a brown sticky mud, thick with algae and bacteria, wherever it crossed. Joe preferred the roofs, even though it meant slower travel without his hoverboard. Here he could still catch a glimpse of the sun sometimes, avoided muggings, and saw less of the despair. He only dropped to the street when he reached his destination.

Rooftop Walk

His boots punched a hole through a thin band of fog, splattering some of the stinking mud on the gray plastered walls. Joe's sharp nose wrinkled at the stench rising around him in the dim heat. Mean houses leaned over the narrow street, seeming to challenge one another as to who could block out the most sunshine. Joe headed to a small house squeezed in between an abandoned butcher's shop and a derelict apartment building. This was one of the forgotten neighborhoods. Not quite in the slums or the Boarding Quarter, a corner of Paradise tucked away between districts, overlooked and mostly ignored. He knocked on the faded gray door a little gingerly, worried he might knock the thing off its rusted hinges. Shuffling came from inside and he waited.

The fog swirled around his boots, searching for holes, trying to grip his feet in its damp smell and leave its ghastly mud. Joe's nose wrinkled again and he shifted his weight uncomfortably. Memories swirled inside him like the nasty fog; an unprotected child coughing in the smoke-riddled dark, helpless, watching friends die from its sickly stench. His spine prickled and his stomach clenched, eyeing it spiral and swirl by his ankles. The gray door opened a crack and a pale face peered out. Joe smiled and gave a little wave. The fear left the man's watery eyes. But his frown stayed, deepening the lines on his sallow face. He opened the door an inch wider and Joe slipped in, feeling in his pocket for his note. The man closed the door and turned to him.

"Hello, little beast. We haven't seen you for almost a year. How have you been?" he grunted in his gravelly voice. Joe considered answering he had been trying to keep alive and barely succeeding, but decided on a non-committal shrug. Anyway, with Mohler that question was just a formality. He didn't hold with GIs. Joe handed over the note.

*Hi, Mr. Mohler. How's the IDP holding up here?*

Kyle Mohler spelled it out slowly, then looked suspiciously at Joe.

"Why are you asking?" he growled, crossing his muscular

arms and glaring down his wide nose. Joe let his annoyance show. He didn't want to play games, especially if this suspicion meant what he thought it did. Mohler backed off immediately and apologized. "I know Paul always wants to know. And Harry over in Story Land, and Charlie in Gaia too. It hasn't been a good year, little beast. And it's gotten worse lately. I thought it was the–" Mohler broke off, his eyes darting around the dirty room, as if someone could be inside the thin walls. He leaned closer and finished his sentence in a hissed whisper. "I thought it was the UPC. But it's not. Something else has been picking up our Christians, and whatever it is it's more efficient than the UPC even. I thought we had it licked a few months ago, but just today another fine family's been snatched." Mohler suddenly stopped and looked at the young man in front of him, one eyebrow scrunched down. "Why am I telling you this? I don't know, little beast, there's just something about you that makes me talk." Joe pulled out his precious paper and pencils to scribble a new note. Using his gloves in this country just seemed like a trick, or someone else's broadcast; people like Mohler wouldn't believe the words were actually Joe's. Notes went over better.

*It's Joe. Who and how many disappeared today?*

Mohler spelled it out, his thick lips moving and his forehead wrinkled as he concentrated. His eyebrows drew together, and his burly arms crossed again.

"Paul doesn't want to know that," he growled. Joe snatched the note back and scribbled on the other side.

*I don't work for Paul. I am a brother, remember?*

A metallic tinkling filled the little room as Mohler read it and he looked back at Joe. The pendant of the flying raven that usually hung around Joe's neck rested on the mute's palm. But it shifted, the metal pieces rearranging in a musical dance. The last piece settled and the intricate, folk-art cross of the IDP rested in his hand. Joe pushed it a little closer to Mohler, a visual reminder he was a part of the IDP, his expressive face telling Mohler to lighten up and be nice. Mohler nodded slowly, but

didn't look pleased.

"I guess no more harm can come to them, anyway." *You want to bet?* Joe thought, but didn't waste the paper on saying. "It was Naman Little and his family. His wife Greta is a teacher at the city's boarding school and managed to keep their children there. Now all six of their children, from five up to fifteen and both parents are reported missing. Gone. Just like they had never been. I know the soldiers have already combed the transports, it wasn't a run. The Littles hadn't shown any signs of that, anyway. They're just gone! Swallowed." That put a lot more on the agenda today. Time to be going. Joe untied the black bag from his belt, dug inside, and pulled out a smaller black bag that sagged heavily.

*From the IDP of Story Land. God bless,* the note attached to the bag said in Joe's scrawl. Mohler fumbled the bag open and placed a watery eye to the opening. A raspy gasp filled the little room. A wash of hot, stinking air swirled in, and Mohler looked up. Joe stood to the side of the open door, checking the outside before he exited.

"Tell them…thank you," Mohler said, a tremble in his voice. Joe paused to look back. He smiled, scribbled a quick note, and handed it over with a handshake.

*I'll relay the message to the Story Land IDP when I can.*

*Don't despair, help appears suddenly sometimes.*

Mohler looked up in surprise. His room stared back at him empty. The IDP branch leader pressed his thick lips together as he carefully pushed his old door closed. Too bad that little one was a GI beast. Something seemed almost likeable about him.

Joe sped along the roof tops, hoping he blended in with the tarred shingles well enough in his black leather jacket and slacks. Heat coursed through him, burning to his bones. He could feel sweat dripping down his body. *I can't wait till this is all over and I can retire in the Sojourner's Kingdom and stop wearing these confounded black long sleeves!* Joe thought as he slid down a roof, flipped onto the next, and began to shimmy up it. *Hey, maybe then I'll stop talking to myself too. And I'll bet mushrooms really will grow down.* He grinned and ran along a ridge, stooping low, leaping over gaps, sliding down steep tiles, and thinking.

*Joe Ravenswing... You know, I like it. I've needed a last name.* He came to the end of a block, dropped to the ground, slipped across the road, gave a leap, and scrambled up the next set of roofs. *A last name...I could take Noble. I know Josh wouldn't mind, and it would be nice to be able to point to a heritage in the name. Especially to point to Josh.* He caught a higher roof with one hand and flipped himself onto the next house. *Boy, I miss him. If people up in heaven really do look down on those still here, like some speculate, I bet I've made him cringe with some of my escapades!* Joe grinned to himself; it only partially reached his eyes. *But maybe, maybe I've become a little more like good old Josh wanted me to be. I wish he were still here. Only Jesus and I know how much I wish it!*

A shingle came loose in his hand, and Joe paused, digging his boots into the roof as he caught his balance again, watching the shingle bounce and jounce, scraping down the old house. It took four more with it by the time it tumbled off. Joe scurried up the roof, gripped the ridge with a black-gloved hand, flipped over it, and landed sliding on the other side, shingles vibrating under him, a smell of warm tar everywhere. *Joe Noble... I don't think I'd like to be called Mr. Noble. Sounds pretentious. Hm. Joe Ravenswing. Joe Black. Joe Ravenswing Black. Joe Raider. I wonder which one Anna would like?*

The connection of Anna and a last name jolted through him, and Joe fumbled in the leap to the next roof. For an instant, his mind filled with the now as gray concrete rushed under him, far, too far, below. A crooked rain gutter leered at him, and Joe flailed a hand, catching it with two fingers. The metal creaked,

shifted with a shriek, and a bolt jerked from the old building. Joe's boots shot upward as he heaved on the gutter, propelling the rest of him straight up. He pirouetted in midair and flung himself to the side. His left ribs bent as he landed with a heavy scrunching thump on the roof. The rain gutter pulled away with a shriek of metal and tumbled toward the street. A woman screamed two stories below him and Joe scrambled to the next rooftop, the wind whipping his shaggy hair at his speed. He spun as he ducked behind the next ridge, and peeked back over the top.

Three stories of frequently patched rain gutter slammed into the apartment house across the street. With a screech of metal and flying shingles, it slid slowly down, caught on the second house's gutter and stopped, vibrating. The street seemed to hold its breath, waiting. A gentle "pop" sounded, and the bolts of the second gutter gave way. The two metal gutters twisted around each other, wobbling like paper, and rammed into the street with a shrieking crash. Shouts, hoverer's horns, screams, and metallic-tasting dust rose from the street. Joe ducked down behind the ridge.

*Oops.* He sped off, distancing himself from the noise, heat-waves shimmering on the rooftops around him. *Joe, stop it,* he told himself as he dropped flat on a roof and studied the streets to be certain no alarm followed him. *You need to focus on what you're doing now. Joe Ravenswing. Yes, that's it.* Joe shook his head at himself as he slid over the hot shingles again, wood biting into him and the smell of warm tar permeating his world. *Stop it! You're a dreamer, that's always been your problem. I've told you again and again, Joe, dreamers and GIs don't mix.* The young man sighed as he pushed off of one roof with his hands and landed lightly on his booted feet on the next. He glanced up at the sun, winced at how far it had moved already, and ran faster, till his actions might almost have been called flying by a watcher in the street below. Only there were no watchers. No one noticed the small black form flipping and scurrying across the rooftops of Paradise.

# Chapter Two: Little Rescue

*"Even so it is not the will of your Father which is in heaven, that one of these little ones should perish."* Matthew 18:14

The bell in the town clock struck noon when Joe finally came to a stop at the end of the roofs. Each toll came as a long, deep, "Gong!" Joe thought it sounded like an oppressive land-owner calling his people to the fields. But that was probably just the atmosphere. He crouched on the roof on his fingertips and toes. He had been digging into his black bag for the last few blocks, and now looked like a pile of elegant soft black leather with two green, shining stars looking out. He wished he had re-membered his eye juice to change his from green to brown. But it couldn't be helped. He panted into his mask, his own hot breath flushing his face. Joe's eyes crinkled in a frown as he let one arm snake around his ribs. He shouldn't be this out of breath after a rooftop walk. Weariness clung to his bones; but he refused to admit it and turned his eyes to the street.

He crouched at the edge of the cul-de-sac. At the very end of the bulge of street, a large rambling house stood off by itself. It seemed aloof from its fellows, as if it somehow knew it was bet-ter than them. The plaster stayed intact, and a fairly new coat of paint even showed through the mud. Joe crouched absolutely still, observing the rambling house and considering. His thoughts moved quickly, so quickly one hardly made it before the next shoved its way into his head, layering so that two, sometimes three and four ideas were there at once, sliding over and into one another.

*I know the FFs are still here. And Simmons isn't (yay!), so that means Nicky's in charge. If it was only today the snatch happened the family should still be here. I miss Beau. Nicky's more of the psychological oppressor rather than the pure violence. Simmons was an expert at both, but he's not around now (yay!). So that means the Littles will be somewhere dark and dirty and secluded to stew in fear. I wonder what Anna and Nehi are up to? I think*

*they'll keep the family together, screaming children aren't really in the FFs style. I remember the day Josh and I accidently crashed the Thieves' party down the street from here, good times. Old and direct methods ought to work for this raid, once I find them in and out fast. First the scouting. I hope the Littles are quick at grasping at strange hope, because here comes one. Joe Strange-Hope? Definitely not!*

The pile of black clothes dropped to the ground and materialized into a supple, small form. He slipped across the street and melted into the shadow of the huge house. Joe slid inside a tiny coal shoot in the side of the building, deposited his hoverboard in a recess leading to the cellars, and began to reconnoiter. He climbed through air ducts, slid into closets, melted into shadows, and found his way all over the house, discovering the occupants and their work. He kept at the nerve-wracking, muscle-wrenching business for well over an hour, till he knew every person there, every corner, every ceiling beam.

Only after he felt free from surprises did Joe slip through the door into Nicky's office. He moved on the ceiling, crawling over it like a gecko. He flipped his jacket sleeve up to reach his tools and gadgets lying neatly in place along his arm. Joe's finger flicked his interferer on. A simple gadget, designed to cause security measures to flicker and falter within a range of twelve feet. Joe detached his gloves and climbing boots and dropped catlike to the floor. He stole to the desk and ran an expert's eye over the contents. It took him four seconds to realize the whole top of the desk lifted up to reveal a secret compartment. A smile flickered under the Black Raider's mask as he glanced over the papers littering the cavity. Nice of Freddy to insist on keeping records of everything. His gloved fingers flipped through the contents swiftly, creating a breeze that cooled his hot face.

His fingers stopped moving. Joe stared frozen at one paper lying in the desk, dated yesterday at noon.

One (1) item, book, received from Will Bonniver. Same item, book, transferred to Frederick Masterson. Item removed to headquarters by means of SOLTD. Wolf informed and stated, "Good." One (1) item, book, settled in place.

Joe gently laid the papers back in their original position. The desk top closed with a tiny click, and he made certain it locked. The Raider stole to the door and slipped out, flicking his interferer off. He made no comment, not even in his own mind. What could he say? Defeat pulled at his limbs, making even his chest seem heavy and his breath hard to catch. The Bible was in the FFs headquarters, in Freddy's own private room. He had missed it by one day.

Footsteps thumped on the stairs and Joe automatically leapt for the wall, slipping his climbing gloves on as he moved. He swarmed up the side and crouched in a corner, watching numbly as two FFs walked past on patrol, chuckling in low voices over a comrade's escapades. Joe gave a shake and his head lifted. So recovering the Bible would take more work on his part. More trouble and... He heaved a tight sigh, but kept his head up and shoulders squared. He could do it. With Jesus' help, he could still get it back. And now he knew where it lay waiting for him.

But right now he had a family to save. Joe scuttled off toward the cellar, ready to finish this. He paused as he reached the first floor, staring outside the large picture windows by the front door. A blue government wagon rested at the baker's at the top of the street. The driver door pushed open and a soldier climbed leisurely out and strolled toward the bakery. A smile quirked over Joe's face. As he crawled upside down on the ceiling, it looked as though the truck and the rest of the world were the ones upside down. He scurried forward, flipped, landed silently on his toes in front of the cellar door, and slipped through.

As Joe ran down the dark stairs he resigned himself to spending some time in this stuffy concrete expanse. There was a way down into a deeper basement somewhere here, and it had to be found before he could declare this house Little-free

and look elsewhere for the missing family. He could always slice a hole in the floor, but that would leave too large a mark of his presence. Anyway the passage might not be down, it might be beside. Joe began to walk around the cellar, systematically pushing walls and stomping floor panels. He was on the third wall when he caught the slight sound of footsteps on wood coming his direction. As the whisper of sound reached him, Joe ducked into the darkest corner in the dark cellar and crouched low, watching.

As soon as he stopped moving the uncomfortable truth hit him; weights seemed to drag at his limbs and his heart labored as it worked. He was tired. No. A grimace cut over his face as he panted and sagged and let himself say it. He was weak. Harry had warned him about this, that if he kept pushing himself, his body would just stop recuperating from trauma. He needed to stop, to give his body time to reset itself and renew its normal strength. Half a year, even a few months, to rest and just be… Nehi's conversation outside of Geatland, about how a settled life calmed his doubts and fears and gifted him strength flashed across Joe's mind. A sharp sigh flew from the mute, a desperate longing twisting his face.

But he couldn't stop. Not now. He had a Bible to recover and a Wolf to catch. Surely this sensation would go away. In fact, maybe it was just because he hadn't had any breakfast since Anna switched his eggs for rubber ones. Yes. Yes, that must be it. Joe dismissed the feeling, too willing to find a probable excuse for the heaviness on him, and went back to his job. Voices joined the footsteps as they grew louder. Joe recognized them. Nicky and Tarin, the two who ought to have been here and he hadn't found yet.

"Are you sure it's a good idea to leave them?" Tarin's voice drifted to the mute. The last time he had seen her she had been in charge of the Killipolis branch, and doing too good of a job at it. He wondered idly what she had done with her giant lizard steed. Joe reached into his pocket and pulled out a small canister and a tiny gas mask.

"Of course," Nicky's nasal voice answered. "The longer you leave them alone, the worse their nerves get. And the worse their nerves get, the easier they are to break." Joe strapped the gas mask on and gripped the canister with his left hand. "Besides, this was just a snatch to occupy that Black Raider annoyance, the boss wanted him busy today for some reason of his own." The voices came from right behind the wall across from him now, and Joe didn't let himself ponder the strange sentence. The Black Raider pulled his arm back, his fingers toying with the canister, but paused. Just throwing it from a dark corner had no artistry, no flare...

"I think the boss is going to be disappointed," Tarin said. "The Raider will never get in this passage." Joe slid into the center of the cellar facing the voices, and waited.

A slit of yellow gleamed along the length of the right side of the wall in front of him, from ceiling to floor. It grew to a crack, and slits appeared at the top and bottom, as the entire wall slid open with soundless, oiled ease. Eight feet by seven feet of well-mortared bricks spun on an unseen axis. Joe pulled his toes back to keep from getting squashed. A dim yellow light came from a passageway and framed two people in the door; short Nicky with his slicked back hair, and Tarin with her too much make-up and sneering face. They apparently didn't see him. Joe was about to throw the canister and give up his professional pride, when Nicky reached over and flipped a switch.

The cellar flooded with light.

Nicky and Tarin fell back, their faces a study of pure astonishment and alarm. Joe smiled at them behind his mask, eyes crinkling in a look a shark might make at a plump fish. He threw the canister. A snarl rippled over Nicky's face and his hand shot to the laser at his hip. The canister rolled against his foot. His eyes rolled up, every muscle relaxed, and he folded over on top of Tarin. A neat pile of villains, snoring gently on their own floor. Joe shot up the stairs, locked the cellar door, slid back down, stepped over the two unconscious forms, and moved down the passageway, still smiling. That had been a beautiful

effect, he would have to remember the light bit.

Joe moved along swiftly, treading lightly and keeping close to the wall to avoid squeaks from the old wooden flooring. The sides of the passageway were the same roughhewn old wood as the floor, and Joe kept away from their splinter ridden sides like he would have an angry porcupine. Closed doors stared back at him as he moved. He flipped his jacket sleeve up and ran his eye over his gadgets strapped underneath the flap. His bio-scanner showed all the expected green dots moving above him in the house upstairs, a blob of green in front of him marking at least ten living bodies, and one behind a closed door in this passageway. Joe rocked to a stop, staring at the plain wooden door. Go in and neutralize it? He only had one canister left, and no dart gun. He hadn't expected to go on a raid today, he left his darts with Beau as an added security for his big friend hiding in the woods. He had his projectile pistol to use on the living green dot in that room... But when he could, Joe chose life. Even a life as rotten as to guard a family for rotters like Nicky. Joe knew of people worse than that his mighty God had redeemed.

He was one of them.

Anna's face flitted into his mind and Joe winced. His eyes darted to his hands and his face twisted, as if he saw something besides the black gloves clutching the pistol. His fingers tightened convulsively around the stock as he suddenly wanted to fling it off in revulsion. So many things in his past...

Maybe the green dot would just stay in the room. Joe made his decision and carefully slid around another skinny corner. The passageway grew tighter. The musty, close air seemed thick and hard to breathe, laden with the stench of mold and standing water. At least the disease ridden fog didn't make it down here. Joe slid his last canister into his hand as another corner loomed up in the dim light. The sound of a hymn drifted to him from around that corner, muffled through a heavy door. Heavy laughter sounded on top of it, un-muffled. Joe tossed the canister toward the sound of laughter, waited a second, and turned to see what he would find.

Three guards sat around a table with a stack of cards between them. Well, they had been sitting. Now Joe's little black
canister rested against a table leg, and the men splayed over
their game. As he watched one big blond tipped over, tumbled
to the floor with his knees under him and the back of his lap in
the air, and gave a gentle snore. Joe slipped his IDP cross and
lock pick set into his hand, eyeing his scanner to be sure only
that one behind the door still remained a possible threat. The
hymn faltered, replaced by a stifled sobbing. Joe cursed his
slowness at this business, whipped his gas mask into his
pocket, and wielded his lock pick.

The door swung open with a dull squeak. A small, wet room
came into view, putrid and dark. Nasty tools hung on the moldy
walls as suggestions for imaginative minds and unidentified
creatures scurried out of the light let in by the open door. The
family huddled in the back of the room, ankle deep in black
mud. All eight of them jumped as the door swung inward,
clutching at each other. Joe stood in the doorway, silhouetted
in the passageway light. He took a step forward and lifted his
hand. His IDP cross dangled from it, catching the light and sparkling as it turned gently. Naman Little (pencil thin, rough fea-
tured, a smattering of black stubble over his face) stared at the
cross and then switched his gaze to the intense green eyes behind the mask. Mr. Little straightened, holding his youngest
daughter in his thin, dirty arms, his eyes snapping with hope
and determination. Greta glanced at her husband and took the
next two children's hands. Tears still stood in her pretty eyes,
but her face was set and determined. Joe smiled underneath his
mask. The Littles would do.

He motioned them out the door and leaned against it as he
began to screw a silencer on his pistol, waiting for them to get
organized. And using the time to just rest. Someone needed to
make a laser light enough to fit in his pockets, the old projectile
guns were small, but noisy. And they ran out of bullets too fast.
A Ruby was too close-range to be worth it, and a Compton too

heavy to be practical for him. At least he had Dark Ray if they needed it. But he liked to keep that for emergencies, as no one really knew the full effects of a PUDRE ray; of those it hit, or those who used it.

Joe leaned against the door, pistol ready, watching the passageway for trouble as the Littles murmured to each other and paired younger children with older ones. No one seemed to be interested in checking on things down here. The FF really needed to keep a better guard if they wanted to keep him out. But then they hadn't really been trying today, according to Nicky. Joe blinked, staring at nothing, his mind rushing off on a thousand possibilities. He shook his head viciously, lips tightened to slits, and told himself to be in the moment. The Littles needed all of him, right here.

A hand landed on his shoulder, tentative, just a quick touch. Joe's lips pursed tighter as he forced himself not to spin and take the man's head off. He breathed out once and turned to look over his shoulder. Naman Little's tight face stared down at him. Joe handed him his spare pistol and started to walk, listening to the creaking floors, shuffling steps, and sniffling following behind him. A little voice started to ask a question, and four other voices shushed them loudly. Were all normal children this noisy? The overhead light spluttered, humming gently as it lit up the passageway. A corner loomed in front of them. Joe held up a black gloved hand, and slid forward alone, spinning around the corner. He couldn't hear with all that going on back there, if the person in that room–

Two brown eyes stared down into his green ones. A long way down.

A gleam of metal caught the sputtering light as the guard jerked his laser rifle up. But Joe's pistol was already lifted and waiting. The mute pulled the trigger. A soft pop, a sharp crack of bone, something heavy toppling, and a black gloved hand moved around the corner, waving the Little's forward. Naman spun around the corner and stopped dead, staring at the thing on the ground. One hand went over his daughter's eyes as she lay in his arms, and he quickly reached back for the next little one in line and lifted him over the huddled heap sprawled on the passageway floor. Greil, the twelve-year-old, gagged as she went by, but no one else made a comment. Joe, snatching his board and flitting back and forth between the family and the way out, considered it as he moved. He couldn't decide whether to be impressed or depressed by their non-reaction to violent death. It came from living in this place, he knew. "Blood will flow and revolution bring progress!" was a national catchphrase here, and revolution always hovered in the wings.

Naman turned another corner, his heart hammering and his pulse singing in his head, and caught his breath in relief. The huge outer door stood just in front of them, granting them access to the dusty cellar. Two more bodies lay in the way. But as he stepped over them and his boots crunched on fallen bricks and dirt, out into the cellar, he saw no blood. His hand came away from his daughter's eyes. Things crowded the room, but Naman only paid attention to one. The little person in black stood at the bottom of the steps, replacing the bullet he had used. He had a hoverboard in a sling on his back now. The small one focused on Naman, the green eyes boring into his. He pointed a finger at the ground to tell them to stay put and darted up the stairs, every movement silent, smooth, concise, and almost a blur of speed. Naman caught a glimpse of metal in the black gloved hand, then the door opened and he went through it into the house. The family huddled in the cellar. Children snuffled. The door swung open at the top of the stairs. Everyone tensed, Naman's gun jerked up and leveled at it.

The one in black stepped through. He waved for them, an urgent motion. Greta ran for the stairs, dragging two little ones with her, wet skirt flapping around her legs. The others fell in line behind her. Naman came last, his hand clammy as it held the pistol.

Joe spun out in front of Mrs. Little, pistol in both hands, leading the way down the green carpeted halls. He moved at a run, cringing at the pounding feet, swishing clothing, and gasping

breaths behind him. A man poked his head around his office door, staring down the hallway curiously. Joe's pistol bucked in his hands. The man's body toppled into the room, flung back with the impact. Joe glanced over his shoulder. Mrs. Little ran two yards behind him, almost dragging her children as they tried to keep up. His lips pursed and he slowed down. His gaze darted out a window as he raced. Heatwaves shimmered as they rolled off the purring engine of the blue government wagon. The soldier had his stock loaded, he was ready to leave. Joe spun on one heel, dancing backward as he motioned Mrs. Little toward the front door, then spun again, and sprinted. Two more heads popped out of doorways. Joe's pistol bucked, twice. He only needed a bullet each.

A giant of a man reared up in front of Joe as he barreled toward the door. The man's laser rifle hummed and glowed red, and it was already leveled at the Black Raider. Fear closed Joe's throat. The man's finger tightened on the trigger.

# Chapter Three: Race for the Border

*"God is my strength and power: and he maketh my way perfect."* 2 Samuel 22:33

The mute's left arm shot up over his face. A flash of light burst in front of Joe's eyes. The force on his forearm burned and sent him staggering back, as he heard four different voices behind him gasp out muffled shrieks. Joe's pistol popped. He couldn't see, the blinding flash had spots dancing in his eyes. But he remembered where the giant stood. Joe blinked hard and fast as he charged forward. His vision began to come back and the mute's hand shot out, palm up. His wrist bone smashed into the man's chest as the guard went toppling, Joe's bullet right through his forehead. He crashed backward out of the way. Joe caught the laser, jerking it from the man's flaccid fingers, and bolted out the door.

The wagon rolled forward, slowly, moving toward the opening of the cul-de-sac. A flying leap took Joe over the porch stairs. He flipped his hoverboard off its sling as he leapt, and turned it on as his feet slid into the slots. Steam wooshed into the cracked, hot asphalt, and he felt his board catch instead of his boots hitting the ground. Joe leaned forward, his hands behind him, body bent forward, every faculty focused on catching that truck.

His arm ached and stung and an acrid trail of smoke rose from the sleeve. But the stumpy tail leather held, still perfectly intact, and it kept his skin and bone from turning to ash and smoke. Joe silently cheered the Geats as he wooshed toward the van.

The driver behind the wheel paused at the street, checking the traffic. He used the moment to lift his clay mug to his lips, blowing on the coffee, relishing the scent that wafted up around him. The door jerked open. The driver started, coffee sloshing out of his mug. A black gloved hand grabbed his cup, steadying it. A force like a blackjack slammed into his chin. The driver's

eyes rolled up, and he toppled gently backward, his fingers slid-
ing off his cup. Joe took a sip, as he bundled the man onto the
road with his other hand, and his eyebrows went up. It was
good coffee. One hand slid the travel mug into the cup holder
as his other pushed off the seat, and he vaulted through the partition from the cab into the back of the truck. The scent of fresh
baked bread and sweet rolls filled the air and Joe's stomach
rumbled. *Why did Anna have to choose today to give me rubber
eggs for breakfast and switch my tea for weeds? Although, I did
deserve it for the mud.* A smile hovered under the mask as his
hand slammed into the door lever and he shoved through into
the sunlight, the guard's laser already jerking around in one
arm as he raised his pistol with the other.

Mrs. Little stumbled out of the house, her children running
beside her. The small one in black raced toward them, waving
at the open back of a blue government wagon. Greta didn't stop
to gawk at their ride, or wonder at how fast their rescuer
moved. She shot down the steps and pelted over the asphalt,
almost dragging her twins. The whine of lasers and the soft,
"pop pop" of the silenced pistols seemed to fill her mind. Naman
tossed Paulsa to his eldest as she rushed past him, spun on his
heel, and took a stand beside the small one in black. His eyes
were bright, his face stiff with the determination to see his family safe as his pistol jerked up, firing at windows, driving back
anyone who dared to cause a threat. A black gloved hand
landed on his arm and spun him around. A palm slammed into
his back, pushing him toward the truck. Naman's lips pursed.
But he ran.

Joe strode backward, moving toward the truck as he faced
the house, firing projectiles and laser bursts steadily, silently
praying they wouldn't leave without him. He had left his board
in the cab, and hadn't exactly been able to ask for a ride. The
engine revved behind him, and Joe's heart raced in time with it,
his eyes darting around the little cul-de-sac assessing his options. He could take to the roofs; it would be a running battle,
with Nicky in his hovercraft, but he could–

Tires screeched as the blue wagon jerked up beside him, the passenger door open inches from his face. Joe sprang into the cab, the laser bouncing onto the seat. The engine revved, the wagon spun on two tires, righted itself, and sped off with another squeal of rubber, fast enough the passenger door slammed shut. Joe scrambled into his seat, breathing hard. His legs dangled like a child's. Hoverers and wagons whizzed past, most of them going the opposite way. Naman Little spun the wheel and screeched into a tiny side street, overhung with tenement houses. The wagon whizzed through the shadows, then burst back into the sunshine of a main road, pulling smoothly into traffic. Naman's foot pressed steadily on the accelerator, and Joe watched the traffic around him seem to melt out of their way as Naman threaded through with an expert's skill. Joe gave a nod, his tight body relaxing visibly. He twisted in his seat and Naman tensed. The sound of the divider sliding back filled the cab, and Naman's throat tightened, wondering what could be wrong now.

The small one in black slumped back into his seat, his mask shoved open a crack and a cinnamon roll sticking out of his mouth. He reached for the travel mug in the cup holder as Naman glanced at him in surprise. The small one smiled, icing on his mouth, and waved a hand out the window, one eyebrow raising.

"I'm a driver for the Calston and Crew garage," Naman explained automatically, and Joe laughed. Of course he was, because that's how God worked.

Naman started, so hard the truck veered left. Horns blared and tires screeched again and Naman jerked back into his lane. He stared at Joe with wide eyes and face tight, as if he was a monster. For a fraction of a second Joe wondered what had startled him. Then he realized he had given himself away with the silence of his laugh.

"You...you're a..." the man stammered, pressing himself into the side of the door as if his rescuer was a wild animal just waiting to tear into him. Joe stared out his window as Naman

worked through his shock, not letting himself grimace. It would be nice if he got over his revulsion too, Joe thought. But that was too much to expect. He took a sip from the coffee and went back to the roll. It was good. Almost as good as Anna's.

"Where do I go?" Naman Little asked after a moment, his voice trembling. It was unnatural, a twisting of the world, for him to be speaking to this creature as if it could understand like a human. Joe pointed at a road sign, a bright white hologram of an arrow standing over the road, the word "Border" under it in thick blocky letters. "Really?" Naman Little blinked. Joe nodded and Naman pushed the truck into neutral, spun the wheel, jerked into fourth, and sped off. The wagon spun onto the road, whizzed through the hologram, and sped out of Paradise. Joe watched Naman's every move, memorizing how he made it around the curves, which pedals he pushed before he shifted the stick. The cracked streets swiftly became towering black pines and bubbling bogs, generating more of the stinking fog.

The empty coffee cup clinked as Joe sat it in the cup holder and swiped one hand over his mouth to get rid of the icing. He readjusted his mask, reloaded his gun, flipped the priming mechanism on the laser, and took Dark Ray from his pocket. Joe pushed the ray to the farthest setting, so the strength of the beam concentrated at twelve feet distance, and lined the three weapons up neatly on the seat. His gloved hand flew up and opened the window separating the cab from the back of the wagon and motioned Naman Little through it.

"What?" the man said, and swallowed visibly, still pressed into his door. Joe rolled his eyes, and squirmed. Naman Little found the small one wormed behind the wheel, and himself pressed into the passenger seat. Naman just sat and blinked at the black form in the driver's seat toying with the stick shift. Joe jabbed a thumb at the connecting window. Naman looked at the small GI, feeling out the pedals and holding himself up by the wheel to be able to see over the dashboard. His Adam's apple bobbed. But he turned and squirmed back to join his family.

Joe slammed the window shut. He pulled himself forward,

pressing against the wheel and keeping his head down so that as little of himself as possible could be used for target practice, and gripped Dark Ray in his left hand. *I'm glad of that driving lesson in Story Land now, even if it was a hoverer,* Joe thought with a grin. He prayed a quick prayer for wisdom and a miracle and spun the wagon around the curve toward the inspection station.

Blue uniformed soldiers scattered in panic as the big wagon shot into their station. Joe stuck his hand out the window and pointed his Dark Ray at the thick wooden post blockading the road. A cone of darkness spilled out of the instrument, aimed at the thick wooden beam. The wood began to splinter and pull apart, drifting into the cone. Joe felt the cab start to vibrate, and the hood had a disturbing crumpling tremble to it. He flicked the ray off with a grimace, jerked his arm back in, and prayed it had been enough. A rending crash jolted through the mute as he sideswiped the inspection booth. He jerked the wagon back onto the road, his eyes focused ahead, and rammed straight into the beam. One side of the beam splintered in a thousand pieces, spraying up into Joe's windshield, the other clattered off the road like a twig. The wagon crashed into the wild lands, bouncing off the asphalt onto the packed dirt, fishtailing wildly.

The driver's window shattered, glass flying. Joe flung his arm over his eyes, desperately trying to hold the big wheel steady. The whine of lasers came from the inspection station, and his stomach twisted in sick fear for the family behind him. That back door had better be lead lined! He kept the wagon at a furious pace for another mile, rocking crazily as he spun down the twisted road. The tall dark pines loomed over the road, casting their shadows deep around the van. A wide, bubbling bog approached on his left. Joe's tongue slid between his teeth as he concentrated, his feet feeling out the brake and clutch. The truck jerked and jumped, but it slowed. Joe tugged the wheel toward the oozing brown. The wagon's tires splashed over a shallow ford in the bog, bounced through a thick mass of climbing vines and overhanging pine boughs, and sloughed to

a shaky stop inside a hill, sand spraying from the tires as the brakes squealed. The engine gave a shudder as it found itself in fifth gear at zero, and coughed out. Joe flipped the switch and hoped he hadn't killed the thing.

The dim light and quiet drip of the cave took over. Joe's eyes closed and he dropped forward, his head resting on the big wheel as he sagged. A silent thank you to his Protector breathed out into the still cab. He allowed himself a few seconds, panting and letting the relief and knowledge of safety spread through him.

It felt so good to be safe.

But he only gave himself a few seconds. Joe began to unwind the leather from his face and stuff it swiftly into his bag. Sirens wailed on the road, but Joe ignored them. The soldiers of the People's Kingdom didn't like the wild lands, and they really didn't like the infected, quick sand-like bogs. They wouldn't try and cross one to check out a quiet little hill, and they never explored longer than they had to. The Littles should be safe enough now that they were over the border. He slipped his hand in one of his cargo pockets and pulled out the black bag Nehi had handed Wiglaf two nights ago. A smile crept over Joe's face as he hefted it. The Geatish Hero hadn't needed it, but God knew someone else would. He scrawled a few notes over the map, and reached for the things on the seat.

Joe's finger hovered over the settings switch on Dark Ray as he shifted it toward his pocket. He usually kept the little instrument on a low range, a six foot concentration in a three foot diameter... His finger slid away without touching the switch and he shoved it into his pocket and reached for his pistol. He had no reason for it, but a quiet something inside him whispered to leave it alone.

Joe shoved his mask and gloves into his bag and went back to looking like an ordinary citizen. Well, except for the high-collared jacket in the summertime. He ran a hand around his collar to be sure it was up out of habit, and moved around to the back. Good, the doors were a little scorched from the lasers, but none

# *Chapter Three: Race for the Border*

*2 Samuel 22:33*

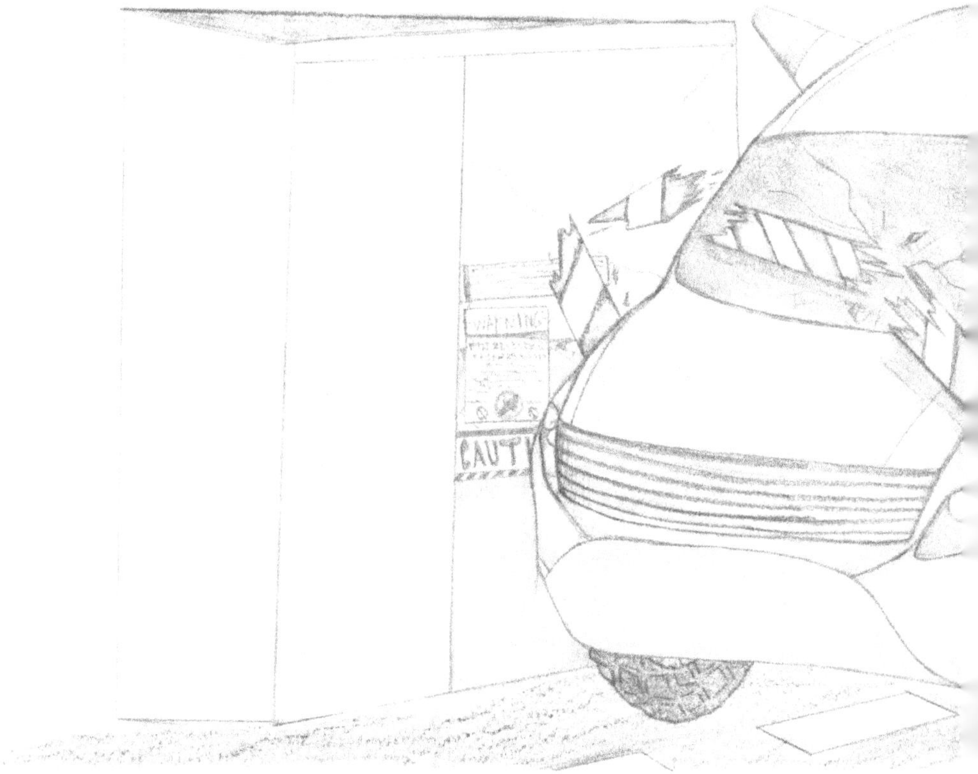

of the beams had gone through. Joe rammed his palm into the latch till it unstuck, and heaved the doors open.

The Little family crouched under the partition window, eyes wide and staring, breath panting out of them in fear. Joe smiled cheerfully at them. Eyes blinked, muscles released their tension, and arms slowly uncurled from around each other as the family came out of their shock. Joe stood by, waiting patiently till they were ready. Naman drew in a deep breath and turned his gaze out the back of the truck, studying the terrain.

"I wish we knew who to thank," he muttered, his voice husky. Joe pushed it away, willing himself not to be offended by the knowledge Naman assumed someone must have trained and sent the Raven, because of course, a GI beast could never have done it on his own. He forced another smile and handed Mr. Little the black bag. Naman took it warily as if afraid Joe's muteness might be catching. Joe decided not to be insulted and waved cheerily at them, turning to go. The littlest girl waved back, but the others just turned their attention to the paper they pulled from the bag. Joe swallowed a sigh and moved off. He had been around Anna and Nehi too long; these small things actually got under his skin now.

The paper crinkled as Mr. Little began to unfold it. Five coins fell out, landing on his damp boots and sticking. Naman reached down in a sort of stupor and his fingers shook as he picked them up. Five coins that sparkled gold, thick and perfectly round; enough to see them through for at least two months. He had never seen so much. Greta poked him in the arm, pointing at the paper. He unfolded it the rest of the way and the whole family leaned over to see what the stranger had left. They stared at a map, a route from the road they were on to the nearest transport line, and directions from there to a kingdom called Geatland. A note was scribbled on the bottom of the map, and Naman and Greta Little leaned closer to read it.

*Contact Wiglaf, Shield-Bearer to the king, he will see you settled. Be polite to the bizarre beliefs of the country, if you*

*can. Later an opportunity might arise to emigrate again to the Sojourner's Kingdom. For now thank Jesus for your lives, build a new one, and God be with you in all things.*

The husband and wife looked at each other in silence for a moment. A shaking, disbelieving laugh slid from Greta, and she hugged the nearest child tight.

Joe stumbled off his hoverboard in a filthy alleyway back in Paradise, a silent groan sliding from him. His muscles twitched and complained. *I wish I hadn't had to speed the ten miles to make my seven o'clock meeting. My face is numb from the wind! I wish I had that orange again. No, it was more needed where I left it. I wish I had been able to eat breakfast; my teeth still feel like their bouncing. Although that was a good cinnamon roll. And I did deserve the eggs for the washing I ruined, and the handkerchief will get me even with Anna.* Joe grinned, mentally running through the battle of pranks he and Anna had been playing. But the sparkle left his green eyes and his face dropped into hard lines as his thoughts turned another direction. *I wish I didn't have to make this meeting at all. I wonder how Nehemiah would look at me if he knew? No, I won't think of that. There's no reason he has to find out, and he trusts me right now. Don't give yourself more worry than you already have by imagining what hasn't happened, Joe the GI.*

Footsteps rang on the pavement as someone came into the square outside of the alley. The strains of "Oh Brotherhood Fair" drifted to Joe. The young man drew in a deep breath and started to move forward. His legs trembled, and he paused, his face tight. Joe steadied his breathing, forced himself straight, and stepped from the alleyway into a beam of sunlight sparkling on the damp, cracked concrete of the square. He walked toward the big, ornate fountain, fitfully spitting out water, its pump abnormally loud as it strained to work. His own whistle harmonized very prettily with the other whistled tune.

Neil Hanson stood by the fountain, staring idly at the moldy water. He straightened at the sight of Joe, his tailored suit falling into place around his perfect form. His eyes raked the young man up and down, and his lips curled into a contemptuous smile. Joe kept his face expressionless and held out a note. The man took it between his thumb and finger, as if afraid Joe had something catching. *That seems familiar,* Joe thought with an inward grimace and silently wished people wouldn't be so rude. He knew he was different, a malformed monstrosity. He didn't need to be reminded. Neil Hanson raised his eyebrow as he read the note, and looked at the small, shaggy headed man in front of him.

*The FFs are in number 47 Proletariat Lane. They had a little trouble today, they may not stay long.*

"Pretty good work for a beast. Maybe there is a reason the UPC keep you around," the man said. Joe raised an eyebrow of his own and held out his hand. "Yes, I've got something for you too. The man you're looking for, that inventor type? He's in the Brotherhood's House. On the no-use-value list." Joe kept his face impassive, but inside he started jumping and screaming in frustration. The man reached into his pocket.

"See the UPC get this, and get it today," he said. "It goes to Damien, and I can't send it by any of the usual channels, but you have your own weird ways of getting messages through. I can trust you to do that right?"

*When have I failed you?*

"Try four months ago," the man sneered. "It would have been one of the best hauls on the IDP ever. Nearly wiped them out here." Joe shrugged.

*Everyone has an occasional bad week.*

"Right. Well make sure this note gets there. If it doesn't, remember the UPC doesn't look lightly on mistakes. You'll find yourself in more trouble than you've ever been in, incomplete."

*Not likely,* Joe thought. *I doubt you can even imagine the trouble I've been in.* Neil Hanson spun away and began to walk down the street. Joe turned the opposite way, his movements graceful and easy. He turned into Bolsom Street, and the overhanging dilapidated houses dimmed the light. Joe took off at a run, almost vibrating in excitement, and spun back into the alley where his hoverboard leaned against the wall. He let his back slam into the bricks and slid down to a crouch, his fingers fumbling the note out of his pocket. Joe slumped on the dirty ground and stared at the plain white envelope. It almost shone in what little light drifted in here.

None of the usual channels and it had to get there today? That meant... He carefully pried open the flap, and pulled out the single sheet of notepaper. Joe's green eyes widened and began to shine as they ran over the notes Hanson had taken of a conversation on the outskirts of town. This almost made up for finding out his inventor was on the death list in the capital building! It had all the important details of the Wolf's next book heist. He planned to take the People's Kingdom book, tonight.

Joe re-folded the note and began to make his way to the Brotherhood's House, the capital building in Paradise and where Quintus Leeman, inventor of the marvelous SOLTD, now resided at the country's expense. Joe knew why, though Quintus probably didn't. The FFs had what they needed now. And they didn't want anyone else getting it. It would be an easy act of bribery to have the People's Kingdom declare him old, no longer a useful worker.

*I can use this.* Joe's mind raced, trying to grasp what he held in his pocket. He stopped in a darkened alleyway across from the Brotherhood's House, but he couldn't take his mind off the note. *This is a shortcut, a way to make everything right tonight! If the Raven goes in, I can catch the Wolf in the act. If I time it just right, I can blow the whistle when he has the book... Instead of the IDP having to hold Wolf, the People's Kingdom can just take care of it instead! Yes, that will work. I can catch Wolf here and the truth will be known and I can stop with the silence–* Joe's lungs constricted and his muscles tightened spasmodically, as if he had just been punched. He shook his head and laughed at himself with no humor in the action. *Okay, wrong phrase, Joe the GI.* He turned his mind to other things and looked at the huge building in front of him.

*No. Too many dangers, too many soldiers. If they caught me again – No, don't you dare think about that. Not a real chance at getting the old inventor out. I miss Beau. I miss Nehi too. If I can actually catch the Wolf tonight it opens up a huge amount of happy possibilities. No, I'm sorry for Quintus Leeman, but I don't think I can do any good here. Wow! If I really can catch Wolf...*

Joe hit his board's switch and wooshed into the streets, his movements supple, reenergized with this news. His thoughts moved faster than his hoverboard. *If I catch Wolf in the act here that despicable person won't be able to deny it. Not if Hanson is there to help with the catch. Could Wolf get out? If they give him time, but it should be a quick execution here. I ought to be able to slip in at the last minute and even get the coordinates if I'm clever with my promises. The IDP frame? I should have a few months to track it down before Freddy gets suspicious and turns the fake evidence in...Yes!* Joe did a sudden flip, his board spraying a circle of steam, then coming down with a little jump and speeding off again. *Tonight I start the long process of retiring the Raven and making Joe Ravenswing alive! Joe, just for this evening, I allow you to dream all you want.*

A small figure rushed through the traffic lanes and around pedestrians, heading out of Paradise. He increased his speed and darted toward a pretty meadow in the woods by the border. A happy smile hung on his face, and his green eyes shone with many a castle in the air.

# Chapter Four: Gone

*"Greater love hath no man than this, that a man lay down his life for his friends." John 15:13*

Joe trotted up to the meadow and stopped dead in his tracks, his smile gone and his face so blank it could have been a white sheet of paper. The meadow stood stark and empty. No wagon crushed its shriveled grass. No giant pig trilled at his appearance, or happy yell came from Beau or the twins...

Joe slipped off the path into the thick woods out of a habit of self-preservation; when something was wrong you got out of sight. Something was dreadfully wrong here. Panic rushed through him, roaring in his mind, twisting his gut. He whistled for Beau. No reply came from the woods around him. *No reply, nothing! What happened, why aren't they here? I never should have left them! Why did they leave me? Alone! Are they safe? Where are they?* Joe ran his shaking, desperate hands through his shaggy blond hair, knocking two pencils out onto the forest floor. He kept moving, not knowing what to do. He shifted through the trees like a silent shadow, circling the meadow. The trees overshadowed him, drawing the late summer evening into a premature darkness that crawled into Joe's throat and stuck there. These black woods, alone, night coming, no knowledge of his friends...

The young man kept circling, trying to calm his choking panic and force his mind back into a position to think. He stumbled, and whistled again for Cobeau, but no answer came, no rumble, roar, or shout. Not even a squeak or a groan. Where were they? What had happened? Why had he left them? The three questions kept circling his mind as he circled the meadow and he couldn't think of anything else. Yes, wait, one more thing invaded his panic. Joe dropped suddenly to his knees, his hands helplessly gripping his hair. *Jesus!* he prayed silently, desperately. *Be with them, keep them safe, where are they?! I can't lose them. I can't lose them all. I don't have the strength to go back to a life alone, I can't! I can't! Alone? No. I'm never alone, for You are with me always, even to the ends of the earth. Jesus, I'm at the end of my earth now. Where are they? What happened? How can I help them, oh Jesus, let me help them! Lord, show me what to do.*

A branch snapped to his left and Joe whirled, hands up in a karate move, stumbling on weakened legs, his breath gasping out of him, his mind screaming. *It's the IK! No, no, focus, not them, focus, Joe, focus. Lord...help. Again. Help me, please!*

"My Joe!" a roar rang out. Joe sprung toward the sound and flew into Cobeau's large, strong arms before the sound of the two words died in the air. "Master, what's wrong?" Cobeau rumbled. He stroked the blond hair gently, letting Joe's face stay pressed into his side.

"Where were you?" Joe signed angrily as he pulled away and slapped his friend on the arm. Cobeau's troubled look dissipated and became a happy grin.

"I found a clean river and have been swimming today. And now you are all wet from me. It's better to get wet by swimming than by Cobeaus."

"How long have you been swimming?"

"All day, Master," Cobeau answered. Joe stomped on his foot. "Ow. I mean, all day, Joe." The mute hugged him again, convulsively, squeezing his friend's ribs together in his fervor. Then he pulled back with his usual swiftness and kept signing.

"You haven't seen Beauty, Knee-High, or D all day?"

"No, Mas– Joe. Why?"

"I've lost them!"

"Not again!" Cobeau said, and Joe had to repress the urge to punch him.

"Glue, when have I ever lost them before?" Joe signed, his teeth grinding. Cobeau considered painfully. Before he came up with the correct answer of never, the sounds of Prissy trilling, squeaky wheeled shoes rotating, and hissing steam came from the path back toward town. Joe and Beau dashed towards the meadow. Their wagon pulled into the damp grass, scattering bugs as it rolled forward. For an instant Joe felt a triumphant

relief wash over him and he sagged back against his friend. He let Beau's solid presence and the return to normal wash over him and felt almost sick with the relief.

But then he looked again. His stomach tied itself in a slow, heavy knot, and dread tightened every muscle. Daniel held the steering stick and Anna sat alone beside him. Tears stained her face, worry lined it, her hair disheveled and dress dirty; Joe's throat constricted so hard he couldn't get a breath as he took it in. He forced himself to swallow, pushed all emotion as far as he could from himself, and began to think. His mind whirled in constructive directions now, swirling and dancing.

Daniel brought the wagon to a stop and Anna dropped off before it had settled on the grass. She darted to Joe, her words pouring out at such a speed they were hard to follow. But Joe didn't need to follow them, and didn't really pay attention, he only listened to Anna when she brought a confirmation or redirection of what he already knew. His thoughts moved much faster than Anna's words, flowing, dancing, concluding, rejecting, arguing, layering so that two, sometimes four ideas danced through him at the same moment, and each one brought a new thought.

*No Nehemiah, a bruise over Anna's temple, a torn shirt on Daniel, they were caught. The only reason they would have been caught as I left them is if Wolf turned them in. So the rage I saw wasn't a sign of Nehi and Anna's safety, I misinterpreted it. Confound it, I misinterpreted it! I should never have left today. Today, that's why the Littles were snatched, it was to keep me occupied while the bigger snatch happened across town. Jesus be with Nehi! He must have been at the Brotherhood's House when I was there, I wish I had known. They haven't seen Nehi since eleven, and Anna and Daniel were left together so Daniel managed to fast talk their way out. Then Nehemiah's still there, at the House, because of that dirty, despicable, rotten, evil – Joe, leave the feelings out of this. Jesus, be with Nehi. He won't make it through the night. They'll know his Christianity. And that's the end. Long before morning they'll know he won't change and doesn't have anything they want. He'll be dead tonight, when they start changing shifts.*

*But tonight Wolf strikes again, the People's Kingdom will die! They have enough trouble feeding their people, Wolf will get impatient waiting for his fee and bring disintegration. So many souls wiped out, so many lives lost! The timing, it all happens at the same moment, Nehi's execution and the Wolf's move. I can't go after Nehi <u>and</u> stop Wolf! Hanson's message. I can send the message to the UPC, if it gets there within the hour they'll have time to stop Wolf's caper tonight. But the shifts change so soon. Again, I can't be the one to deliver it <u>and</u> get Nehi out. Beau can't go alone, not after Darwin Hall. To stop Wolf here... I'll have to send the message with Daniel and Anna. Anna! She'll never speak to me again, not after she finds out I've been working for the UPC, and Daniel, he'll turn me in as a traitor! I could tell at least Anna before I send her? No good, I'd have to explain it, no time, and if I explained first Daniel won't go. Jesus be with Nehi! It's already getting dark, and he's still in there. Because of that – steady, Joe. You never should have left them.*

*But I can't let my connection with the UPC come out! I know everything about the IDP, I was a co-founder. If they think I'm a traitor (and Daniel will be sure they do) I'll be the one dead! I can't just run, I have to bring the Hillsons back together, to somewhere safe, and Daniel will see I'm caught. I could just shoot him? Bad idea. Then Nehi and Anna would see me caught and killed. And... No good. Daniel will see me caught. I won't have time, or the words, to convince them. They'll execute me. Shoot me with a laser in a dark cellar, and leave my smoking body to rot, I know they will. If I tell my UPC connection, I die! But I promised Halbred I'd hold the breach, who will do it if I get executed as a spy? Jesus be with...Nehemiah.*

*He can do it. He would listen, and understand the danger. I'll leave my notebook behind, and he'll have good old Beau. And I'll start the end before...my end. Yes, he can do it if I start it. No more hope of that lovely idea of the books, no way he'll be able to save that. And only a chance he can stop the IDP frame, but I'll take*

*him to Harry and I think they could handle that. And the end of so much more, of everything I've ever hoped for, of my own life– Joe, you shouldn't have hoped, you know better, you idiot dreamer.*

*What about the Bible? I'm the one who knows where it is, how to get to it...* "He said heaven and earth would pass away before His word would be lost.[3]" The verse came drifting through Joe's mind in Nehi's voice. Gentle and firm, twisting with the memory of the first time he had let his friend inside; and Nehi had given him more consolation and wisdom than Joe had felt in years. The mute let the truth sink into him again, and felt the comfort.

*Yes. God can rescue his Own words, even without me. Nehi can handle the rest. It will be hard for Nehi, very hard, but he can do it if I get him to Harry. And I'll want to see Harry before...the end. The end of my story, already! Already? And to go out despised by everyone as a rotten spy, even Harry, and Nehi, even Anna! Oh, dear Jesus, even Anna. They won't understand, and the way they'll look at me, I– Hated and alone even at the end, by everyone, can I, is there any other way, any way for me?*

*The timing's all wrong. I can't let Wolf steal the* <u>Manifesto</u> *(so many souls!). Nehi needs me now. And if my UPC connection comes out, I'll be killed as a traitor. The People's Kingdom, Nehemiah, or me. One of us has to die tonight.*

A black gloved hand touched Anna's lips. The soft leather pressed gently, stopping her torrential outpour. Joe crouched in front of her as she kneeled in the damp grass of the meadow, and he started to sign, green eyes boring into hers. Something hovered behind his intense gaze, his stiff muscles and strangely smooth signs, something she didn't really understand.

"Beauty, I'll get him out," Joe signed. "Don't worry, I can do it."

"You think he's still there?" Anna said, her beautiful eyes staring into his in trust and friendship, and making Joe's job so much harder without knowing it. He couldn't help thinking

---

[3] Matthew 24:35

how she would look at him tonight, and it broke his heart, and very nearly broke his will, as his mind cringed and his heartbeat thudded and physically ached inside him. But he knew how to cover it. Joe just nodded, and went on, his gaze so intense it almost hurt.

"Beauty, I need you to handle something for me. I had a very important thing to do tonight, and now I'm going after Knee-High instead. You have to deliver a note for me to someone who can take over my job. Glue can't do it on his own, and look at D, Beauty." Anna glanced over at her brother slumped in the wagon's seat, his face pale and his breathing strained. "He's too exhausted to do it on his own, too. You have to take it for me."

"I can't leave you and Nehemiah here!" Anna cried, feeling as if she was being jerked in two directions she didn't want to go and was about to come apart at the seams.

"You can and you will, because you're the only one here that can see this note is delivered and delivered well. Beauty, if you don't either Knee-High dies or a whole country dies. You taking this note should stop disintegration from coming on the People's Kingdom." Anna almost said let it come, but stopped herself in time. She had seen what it did to a people to have their country die around them. Anna looked up at Joe. He smiled at her, almost his usual carefree smile that made her so happy to see. But there was still something in his face... Joe laid his hands on her arms and pulled her gently to her feet.

"Beauty, I'm deputizing you to work as my agent, think you can be the Raven's second lieutenant?" he signed in his half serious half silly way. Anna tried to smile and nodded. "Then raise your right hand." Joe paused and looked at her pointedly. Anna raised her hand. "Fine. Now sign after me. I will deliver my note and go where my leader, the Raven, tells me to, come rain or shine, and whether his mode of transport blows up on me or not."

"What?" Anna blinked, but Joe had already disappeared into the wagon. Thumps and bangs rang from inside, things rattling onto the floor as he hunted for items. She was about to follow

him in when he popped back out again. Anna noticed his shoulder bag bulged when it had been sagging before. He dived under the wagon, and Anna heard a familiar click of a cubby hole opening up. Beau slid up next to her and hugged her tight.

"Don't worry, Miss Beauty. God's still in control," he rumbled, and a whelming gratefulness made her hug him back. Joe wriggled out into the twilight air. He came out holding a wand, about a yard long, with a large copper colored ball on each end and two small black boxes on the center. The metal was soldered together rather crudely, and it looked old and nearly homemade.

"What is that?" Anna asked. Joe handed it to her gingerly, as if afraid it might bite.

"An early version of the SOLTD," he signed.

"What?" Anna yelped. Daniel looked up from where he slouched on the wagon's seat. He began to slowly come down to join the group. "Why did you never mention you had this before?"

"Because I don't know how well it works," Joe signed, "and I didn't want to risk it. And now I'm asking you to risk it, and I really, really, really wish I had tested it more than once before sending you."

"What's going on?" Daniel asked, his voice strained with exhaustion.

"Beauty's running an errand for me," Joe signed at him and Beau rumbled dutifully. "You don't have to go if–"

"She's not going anywhere alone tonight, especially not on mysterious errands!" Daniel growled. Joe just shrugged, outwardly uncaring; inside another little weight of hopelessness sank into his stomach and burned. "What errand? And what is that stick thing?"

"I'll explain later, Dan, just go along with it for now," Anna said quickly, and spun back to Joe. "Why again haven't you told us about having this?"

"Look, some things are best kept quiet. I've used it once, it should work fine for you. Beauty, here's the note you have to deliver for me. I wrote some important stuff on the envelope, read it and follow it please, lieutenant. For this country's sake, don't lose this note and only give it to who I told you to on the envelope. And for your sakes, read the rest." Joe handed Anna a white envelope with his distinctive scrawl splayed across the front. As she took it her hand closed on his for a moment.

"Joe, you're shaking," she said, looking at him closer.

"I hugged Glue and he got me all wet," Joe signed and quickly started scribbling something on one of his papers.

"That's not it," Anna prodded in concern. Joe froze, his fingers hovering over his writing. His thin shoulders hunched as if he was too tired to hold them up anymore, his green eyes staring at nothing, face twisted and lined.

"Glue, tell me God really does know what He's doing, will you?" Joe signed, and to Anna his motions felt like a whisper, words he fumbled to get out.

"Of course He does," Cobeau rumbled, disbelief in his voice that anyone might think otherwise. "God always knows what He's doing." Joe took a deep breath and nodded, his usual competence flowing over him again like a blanket. His shoulders were squared as he handed Anna the paper.

"This is the co-ordinance for where you go after you've delivered the note and gotten back out again. That last is important, don't forget to get back out before you leave. As soon as you get to where you're going, put this co-ordinance into the boxes. See there's a little keypad on each, make sure you program both of them. One makes the dark energy go, and one makes the dark matter go, and if you forget one you're liable to die a gruesome death. And get rid of the note. That means destroy it really well." Anna nodded trying to remember everything as Joe kept explaining the workings of this strange gadget. But he finally wound down, pointing over his shoulder at the big Chimera. "If you get stuck, Glue knows more than he lets on. Thank you, Beauty," he signed, and knelt down to reattach his bag on his belt. Cobeau leaned over and grabbed him, lifting the mute's feet far off the ground as he held his little friend to his

huge self. Joe gave in for a moment, giving his Glue a fond squeeze back. The young man squirmed out of his friend's arms, signing vehemently as he moved.

"You take care of her for me!"

"I do," rumbled Beau. "You go get Nehi." Joe grinned at his friend. Cobeau wrapped his great arms around Anna and Daniel's waists. Joe stepped back and nodded at Anna, giving her his encouraging wink. Anna took a deep breath and pressed the large black button.

Joe darted behind a great pine tree and held on as the SOLTD began to work. Two shooting stars flashed out of the black boxes, carrying the tiny bits of dark matter and energy, darting off too quick to even register, to plant themselves where they were programmed. Then the rest of the SOLTD longed to follow. The hissing of the dark energy and matter escaping out of the balls whipped through the darkening air, drawing itself into a swirling black ball of pure power. Then the gravitational manipulation started. Joe clung to his tree as a huge drawing force began to suck everything to itself; pine needles swirled into mini tornadoes and whistled toward the blackness, the trees bent toward it, the ground itself began to be sucked up by the colossal immensity of the blackness.

And then it was gone. Joe sagged gasping against his pine, vaguely wondering if he still had all his sinews attached in the right place, and watched the misplaced needles and boggy ground collapse under normal gravity's laws. It had taken all of three seconds from start to finish. And now they were miles from him. He crouched alone in the meadow. Night pressed in. The trees loomed ominously near him. Joe hugged himself almost unconsciously as he staggered up and trotted to the wagon.

The mute pushed through the pointed door and his finger

shoved into the switch. Warm, homey yellow light spread around him, infused with the scent of Anna's cooking. Joe's hand rested on Anna's painted raven as he shut the door on the glowering forest. The SOLTD seemed to have worked; at least it hadn't exploded. *Let's just hope it works the second time now,* Joe thought as he dug into his raven stash, pulling out a handful of raven snacks, a small bag, and two sheets of paper. He poked his head out of the skylight, gave a series of piercing whistles, ducked back in, sat down at the little table and quickly began to write. He had filled the two pages with his distinctive scribbling when a fluttering of wings sounded. A pretty, black raven flew in to perch on the twig sticking out of the painted oak tree.

"Hello, Jewel," Joe signed fondly. He rubbed her slick black feathers as he filled the small bowl attached to the perch with raven snacks. Joe quickly folded the two papers, slipped them into the little bag, and tied it to Jewel's leg. The raven's head bobbed up and down, and Joe watched for a moment as he sat at the table. His shoulders slumped, head bowed, and he splayed over the table. Just lying there. Three, four deep breaths pulled into him, his face crinkled with a sorrow too deep for mere tears, his eyes running around the wagon, trying to drink it all in. Then he straightened smoothly, took the raven on his arm, pushed the door open, and leaned out. A series of clicks, rising and falling in pitch, quick and slow, flew from Joe. The raven tipped her head as she listened to the complicated pattern. A great caw broke from her, wings lifting. Two flaps, feathers beating into the air, and Jewel soared off. Joe watched the black raven cawing at the sky with a mixture of emotions rolling inside him, too strong and strange to sort out.

The end had begun. Now he just had to go retire the Black Raider, infiltrate deep into the last place he wanted to go, get Nehemiah out, and back to Anna and Cobeau. And Daniel. And take what came next. Not too much for a night, right? Joe gave half a chuckle at the crazy things he did in this life, shakily tugged his bag tighter against his back, leapt on his hoverboard, and started toward town. *I hope everything goes well at that*

huge glass house of the UPC's. *No, not hope, pray,* Joe corrected himself, and began to take his own advice. He prayed all the way into town, and kept it up as he caught a ride on an omnibus, a black shadow lying curled on the black roof. Thirty minutes of lying flat, praying no one looked too closely and thanking God few of the street lights worked properly, and Joe suddenly arched up. He leapt from the bus like a monkey, skimmed up a building, slid down two roofs, and paused across from number 47 Proletariat Lane. He crouched there, a pile of black fabric on a rooftop. A yellow light shone from the second story study. Good. Joe pulled out his papers and scribbled a note, slipped it over the blade of a throwing knife, held another throwing knife in his left hand, and stood up.

He looked at the window, gauging his distance, then took a few steps back. Joe darted forward and leapt through the air. He flung his knife just before he hit the window and glass shattered, spraying into the room. Joe rolled over it to gain a crouch. His green eyes burned, set in his elegant black fabric. Nicky sat at his desk. He stared in frozen fear as the Black Raider raised his hand, a knife clutched in the lithe fingers. The slim weapon left the hand in an instant, whizzing toward Nicky's head, and the man's own strangled gasp was drowned out by the thudding of his pulse in his ears, as his eyes screwed shut involuntarily. A plunk sounded beside his right ear and...he was still breathing. Opening his eyes, Nicky saw an empty office. He started to his feet, looking wildly around him. The only sign the Black Raider had been there was the shattered glass and a knife embedded next to his ear. His breath rattled out of him, and he focused enough to see a note attached to the blade.

*Tell Freddy he wins. If he leaves the IDP alone the Black Raider will retire.*

# Chapter Five: The Council

*"The wind bloweth where it listeth, and thou hearest the sound thereof, but canst not tell whence it cometh, and whither it goeth: so is every one that is born of the Spirit." John 3:8*

A shriek ripped from Anna as the freezing darkness wrapped around her. The air spun and hissed and froze, the noise kneading her brain and shaking her insides. She clutched at Cobeau's arm as her knees sagged. Cold, so cold! Her feet slammed into something hard, the hissing wind changed to a feverish howl that rang in her ears till nothing else could be registered. The black peeled away, and balmy, humid air swirled around her. The wind cut off and Anna stood shaking, her mind spinning, ears ringing, and stomach boiling with bile. The scent of bruised grass swirled with the breeze. She stood and shook and gasped for another five seconds, then slowly un-clasped Cobeau's arm.

"I feel sick," Daniel muttered thickly, his teeth chattering. The chimera grunted. Anna opened her eyes and looked around her. The landscape spun in her vision and she caught a con-fused glimpse of green grass and a hill, before she shut her eyes. Another ten seconds, and she tried again. This time the world was back to normal. She stood in a dip between two hills and could see nothing but the green grass rising up around her. The warm air swirled around her with the sweet scent of tall grass and fresh dirt. The relief of getting away from that fetid bog smell poured through her. Anna slid Joe's note out of her pocket and plotted the new co-ordinance into the two little black boxes on the middle of her stick. The tiny screen on the top of the box blinked blue at her, then shut off. *I guess that means it worked?* Anna thought to herself. She looked at the little piece of white paper in her hand, wondering how to destroy it. Cobeau en-closed the note in a huge fist, and ate it. Anna giggled.

"Thank you very much. Where are we, Beau?" she asked.

"Wild lands. Just pretty wild lands. Come on." He began to

stride up the hill, his unconcerned tuneless hum drifting into the air. Anna took Daniel's arm and hurried after him. Her boots sank into the soft dirt as she climbed and filled Daniel in on the mute's errand. Daniel's jaw tightened and his eyes flashed as he listened. She had accepted an undefined task from the mute and even let him send them somewhere unkown? His words came in a sharp hiss, his wit less rare and caustic but more sincere, as if he cared too much about the subject to try and be smart. Anna listened quietly as she topped the hill and looked around. Plains stretched out in front of her, rising into small hills occasionally. Waist high grass waved everywhere she looked, turned soft and beautiful by the glowing sunset.

Something twinkled at the corner of her eye, and Anna lifted her gaze. On the horizon a building caught the light and sent it glinting back out again. It looked like a huge, many faceted jewel, shooting the sun's rays back out into the world. Beau strode for it, and Anna trotted to catch up, dragging the complaining Daniel with her. A sharp squawking split the night from just in front of them, a flurry of flapping wings started up, and a flock of white birds darted out of the grass and into the darkening sky. A few more yards and a brown rabbit hopped over the top of the grass, twitching his six-foot ears. Anna smiled and wished she had time to pull out her drawing pad and sketch the scene. It was with difficulty she pulled her mind away from the pretty landscape to Daniel again. His words flowed out of him in a tirade, hot, fast, and low, just to her.

"All right, Daniel," she broke in. "I suppose I should have told you what was happening before I said yes and sent us all here. But Joe was insistent and you were exhausted."

"You do realize we could be going to our deaths right now, don't you?" he muttered, panting as they walked a little behind Cobeau. "We're blindly following an untrustworthy person's slave to who knows where. We don't even know what country we're in or how we got here!"

"I told you, wild lands," Cobeau's rumble shook the air around them. Daniel jumped, starting backward and one hand going to his heart as he barely swallowed a curse. Cobeau stopped and glanced at them. He stepped back, swept Daniel up in his arms and started walking toward the building again. Daniel went stiff for a moment, his jaw clamping as he glowered at the chimera. Then he gave a mental shrug and relaxed, slumping back; tonight he was glad of the ride. Shame and sorrow flooded Anna as she realized Cobeau had heard Daniel's insinuations about the Ravens. She hurried to catch up and slipped her arm through his. Cobeau looked down at her and beamed. Apparently Daniel's tirade didn't worry him. She put it out of her mind and started paying attention to her surroundings again. Anna realized these plains were not flat but rose steadily upward to the strange glass building. Cobeau kept striding toward it, humming to himself.

"I miss her hisses," he said suddenly, and it took Anna a moment to grasp his meaning.

"You mean you miss Wara hissing at you?" she asked incredulously. Cobeau nodded, a frown on his hirsute face. Anna chuckled.

"Oh come on," Daniel muttered, "you were furious every time she did it."

"Not furious, upset," Cobeau corrected. "I miss it."

Eight black forms shot up out of the grass, shifting just enough they surrounded the little company.

Silent, supple, competent, each leveled a Krackman ruby laser, primed and ready. They stood stock still, staring at the newcomers with no expression showing through their trained competence. Anna bit down a squeak and jerked to a stop with Cobeau as Daniel scrambled to the ground. The strangers were dressed all in black, but not elegantly like Joe in his Raider outfit. These clothes were one full body outfit, tight fitting to the point of being idiotic, and with funny black zippers in the strangest places. Anna had seen outfits like this once before, and her heart began to beat wildly. UPC! What on earth? Where had Joe sent them? A woman stepped forward, her straight brown hair cropped close around her beautiful, stern face.

"Hello, Gana," Beau said cheerfully. Anna and Daniel gaped at him.

"I know you, chimera," the woman said, her voice disdainful and cold. "But you always come with the GI beast. After you wrecked Darwin Hall you are not allowed in alone. Now you come unexpectedly, bringing two...strangers." Her eyes darted up and down Anna, taking in her black hair pulled loosely back in a clip and her long dark blue Geatish dress; a pitying smile that was more of a sneer cut over her perfect face. Anna took in Gana's ugly outfit, her hard eyes and controlled features, and felt sorry for her. It must hurt to pluck your eyebrows to that kind of perfection.

"Joe couldn't come," Cobeau rumbled. "He sent us with a note."

"A note? Let me see it," Gana ordered, holding out her hand. Anna took the envelope half out of her pocket, then pushed it back again.

"I'm not going to give it to just anyone," Anna said quickly, as Gana's perfectly plucked eyebrows came together in a furious frown. "Joe deputized me as his agent in this matter, and I don't know about you. Especially as you just leapt out at us in a very rude way."

"She has a point," Daniel drawled. Cobeau shifted from foot to foot, impatient. "It isn't exactly easy to trust someone who's idea of fun is to lie in the grass in the dark and jump out at people waving lasers."

"We are on patrol," Gana said, studying Daniel. Beau's huge hand closed gently over Anna's arm, and he began to move forward, taking the young woman along. Anna snatched Daniel's arm, he jerked forward with an undignified stumble, and fell in line a little reluctantly.

"Wait!" Gana ordered, her stiffness cracking a little as she blinked and had to break into a jog to catch up to the big chimera. "My patrol and I need to question you."

"No," Cobeau rumbled, and kept walking. "Joe's note goes to the council, and I am in a hurry." Anna and Daniel glanced at each other. Apparently Joe was right about his Glue knowing more than he showed.

"But..." Gana started, then grimaced and motioned her patrol to circle the group. Beau made no objection to being surrounded by an escort. He just kept walking toward the big house with Anna's arm firmly in his own. Clear glass twinkled in the last shards of sunshine, held together in geometric shapes by black iron bars. A slick modernity gleamed in it, but the overall affect made Anna want to laugh over how pretty they could have made the large building for the same price this ugly thing must have cost. To her it seemed like someone had been conned by a quick-talking amateur architect.

More of the black outfitted people stood guard at the entrance. Anna found her amusement at the strange style of this house change to surprised amusement at God's movement of human lives. In her lifetime she had glimpsed one UPC agent in the entire world, while racing out of a house in KAM. A handsome, muscular man with gold-flecked eyes set in a dark-skinned face; and here he stood guarding a door she was walking through voluntarily. Tanzid, someone had called him? Joe had better have a good reason for sending her to this place.

Joe. These people knew him.

The thought hit her like a punch in the gut. She reeled, her ears humming. Anna shoved it away and hopped forward to catch up to Beau again. Tanzid stepped in front of the door and pulled an enormous black laser rifle off his back, nearly a yard long and almost a foot in circumference. The muzzle swiveled to point at Cobeau. A deep rumbling, overlayed by a whine sounded from the rifle and a red glow came from four slits in the side. Gana glanced at the chimera and saw he wasn't going to stop.

"Don't you recognize the incomplete's chimera? The strangers are with him bearing a note for the council. Let them through, Tanzid." The young man pursed his lips, his eyes on Anna. This man had glimpsed her in KAM, running from a Christian's home. He knew enough to accuse her of being one of the

hated and hunted of the UPC. Anna stared back into Tanzid's gold-flecked eyes, waiting, her prayers all for the man in front of her. He hadn't turned her in last time. Maybe something in his soul was in the process of twisting the right way up…

"The chimera isn't allowed in alone after Darwin Hall–" Tanzid started, his voice rich and deep, but Beau wasn't in the mood to wait. Cobeau's fist closed over Tanzid's collar. The chimera lifted him and the huge laser till the man's feet dangled. He moved him to the side, sat him down gently, and reached for the door as Tanzid stood with his mouth half open blinking at the chimera.

"But–" Tanzid stammered.

"Not alone," Beau rumbled, and swept through the door with Anna, as she dragged Daniel after her. With a few swift motions, Gana stationed her patrol at the door and swung after Beau and the Hillsons, with Tanzid as her backup. The Chimera marched on, through one clear room after another. Anna silently tried to decide if she could do anything about Tanzid… No, he would either denounce her and she would die, or he wouldn't, and no action of hers would change that right now. Anna left it in God's hands and turned her mind to the people they passed. They seemed a very mixed group. There were old and young, men and women, and all but those in the ugly black suits wore badges that said their name and what country they were from. Gaia, the People's Kingdom, the Kingdom of Autonomous Man, Story Land, the Kingdom of the Wise, the Battle Kingdom, Kallipolis, it seemed like every kingdom had a representative here. Anna even spied two kingdoms she had never heard of.

Cobeau didn't glance at the people as he marched. Gana and Tanzid walked after the little group, trying to appear as if they were in charge and doing a good job at it. Cobeau turned into a hall and dark, carved wood confronted Anna. She rocked to a stop in front of two large doors set in a wall of steel. Gana glanced at Beau's hand moving toward the handle, and deftly ducked in front of him. As the chimera flung the doors open,

Gana stepped in, competent and stern, and her voice rang through the chamber.

"Excuse the interruption, Council, but the incomplete's chimera is here. He says the strangers he brings with him have an urgent note from the GI beast." Cobeau brushed around her, pulling his two charges through the heavy doors. Anna found herself in a large, plain room. A set of rising platforms took up half the room, with chairs set in a semi-circle. People filled the chairs, of the same eclectic variety Anna had seen moving through the building. All of them stared at the newcomers. Cobeau marched in front of the semi-circle, pulled his arm away from Anna's, and moved into a corner, leaving Daniel and Anna faced with fifty suspicious pairs of eyes. A gray-haired man in a pinstripe suit sat at a small polished desk in the center of the horseshoe facing the other people. He stood up, slowly, impressively, his gaze on the Hillsons.

"You bring a note from the incomplete? Let me see it, if you please," he said, holding out his hand.

"Now wait a minute," Daniel said, "we don't know who you are. In fact, we don't even know where we are. (It's been an interesting day, all right, don't judge.) We aren't going to hand over an important note to anyone. What do you take us for, utter fools?" A murmur ran around the crowd, but Daniel didn't back down. His chin rose and he eyed the pinstripe suited fellow, glare for glare. The man studied Daniel for a moment before he spoke.

"I recognize you now. I take you, sir, for two of the Judge's children from the late Sojourner's Kingdom." A louder murmur sounded in the hall, clothing whispered and chairs squeaked as the crowd shifted. It wasn't a friendly sound. "It has been four years since I was there, and you have both changed. But I remember your voice, and your father's likeness remains."

"Yes, I remember you, a visiting dignitary who declined to state his country," Daniel said, outwardly unabashed. Inside he cursed how easily recognizable their family's prominence had made them. "Yes, we are two of the late Judge's family. Now,

who are you and where are we?" A smile cracked over the man's thin face.

"You have a commanding way about you, Sojourner. You are in the council chambers at the United Peoples Commission headquarters," he said. Anna saw Daniel clamp his jaw shut to keep it from dropping in his shock. She felt almost as shocked, even with having recognized two members of the UPC here. They were actually at the headquarters! Joe was known here, he...Joe worked with these people! "I am Damien, the leader of the Council. We are a group dedicated to seeing peace stays in this world between kingdoms, and inside of kingdoms, and communication is kept open. We are made up from all walks of life and nearly all places in this world. Our agents are the best any has ever seen. Gana and Tanzid, whom you have met, are two of our most qualified. We are the real power behind the movements of this world. It is the UPC that makes kingdoms rise and fall, that keeps the advancement of science and society always before our people's eyes, that sees no individual is made a victim in this dark world. We are the silent workers of good, however you may define that term. We go about our work secretly, for there are many less enlightened people that would object if they knew. Does that satisfy you, Daniel Hillson?"

"It helps," Daniel answered, his face showing no hint of surprise.

"Now I would like you to answer a question, Mr. Hillson," Damien said, stepping down from the platform and moving to stand in front of the tall young man. "How did you get here? I believed we had a very clear view of all the land around us and could not be approached as you have done. How did you do it?" Daniel studied him again for a moment, his jaw tight. Then he shrugged and took the heavy black stick from Anna.

"It's called a SOLTD, Speed Of Light Transportation Device," he began, and pointed to the two boxes in the middle. "These have small bits of dark matter and dark energy in tiny cases designed to flit to where you want them to go using coordinates according to the draw of the magnetism of the earth. You program each separately, and zip, they're off, using the combined energy of excited dark matter and energy to move. And of course dark matter is attracted to dark energy like an unerring magnet, and dark matter to dark energy respectively, especially when two pieces have already been introduced; so when you open the dark energy ball on the end and let a whole mass of the stuff out, it wants to zap off to the tiny square of dark matter you already sent flitting to your destination and join in the fun. But first, the dark matter and dark energy from these two big balls on the end ram into each other when you let them out. It creates a small black hole effect and uses the energy of it to travel, and the quirk of a human's body heat, to create a space warp around travelers. A black hole generates cold internally, and warm bodies inside of it create a sort of eye-of-the-hurricane calm that the SOLTD utilizes to make the bubble. It literally takes the ground you're standing on and drops you with the two little boxes you already sent to your destination. Not too comfortable of a way to travel, but it gets you places quickly."

While everyone's attention was focused on Daniel, Anna took the opportunity to pull out Joe's envelope and read the scrawled words. With the crazy ride to get here, Daniel's lecture, and then Gana jumping out at them, she had forgotten about it. But the sight of Joe's distinctive scrawl on the front of the envelope stopped her. She felt her heart swell and pulse in an agony of doubt. The UPC. Joe was part of the United People's Commission, the sworn enemy of the IDP, merciless murders of the little mute's Christian brothers and sisters! Was he really a Christian at all, or an unbelieving spy, a wolf in the middle of the unsuspecting flock? Or did he just use whichever side suited him at the moment? He admitted to being a minute by minute sort, was he a selfish brute who just used people?

But even the ferocious heat of that first shock came tempered by a wave of doubt. Was the young man she had joked with and traveled with and watched fight for their lives again and again really such a despicable liar? Could her little Joe be

that bad of a man? Or was this just another layer to the same sweet young man who hid shyly behind mask after mask? Either way, she was furious at him. If he was still the same old Joe, tossing them into this situation of wondering if he was a traitor out to kill them was downright mean. Anna steadied herself, turned in toward her brother to mask her reading from the councilmen, and focused on the words.

*Anna, remember neither height nor depth can separate us from God, and that includes Nehi.* Anna frowned and smiled in almost the same instant as she felt the comfort hit home. *Joe, you obnoxious riddle, why do you have to be so sweet and at the same time so secretive no one can be certain who you are? Watch what you say, they don't like Christians there.* This she knew. *Give the note to Damien and no one else, and be careful, there's an FF there that would love to get you and the note. DON'T tell them how you got there, whatever you do, and remember to get OUTSIDE before you press the 'Go' button again. God bless, Ann, and thanks.* Anna looked up at Daniel.

"And that's how we got here without you seeing us. Pretty ingenious if I don't say so myself." Anna cringed and prayed that wouldn't come back to haunt them.

# Chapter Six: House Raid

*"Peace I leave with you, my peace I give unto you: not as the world giveth, give I unto you. Let not your heart be troubled, neither let it be afraid."* John 14:27

Back in the alleyway in front of the Brotherhood's House, Joe leaned against the wall and watched the gate, the only way out of the great building. A massive ugly iron thing that took three strong men over a minute to open, and just as long to close. No one came in there who wasn't cleared, and getting out again was generally considered impossible. A little door cut in the side of the wall stood a few yards from the gate though, guarded by one soldier. He could get in that way on foot. But he couldn't get out again without the proper papers. Joe's eyes lifted over the electrified wall to the vast square building shut inside. It's coat of white paint hadn't been allowed to turn gray yet. The top of the Doric columns could just be seen from where he stood, as they shouldered the weight of the third and fourth stories of the massive structure. Joe shuddered and dropped his eyes to the dirty ground. He had been there when this building was erected and the scenes of forced labor flashed back in fresh relief in his mind. There could be no beauty for him in that vast expanse, painted white to cover the blood stains.

Despite himself, his mind leapt to the thought of those laughing and talking just beyond the massive gate, of the future waiting for him if just one person in there latched on to his forced silence. A cold chill ran down his spine making him shiver and huddle against the dirty wall. But Joe was smart and strong, and didn't dwell on the possibilities. He forced his back straight and began to dig into his things. He had been elated when he stopped here earlier. Though he certainly wasn't now, Jesus had implanted a peace, and even a kind of joy. Joe's mind rested, at ease and able to dwell wholly on the problem of getting in and getting Nehemiah out. *Well, I did retire tonight. Just not the way I'd hoped,* Joe thought to himself as he watched the

gate for ideas. *It couldn't be helped. When I'm put on ice as a spy tomorrow I can't leave the IDP guessing and still in trouble with the FF.* A boy in a light blue shirt ran up to the gate and held up a yellow card and a piece of paper. The guard let him in.

*Joe, you never should have left them today,* he told himself as he pulled out a light blue turtleneck and slipped it on over his black jacket. *And no more dreaming. It only makes real life harder.* He put his dart gun, pistol, and two extra clips in one pocket of his cargo pants, and filled the other pocket with miscellaneous items that might be useful in this caper. *I've told you again and again, Joe, dreamers and GIs don't mix.* He pulled out a yellow card identical to the one the boy had held up and scribbled on one of his papers. *Oh well, I guess you won't have much of a chance of mixing them after tomorrow.* Joe paused and sucked in a breath. He let it out slowly, checked to make sure his collar was up, and shoved his bag behind a dumpster with his hoverboard. *Bad call, Joe. No thinking about tomorrow. This is a minute to minute night, forget the future and focus on now.* Joe stood still for a moment to steady himself, eyes closed, fists clenched. The breath rattled out of him in a long, slow hiss, and his fingers uncurled. Joe's eyes shot open. There was no trace of the cheerful musician in the steely determination on the mute's face.

Joe scurried up to the roof, dropped into a street, and loped through it up to the gate of the Brotherhood's House. He held up the yellow slip and his piece of paper. The guard glanced at it and motioned him in. Joe crossed through at an easy jog, and was inside. People milled everywhere, despite it being after eight, dignitaries, elite, soldiers... lots of soldiers. Quiet terror mounted steadily higher in the mute as he dodged in and out of groups. Every moment he expected one of them to call for him to stop and explain his business, and then where would he be. "He can't talk. An incomplete!" the hated, inevitable cry would sound, and he would be whisked off to a station again. Scenes as fresh in his memory as the reality he walked through now flashed through his agile mind; stinging smoke that wouldn't let you breathe without pain, starvation cowing every strong thought, the work glue that ripped off patches of skin, companions dying slowly all around him of disease and abuse, the torture stake and dark cabinets, sticks and harnesses, that racking pain that grew and grew till – Joe gritted his teeth and willed the memories away. If he got lost in them now he would lose his nerve, and then where would Nehemiah be? And Anna. And Daniel and the IDP, for that matter. No, he would figure a way out of it if he was discovered. He had to.

Across the courtyard, through the Main Hall, the Decorations Room, the Proletariat Gallery, Joe moved steadily, always looking about him as if searching for the right person for his note. The plaster was all new, and the paints even varied in color with a fair amount of taste. Joe came to a tightly packed hall and dived in without hesitation, ducking under legs and around bellies, thanking God for his small size. He made it to the end of the hall and around the door. *Wow, when even the Brotherhood's House mess hall smells good, you know you're hungry. Why didn't I grab something while I was at the wagon?* Joe chided himself as he weaved through tables and around more soldiers, still sending his eyes darting back and forth in search of his elusive (and non-existent) note recipient. Once through the mess hall, the soldiers began to thin out. As Joe dived deeper into the building, they became fewer still. Finally he reached a hall with no one in it but a single guard at the end, standing in front of one heavily padlocked door. Joe prayed another silent prayer and loped toward him, holding up his note and raising an eyebrow in an easy way. The soldier waved him away impatiently, then glanced at the note and hesitated.

"*Major* Urick?" he asked. Joe nodded emphatically and moved toward the door. The soldier hesitated, then pulled out his keys and slid it into the lock. The click as it turned seemed to ring in Joe's head in time with his ringing ears. The guard dragged the door open. A bare, metal landing at the top of a long flight of stairs faced the mute. Joe stepped past the guard onto the landing, and cringed involuntarily as the door crashed shut

behind him and the heavy lock clicked into place.

He stood still on the top of a long spiral staircase, a single blue bulb hanging down as lighting. It only made the darkness below seem deeper. He took a deep breath and stepped down. Black boots shot out, padding down the spiral staircase, silent even on the metal stairs as he moved swiftly downwards. He slipped off his blue turtleneck, rolled it into a ball and stuffed it in a pocket, pulled a black wad of soft black leather from the same pocket, and wound it quickly around his head. By the time he stepped off the stairs into the pitch blackness of the entry to the Brotherhoods' holding cells, Joe had become the Raven again and slipped through the darkness as if he were a part of it.

He found the door and put an ear to it, using a simple ear funnel to hear through the thick metal. One set of heavy, rhythmic breathing came from the other side. One guard, just like at the top. Joe loaded his dart gun and hefted his drill. The bit cut through the door for a brief two seconds, a tiny whine invading the entry. A beam of clear yellow light spilled through from the room on the other side of the door. Joe clicked off the drill, his throat hot and ears singing; the guard must have noticed the disappearance of part of his door! But no outcry, no alarm… Joe leaned forward and put his eye to the hole. The guard slouched in his battered swivel chair, fat chin on his chest, his eyes closed. A snore rumbled from him and a line of drool slithered from the corner of his mouth. The Raven smiled, breathed a prayer of thanks, and used his dart to be sure the guard stayed asleep.

Joe had the door open in a trice and moved into the glaring light of the passage. He wrinkled his nose and was glad he hadn't had dinner after all. This place stank worse than any bog in the forest, or even the crawling fog. A group of lockers caught his eye and the young man moved quickly around the guard to glance in them. He pulled out Hope and its holster, pocketed them, and began to move down the rows of cells. Stark, filthy, gray emptiness stared back at him from each tiny room. He tried to decide if that was a good thing and they weren't taking many in, or a bad thing because the ones in them had already been dealt with. Only one cell held an occupant in this area. An old man sat huddled on the metal cot, his gray head slumped on his thin chest, his hands in the pockets of his dirty white lab coat. Joe pulled out his paper and pencil and began to scribble. The man looked up at the slight sound of the pencil scratching. His eyes widened and he stared at the small, black figure in front of him. Joe handed him the note through the bars.

*You're Quintus Leeman. You invented a device that can transport whole armies faster than the eye can see. Now you're in the death block because of old age.*

Quintus Leeman's mouth dropped.

"Who are you?" he breathed. Joe held up a hand for silence, his head cocked on one side as he listened to something. He grabbed his note, scribbled on the other side and shoved it back into Quintus' hands.

*I'm a friend of Paul Sireton. Don't let on I'm here.*

Quintus' head shot up from the note, but no black figure stood in the hallway. The thud of heavy soldier's boots reverberated from the direction of cell block three. Clothing swished as something dragged between them. Quintus winced, stuffed the note into the pocket of his lab coat, and moved back to his cot. A key clattered into the lock of the door leading to that horror of cell block three. The click of the tumblers rang loud in the stark hallway, and the clang as the metal door opened seemed deafening. Two soldiers stepped through, dragging a dark young man between them. A very young man, Quintus noted, the wrinkles on his face deepening. They dumped him on the floor in front of the execution room, across the hall and one cell to the left of Quintus. The old inventor looked away. He didn't want to see that handsome young man's end. He had seen so many over the past few days! The soldiers stood impatiently by the locked door. One began to call for the guard at the end of the passage to come and open up.

A glimpse of movement above the soldiers caught Quintus's eye. He glanced up, and saw part of the dark ceiling shifting and moving. He blinked, lost the movement, found it again, and watched in awe as his mysterious black figure moved upside down along the pipes as if he were a bug or a gecko. Paul's friend paused directly over the two soldiers. Annoyance showed in the man with the officer's stripes and he heaved a huffing curse. He took a step toward the jail door, raised his foot for the second step, toppled forward, and lay still, face down on the cold floor. The other soldier whipped his luttle rifle off his shoulder. The whine of the priming laser filled the cell block, the light glowing eerily. The man spun around, his face working in fear, looking everywhere but up. His feet stumbled. Every muscle went limp. He toppled quietly forward, slamming down on top of the whining luttle. Quintus squinted through his bars and thought he saw a tiny piece of something stuck in the soldier's neck.

Joe dropped catlike to the ground beside Nehemiah and rolled him over gently. Nehi stirred and a gasp came from him. Joe's lips pursed as he pulled his friend into a sitting position, propping Nehi up, assessing the damage. They had been even rougher on him than Joe had expected. *Nehi is tough, he'll be all right.* But Joe suddenly found that made little difference as his best friend slumped against him gasping and only half aware of his surroundings. Quintus blinked and stared hard at the black clothed figure; surely that hadn't been a sniffle he heard from him. Joe rested Nehi's dark head on his left arm, ignoring the blood dripping onto his clothes, and began to dig into his pocket with his right hand. *Wolf knew this would happen. He meant him to die, and didn't care how nasty it got. That dirty, vicious, evil, despicable– steady Joe. It's not time. Besides, it's not your problem anymore.* A bottle appeared in a black gloved hand, and a little pop sounded in the quiet cell block as the stopper came out. The mute held it under his friend's nose.

Nehemiah coughed and pulled away, an arm clutching his stomach and his eyes jerking open. He retched and doubled over. Joe's arm shot around Nehemiah's chest as he began to fold onto the ground, pulled him back up, and leaned him against the cell door, pressing an antiseptic soaked bandage to the gash on his forehead. The mute caught his friend's eyes and winked as cheerfully and positively as he could manage. Quintus hadn't expected that and sat back, pleasantly surprised. Nehemiah forced himself under control, making himself breathe and focus on the black form in front of him. He gave a weak laugh.

"I was wondering when you would show up," he muttered, his voice thick and hoarse. "Thanks for coming to the rescue again." A black gloved hand patted him on the shoulder and held a flask to his lips, forcing a drink down him. Nehemiah felt hot fire running through his throat. It spread into his veins, tingling through his whole body. He doubled over in a cough, his head spinning uncontrollably. Joe shoved him back against the iron door, forcing him to straighten out, and he could breathe again. Nehi's head cleared, and he found he could sit up on his own. He gripped his friend's arm, his raspy breathing speeding up, and his eyes boring into the mute's.

"Anna and Daniel, Joe, they aren't used to this, did you–" Nehemiah choked.

"They're fine, Knee-High," Joe signed. Nehi slumped back in relief. "No one hurt them, not really. They're out, and safe as far as I know."

"They keep a database of known Christians here, complete with sketches. The Judge family is still in it." Nehi paused, a short, tight breath hissing from him. His eyes opened again and focused on his friend, his voice dropping to a hoarse murmur that he knew couldn't reach Quintus. "The officer in charge shoved everyone else out about four hours ago. He's an FF, Joe, and they really want that cursed treasure." The mute's shoulders slumped, his face lined behind his mask.

"I'm sorry, Knee-High, so sorry, I thought you were safe here. I misread–" Joe's signs broke off mid-thought as a choked gurgle came from Quintus, his eyes riveted on Joe, his body

tense.

"You're a GI!" Quintus burst out, his voice echoing off the walls. His lip curled as if a fetid smell wafted past, his eyes wide in his shock. A black gloved finger shot to Joe's lips as he scuttled over to the door of the cell, pulling his lock picks out as he moved. Quintus steadied himself, and lowered his voice. "Sorry. I was shocked. He is then? An incomplete?"

"Don't call him that," Nehemiah gasped. "We're all made precisely how God meant us to be." Joe spun around to face Nehi, the finger to his lips again.

"Sorry once more," Quintus murmured, leaning on the door, his eyes dulling. "Forgive an old man set in his ways if I gave offence. I won't be around much longer to offend, anyway." The door suddenly swung open, and Quintus pitched into the hallway, his chest ramming into Joe's head. The two of them slammed into the ground, a tangle of arms and legs. The mute squirmed out from under him and pulled the inventor to his feet, laughing at the mishap. The little mute gave a low whistle and began to move his hands. The movements were more than swift and smooth, Quintus noted this time, they were elegant and beautiful.

"Joe says hello," Nehemiah interpreted, his voice gravelly and deep. "And to tell you I'm Nehemiah, and that you aren't as old as they've made you think you are, and do you want to try and escape with us tonight?"

"What? Well, yes, thank you for the offer," Quintus Leeman stuttered. He collected himself and gave a little bow. "I would be honored to be counted as one of your company. So when do we leave?" Joe began to sign again, but Nehemiah didn't really pay attention to the signs, he was watching Joe's eyes, his mannerism. Whatever Joe had made him drink did its stuff, strength and clarity flowed back into him. He could notice details. Like the strange light in his friend's face... Joe stared at him, one eyebrow raising in a look that said, "Snap out of it and translate, do you think I have all day?" Nehi put it out of his tired, tired, aching mind and spoke Joe's words for Quintus.

"We have a ways to go and lots of soldiers to pass through," Joe said through Nehi. "We need a good cover for the three of us to use, either of you have any ideas?"

"Cover?" both men said. Joe chuckled silently and shook his head in mock despair. He tweaked the lock on the execution cell door, dragged the two unconscious soldiers in, locked it again, and spun around.

"New plan, you two stay here and get acquainted. Quietly. I'm going to go see what I can find. Oh, Knee-High, I have a present for you." Joe reached into his pocket and pulled out Hope. Nehemiah's eyes brightened, even the one swollen nearly shut. Joe grinned behind the mask as he handed it over.

"Thanks, Joe! Boy, I feel better having my Compton near," Nehemiah said as he slowly strapped the holster back on his leg. "Her name really fits."

"Very useful in a tight scrape," Joe signed with a nod. "Pray you don't get into one while I'm gone." Joe turned and disappeared into the darkness to find a way out.

Nehemiah and Quintus looked at each other. How did one start a conversation with a stranger in the stinking holding cells of the Brotherhood's House?

# Chapter Seven: Tanzid

*"Therefore being justified by faith, we have peace with God through our Lord Jesus Christ."* Romans 5:1

Remarkable. Especially for a Genetic Incomplete," Damien commented as Daniel finished. Damien's dark eyes turned thoughtful and scheming as he gazed at the SOLTD in Daniel's hands. They darted suddenly to Anna, and she felt like the rabbit under the gaze of a green back. "May I see that note please, child of the Sojourners?" Damien held out his hand and Anna took the note out of the envelope and handed it over. She stuffed the envelope back in her pocket and waited to see what would happen now. Damien stepped aside to read the note and Cobeau strode out of his corner toward the Hillsons.

"Time to go," he rumbled. His palms pushed into their backs and he began to herd them toward the door.

"I'm afraid not," Damien called, looking up from the note. "I don't want these three leaving. Not yet, possibly not ever. That SOLTD could be very useful indeed in our work, and after all, you are Christians and chimera. Gana, see that they don't leave and get that remarkable gadget will you?" Gana whipped her Compton pistol out, a pair of black laser goggles flicking over her eyes. Tanzid lowered his huge blaster from his shoulder and leveled it at Daniel. Gana moved forward, her pistol at the ready and her hand out to take the SOLTD. Cobeau's huge fist closed over the stick. His short rifle glowed red and pointed at Damien's chest. No whine invaded the room; all three lasers were primed and ready.

"You can't have it," Cobeau growled as he slipped the SOLTD under his coat. "Not yours." The two UPC agents paused, studying the chimera calculatingly. A snarl rippled over his face, and Gana's eyes narrowed. Anna stepped between them, her hands coming up palm out.

"Now look, all of you," she said quickly, "you aren't going to get our SOLTD by waving guns around, believe me. I know Beau better than that, we'll all end up dead and he'll fall over on the thing and smash it. If it hasn't already been hit by a laser beam and loosed the dark energy and matter right here in the middle of your council chamber. Besides, I have a feeling the council has a great deal to discuss now. Is that right, Mr. Damien?" Damien looked up again and let his arms drop to his side, the note held in his cupped hand, his face completely emotionless.

"She has a point. Take them somewhere else, Gana, and leave Tanzid on watch. I may have further questions for them later." Gana waved her pistol at the door and Tanzid stepped aside, his huge laser glowing red. Cobeau still stood with his laser pointed at Damien.

"Lay off, Beau, Anna just bought us a reprieve on life," Daniel muttered, pushing the laser muzzle towards the ground. Cobeau looked at him uncertainly.

"Come on, Beau, keep the SOLTD in your coat and your rifle still, and we're going to quietly follow our captors for the moment," Anna ordered. She took his arm and walked out the doors. Daniel followed and Tanzid slid into place behind them, marching just out of reach of any possible funny stuff from the prisoners.

The envelope seemed to burn in Anna's pocket as Joe's face burned in her mind; laughing, teasing, exhausted, frightened, blank...so many Joes. Which one was real? It rolled through her, tightening her stomach and pulsing in her mind till her head began to ache with it. Anna gave a sigh and straightened her spine, willing Joe away. She couldn't deal with him now. She glanced to the side, at Cobeau's simple face crinkled as he tried to understand what was going on, and Daniel's half-closed eyes and exhaustion. Her brother's silence told her all she needed about his condition. She had to get them out of this mess. Which seemed only fair, considering it was her fault for not reading that note in time.

Gana shoved a shiny metal door open and spun through it onto a stairway, her hard boots ringing on the metal stairs as she marched down. Anna let go of Beau as she followed and

took in the area. She craned forward as she walked, glancing over the simple metal railing. Three stories of stairs twinkled in the bright white light below her. Above, another four stories twinkled and glimmered. The place was empty. Only their footsteps rang in this echoing stair. Anna steadied her breathing, studying the woman in front of her. Gana walked two yards ahead, her Compton out, steadily marching; but her attention stayed on Beau, as if he were the only threat. A skip and Anna came a stair closer to the woman. Another skip, and Gana still hadn't glanced at her. Anna stepped down another stair, and jumped.

She collided with the woman's arm and found Gana's thumb. Anna pulled back with all her strength, bending it over her arm. A sickening crack, a strangled scream, and the Compton was in Anna's hands. A well aimed shove sent Gana stumbling down four steps to a stairwell, bent almost double, struggling to regain her footing. The Compton jerked up, aimed at Tanzid's head, as Anna's foot shot out with a judo kick. Her steel toe smashed into Gana's temple. Gana's dark eyes dimmed, rolled up, and she folded into a pile on the metal stairwell. Tanzid's arms shot over his head, his eyes bright as he stared into Anna's.

"Easy," he murmured, his voice low. "I'm not sure, 'on your side,' is quite the right way to put it yet–" He broke off his eyes darting away.

"Shoot, Ann, he's buying time." Daniel's hiss reverberated around the stairwell and vibrated in Anna. Her gaze never left Tanzid's dark face.

"Beau, take his gun," Anna ordered. The chimera's massive hand shot back and wrapped around the blaster. The shoulder strap snapped as Beau pulled it, and Tanzid stumbled down a step, his shoulder throbbing. Anna made a noise at him and he froze. "Quick Beau, tie up Gana, then catch up to us. Tanzid, turn around and up to the roof." The chimera slid past Anna as Tanzid spun with cat-like quickness and started to trot up the stairs, his hands still held carefully in view. Anna ran past

Daniel, ignoring the way her brother held out his hand for the laser, and trotted two yards behind Tanzid. Daniel started to mutter under his breath as he trudged behind Anna. "Ok, we're moving again. Now what did you mean, what were you going to say that you cut off?"

"I was going to let you go," Tanzid said, his voice still unnaturally low. "After Gana left me on guard with you."

"I would say that's ridiculous," Anna said, cutting off Daniel's bark of incredulous laughter, "except that you saw me in KAM." Silence dropped behind Anna. "Why didn't you send out my description?" Nothing came from the agent. Daniel felt soft breathing on his neck and spun with a stifled curse. The chimera stared back at him, eye to eye though he padded along two stairs lower. Daniel looked over the banister. Gana lay trussed like turkey, a white gag protruding out of her mouth. Cobeau worked fast. "Oh come on, we don't have all day for this! Just tell me, you didn't turn me in because..."

"I didn't want to," he snapped. A low curse came from him and he sped up, his muscles bunching under the weird tight suit. The stair in front of his feet disintegrated into a mass of molten metal. Tanzid gave a sharp curse, leaping back out of the way.

"Not an answer," Anna growled, letting her finger off the trigger.

"I'm haunted at night by all those like you I've killed, all right?" Tanzid almost shouted, spinning toward her. His face worked, but Anna couldn't decide what emotion moved it. "People who have never done any harm except disagree with the way Damien and the others want their world to be, and I've–" His jaw clamped shut and his fists balled.

"May I remind you, little sis," Daniel drawled, "that we're standing on a staircase inside the most enemy territory we'll probably ever get into?"

"Move," Anna told Tanzid, motioning back up the stairs with the pistol barrel. Tanzid turned and moved.

"There's no way out up here," he growled.

"Wait, no way onto the roof?" Anna asked.

"Roof access is via the south staircase, on the other side of the building. This way dead ends in a steel ceiling ten feet above the stairs." Another curse spilled from him. He spun onto a landing and stopped beside a door. "Come on, I'll lead you out. But I'll need my blaster back, we have to look the part."

"Oh sure, right, yeah," Daniel said, his voice quick and amused.

"Shut up, Dan," Anna snapped at him. "Look, Mr. Tanzid, we need to clarify some things."

"Enemy territory!" Daniel almost yelped. Anna waved him quiet, not taking her eyes from the stiff agent.

"The Spirit's obviously calling you, are you going to answer or not?" Anna demanded, her chin lifting. Tanzid blinked at her.

"What?"

"You're being dragged to Christ. He's calling you, telling you turning in His people is wrong, giving you that haunted feeling you just mentioned. Are you going to answer?"

"Your Christ doesn't want me!" Tanzid hissed, his fists balling again. His face worked, but this time Anna could see the liquid pooling in his desperate, despairing eyes.

"Unconscious commando, on the stairs below us!" Daniel said through clenched teeth, jabbing Anna in the shoulder. She ignored him.

"You've obviously been around people of the Way, do you know the truth we preach, about Christ's death that saved us?" Tanzid nodded, and Anna swept on. "We don't have much time, listen and don't interrupt," she said, her words quick and clear, little staccato sentences of distilled truth. "God uses sinners, that's what we all are, none of us are good without Christ. Ever heard of the Apostle Paul? He was a man who turned in Christians too, he destroyed people, hunting down members of the Way mercilessly, zealously. Till Christ met him on a road and fried his eyeballs so he would listen. Then Paul became one of the strongest pillars in the church, and wrote a good portion of our Bible. Tanzid, God says come. Now. While you're still dirty because you'll never be clean without Him. Christ says, 'Behold, I make all things new.' So are you switching sides or what?"

"I can just come?" Tanzid blinked. He was bewildered, a whole new world opening to him. Daniel hopped from foot to foot, eyeing the Compton in Anna's hands, obviously considering making a grab for it. Anna ignored how stupid it was to just stand here.

"Yes. Tell Him you're switching sides, now. Pray with me." Anna tossed the heavy pistol to Daniel, stepped forward and took the agent's shoulder. He flinched, pulling back and staring at her with wide, shocked eyes.

"You do realize I could snap your neck with one move, right?" he said, a kind of worried awe on him as he stared at this madwoman.

"Yes. And that it would be your last act, with Dan and Beau there. Come on, stop stalling." Anna's head bowed, her curls sweeping her cheeks. For one blink more Tanzid stared at her. Then his head dipped, his shoulders slumped, and he gave up the fight. His voice came husky, almost indistinct as he muttered after Anna. It told her he wasn't just acting it to gain their trust; he had no bravado during that prayer. "Lord Jesus, forgive me for the evil I have done to You and Your people. I believe Christ died for me, and trust Him completely to bring me to heaven, and to help me live here. Make me new, make me into a servant you can use. Amen." Anna's head shot up and she took a step back. "There, you're covered in case this thing all goes wrong. Now get us somewhere outside into the open air, and we'll take care of the rest."

Beau tossed the blaster to Tanzid and the agent staggered back, his shoulder ramming into the metal door. Daniel's lips were so tight they could hardly be seen. But he tucked the Compton into the pocket of his long leather greatcoat and shot up past Tanzid. He jerked the door open and strode out, his facial features and manner changing as he walked into a dark, empty office. Anna trotted to catch up and glanced at him as her brother pulled open the connecting door and strode into a

hallway. Resignation, quiet despair, anger, bravery, it all played over him, and the story could be read at a glance; prisoners being escorted out for execution in the open air where the smell would be carried away by the breeze and the stains wouldn't matter.

"You're a really good actor," Anna murmured to him in surprise.

"Just pray your little lovefest on the stairs holds out and we're not actually marching to our deaths," he muttered back to her. Two women in flowing white robes passed them, glancing curiously at the group. Tanzid's huge gun prodded Daniel's back.

"No talking! Faster," the agent ordered. Anna could feel the heat coming off the blaster in waves. Sweat began to roll down her spine, and it wasn't from the laser's heat. One quick prayer versus years serving the UPC... Just at that moment, with the primed laser casting an eerie red glow on the glass walls of their dim hallway, it was hard to imagine him being sincerely on their side. Beau strode in front of her and took the lead. These upper floors were starkly empty this late at night. Daniel glanced back at their guide and his normal self came back over him as he dropped the acting. Joe sprung to Anna's mind as she watched it, and her gut twisted.

"Don't get me wrong just because I'm impatient to get out of here, I am happy you've seen the light. Welcome to the family, and all that," Daniel drawled. Tanzid blinked at him, his face wrinkling with confusion. "This Christianity you've jumped into is a family, you'll see soon enough. Now listen, you're one of these UPC characters. Do you know Joe?"

"Joe?" Tanzid asked. His eyes snapped around the hallway as he marched, and Anna wondered what went on behind his tight features.

"The incomplete," Daniel supplied, and Anna winced.

"Oh, the little GI beast," Tanzid said, a little absently. "Yes, I've worked with him on a few assignments, he and Gana and I. And the chimera, of course. I didn't know the two were ever separated."

"What assignments?" Daniel asked quickly.

"Things like last year when the KAM book was in danger and we had to run the parties off who wanted it. We did, that time. The GI can be pretty impressive, I have to admit."

"Wait, you work on keeping books from being stolen too?" Anna asked.

"I'm not sure what you mean by the 'too,' but we try, yes. It shatters peace to have a country go into disintegration. We've been after the group doing the blackmailing and theft for years, but still haven't found anything about them. What little we know comes from the GI, actually. As soon as one of our agents finds something out, they die. It's creepy how quick that group moves."

"You said you worked with Joe a year ago?" Daniel asked. "How long has he been a part of this?"

"He's never been a part of us, not really. He's a genetic in-complete. He does some work for us and he carries news and messages sometimes. He's been around here for about two years now. Wait a minute." Tanzid's gold-flecked eyes stopped flicking around the hallway and focused on Daniel, his voice suddenly interested again. "If you two know him well enough to call him a name, he must know you're of the Way. Why has he never turned you in?"

"I don't know why he does anything," Daniel growled, "but he is deep in the IDP, and knows a lot more Christians than just us."

"He's in the IDP?" Tanzid gaped. "Why that little traitor!"

"My sentiments exactly," Daniel growled.

"You realize you both just called him traitor, and you're speaking from opposite sides," Anna said. Silence slid into the hallway.

"So who is he actually working with?" Daniel murmured.

"You mean who is he working for," Tanzid corrected grimly. "Now be quiet, all of you, you're condemned prisoners and I'm taking you outside to shoot you, act like it. And keep moving.

We have to get out fast, Gana tends to escape quickly from things like that." Cobeau sped up, winding his way back through the clear rooms. Most stared back at them empty, but as they stepped off the sweeping main staircase onto the ground floor, plenty of people looked up at them. Dignitaries huddled in little groups, students studying papers in comfortable arm chairs, a few laughing over glasses as they leaned on an oak bar; business went on late into the night here. Anna tried to look frightened and upset, and wondered if it worked. Daniel did the acting for her, and Beau moved quick enough they only had a glimpse of the open area, then they were pushing through into the balmy breeze and swishing grasses. A bird sang somewhere to their left. Anna let herself smile as the fresh breeze and openness rushed over her. Cobeau trotted on two more yards, spun, and shoved the SOLTD at Anna. The big man wrapped his arm around Daniel and Anna's waists again, then he looked at Tanzid.

"Come on," he rumbled. Tanzid stared at him from a pinched face, then his eyes swiveled back to the glinting building. But his thumb absently hit the safety on his blaster. The red dimmed and died. "You have to be touching," Beau prodded. Tanzid stood looking back at the big ugly building.

"Oh come on, what are you going to do, wait till Gana wakes up and asks those people we just strolled by if they've seen you?" Daniel said. He reached over and grabbed Tanzid's arm. Anna hit the large black, 'Go' button, and screwed her eyes shut. The hissing wind, dizzying darkness, and debilitating cold wrapped around her in a ferocious spinning nightmare.

# Chapter Eight: Trio Trouble

*"And the multitude of them that believed were of one heart and of one soul: neither said any of them that ought of the things which he possessed was his own: but they had all things in common."* Acts 4:32

Joe's fingers tingled as he lifted the GI harness off the wall and he felt his stomach clench. He really didn't like this idea. But it was their best chance for getting out. He plopped the IK hat on his head as the easiest way to carry it and hunted in a pocket for his black material as he padded along the corridor with his finds slung over his arm. His eye fell on a ticking clock at the end of the hall, and his expression tightened.

The Wolf hadn't given a time for his infiltration tonight. But to Joe the timing seemed obvious. A frown cut over his face as he calculated when Anna and the others had zipped off, and how long it would take the UPC agents stationed in town to deploy. If the Trio succeeded in tripping the book alarm, everything would immediately lock down and he would never get Nehi and Quintus out. He would have to do a little slowing down and prep things for the UPC teams coming in. Once here, "discretion" played a main role in the UPC's training. They won't trip any alarms. But a little interest away from where Joe and his charges headed tonight might be nice...

Joe pushed his pile of things into a dark corner, draped it with his black cloth, and leapt onto the pipes running along the top of the ceiling.

The Brotherhood's House boasted regal meeting rooms, well-kept barracks, and even a clean white façade outside. Very few people who walked through its door knew about the inner places. Pipes and bundles of electrical wires ran through every part of the building in stark, small passageways. Most were too thin to fit a grown man. But Joe fit just fine, and down here the lower jails granted easy access. He scrabbled along the pipes,

skimming up to the higher parts of the house with the speed of a flying bird. The world around him stayed in pitch blackness, but he could feel the air currents, hear the conversations through the walls, and knew where he moved. Joe didn't stop till he had reached the upper level of the house. He clung to a pipe, his arms trembling as he blew hard into his mask. But his eyes shone and a smile hung on his face; he could enjoy this part of the game. The tiniest hint of yellow light shaped a square on the wall, and he knew he had found his entry point. He gently pushed against the square.

It swung open, spraying light into the passageway. Joe slithered through into the room beyond, his eyes slits against the bright glare. His toe closed the square as he moved, and he scuttled forward.

The book room stood just behind him. He could see the relic in its glass case, the paper crumbling and discolored, the cover nearly disintegrated. A part of him wanted to stop and ogle it; every book looked so beautiful to him. A passage to past worlds, a way to step into another person's mind, to see things as they saw, and gain a glimpse of a whole different generation.

But not today. He knew the cameras caught every move he made, and in this glaring light his black against the red-painted ceiling wasn't exactly discreet. If the guard on duty actually paid attention, alarms should go off any second now. But Joe's smile stayed on as he skimmed over the ceiling of the outer room. He knew no outcry would follow him. This was the moment the guards changed. It ought to be a quick thing, two people switching seats, a new pair of eyes glued to the monitor. But that would be automatons, not humans. Humans stopped to exchange news and jokes, settled their coffee mug in its spot, probably unbuttoned the bottom button on their vest... And the guard shift always changed at the same time each night. When the Sojourners came back alive, he needed to recommend randomizing the guard changes.

If. If the Sojourners came back alive. And besides, he wouldn't be around to recommend anything.

Joe scuttled to the corner where the shadows gathered, his smile gone. He shouldn't think about the future. He needed to focus on the now. But his mind drifted to Nehi's trusting eyes, the way his battered face had lit up at the sight of his friend there to get him out. Bile rose in Joe's throat as he thought of the way those dark eyes would look at him later tonight. He shook himself like a dog coming out of a pond, and got his mind back on the business.

A movement caught Joe's eye. The Trio strode toward the book room. Their black suits pulled tight over their bodies, their shiny oval masks hiding their faces. Jill held her Personal Pad in her hands, interfering with signals as they moved through the halls. The shifting fuzziness in the signal should have been noticed by the guards on duty. But the Wolf chose his time well, and the Trio moved quickly. Their path would be noted, all right, but after chaos broke loose and security started raking every feed looking for abnormalities. Then precious time would be lost following their path in and out, while the trio skimmed over the rooftops of Paradise and disappeared into the night. Joe flipped till he hung by one hand, the fingers of his gloves sticking to the ceiling. He hung just inside the door to the room, out of sight of the Trio. Jill strode past him, her fingers still moving over her screen. Bill moved just behind her, his muscles tight as he held his bow ready. Joe hung and waited. Will stumped in after Bill, the man's feet clumping into the floor in loud staccato beats.

Joe's legs shot out and locked around Will's neck. The big man gave a tight gurgle as his neck twisted and a weight slammed into him. A taser shoved into his ear and sparks shot through Will's system.

Bill spun at the sharp buzz of the taser. He found his companion a twitching heap on the ground, and a black form sliding off into a smooth Kungfu five elements pose. Two bright green eyes stared into Bill's for an instant. Then the black one moved. Silent and swift, he darted around the twitching Will and made a diving kick at Bill's shin. He came so fast, a blur of movement.

Bill slashed out at the figure with his bow. He felt it strike; and stick. Then he focused and saw the black glove clutching the end of his bow. Those two green eyes burned into his own. A twist, a spin, and the bow jerked and bent around the figure's arm. Bill clutched at it and did a quick spin of his own, a growl rising in his throat. The supple wood trembled, bent nearly double, but held.

Joe stepped back and let go. The bow twanged straight into Bill's midriff, and a sharp woosh came from him as he doubled over.

The rasp of metal on metal came from the left. Joe spun, his left arm coming up over his face. A sharp impact jarred into his jacket sleeve. He could see a blur of silver as another throwing knife left Jill's fingers, and his arm slashed down. A knife sailed for his abdomen, then another at his face, and another for his belly, in blurring succession. Joe caught each with the stumpy tail leather on his sleeve. With each block he danced a little closer to her. With each strike her foot moved back, inching her toward the door to the book room. All she had to do was brush her hand over the door…

Behind him he heard Will's sharp gasp as he gained his feet.

He caught a glimpse of wood as Bill's bow struck out for the Raven's ribcage.

Joe launched himself into a flip. He slapped his right arm into his left, giving the bone added strength. His forearm smashed into Jill's throat. His legs kept moving in his flip, and she went backward at the force. Her knees slammed into the floor, and her head touched the ground, her spine bent in a C as she gagged and gasped. Movement caught Joe's eye, and he saw Bill knocking an arrow, aimed for the glass case where that beautiful pathway to another mind lay protected. As he felt Jill's head touch the ground and his feet still spun in midair, Joe analyzed the trajectory, the weight of the bow, the speed of travel. Joe cartwheeled off her and his boot struck out. It hit the shaft and deflected Bill's shot. The arrow slammed into the wall and stuck there quivering. Joe's feet landed on solid ground, and he slid into a fighting stance, one palm up ready for a strike.

Will charged toward him, his face rippling with fury and still twitching with the impulses from the taser. He swung his laser up as he moved, the red bright and silent in the Krackman rifle, already primed and ready.

A kyoketsu-shoge rope dart sailed into the room and wrapped around Will's thick chest. It pinned his arms to his side and the Krackman bounced out of his grasp and hung on its shoulder strap. Five black-suited figures moved into the room and chose their targets with silent precision. The Trio spun toward the new fight. An arrow sprung to Bill's string, as Jill snatched up her knives. Will flexed his arms and snapped the rope around him.

As the fight shifted, the Raven pushed against a small square in the wall. It swung inward, and he melted into the inner workings of the Brotherhood's House.

But as the door swung, he flicked a metal pellet at the camera mounted in the corner of the room. Joe didn't want an alarm over the book tonight; that meant automatic lockdown. But now that the fun had begun, he wanted it noticed. That should cause just enough confusion to get everyone's focus away from the Raven's little escaping party.

Five stories below, Wilhelm Neeander sloshed coffee out of his mug as his screen gave a sudden beep. His mug clunked onto the desk and his fingers flew over the screen till he found the source of the beep. Eight black figures spun and struck and fought in the outer room to the book. Wilhelm's jaw dropped onto his chest as his eyes nearly bugged from his face. He caught one glimpse of the scene, then the camera went dark. Wilhelm spun from his chair and sprinted to go find his officer.

Five minutes later, a squad pounded up the stairs and into the outer room leading to the book.

Everything looked pristine and in order. A red light blinked gently on the camera, suggesting it needed service. Wilhelm's officer turned slowly on the young soldier, his face darkening with anger. Wilhelm's arm lifted and he pointed just to the side

of the book room.

An arrow stuck deep in the wall.

"Fan out," the officer shouted, "find out what's going on!"

"Hello," Nehemiah croaked. Might as well start off on a conventional note.

"Hello," Quintus answered, trying to decide if he was awake or dreaming this whole strange affair. After this brief exchange there didn't seem to be much else to say. Nehemiah drew his knees up to his chest and let his hot, heavy head slump on them, wondering idly if he had to stay awake or if he could go unconscious like he wanted. Joe's wish to get this Quintus Leeman "into their ranks," as the mute had put it, flashed into his mind. Nehemiah shifted his head and looked at the inventor. His wasted face was confused, and his watery eyes kept darting around the bare, stinking hallway, as if he couldn't focus on anything. He looked so lost. Christ's reminder to swell His own ranks flew into Nehi's mind. *"For whosoever shall call upon the name of the Lord shall be saved. How then shall they call on him in whom they have not believed? and how shall they believe in him of whom they have not heard? and how shall they hear without a preacher?*[4]*"* Right here he was the only preacher available. Quintus' flitting gaze focused on Nehi and the inventor's lips pursed with concern.

"I would like to ask if you're all right, young man, but I am well aware of the stupidity of the question," he commented, and it drew a smile from Nehi. "I hope you're recoverable though?"

"I'll be all right. And even if I don't recover, I've got my place in heaven settled," Nehi murmured, his voice scratchy and deep.

"Heaven?" Leeman asked. His Adam's apple bobbed on his

---

[4] Romans 10:13-14

skinny throat. "You're a Sojourner then? I suspected when I saw your treatment, but one hates to assume."

"Yes," Nehemiah muttered, letting his eyes close. He wasn't about to try nodding. "You sound interested. Curious about it?"

"I've been sitting in front of an execution room for ten days, waiting for my turn. Yes, I'm curious what Paul held to so tenaciously, I never really paid attention to it when he tried to explain. But are you sure you're up to questions?"

"I'm not dying, I just sound like it," Nehi smiled wearily. "First question?"

"Why did the Sojourner Judge condemn the People's Kingdom ideas so harshly?" His hand rose and he stuttered on in a rush. "Don't misunderstand me, I've been here long enough now to despise these cells, the thieving, the work permits that only go to the favored, and even to view the work stations as the horror they are. What I mean is, why do the Sojourners disagree with the basic beliefs of the country? You even call yourselves 'brothers,' and I've heard your early church fathers shared everything communally."

"The thing about sharing is you have to own it first," Nehemiah drawled, and in that moment he sounded just like Daniel. "I know what passage you're talking about, I remember the Judge reading it to someone." Nehi didn't mention it was his own father reading to the president of the People's Kingdom. "The early church brethren owned the property they shared. You have to own it before you can voluntarily share with those who need it. God has a lot to say on personal ownership, and a whole lot on sharing what you have with those in need. God commands us to be generous, as a way of physically expressing all He's given to us. But sharing what you have, and the government owning everything, are two very different starting points."

"Yes...I do see what you mean." Quintus shifted on the hard ground, staring at the splattered bloodstains. "Most people are unwilling to offer what they have... but I recall hearing gratitude plays a part in your religion. And gratitude for a gift makes

a person more willing to give gifts of their own."

"Sounds like you've got it. Let me tell you about that gift," Nehi wheezed. He swallowed and began talking, explaining how he could still have peace even when sitting against the door to the Brotherhood's execution cell. He found Quintus Leeman very willing to use the time well. The two men waited for Joe, and covered the Bible's teachings on charity, wrecked the idea of incompletes and chimeras and turned them back into humans, dealt with the correct view of life and death, delved into science and why it mattered, and ended with Quintus deciding his old friend Paul and this new, battered friend were right. Quintus Leeman admitted it, and followed in a prayer very similar to the one Anna led Tanzid in miles away in the stairwell of the UPC's headquarters. The gray head of the inventor lifted with a joyous hope after his first prayer, and Nehemiah broke into a smile to see it. But the next instant a cloud covered the inventor's face again. The old man drooped beside his new brother.

"What's wrong?" Nehemiah asked. As soon as the words left him he knew the answer; the same feeling had been growing on him for the past few minutes. He let his eyes turn away and tried not to frown too heavily. He really, really didn't want to have to get up and go looking for Joe.

"I'm sorry, lad," the inventor answered. "It's just I've been an enemy to Jesus so long, and now, when I finally want to serve Him..."

"I know. I hadn't expected to leave this earthly battle ground so early myself. But don't give up yet. We're not locked in and I'm armed, we can make a run for it together if we need to. And Joe might be back any time now. He's a pretty impressive character."

"We haven't heard from him for nearly twenty minutes now, Nehemiah. Nothing in these cell blocks is large enough to justify that kind of time gone." Nehi looked away and didn't answer. An uncomfortable silence fell, as Nehi tried to talk himself into getting up to go find Joe.

"I cannot believe it has taken me all these years to admit the truth!" Quintus burst out. "And now I'm an old wreck. How could I have been such a fool?"

Joe's whistled translation request sounded in front of them. Nehemiah and Quintus leapt a foot, starting so hard they almost fell over. Joe stood in front of them, his green eyes crinkled as he grinned at their shock. A large bunch of cords and blue fabric lay slung over his shoulder and one of his hands clutched what looked like two sticks. He threw the stuff on the ground and began to sign, Nehemiah translating.

"We're all fools, Quintus. You still have much to give our Savior, I don't classify you as a wreck. I'll have no despair from you two, not tonight. If I see either of you giving in to our enemy despair, I'll knock you off your feet. Got it?" Joe's green eyes were cheerful and confident, and both the men in front of him relaxed visibly as they nodded.

"Where have you been?" Nehemiah wheezed, a little sharply.

"Later," Joe signed in his infuriating way. "We're in a hurry. Knee-High, do you think you can walk on your own?" *Confound it,* Nehi thought.

"If I have to," he answered, his voice quiet. "Abid's training is still in my bones enough for that. But I hope you're not planning on racing out of here. I'm not up to anything quite that energetic."

"I haven't been up to racing for decades, even before days on prison fare," Quintus put in. Joe picked up the cords and shook them out till they fell into shape. Nehemiah's nose wrinkled with loathing and his face steeled as he recognized them. A stiff tether that shoved over a person's elbows to pull on their shoulder joints, clamping their arms tight against their back. He had worn one most of today. But the other... As Joe shook out the mass of strong, black cords, Nehi watched an incomplete harness take shape. He had seen one briefly on his friend in KAM and had hoped he would never see another. Joe suddenly produced a blue officer's uniform with one of the tall green hats

with the badge marking it as an Incomplete Keeper, or IK, and dropped it in front of Nehemiah. Nehi wondered where it had come from.

"Get the picture?" Joe signed to Nehemiah, his green eyes crinkled with an impish smile behind the black mask. But a flush painted his face, and something...almost a glow in the eyes that Nehi didn't understand...

"I'm denser tonight than usual, Joe, you'll have to explain," Nehemiah wheezed. Joe nodded and plopped cross-legged in front of his friend, unwinding the black fabric from his face and stuffing it into a pocket. Quintus' mouth dropped open in surprise when he saw the one they were relying on to get them out of this place was little more than a boy. He looked younger than Nehemiah. No. His scarred face looked older. Much older. And yet so joyful and so steady... Quintus found himself wanting to know more about this young man.

"I'm a recaptured incomplete. You, Knee-High, are transporting me back to my station and were asked to take Q along–By the way, brother, welcome to the family!" Joe interrupted himself, leapt to his feet to give the old inventor a bone crushing hug, and dropped back in front of Nehemiah. "You were asked to take Q to the next cremation facility. (They use a cremator to get rid of the Brotherhood's victims, Knee-High). The one at this facility just broke." Joe flipped Dark Ray and grinned mischievously. He slipped his ray back into his pocket, along with his gloves, ripped his collar and flipped his hair back so that his GI mark showed plainly, and began to dig in his pockets again.

Two minutes later the three had been transformed from Joe's capacious store of stuff. Nehemiah found himself walking down the hallway toward the outer office, with Hope on his hip and Joe's ray in his pocket. Joe had erased Nehemiah's visible bruises and other marks of his interesting day by means of a strange make-kit, created a few bruises and wounds on himself with the same kit, and carefully fitted on Quintus' tether. They looked like they were supposed to now, condemned and executer. In fact Nehemiah looked enough like an IK in the suit, with the cap tilted to cover the swollen eye, Joe felt the urge to punch him and start running every time he looked at him. The mute studied Nehemiah as they walked. He would do, poor fellow.

"Don't let go of the sticks attached to Q and me," Joe signed, "but don't press the buttons on the ends. What happens if you press the button?"

"It shocks you two," Nehemiah answered, thinking he must look as bad as he felt for Joe to make him recite things back.

"Right, very unpleasantly, and if you accidentally slip it to a higher setting it does worse. So watch that knob on the top! Knee-High, I can't sign in this harness and I'm going to be looking as desperate as I can, so you're going to have to watch carefully to follow my leads and hints." Joe paused beside the snoring guard, fished the keys out of one pocket, and a thin paper out of the other. He handed it to Nehi. "That's for the gate. Get us all back to the wagon. Get Q and I out of these ropes." The mute opened the heavy door and led the way into the deep darkness of the stairwell. He looked back over his shoulder at Nehi, raising one eyebrow.

"Get us all to the wagon, get you two out of the ropes," Nehemiah repeated dutifully. "Stairs?" he added unhappily, staring at the bleak metal staircase winding up till it was lost in the darkness somewhere high above them. Joe shook his head and led the way to the other side of the little area, revealing an elevator underneath the stairwell.

"But it requires a card," Quintus pointed out. "An ID badge from an officer, probably." Joe pulled an officer's ID badge out of his pocket, swiped it through the slot, and the elevator began to hum as the cage lowered. Nehemiah started laughing at Quintus' expression and ended up gasping and leaning against the wall, Joe's arm around his chest the only thing keeping him on his feet. Joe's flask pushed against Nehemiah's teeth, and stinging liquid streamed down his throat. Nehi gagged and shoved the flask away, taking his own weight again. A moment, and he stopped hacking and started breathing again.

"Neither height nor depth, remember?" Joe signed. Nehi focused on Joe, and realized his head had cleared again and he could stand up with less effort. Those green eyes stared back joyful and bright, but...sadness. That was the strange glint, or at least a part of it. A deep sorrow that the mute's joy only just covered. Nehemiah nodded slowly.

"Right," he said softly. "We're in God's hands, little friend, and no matter what we'll make it home to Him. Keep that vision." Joe nodded and motioned for help into the harness. For just a moment, as the ropes began to settle around his torso, and Nehi tugged them tighter through the series of s-hooks, Joe felt his throat tighten with panic. He almost jerked away, and toyed longingly with at least holding a razor in his hand to cut his own way out when he wanted... But the soldiers up there would notice if a GI held something. And notice would bring questions. He stood still, let his arms lock tight against his chest, and felt the stick click home at the small of his back giving Nehi perfect control over the mute. Joe stepped into the elevator, head high and prayers strong inside him.

A moment later Nehemiah found himself holding a pair of sticks attached to two brothers, riding up an elevator that would open on he didn't know what. He prayed a silent prayer for strength and waited.

The elevator opened on nothing but emptiness. An empty hallway stretched in front of them, and Nehemiah followed his two friends out and began to walk. He focused away from himself, letting his eyes lock on Joe's back. They came to the end of the hall and Joe's head dropped and waggled back and forth as if his neck had just come loose. He began to stumble, and a look of desperate horror contorted his sharp features. Nehemiah reached forward to help, afraid he was about to have a fit or something. Joe shot him a look that said, "I'm doing my part, why aren't you doing yours?" Nehi dropped back again and held the sticks, carefully keeping the little knobs at the top still. They turned another corner and Nehemiah's forced his spine straight and a march into his steps. Soldiers eyed them without much interest as they walked through the stark hallway.

Quintus didn't have to act to look scared. He was used to element tables, energy balls, and test tubes, this type of thing was an entirely new experience for him.

They made it through the halls and into a large room filled with tables and chairs, only a few of them occupied. A general movement seemed to be drifting toward the left... The smell of something cooking wafted to Nehemiah and his stomach knotted with nausea again. Joe carefully led the way through the mess hall towards a tall wooden door. A stocky soldier in a dirty IK uniform lolled there. Watching Nehemiah. The door loomed over Joe, and the soldier straightened up, took a stride forward, and tapped Nehemiah on the shoulder.

"Where are you going?" he said.

*Good question, why didn't I ask Joe that?!* Nehemiah thought. He just grunted a rude reply and brushed through the door into the Proletariat Gallery. The soldier followed him. Portraits glowered at Nehi from frames on the wall as he walked. The soldier swung into the hall and strolled behind him, hands in his pockets.

"Okay, you don't have to be suspicious of a fellow IK," the stocky soldier chortled. "I was just going to say, your odds aren't what I'd like."

"What?" Nehemiah growled.

"Two to one. Two prisoners and one guard isn't always a safe equation. Something's happening tonight, the high ups are suddenly looking nervous, and I don't want our squad caught in whatever it is. You're a little young, you know. You'd better have me along to even the odds. You're in my detachment according to your uniform's badge, and we look out for our own," the soldier explained.

"What?" Nehemiah growled again, then decided he'd better say something else. "I'm fine, I don't need your help."

"Don't get so up-tight, brother! Believe me you don't want to lose either of those two." The soldier laughed and one finger flicked at Joe. "Haven't you even noticed the beast is looking a

little desperate?" Nehemiah felt his fist itch in the wild desire to break this fellow's nose for calling his good little friend a beast, knowing he didn't consider it a character description; to this man it was a fact. But now that he mentioned it, Joe did look desperate, his whole body almost writhed with it.

"So what?" Nehi growled.

"So that's when they're the most dangerous! I knew you were green. Better let me come along," the stocky IK responded. They stepped out of the glowering gallery and into the wide entryway. Nehemiah hardly noticed the checkered tile under his feet or the towering Doric columns beside him. The busy courtyard loomed just through that wide doorway, and dismay crawled through him as he realized he had no idea what to do when he got there. And this soldier wouldn't quit! Nehi walked onto the wide, white porch, on down the shallow staircase, and felt his boots crunch on the gravel of the courtyard. Soldiers flowed steadily into the house, always headed up the grand staircase toward their left. A general feel of urgency moved with them.

The stocky IK kept on his heels, insisting the odds were no good.

Nehemiah paused, forcing himself not to sway. He watched Joe carefully and tried to keep his brain from numbing over like it kept trying to do. Joe led him toward a small armored wagon, a nifty little job, if a bit outdated. But then all the vehicles looked older in this kingdom. No hoverer graced the line of vehicles in the courtyard, and Nehi could have cursed. A wagon tied to the ground was a slow way to travel, and easier to track.

Joe stopped at the back door. His wild eyes shone and snapped everywhere with the light of a person crazed with terror and hopelessness. The IK pointed at him with a leering grin and opened his mouth to say something. Joe spun with a desperate, mad, fury in his manner. Nehemiah found himself clutching the stick to ward off the little mute, out of instinct. Joe's face contorted with agony. He screamed silently and crumpled to the gravel writhing, twitching, and convulsing as the silent screams twisted his features. His fingers formed into claws as his muscles seemed to tear at each other, screwing the mute into an unnatural, thrashing heap. Nehemiah stood staring at him in shock.

As he went through the motions, Joe used his new position to rake the top of the Brotherhood's House with his gaze. Just barely silhouetted against the dingy gray of the city at night, he spied them; eight figures, still moving in a fight over the house. As he watched, one went down with two sitting on their chest. He hoped it was one of the Trio. Darn it, why were they still here? The Trio must be putting up quite a resistance. Some smart soldier would find the party on the roof, soon. Then the fun would spread to the whole house, lockdown would come after all, and they had to be gone before then. Joe slammed his thrashing foot into Nehi's calf.

Nehemiah collected himself and reached for the back of the wagon. The door pulled against his muscles and his body screamed in a duet with Joe. But he locked the scream in his throat, wrenched the door open, and bundled the twitching mute on the floor.

"Well..." the IK soldier said grudgingly as Quintus' slid into the back of the wagon, his eyes glued on the twitching, curled mute. Nehemiah slammed the door shut on them. "Okay, so maybe you have more experience at this than I thought, I didn't know you had the harness at level eight. Actually I didn't think you had it in you to push it that high. Okay, so go ahead, but if you get into trouble I won't stick up for you."

Nehemiah just grunted and slid into the driver's seat, slamming the heavy door in place. His mind spun with the relief of having the soldier out of his hair, hoping like mad he could get through that gigantic gate, and stomach-churning horror that Joe knew just how it felt to have that little knob twisted and pushed. The mute knew it well enough to act it to perfection. How many times had that really happened to him? Shudders shook Nehemiah and his heart missed beats. He put the thought of Joe's past firmly behind him and started the wagon. The

engine purred and it sounded like a good one. Nehemiah rubbed the steering wheel and looked at the gate, feeling helplessly weary and pained and alone.

"Jesus, help us now!" Nehemiah prayed into the darkness of the cab. "It's going to take your power to get us out of here. Please show Your strength in your people's lives again." He laid Hope and Dark Ray within easy reach and slipped the car into gear. That gate looked like it would take a long time to open. Maybe if he took it slow. He did take it slow, and the van crawled toward the mass of iron. It had the effect he had hoped for. Or had he hoped for it? Maybe the thought had been transplanted there, but however the idea came, it worked. The massive gate swung outward, slowly, ponderously, as the guards shoved at it in an effort to be efficient. It stood a third of the way open and getting a little wider every second as Nehemiah pulled the wagon to a stop beside the inspection station. A soldier stepped to the window and held out his hand.

"Papers?" the soldier said, smothering a yawn. The gate neared the halfway mark. Nehemiah estimated he could slip through if it would only open halfway.

"Papers..." he muttered, and fished into his coat pockets. He found the paper Joe had handed him and passed it slowly to the guard, his eyes never leaving the gate.

"Brother," the soldier said in an exasperated voice, "this is for a single transport, not a wagon."

An alarm blared through the courtyard.

"Lockdown, everything lockdown!" a voice blared over a loudspeaker.

Nehemiah slammed his foot onto the accelerator. One hand darted to Hope as the other gripped the steering wheel, and he took out those his training automatically picked out as the worst threats. The laser bit through walls and flesh, silent and invisible, leaving dead men and molten metal. Soldiers spun as their companions fell beside them, raking the area for the enemy. The light and whine of priming lasers dotted the courtyard. The truck shot over the four yards to the gate and slammed into the opening that meant freedom. A squeal bit through the night, horrendous metal on metal, as the wheels tore into the asphalt and the engine revved.

The truck stuck there, half in half out.

# Chapter Nine: Running the Gate

*"I go to prepare a place for you."* John 14:2b

Whining lasers hit the back of the wagon, pulsing again and again. Nehemiah shoved his foot down on the accelerator. Wild squealing covered even the alarms and shouts behind him. The truck inched through the metal gate. The noise tore at Joe and Quintus, locked in the back of the metal truck, and the mute's writhing was no longer an act. Acrid smoke billowed from the tires. Another inch, another squeal of smoking tires, and the wagon shot through the gate. They jolted and jumped into the street, and a gasping yell broke from Nehi as he desperately tried to control the rocking van. Joe and Quintus slammed helplessly into the back doors. A tall gray building loomed in the headlights in front of Nehemiah. He spun the wheel left and the truck rose dangerously on two wheels. But it turned. He spun into the road, the truck jolted back to all four tires, and he managed to spare a glance behind him.

Two blue government cars shot through the gate just before it closed, red lights revolving steadily on their roofs. Nehi's hand shot toward Dark Ray as he spun the van into a tight little road.

Joe and Quintus banged against the right wall with a clang. The van spun with a squeal of tires, and the left wall met them, then the right, then they were flung against the back of the wagon. Nehi slammed on the brakes and Joe tumbled across the floor to smash into the front. Quintus slammed into him and the mute's neck bent under the weight. The wagon jerked off again. Joe's boots jammed into the bench, pressing his back against the wall. He could feel himself slipping, as the truck jerked and jolted. He gritted his teeth and wished he hadn't given Nehemiah Dark Ray. He could really use that beam to get out of this horrible harness!

In the driver's seat Nehemiah silently thanked Joe for giving him the ray as he slammed on the brakes again, spun in his seat, and shot the dark beam behind them at the two red lights rushing down the road. The ray's blackness enclosed the first vehicle. The red light popped and went dark, and he heard the satisfying sound of metal scrunching from the cone of darkness enveloping the car. His own door wrinkled. Nehi shut the beam off and stared behind him to see the effect. The first blue car slid under its earlier momentum, a crumpled wreck, bits of it lying about the street. It twisted sideways till the buildings surrounding the road caught it and held on. With a screech of tires the second car veered to a stop behind the new blockade of crumpled blue metal. The second vehicle's spiraling red light reflected off the walls like an angry firefly. Nehi shoved his foot down and shot forward again. A soft "boom" came from behind him, and Nehi found himself enjoying the sound of the vehicle's explosion more than he perhaps should have.

Nehi pulled into a busy street, shifting between the trucks and hoverers, trying desperately to find his way in this strange city. After six streets he realized he moved in a grid. Not a perfect grid, but close enough to let him find his way to the right edge of town. He could hear alarms coming to life throughout the city. The streets emptied around him, as the citizens quickly realized they would do better out of the public eye. Nehi pressed the accelerator harder and felt the van leap through the night.

In fifteen minutes, he turned out of the city toward the peaceful little meadow and the Ravens' wagon. Oh that deliciously peaceful Ravens' wagon! Ten minutes later, Nehemiah jerked into the clearing and slammed on the brakes. He could hear sirens wailing back toward town. The van would be easy to track with its four tire marks and bright blue color, they would be here in minutes. His shoulder pushed into the door, and the metal seemed so heavy.

He staggered out of the wagon, his legs quivering and his body shaking. His mind numbed. But the mute knew the type of master Al Abid had been. Now, when nothing else could have kept him on his feet, the orders Joe had hammered into his head

played through his marrow. Nehi obeyed. As long as he had any molecule of strength, he would obey what had been ordered. Nehemiah stumbled to the back of the wagon. The catch bit into his hand, cold and hard. His muscles screamed at him as he dragged it open. Two heavy bodies tumbled forward, and a hoarse yell quivered from Nehi as they crunched into him, knocking him flat.

"Sorry about that lad, but it was you that stopped so suddenly," Quintus said breathlessly somewhere above him, and Nehemiah breathed again. His recognition of that voice came dim and fuzzy; but it wasn't Abid or Simmons. Quintus and Joe scrambled off of him, and the mute snatched Hope from where it stuck out of Nehemiah's pocket. Two seconds later Joe stood free, with a black scorch mark raking up his jacket, and a smell of burnt flesh under the melted leather. He jerked Nehi up to lean against the van, shoved the flask into his friend's shaking hands, grabbed Quintus and dragged him towards the wagon, undoing the inventor's tether as he moved. Nehemiah raised the flask in the numb haze of obedience. The liquid fire poured down his throat and Nehi doubled over, gagging and coughing, his body quivering.

"Joe, what is in that!" he gasped. His mind cleared, like a frosted pane of glass lifting from his vision, and he felt as if he could move again. A little. He lifted his head slowly as he heard no answering whistle or click. For a moment, the world spun. But then it calmed, and he saw his friend's feet sticking out from under the wagon, and Quintus blinking at the black boots. Nehemiah stumbled up and wove his way toward them. A familiar black bag shoved from under the wagon, the one he had carried to Geatland. It clanked as it moved. Joe squirmed out and shoved the bag at Quintus.

"Hadn't we better start Prissy on our way out?" Nehemiah murmured. He stood swaying on his feet, his eyes half closed, his voice gravelly. "I shook off our hunters, but they can follow our tracks. Joe, what's wrong, why do you look so sad?"

"Just some silliness, Knee-High," the mute signed, forcing a smile. He grabbed Nehemiah's arm and tugged him toward where the giant pig grazed on the meadow, staked comfortably in her harness. "I'm just a little sad to leave it all behind. You unhook that side."

"Wait, we're unharnessing Prissy?" Nehemiah asked, rubbing his hand against his forehead. A siren ripped through the air and he whipped toward town instinctively, stumbling back a step. Joe's 'listen-up' whistle sounded and he stumbled around again.

"We're not taking the wagon, no time. We've got to let her go," the mute signed steadily. "Unhook it." Nehemiah began fumbling with the harness, and fumbled in his fuzzy mind.

"What will happen to her?" He thought it a silly thing to ask as soon as he said it. Just at that moment, with all their lives hanging on seconds, to ask about a giant guinea pig seemed idiotically sentimental. But he didn't want to retract it.

"She'll be all right," Joe signed. He pulled the harness off her back and rubbed her nose fondly, that sad look back on his face. "We got her around here, there's an old farmer who will be glad to have her back. A nice old guy. You know where it is, Prissy, go on." The mute led the pig a few steps on her way. Her ears twitched and she started to trot, squeaking happily, pine branches swishing away as she shuffled into the woods. Her white and brown back disappeared into the dark trees, and sorrow settled deep in the pit of Nehemiah's aching stomach. Then he connected with the sirens behind them again and remembered he didn't have time to be sad. Not yet.

"What about us, into the woods?" he rasped. Joe shook his head and trotted back to Quintus. The inventor knelt beside the black bag, digging into it and muttering things to himself. He heard the young men coming and looked up, his eyes bright and face lit with curiosity.

"Where on earth did you get this?" Quintus asked. "I know I didn't make this SOLTD, but here it is, nearly complete and with the parts needed to finish it!"

"A SOLTD? In that bag?" Nehemiah blinked. His brain spun

again and he swayed in time with the rocking world. Joe whistled for translation.

"Q, we need that now. Can you finish it in fifteen minutes?"

"Fifteen minutes?" asked the inventor in shock.

"Okay, eight," Joe signed and Nehemiah said. Quintus started to stammer something about connections and credinces but Joe cut him off, his signs hard and fast. "We have five minutes before they get here, Q."

"Oh," Quintus muttered. His Adam's apple bobbed again. Then competence seemed to flood over him, and Nehi could see his scientific mind taking over. "I'll need the blueprints, the latest model has a complicated pattern to the aiming mechanism, I have to–" He broke off as Joe pulled a large blue paper from his jacket and handed it over. "You do realize this has to be stolen property..." the inventor murmured in a kind of awe as he took it. Then he snapped back to business. "Joe, lend me your hands, I don't have my tools and your fingers are small enough to fit where mine can't."

Joe nodded, but turned to Nehemiah first and began to sign a list of things he needed from the wagon. A very small list, considering it was all they were taking with them, Nehemiah reflected as he stumbled inside and began finding things. He went first to the drawer he didn't know; his fingers ran under the rim of the table, feeling for a tell-tale bump as Joe instructed. His pointer finger brushed it, and he pushed. A drawer shoved out, just missing his hip. Nehi fumbled inside the small space and pulled out the black cloth Joe had requested. Something small and heavy lay inside it. As Nehi moved toward the night room for a bag, the cloth shifted, and he saw silver sparkling under it. He moved the cloth aside and stared at a man's ring, a cross etched in gold filagree over the front. Images of Joe's sketches filled his tired brain, and he saw a penciled figure with large ears and a button nose, and this cross on hands lifting a broken mute into his arms. Joshua Noble's ring.

A siren wailed, close enough it drifted through the wagon walls. Nehi wrapped the cloth back over the ring and shuffled

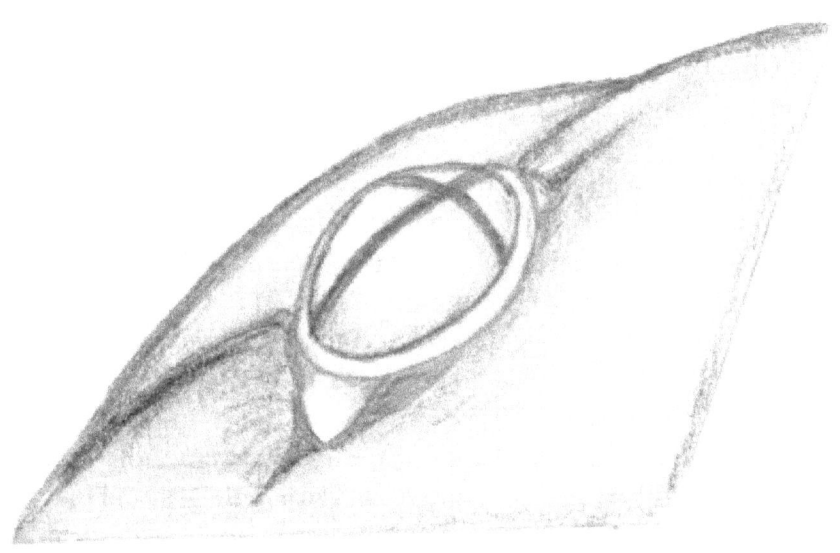

*The Ring*

off to finish his task. Five minutes later he stepped out with a bulging black bag and moved toward the two surrounded by piles of metal and wires and gears. Joe's hands darted away from the copper balls to shove the flask into Nehemiah's hands. Nehi looked down and caught the mute's eyes. The scarred face shifted in a smile, but it didn't touch his green eyes. There was that glow there again, an almost unnatural heavy something...and his breathing pattern came strained and short...

"Shut up and drink it," Joe signed. Nehi stopped staring, steeled himself, and swigged it. The fire poured into him, racing through his limbs. He gagged and wretched and stood shaking. But then it stilled, and he could move again without the weights dragging at his heavy limbs, or the frosted glass over his brain. Joe slung the bag over his shoulder with his usual lightning rapidity and his fingers disappeared inside the little box Quintus leaned over. Wheels crunched on soggy ground. Nehemiah turned toward the road, and slid his goggles over his eyes.

"They're here," he said. Quintus and Joe scrabbled on the ground, grabbing their stuff, and moving behind the wagon. Nehemiah stepped around the beautiful wood and dropped in a crouch next to the frantically working inventor. Quintus rattled off things to Joe that made no sense to Nehemiah. But Joe seemed to understand all right. The two of them soldered and connected, swore, and started again, smushing things into the two tiny boxes and affixing the two large Z shielded balls to the wand. The copper on the last layer of the balls glinted in the moonlight. Their movements blurred, but a glance at all the wires and gears and the two little copper balls still on the ground told Nehemiah they weren't going to be ready in time. He plopped on his belly and stared under the wagon. He could see the road snaking into their clearing, a ribbon of rutted mud, puddles shimmering in the moonlight.

The lead wagon in the chase bounced down the path through the woods, following the tracks of the escapee's wagon. The soldier riding shotgun spotted it first, sitting skewed off the road in a little meadow with some kind of shack thing. He pointed and they jerked and bounced toward the stolen blue van. A sharp bang of a blown out tire rent the air, the wheel jerked out of the driver's hands, and the wagon jolted off the track. The exposed wheel hit a hole, the van reared up, teetered, and toppled to its side. The soldiers in the back yelled and cursed in a medley of confusion.

No whine of a laser recharging, no burst of light, no sound of a projectile shot... and yet that tire smoked and steamed in a melted heap. They were up against a professional, with a weapon most of these soldiers had never even heard existed. A round hole melted in the windshield and the driver slumped forward, a burnt patch on his temple and the force of the silent laser beam knocking him out cold. The soldier riding shotgun yelled a warning to the troops in the back as he slid his rifle off his shoulder. Another hole of melted glass, and the man slumped. A screech of metal hinges broke the night, and soldiers poured out of the back of the truck. A young soldier pulled his rifle from his shoulder and stepped around the open door of the truck, crouched low and peering around him for the enemy. The man slumped forward. A dull splat drifted into the night as he faceplanted into the wet ground. Another soldier leapt forward wrapping his arms around the fallen comrade to drag him back. A smell of scorched hair, a blackened patch on his head, and the second soldier folded gently up onto the first.

"How's it coming?" Nehemiah asked as he steadied his heavy Compton laser. He could see legs shifting under the wagon, soldiers milling in panic, staring at their two comrades laying in the mud. The legs stopped shifting and stood still. Someone over there fed them a plan. A rush of bodies raced for the trees. Nehemiah lowered his aim and squeezed the trigger. Screams rang through the night, hideous sounds, as the smell of cooked meat lifted up. Ten soldiers collapsed, writhing and clutching at the burning holes in their legs. Hope heated in his hand. She tingled under his touch as the energy built, and he lifted his finger from the trigger.

"Coming, coming," Quintus finally answered, his voice

absent. Nehemiah wished he was a little more informative. Another wagon clumped to a stop behind the first, and Nehi thought he saw a third through the trees. Soldiers poured out, too many, faster than he could bring down. Blue uniforms deployed into the woods, and at least two dozen made it unscathed. Nehemiah lay alert and steady, whether from Joe's juice or natural adrenaline he didn't spare the time to consider. His finger almost spasmed on Hope's trigger, firing again and again. Blue uniforms dropped everywhere she pointed. But the massive black trees towered on every side, and the soldiers of the People's Kingdom knew how to use their cover. He slowed them down, but he couldn't stop them.

"We're being surrounded," Nehemiah informed the two behind him. He lay his steaming gun on the soft ground for an instant to pull on a pair of black leather gloves.

"Almost there, just keep them back," Quintus answered. A sharp whistle came from Joe and Quintus cursed, something about a dropped piece. Nehemiah spun to look at the mute.

"Aim for the bog," Joe signed. Then his fingers disappeared inside the little box again, and Quintus leaned over it, sweat pooling on his face. Nehemiah spun back toward the woods and shoved his goggles up, raking the trees to find the telltale brown fog lifting from the stinking bogs. The soldiers on the left had almost made it around the edge of the wagon, the little hunted group's only cover. Nehi spotted a tendril of brown smoke undulating just behind the line of soldiers. He snapped his goggles down again and fired, holding Hope's trigger down. He could feel the weapon vibrating and heating as the energy surged from her.

The bog boiled. Fog poured off it in a brown cloud, heavy and damp, shifting over the ground and twisting in the soldiers' legs. Something else moved out there in the bog. Nehi lifted his finger off the trigger and spun, searching the other side of the woods. He spotted another bog immediately and Hope opened fire. It boiled, and the fog started to bubble out onto the forest floor just as the soldiers reached it.

"We need to move," Nehemiah said as he spun again, trying to ignore the sharp ache of his muscles, and taking out a soldier aiming at Joe's back. Quintus only grunted. Two rifle shots spluttered mud on Nehi's face and over his goggles. The bullets showed him the direction of the shooter, and the mud didn't bother him enough to shake his perfect aim. Hope leveled and the right line fell back again.

"We need to move!" Nehemiah grunted urgently. He spun on his back, ignoring the fiery agony as the mud got into his whip cuts, and fired to the left, dropping the rifleman who had snuck around their cover and aimed at Quintus' head. "I can't hold them, they're coming too fast. We've got to–"

A scream rent through the night. High and riddled with terror and pain, it rose from the forest like a nightmare. Another followed it. Then hoarse shouts came from every side, the sounds of panic, smattered with the sharp reports of rifle fire.

A deep, menacing sound underlaid it. Nehi concentrated on it, trying to pick it out amidst the clamor. He could see something moving out there. Lots of somethings, black lumps leaping above the curling brown fog for an instant, then disappearing again underneath it. The sound rumbled and...croaked. He sat up slowly on his knees staring into the woods. Their little party had been forgotten, he knew that much.

A black lump plopped onto the grass a yard from Joe, and Nehi gaped at it. A warty, black frog, at least three feet long, with muddy brown eyes and the biggest, ugliest head he had ever seen. The mute spun on Nehi, a hissing whistle breaking through his teeth and his eyes shining in panic. A black tongue shot from the frog and wrapped around Joe's ankle. As that tongue shot out white teeth glinted in the moonlight from the frog's mouth, rows and rows of them. Hope's silent beam hit it in the face, and it melted into a steaming black puddle.

"Frogs with teeth," Nehi muttered, his own voice a slow, slurred croak. "Really big ones. Not expecting that."

"Neither were the soldiers," Quintus grunted. He sat up suddenly and picked up the wand. Joe grabbed his friend's arm.

Nehemiah caught a glimpse of Quintus wincing as he pushed a black button on two small rectangular boxes stuck on the copper colored wand, and just had time to notice the black tongue still curled around Joe's boot. A freezing wind wrapped around him, cutting into every wound. Nehemiah felt himself screaming as he curled on frozen ground, but had no control over it. A wiry arm shot around his chest and held him tight. Blackness closed over his world, hissing and whistling, and the cold, the cold was indescribable. Everything spun out of focus. Nehemiah clutched at Joe, unable to even breathe the whistling, battering air.

A small, calm part of him deep inside wondered if he was dying of a bullet wound, or riding Quintus' SOLTD.

# Chapter Ten: Story Landing

*"Be kindly affectioned one to another with brotherly love...Dis-tributing to the necessity of saints; given to hospitality."*

Romans 12:10,13

Anna gradually released her death grip on Cobeau's arm as her head began to slow its spinning. She cautiously opened her eyes. A concrete wall stood about four feet from her face, an obscene word scrawled across it in colorful graffiti. The scent of filth and rotting refuse struck up at her, and Anna gagged, clutching at her already nauseous stomach. She looked around, moving her head with caution, and saw more concrete, graffiti, garbage... She stood in a dead-end alleyway, with a glaring streetlamp all she could see out the only opening. The lamp hummed and sputtered and the light seemed swallowed by the thick humidity in the air.

"Where are we now?" she asked Cobeau. Her voice sounded slow and distant to her ringing ears.

"Don't know," he rumbled, and her heart sank.

"You don't know?" Daniel burst out. He leaned against the wall behind them, trying to make his head stop spinning. His slitted eyes stayed on the concrete wall four feet in front of his face, covered in swirling lines of iridescent spray paint. Daniel remembered Joe suddenly. He straightened and pulled a deep breath into his lungs, drawing himself back into control. The mute would show up again soon. Daniel's hand slid into his pocket. A grim satisfaction filled him as he cupped the little box in his palm; sometimes pickpocketing skills really came in handy.

"It's an alleyway," Tanzid commented shakily from beside him.

"This I could see," Daniel muttered.

A pile of black fabric with two shining green eyes dropped in front of him. Daniel shouted despite himself, staggering off the misplaced grass and dirt that had come with them from the

plain. Tanzid jerked his huge blaster around and the whine of it cut into the alley. But Cobeau shot forward and swept the soft black leather into his arms and squeezed, a happy smile on his simple face. Daniel stumbled again, still trying to regain his shaky footing as his head spun. For an instant his hand brushed the black leather.

Joe felt it slip onto his lower left rib cage, pinching the skin. A sick weight slid into his heart as his mouth twisted, his eyes screwed shut. For an instant, skinny arms tightened around his big friend's neck like a terrified little boy. Hope had finally deserted him. But Joe knew this had waited for him here. In a flash his manner shifted to the blank cheerfulness of Joe the GI. He pulled back and jerked Beau's beard like it was a bell-pull.

"My Joe my Joe my Joe!" Beau rumbled happily. Joe pulled harder, squirming and grinning. Cobeau quickly let him go, and the mute dropped to the alleyway gasping for breath and laughing silently. A red glow fell over him and he spun on his heel, suddenly lithe and dangerous. Green eyes met gold-flecked brown ones. The two men stood stock still, black outfit facing black outfit.

"Joe, I hear you've already met Tanzid, and the other way around," Anna said quickly, a tremble just under her voice, "Joe, you're alone. Nehemiah, he's not...you did..."

"I did and he's not," Joe signed at her, his eyes not leaving Tanzid. "He's fine, Beauty, I left him in a street a few blocks away with a new brother. Or nearly fine, anyway." Anna wanted to ask what "nearly" meant but Joe's hands moved too quickly. He indicated Tanzid, gave his translating whistle as he whipped his mask off, and spoke through Beau. "I know Blaster. And I know he wasn't a friend of the Way when I saw him last, even though he was thinking about it."

"Are you so sure you'd recognize a friend if you saw one?" Daniel asked acidly.

"I don't think I was thinking about it," Tanzid frowned. A slight smile cocked over Joe's face.

"You can sometimes tell when the Spirit is working in a man,

He was stirring you. But you were still far from a friend. What are you doing here?"

"He wasn't a friend," Cobeau answered, and draped a huge, muscular arm over Tanzid's shoulders. "Now he's brother." Joe kept studying Tanzid, his green eyes searching.

"It's true, we wouldn't have gotten away without him," Anna put in quickly, and Daniel spun on her, about to object; her swift action would have gotten them out anyway, and the big brother in him wanted it known. Anna's words came faster, shutting off Daniel. "I'm satisfied he's one of us. But I'm not so sure about you! And what is that stinking thing around your boot?"

"Tanzid, what happens to you when you die?" Joe broke in through Cobeau, ignoring Anna's remarks.

"I go to heaven," the former UPC agent stammered.

"Why?" Joe signed and Cobeau said.

"Because of Jesus' blood. He knows I have no reason in my-self," murmured Tanzid with no hesitation, though you could see the blush even under the black skin, and his face held confusion as he looked away, unused to talking about these things. Joe's signs flashed on. He plied Tanzid rapidly with question after question, the agent stammering out what first came into his head. He understood the test and played fair. Joe watched the fury building in Anna and Daniel as he rushed on, ignoring them and interrupting when they tried to get a word in. Daniel took a step forward his eyes burning and face hard, and Joe saw his gaze flick to the mute's ribcage; the one reason Joe couldn't refuse him. The mute spun to Beau, changing the scene and buying more time.

"You trust him, Glue?" he asked. The chimera's big, simple face flew into a delighted smile, and he squeezed Tanzid's shoulders in friendly glee. Tanzid yelled in pain and pulled away. Joe forced himself not to smile and stepped forward, offering the agent a welcoming handshake. He gripped Tanzid's hand as the agent began to pull it back.

"Blaster, I'm trusting you," Joe signed earnestly, Cobeau's rumble filling the little alley as he translated. "I'm trusting you

with more than just our lives. I'm the one that's going to have to speak for you, to bring you into the IDP. Can I trust you?" Daniel began to mutter something about hypocrites and even Anna's eyes flashed dangerously. Tanzid met Joe's gaze and nodded.

"You can trust me," he said steadily. The agent leaned a little closer and spoke quietly, just to Joe. "And I won't mention your association with my old firm, you don't have to worry about that." For a fraction of a second a look of painful, sardonic humor flew over the mute's face. But it was gone before Tanzid could be certain it had ever been there. Joe nodded and relaxed into a smile. He shook Tanzid's hand cheerfully.

"Welcome, brother," he signed. Joe suddenly spun around to Anna, his green eyes fixed on the ground to avoid meeting her gaze. "Sorry to keep you waiting so long Beauty, we'll go collect Knee-High now." He slid up to the alleyway entrance and slowly pushed his head around the corner. The spluttering light glinted on an old projectile pistol in his hand. Tanzid flipped his blaster on again. The priming whine cut into the alley, and he slid the shutters closed, blocking the red glow.

"Where are we, incomplete?" he asked.

"It's Joe. We're in Story Land," Joe signed.

"That's what I was afraid of. I'll take the back," Tanzid muttered. The former UPC agent moved behind Anna and Daniel as the group walked out into the street.

"I didn't think Story Land was that bad," Anna said quietly as she followed Joe down the block past dark, crumbling buildings. The street stared back at them empty. "When we were here earlier you weren't this worried."

"Another regime's taken over since then," Joe signed. "And it's night."

"It's totally unpredictable," Tanzid answered her. "You never know who or what you'll meet with here, and no law stands for more than a month."

"How can a country survive like that?" Daniel muttered.

"I have no idea," Joe signed. "One of the mysteries of this

world, Story Land is still standing. Mostly." He stopped beside a sharp corner and motioned into another tiny alleyway. Anna stepped past him, and saw two figures sitting in the far corner.

"Nehi!" The word came as a joyful yelp, relief almost tangible in it. She darted to her brother, hardly even seeing the old man beside him. Nehi lifted a battered, exhausted face at the call, and it lit up with a smile at the sight of his twin. Nightmares had claimed his mind; Anna and Daniel, safe and here, seemed to float to him on wings of light. The nightmares dissipated. His vision focused again, and his mind went pleasantly blank. Anna brushed her hand gently over Nehemiah's swollen eye. As Daniel stepped up for his own perusal of their hurt sibling, she stood and spun to Joe. He stayed at the top of the alley, a dark shadow on the edge of a pool of lamplight, watching them.

"That's what you meant by 'nearly.' Thank you," she said. Something flashed over Joe's face, but he replaced it so quickly with his friendly, dim look she couldn't define it. Nehi fuzzily introduced Quintus, Daniel introduced Tanzid, then Anna interrupted.

"You're wearing one of those horrid uniforms of the People's Kingdom, what on earth are you doing that for?" Nehemiah's face wrinkled in effort, working on bringing his blank mind to bear, but Joe gave his quick 'listen up' whistle before he had to form the words. He signed they needed to move on, and motioned Cobeau to Nehemiah. The big man scooped Nehi up with a friendly grin, and the whole group moved slowly but steadily back into the street. Daniel stepped up behind Joe as the mute led the way.

"That surgeon's," Daniel ordered, his face a dark glare as he stared at the back of the mute's head. "We go there." Joe's blond head nodded and Daniel let himself be content with it. Nehemiah began to answer Anna's question as he nestled in Beau's arms, his words slow, slurred, half-conscious, explaining about that hectic night and glad to get to leave out the horrible day. When he got to where he shut the wagon door on Joe and Quintus, Tanzid interrupted, professionally interested by the story.

"But you were still inside the gate?"

"Yes, but Joe had passed his PUDRE to me and I had Hope (my Compton laser), so it wasn't too much trouble to get out and back to the Ravens' wagon," Nehi mumbled, his eyes closed as he curled in Beau's strong grasp. Tanzid's eyes flashed to Joe, shock shining in his face. How did a GI get his hands on a PUDRE?

"I like your definition of not too much trouble, Nehemiah," Quintus chuckled. "I'll have to remember that next time anyone asks me to fix something and says, 'if it's not too much trouble.'"

"You're like your sister, more than what you appear," Tanzid said, switching his curiosity back to Nehemiah. "I've only known a handful of people that had the skill and courage to run the House gate like that and get away with it. And I don't know of any who could do it in your condition."

"You forget I don't work alone, God moves with me," Nehi murmured.

"What happened next, Nehi?" Daniel prodded. A sharp sigh slid from his brother and no other response. "Oh shoot, he's out," Daniel grumbled. Joe's hand suddenly appeared by Nehi's face, he tilted a copper flask up, and Nehemiah spluttered and jerked, his eyes shooting open, coughing and gasping at the effort each breath took. "That wasn't a request, he could have slept!" Daniel shouted, menace dripping from him as he spun on Joe. The mute didn't look at him and slid back to the front of the group.

"We made it to the wagon," Nehi spluttered with an effort, going on as if there hadn't been an interruption. There probably hadn't been in his mind, the others knew. "Joe pulled out that black bag I carried to Geatland from a cubby under the wagon, and he and Quintus went to work on a bunch of metal and wires and other junk to make a SOLTD. Joe already had all the things, apparently, and the blueprints, though he didn't tell us–"

"That's not all he neglected to mention," Anna muttered. Something in her voice made Nehemiah pause. He could think again after another draft of that disgusting stuff Joe carted around, and notice things. His eyes flitted open and focused on Anna. Her eyes were reddened and a little puffy, and anger and worry mixed in the drawn lines cutting over her face. Someone had really hurt her tonight. His gaze flitted to Joe, and caught him at a moment the mute had turned to glance over his shoulder. Joe was blank, no emotion at all on his sharp face, a sure sign he was upset. A smell like rotting meat and fouled water hit him and his eyes flitted to the source as one hand clamped over his belly. The frog tongue dragged a yard behind Joe. It left a slimy trail that steamed on the bricks.

"You created a SOLTD in a night?" Daniel asked Quintus, obviously impressed.

"Well, the GI – I mean Joe, already had one mostly made. It just needed some tweaking and finishing," Quintus said. "And I would very much like to know how he knew how to make my SOLTDs. To my certain knowledge only three of them were made and went to an anonymous donor. While the plans, well, those were plainly..." He coughed a little uncomfortably and murmured the last word under his breath. "...stolen."

"We're here," Joe signed ignoring Quintus' look, and stopped at an ornate, wrought iron gate.

"Yes, I know this place," Daniel said to the others' surprise. "Joe and I came here last Story Land visit. It's a doctor's house, name of Harry. Nice, competent character. I'm all right with this place." Anna peered through the bars and saw a large, old fashioned house set back from the street, two apple trees standing on either side of a set of steps leading to the ornate wooden door. It was a pretty, professional, lived-in looking house, and she liked it. Much better than the falling down brick ones she had passed on the way.

"Doctor Harold Pablo, Surgeon," Nehemiah read off a plaque on the gate from where he lounged in Beau's arms. Joe pulled the gate open from the inside and trotted over to the door of the house. As the others shuffled toward the porch, the mute pulled the bell. Something thumped inside a second story room

above them, as if a body rolled off a bed. The group converged on the wide porch and waited. Anna tried not to look at Joe. She wanted to find a dark corner and cry for a while. Then she could think clearly about this mess and decide what to think about the sweet, awful mute. Someone grumbling and thumping could be heard coming toward them from inside. The door swung open and a man in his mid-thirties stood framed in the doorway, a dressing gown pulled over his pajamas, a very grumpy look on his ordinary face, and his brown hair sticking up in messy disarray. Joe stepped into the square of yellow light spilling from the doorway and the grumpy look flew into one of joy.

"Joe!" Harry cried, and his arms flew around the young man in a bear hug. The mute's feet dangled a foot in the air, and the doctor didn't seem to notice.

"Hello, Doctor," Joe signed with jiggling hands as Harry ruffled his hair vigorously. "Beau and I are back just in time for breakfast." He winked as the doctor let him go, and Harry laughed.

"I've got you beat today, I actually went shopping last night," he said, his voice cheerful and competent. Anna thought it matched the house very nicely as it began to pour out in a steady flow.

Everyone focused on the surgeon and mute, but Anna noticed Daniel stepped forward, his jaw tight. She saw his IDP cross clutched in his hand and knew he meant to accuse Joe of being a traitor right there on the porch. Her hand clamped on his shoulder and jerked him back.

"Let him have a chance to answer it first," she hissed in Daniel's ear. Her brother shot her a look with lingering fury still smoldering in his eyes. "Give Joe that one chance. Please." Daniel's fist curled around the token in his hand till his knuckles were white. But he kept his mouth closed and let the doctor's swift chatter keep the conversation.

"Joe, you old scoundrel, this is the second time in two months, that's good! And Beau, still as big and hirsute as ever,

why didn't you come with your good old master last time? Oh
no you don't, I know what your hugs do to the rib cages of your
victims! Besides, you already have your arms full. Hello again
Daniel, nice to see you. Well Joe, I see as usual you bring me
needy ones for sanctuary and repair. At least this one's con-
scious, that's a pleasant change," he said, his bright hazel eyes
twinkling cheerfully at Nehemiah. He looked at the rest of the
people outside his door. His eyes rested on Tanzid and his ugly
outfit and the ordinary, friendly face hardened. He leaned toward Joe.

"That's a UPC," Harry said quietly to Joe.

"He was," Joe nodded. "He's a brother now. Just tonight, a
little earlier. I'm satisfied."

"Well, Joe, littlest founder of the IDP," Harry murmured,
studying Tanzid, "I'll be the last to question anyone you vouch
for." He straightened up and his smile flashed again. "Come on
everyone. A friend of Joe's is a friend of mine. Inside all before
a marauding band catches sight of the beauty you have in your
midst and we have an all-out battle before it's even properly
morning. Introductions on the way." Embarrassment flew over
Anna and the rest grinned and moved into the house. A deep
breath, scented with vanilla potpourri and old wood, went in
and out of her lungs, and her swollen heart shrunk a size. The
inside was as old fashioned, pretty, and efficient as the outside
looked, and Anna felt pleasantly surprised by this spot Joe had
taken them to.

Joe. A sigh pulled from her, and she glanced over at that riddle of a person. She caught him staring at her; his sorrow bit
into her heart, a hopeless, tired, twisting of the scarred face, an
unnatural glow in eyes that were crinkled in weariness instead
of humor. His face was turned toward the doctor now and the
green eyes were cheerful. It had been so quick Anna would
have dismissed the look as a fancy, but she knew Joe better by
now. She followed the group through the house to a comfortable den behind a pretty kitchen. Anna would have liked to stay
and putter in that kitchen. It would have soothed every ruffle

in her confused, weary soul tonight. But this wasn't her house. She didn't have a house. Anna followed everyone into the den, her usually cheerful face drawn.

As soon as he had everyone settled on the worn, comfortable couches and chairs, the doctor shooed Nehemiah out again, into one of his surgeries that adjoined the wood paneled den. Doctor Pablo swung the door to a crack discreetly, assisted his patient out of most of his clothes, and began 'repairing' as he put it. Nehemiah felt himself relaxing under the doctor's care. The sharp pains dulled to mere aches and his body slumped in relief, suddenly able to rest. This guy was good. And nice too. Joe slid in after a minute, allowing the door to open a little farther. The mute sank onto a wooden chair, resting his chin on the back as his legs splayed around it, and chatted with the doctor as he worked. Nehemiah noticed Anna and Daniel both looked daggers at Joe's back as he slipped into the surgery and Joe nervously ignored them. Joe nervous? What was going on? He felt too tired for this. He just wanted to lay down and not move for weeks, and instead it looked like he had a heated confrontation to face.

"There." The Doctor tossed his own dressing gown over Nehemiah and smiled. "You'll live. You may not feel like it now, but you'll live. Beau, come and move him to the couch, I don't want him falling over and knocking his head on my baseboards. He might dent them and they're antiques." The teasing note in his voice forestalled any hard feelings about the remark, and kept Nehemiah from any embarrassment about being carried from place to place like an invalid. He was grateful and said as much to the doctor as Cobeau swept him up and moved back to the den.

"Harry, please, always Harry to fellow brothers in Christ," was the only response from the doctor. "All right Joe, your turn."

"My turn?" Joe signed, sitting up with an effort. "What's wrong with me?"

"Well, exhaustion for one, and what about that nasty bruise

over your temple?" Joe laughed his silent laugh, grabbed a towel off the sink, and rubbed the makeup off. His fingers closed and opened again as he moved his arms smoothly outward and his face looked mysteriously surprised.

"Poof!" he mouthed.

"All right, so it wasn't a bruise," Harry said, unable to hide a smile at the indomitable mute. "But I've been your doctor for eight years and I can tell by now when you need something. You definitely need to get that disgusting black bit of animal tissue off your boot, did you even know it's making you smell like death warmed over?" Joe shook his boot and stared at the wiggling tongue with a wrinkled nose.

"Black frog," he signed. "These things don't cut even with a titanium blade, and they're coated with an acid that fuses to whatever it touches. It's not coming off."

"Great, that makes me happy about my floors," Harry snorted. "But you're not getting me off the subject that easy, you're more than exhausted, and I'm going to tell you once again. You need to stop." He annunciated the words slowly and earnestly, each one almost a sentence in itself. "A human body can only take so much pounding before it wears down and loses the ability to repair itself. You need to stop this madcap rushing about and give yourself a year or two to recover. Even a few months would help!"

"Doctor's orders noted," Joe signed airily, and Harry rolled his eyes.

"Well, you need something now. A good dose of aspirin (never mind, no pain pills, I forgot for a moment). Maybe a good meal, a good hug, or a good night's sleep, I'm not sure."

"How about a good kick?" Daniel drawled from the den, and everyone stared at him. He and Anna perched on the couch next to Nehemiah, both of them glaring at Joe. The mute sighed and looked up at Harry.

"I don't suppose you have a surgery or something to do for a while, do you?" he signed wearily. Harry glanced from the uncomfortable confusion on Tanzid and Quintus to the three

Hillsons (two of them fuming and one looking worried), back to Joe's tired, blank face.

"Hm," he said. "No, no surgery at this time of night, but I can take a hint. Come on Tanzid, Quintus, you're both about my size and could use a new set of clothes. Let's go see what my wardrobe holds and let them have their say." The three men walked out, Harry's swift conversation leading the way. Tanzid and Quintus' replies noticeably relaxed at the other's easy hospitality. Anna stared at the blank mute sitting in the surgery and waited until the voices disappeared up the stairs. Then she blurted it out through clenched teeth.

# Chapter Eleven: Traitor or Trusted?

*"But mine eyes are unto Thee, O God the Lord: in Thee is my trust; leave not my soul destitute."* Psalm 141:8

"The UPC? Joe, you've been working in the UPC for two years?" Anna snapped.

"What?" Nehemiah blinked, his mouth dropping open and his eyes widening.

"And we've been wondering who the dirty wolf in our midst was. The whole time he's been right with us!" Daniel spat.

"What?" Nehemiah gasped.

"Joe, they find Christians and turn them over to the states, it's one of their main functions! And you help them?" Anna cried.

"What?" Nehemiah's voice strangled in his throat.

"Nehi, you sound like a three-year-old," Daniel growled.

"Then explain what this is about," Nehemiah pleaded, only one thought shining on his battered, open face; disbelieving horror.

"I've been in and out of the UPC for two years, Knee-High," Joe signed. The room dropped into silence so deep it was hard to breathe. The mute stood and padded into the room, stopping in front of the couch like he was at a tribunal. Daniel nudged his sister, and Anna's wooden translating relieved a little of the shocked silence as the mute went on. "Yesterday I was passed word about a book heist, the People's Kingdom book was about to be stolen. I planned to stop it myself and hoped to catch the would-be thief in the act, but I ended up having to go after you, Knee-High. I couldn't let the book be stolen, so I sent the note to the only people I knew of who might be able to stop the FFs; the UPC. I sent it with Beauty and D. I'm sorry it put you in danger, I didn't mean that to happen."

"Oh, but you're not sorry you're a part of that murderous bunch of anti-Christ's?" Daniel growled.

"I'm not a part of them and I never will be," Joe signed.

"No, you're not. You're an incomplete, a GI, and they won't allow you to join them all the way," Daniel scoffed. "So you let yourself be used, like a miserable, fawning slave."

"I'm a slave to the right One," Joe signed, his eyes flashing with the first real emotion he had shown since meeting up with Anna and her company tonight. It burned fierce, a flame inside him, launching up and shooting from his eyes as his face steeled and his stiff muscles almost vibrated. "I'm a slave to Jesus, and that's Who I will always serve! That's what I'm made for, knowing I belong to Him is my only comfort. And service to Him looses me from every other bond. That's Who I serve in the UPC." The mask fell over him again, a blank shield snuffing out any emotion. "There are some things they work on that are good. Keeping peace is good, trying to catch the FFs and keep them from tearing the world apart from greed is good. I've served with the UPC on those kinds of tasks."

"But what about the IDP, Joe? What about the UPC's intent to destroy your brothers and sisters?" Nehemiah asked. His voice trembled with the intensity of his hurt, and it wasn't from the pain in his body. Joe couldn't completely hide his own smart at Nehemiah's tone, but he covered it with his customary quickness and answered a question with a question.

"Beauty, when did Blaster say I showed up at the UPC?"

"About two years ago," Anna answered, searching Joe's blank face for some hint of what went on behind it.

"Knee-High, when did P-a-u-l say the IDP's trouble with the UPC started to die down?" Joe signed at Nehemiah.

"About two years ago," Nehemiah answered, searching just like Anna, but his open expression said more. It held accusation, intense feelings of betrayal. Even clear disgust plastered through the bruises and cuts. Joe just shrugged, but Anna saw a muscle by his eye twitching under Nehemiah's stare.

"That's my defense," he signed. "The best I have and the best I'll ever have. I've worked alone except for Glue, and dear old Glue can't remember what day it is. I won't say you'll have to take my word that I've been helping the IDP's cause by working in the UPC, because I know at the moment my word doesn't mean much to you. But I have. I've been dropping the messages that would hurt the IDP and delivering the ones that would help, finding out where the UPC is going next and alerting the IDP there, and helping the UPC when they needed it on the right things. And I haven't told either side what I was doing. Look, it's been a long day and a longer night, and I want to go collapse somewhere."

"Running away with your SOLTD?" Nehemiah asked. Joe met his gaze, a tired, quiet sorrow showing through his blankness. The mute just raised the left side of his black jacket and sleeveless turtleneck. A small black rectangle attached to his ribs, the white skin pinched and discolored under it. A red light flashed briefly in the room, and then Joe dropped the jacket again. It was a Meslee control, already armed. A sophisticated bomb, only large enough to do damage to the one wearing it. But to that person it brought sure, messy death when activated. The bomb fused to skin automatically when armed and took the DNA from the fingers of the one who attached it. Only that person could activate the Meslee, or remove it. Joe's gaze went to Daniel as Nehi's mouth dropped open for the second time that night. He and Anna turned shocked faces to their brother. Joe and Daniel just looked at each other. One blank and tired, the other disgusted.

"I won't be leaving, not unless you say I can," the mute signed, and Anna's sweet voice continued to translate. "Besides, even without this thing on, I have nowhere to go. I can't survive entirely on my own. I've tried, I know. We had to turn Prissy loose and leave the wagon behind, and that's the only home I have. Had. I'll stay in sight, I'll go collapse on Doctor's surgery cot while you decide what you're doing with me." He turned, shuffled into the surgery, and slumped down on the squeaky cot. He looked utterly worn out, in mind and body, but he didn't lay down to sleep. He sat with his legs crossed in front of him, his back against the pretty green painted wall, staring listlessly at the ceiling. The yard of black frog tongue dangled

off his boot and curled on the floor under him.

"I don't understand," Cobeau's rumble came from a corner of the room. The couch squeaked under the combined starts of the three Hillsons. They had all forgotten him.

"It's not hard to understand, Cobeau," Daniel drawled. "We just don't know who your master is, and happen to think he's proved himself a rotten traitor."

"You know Joe," Beau said, his face wrinkled as he watched the twins and tried to make sense of it. Daniel was about to interrupt when the big chimera stood up from his crouch and began to move toward the surgery. He paused at the door and turned back to the couch. "You may not know why Joe does things. And you may not know what Joe thinks. You may not even know what Joe feels. But you know Joe." Cobeau walked into the surgery and the door swung on its hinges at his movement. He sat down on the old cot, Joe scrambling to the side to make way for him and the cot creaking dangerously at the added weight. Beau draped his arm over his little friend. Joe laid his shaggy, blond head gratefully on Beau's side, and closed his eyes with a sigh.

"Tell me a story will you, Glue?" he signed listlessly. Beau smiled and began to stroke Joe's hair.

"There once was a pretty lady who liked to hiss," the chimera began. The door had been swinging back and forth in Beau's wake, and now it closed with a click and blocked out all but a few of Beau's louder rumbles. The three siblings looked at each other.

"A bomb, Dan?" Anna asked, sharp, accusing.

"I picked it from a SW's pocket when we were here last, and put it on to keep that little villain from running off to our enemies. I'm not apologizing. He's dangerous. I've wondered if *he's* this Wolf he has everyone so up tight about. Joe is a vile traitor and we need to turn him in to the IDP before he kills it," Daniel said. Then he turned quickly to Nehemiah and began checking over his facial wounds. "That doctor he brought us to does pretty good work though. Are you all right, Nehi? Boy, it made me ache to leave the Brotherhood's House when I didn't know if you were still in there or not, but I had to get Anna out! I've hardly breathed since they dragged you out of sight. Are you recoverable? They really hurt you! If I ever see any of those green coated soldiers again, so help me I'll–" Daniel snapped his jaw closed on his furious growl.

"I'm recoverable," Nehemiah smiled, enjoying having a protective older brother around. Even if he was an old goat who refused to show affection or worry around anyone but his family. "Besides, it's not like it's a new feeling. I have practice in handling it Danny, I'll be fine."

"That's not what I wanted to hear!" Daniel almost yelled.

"I have to agree," Anna frowned. "Get unused to it, Nehi, that's an order."

"Okay, okay," Nehemiah chuckled, one arm stealing around his rib cage. "But about Joe. You shouldn't have bombed him, Danny. He has enough normal fear to work through without you adding to it."

"He's a traitor," Daniel stated, sharp disbelief in his voice at Nehemiah's reaction.

"I can't believe that." It came as a statement, and the others knew Nehi spoke only the truth. He couldn't bring his battered mind to believe it.

"If he wanted to kill the IDP, Daniel, he would have done it a long time ago," Anna objected, her forehead creased with her frown. "He knows everything about it. In fact he helped set it up."

"He was one of the co-founders, Harry confirmed that tonight," Nehemiah put in, rubbing his aching head in an effort to make it work right. "Anna's right, if Joe wanted to see the IDP die, he wouldn't have helped it live like he has."

"Okay, so he likes the IDP as a whole," Daniel conceded. "(And quit with the 'Danny' Nehi, or I'll come up with something nasty to call you.) But what about the individuals in it? There's no getting around the fact that the UPC has picked out members of the Way and turned them into states that hate

Christians. During the two years Joe's been working there."

"Yes, but not as many as before the two years, according to what we've heard. And not heard from Joe, either," Anna put in.

"I didn't say it was many, I said it was some. What if Joe's been picking and choosing, getting rid of the ones he doesn't like?" Daniel said.

"Oh that's a horrid idea!" Anna burst out.

"Horrid yes, but there are a lot of horrid people in this world. Face it, sister, a life like Joe's had would almost certainly lead to some sort of brain damage. Have you ever thought of that one? What if he's a genius in most things, but has that one piece a little wrong in his brain from too much childhood abuse?" The thought that this could be true was too much for the sleep deprived Anna, and a sniffle broke from her. She reached into her pocket for a handkerchief and put it to her nose. Anna's arm jerked, throwing it convulsively toward the far wall, as a sneeze shook her whole form. Her head lifted and snapped down with alarming frequency as her explosive sneezes kept coming, her face flushed with lack of breath.

"What is it?" Nehemiah gasped, swinging into a sitting position, his eyes wide.

"Breathe, Ann, breathe!" Daniel ordered, his eyes snapping in alarm, untangling his legs from the couch's throw and staggering up. She was trying to say something between her sneezes but couldn't. "I'll go get the doctor, keep breathing–"

"She's laughing!" Nehemiah cried in surprise. Daniel looked again and saw it too. Between the constant sneezes, Anna's eyes danced and hiccupping giggles broke out. Daniel moved over, picked up the handkerchief, and sniffed carefully. An explosive sneeze shook his whole body. Another hit, one leg coming up and slamming back down again with its violence.

"Powder," he managed to get out. Nehemiah grinned and sank back against the couch, his arm snaking around his ribs again.

"I guess that makes up for the rubber eggs you served him at breakfast, eh Ann?" Nehemiah wheezed. Anna nodded, sucking in air, her face still suffused. She couldn't decide whether to cry or laugh at the practical joke, it reminded her of the Joe she thought she knew. It reminded Nehemiah of the Joe he did know.

"Daniel," he said, "if Joe has something wrong in his brain, it's wrong the opposite way. He's tough, and brave, and brilliant, and almost fanatic when it comes to saving others. He wouldn't risk himself like he does for some and then turn around and kill others mercilessly. Think about tonight. He didn't have to come after me, and he didn't have to send word to the UPC too."

"That's a good point," Anna gasped hopefully. "He could have kept his association with the UPC quiet and himself safe, and let you or the kingdom die. It was either you, the People's Kingdom, or Joe."

"And he picked Joe," Nehi nodded. A groan slid from him and his hand went to the top of his head as if he needed it to keep his brain in.

"I think Beau's right. We do know Joe," Anna said.

"Right," Nehemiah wheezed, blinking painfully and hoping this conversation ended soon. "We may not have a clue what he's up to, and I won't dare guess how many secrets he's hiding. But I know him, and I love him like the brother he is, and I trust him with my life. After all, he's already saved it six times that I know of."

"Yes," Anna nodded.

"That's it?" Daniel growled. His arms were folded and he stared at the twins in surprise. "I mean, I knew you two were gullible, but to trust him again just like that?"

"I've never stopped trusting him," Nehemiah said, and you could hear the truth ringing behind the simple words. A ripple of homesickness, pleasure and pain and surprise all boiling in it, went through Anna. That tone sounded just like their father. "It shocked me pretty good tonight, but not enough to break that trust. And he's never really betrayed it. Not completely."

"Oh, so turning you in to attempted murderers in Kallipolis

and being a self-confessed slave for an anti-Christ organization doesn't count as betrayal?" Daniel drawled. You could see the astonishment in him. He didn't understand this, couldn't comprehend his siblings' mindset.

"No, actually it doesn't," Anna said, her usual calm smile beginning to creep over her face. "In Kallipolis he had Beau with us the whole time to get us out and make sure we were safe. And I believe him about his UPC involvement. He's been a spy working for the spies, rooting out ways to help the IDP and serving the UPC only where he agrees with them. Do you remember Tanzid's comment, Daniel, about the FFs? He said practically all they know about them is from Joe. That's the type of involvement he's had with the UPC."

"Yeah, but what if Joe's an FF too," Daniel countered. "What if he's the Wolf he keeps going on about? Bi-polar maybe, his own worst enemy?"

"Oh come on, getting a little far-fetched aren't we?" Nehemiah grinned, his voice hoarse.

"I don't know, you two who immediately trust a self-confessed member of the UPC tell me, what is far-fetched?" Daniel's voice came confused and caustic at once, and Anna bit back her quick reply and thought for a minute. It didn't take long to spot the disconnect between the twins and their brother. Joe never opened up around Daniel. Ever. Dan had only seen the blank mask.

"Listen, Daniel, I think I see some of your problem," she started slowly, and held up a hand when he went to interrupt heatedly. "Beau was looking at Nehi and I when he said, 'You know Joe,' and it wasn't an accident. The mute runs scared from everyone. He's been hurt so much he doesn't trust anyone, and it's taken Nehi and I over a year to get past his outer layers and meet just a little of *him*, who he is on the inside. *He* never comes out around you. You're too caustic, and you don't trust him, so he doesn't trust you back. You've never even met the Joe Nehemiah and I are talking about." Daniel made to interrupt again and Anna held up her hand to stop him. "I can't explain it, not fully, and not right now. You're swaying on your feet and Nehi is already almost unconscious. But I know you're confused, so just ponder this for a minute; you're talking about a Joe that's only a mask. An outer layer. An actor that can put on any face he wants, and that's what you've seen, and what you mistrust so much. The Joe you're talking about is fake, he is hiding things, just like you've been telling us. But it's not the secrets you think it is. Joe's hiding himself. Nehi and I have met the real Joe. He's sweet, and incredibly shy, and a little silly, and faces every day willing to give up his life in the fight for Christ's own. He's proved that. He's also a genius, in quirky ways that I don't always understand, an artist, and even moody sometimes. But I trust him. So does Nehemiah. You've never even met him."

Silence fell around the room and stretched on, and Anna could watch Daniel thinking back on the past months. He had noticed the incongruities in Joe. How he seemed to be one person around the twins, when Daniel had seen him from a distance talking and laughing and relaxed, and someone completely different whenever Daniel actually came on the scene. Anna's words made sense. Actually, they explained almost everything he had been so confused about these past months.

"So there's a Joe I haven't even met," he said slowly, as if tasting the idea, mulling it over in his head.

"Yes," Anna said. Nehi's eyes were closed, his breath wheezing out of him. "But we know him."

"You two know him, the actual Joe. How do you know it's the real one, and not just another actor put on to fool you?" Daniel asked.

"I know." She looked just like their mother when she said that, so certain, so sure of her facts when there were no actual facts to point to. It convinced Daniel, when no other words or arguments could have. Call it womanly intuition, or something that ran deeper than explainable factual knowledge, every time his mother got that look, she was always right. "The real Joe is a good man, and we trust him. Don't we, Nehi?"

"Hm, what? Oh, yes, we do." Nehemiah sat up a little

straighter, wincing and blinking, obviously forcing his mind back on the conversation. "Listen, Daniel, Anna's right. We know Joe, you don't. It's been a hard won war to get to that point, where he opens up around us and we aren't constantly fretting over his secrets. And one little added on layer like this isn't going to break that trust."

"Little added on layer...his being a member of the UPC, you mean," Daniel clarified. "It's...really no big deal."

"Not compared to what else we know about him," Nehi wheezed. "No, it's not that big of a deal once I got over the shock." That did it. Nehemiah's off-hand treatment of the situation, added to Anna's certainty. Daniel accepted their case. Though he often teased them over their naivety, he knew better. The twins were smart, savvy about the world, and especially about people. If he was honest with himself, they were better with people than he was.

"I think if we stopped mistrusting him and just let it be till he's ready to tell us whatever *it* is, life would be a lot easier for all of us," Anna put in. They all knew she meant if Daniel stopped accusing and pushing constantly. "Joe's not only safe to be around, he's the one who's sacrificed to keep us safe again and again. What do you say, Dan? Are you really determined he's such a threat?" Daniel looked from one sibling to the other for a long moment. A deep sigh welled from him.

"I'm outvoted," he said with a shrug. Anna grinned and hopped up to give Daniel a quick pat on the cheek.

"You old goat, you're happy to think he's not a traitor too, you just won't admit it," she said. Nehemiah laughed, coughed, and groaned.

"I'm going to faint now," he informed his siblings, leaning his head back on the arm of the couch and sinking further into its green pillowed comfort. "Just so you know. And then I'm going to sleep. Don't wake me for at least a month, please." Daniel grinned then covered it with an ill-tempered frown. Anna laughed at him, but he interrupted it quickly.

"Hold on a little longer, Nehi, I have one more thing to

mention before you drop into oblivion."

"Can you make it quick, please?" Nehemiah sighed from the depths of the couch.

"When we were here earlier I met this Harry character, and I liked him. Our talk drifted onto the FF Wolf and I brought the subject up again when we were at the Ravens' beach because...well, just because."

"And?" Anna asked.

"I was just trying to get Joe to talk. But I mentioned it could be Harry, and he jumped."

"You said the Wolf could be Harry and Harry jumped?" Nehemiah muttered.

"No, Joe jumped," Daniel corrected quickly. "At that beach, I mentioned the FF Wolf might be Harry, and Joe jumped like I had hit it on the head. I mention it now because the little scavenger doesn't usually get disconcerted like that, and there might just be something behind it."

"Something behind it, like Harry actually being this FF Wolf?" Anna asked skeptically. "But Joe seems so happy to see him."

"Joe could seem to be whatever he wanted, you just said so," Daniel answered. "What do you say, brother?"

"I'm not really here," Nehemiah murmured thickly. "Ask me when I wake up."

"It's a good thing to keep in mind, Daniel," Anna took up thoughtfully. "But there could be lots of reasons why your comment disconcerted Joe, or maybe it was a different comment in the same conversation that got to him. Right now I'm more concerned about you two, and Joe still having that horrid thing on him and thinking we think he's a traitor. You go tell Joe he's free to do what he wants again, and get that bomb off him now, Daniel, before I yell at you. I'm going to see Nehemiah situated, then go tell Harry he can come down again, and figure out where to let you collapse before you do it on the floor."

"I'm fine, no collapsing for me," Daniel said with a wide yawn. Anna shooed him toward the surgery door and turned to

Nehemiah. Her smile faded.

"Nehi, is even Prissy gone?" she asked softly. Nehi's eyes opened slowly and he stared at the wall across from him.

"Yes. Joe said she'll be all right, we sent her off into the woods because apparently there's a farmer she knows nearby. Everything's gone. Again." Nehi's voice came tired and hoarse. Anna drew in a long breath and let it out slowly. Her chin lifted.

"But we're all here, alive and able to build a new life, again. It's all right, Nehi. God's holding our real home firm, and here we still have each other. Tomorrow will be fine, whatever comes next. Now go on and faint, it'll do you good." A smile flitted over Nehi's battered face. He let his eyes close and Anna watched his breathing pattern change as he dropped into unconsciousness. She spun on Daniel and shooed him toward the surgery impatiently as she trotted off to go find the doctor.

Daniel obediently pulled open the door to the surgery.

Beau sat fast asleep and snoring, sitting up against the wall. The mute huddled next to him, definitely not asleep. Joe's eyes met Daniel's and the eldest Hillson suddenly remembered how serious their debate had been. And that Joe knew his life hung in the balance, and had known it for some time. All night. The mute had known it all night. He hadn't responded at all when Daniel had stuck that bomb on, and knew who had done it in a dark, crowded alley... Joe had expected it. His siblings' argument seemed more certain as that knowledge hit home.

This shrunken young man had known he was killing himself by saving Nehi and the People's Kingdom, and chosen that. So someone was in there he had never met, a deeper Joe... Someone who talked to the twins, even if he didn't to him yet. Interesting.

Daniel stepped closer, till he towered over the mute. Joe flinched. His shoulders hunched, his head ducked, and his eyes screwed shut as he turned into his friend, a cold sweat sparkling on his forehead. The kid thought he came as an executioner. Joe expected Daniel to start the timer, and in ten seconds his heart, left lung, and a good portion of his spine would be

# Chapter Eleven: Traitor or Trusted?

Psalm 141:8

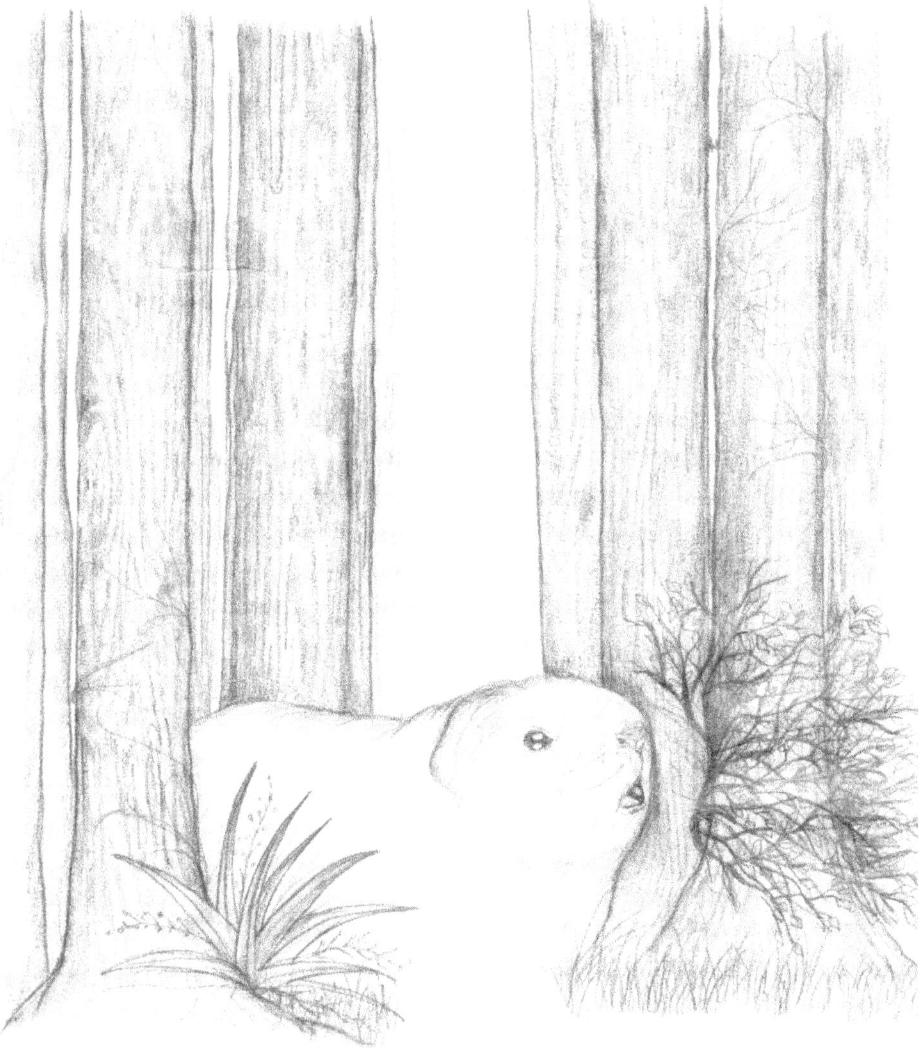

Saying Goodbye

blown out of his body. Daniel dropped to his knee and flipped Joe's shirt up. He glimpsed a silver ring hanging on the chain with Joe's IDP token, a ring with a thick gold cross over it. Another little curiosity about the mute. Daniel brushed his thumb against the bomb. The thing gave a beep and clattered onto the ground. The two men's eyes met for an instant.

"You've been reprieved," Daniel said. Joe gawked at him, blinking rapidly, his mouth parted. Daniel straightened up slowly and walked toward the door, tossing more words over his shoulder as he moved. "The twins say you're still to be trusted no matter what evil, Christian hating groups you're a part of, and it's two to one. Get some sleep." A smile broke slowly over Joe's pale face. Daniel looked over his shoulder as he reached the door. The mute nodded a heartfelt thank you. Daniel nodded back, allowing a little smile to cross his face to bring peace, and closed the door.

A shaky laugh slid from Joe and he laid his head on his knees. He felt lightheaded and giddy. Of course some of that might have been he had only eaten a cinnamon roll for sixteen grueling hours, but most of it was shock and joy. He had his life back. Beau had told him not to worry, that Anna and Nehemiah won't dump him, but he couldn't believe it. Not completely. But they trusted him. Even after they found out about the UPC. A soft, shocked, delighted laugh split the mute's face, and his head shook slowly back and forth in disbelief. Exhaustion climbed over him like a living thing as relief poured out of his soul, and he couldn't stay awake any longer to realize his joy. Joe squirmed till he could lay his head on his Glue's lap and closed his eyes, letting the exhaustion take him over.

"Thank you, Jesus. Thank you," Joe breathed into the quiet room. His Savior heard his silent voice as clearly as He hears all the prayers of His saints. Joe felt peace and joy steal over him even deeper than oblivion, and smiled in his sleep.

# Chapter Twelve: Harry's House

*"For ye have not received the spirit of bondage again to fear; but ye have received the Spirit of adoption, whereby we cry, Abba, Father."* Romans 8:15

A yell vaguely registered in Nehemiah's mind. He shifted to a different position and realized three things; he lay on something soft and very comfortable, his stomach was very empty, and his body ached almost as bad as coming out from under one of Abid's sessions. He let his eyes flutter open. A warm room with light wooden panels running along the wall and worn, comfortable furnishings greeted his gaze. Morning sunlight streamed through a screen door, and he could glimpse a well-tended green lawn through the wire mesh. Memory returned, and Nehemiah smiled. He let himself rest easy for another moment, his mind going comfortably blank. He realized he only took in the scene with one eye. Nehi raised his hand slowly and gingerly felt his eye that hadn't opened on command. A bandage covered it, and as he touched the white fabric, Nehi felt something cool and nice slathered underneath the patch. A yawn broke from him as he let his arm drop comfortably behind his head, and wondered why he was awake when he still felt this awful.

Joe popped partially out from behind the arm of the couch by Nehi's feet. His eyes laughed and his face looked playfully frightened.

"I'm not here, remember that if anyone asks," he signed, then popped back again. Nehemiah was awake enough now to notice a strange sort of bubbling coughing coming from the kitchen. Curiosity began to tug at his tired heart and get his blood pumping. Joe popped out again, obviously having to hold back laughter.

"I'm especially not here if Beauty asks. Or Blaster. Or Doctor, for that matter. Never mind, I revert back to my old statement, if anyone asks." The door to the kitchen swung open and a cloud

of bubbles and flour flew into the room.

"Joe!" Tanzid's fine voice bellowed from the doorway, then started gurgling and coughing. A slim white form that seemed to be blowing bubbles with every breath stormed in and Nehemiah looked at it in surprise.

"Anna?" he asked.

"Where is he!" Anna burst out, several soap bubbles coming out with the words. "Joe, you get in here and help clean up the mess you made of breakfast before I–"

"I made!" Joe signed, popping up from behind the couch. "You're the one who told me to go try to make pancakes while you finished straightening up, and it was you that tripped your wire, not me–"

"That wire was no longer mine after you moved it to get me, and after all, it was meant for you for your sneezing powder on my handkerchief and you know–"

"Okay, I take responsibility for it, sorry about that," Joe interrupted, the wide grin covering his face ruining all attempts at a decent apology. "How did you know I was in here?"

"You're always in here when we don't have you busy," Anna answered, "watching over Nehi." Joe gave his "awkward" click, glanced at Nehi a little shyly, and rushed the conversation on.

"You have to admit switching the water for flour was a good touch considering what started this war, and if you think I'm going to clean up the mess–"

"Did someone mention pancakes?" Nehemiah broke in, his hunger drawing him up on one elbow.

"You don't want them, believe me," Tanzid coughed from the doorway. Joe bit his lip.

"I'm sorry, Blaster," he signed. "I knocked the box of dish soap into the batter and didn't realize it until the first batch started blowing bubbles while they cooked."

"How can you not notice you knocked dish soap into the batter?" Tanzid asked when Anna had stopped grinning and translated what he said.

"Well...the cabinets have a very nice resonating tone when

you kick them just right. I was dancing, and–"

"What happened to my kitchen!" Harry's bellow blasted through the doorway. Nehemiah started laughing.

"Good morning to you too, everyone!" he said, slowly climbing to his feet. "Let's all go clean up the mess and start a new batch of pancakes. I'm starved!"

Soon they were all busy with the soap blowing pancakes and flour. Joe demonstrated the resonation of the cabinets after a moment. Anna started up a favorite hymn to the rhythm, and Nehemiah joined in from where he stood at the sink trying to get the soapy batter out of the bowl. Tanzid marveled, the doctor said to be careful of the woodwork, and all enjoyed as they helped get the flour off the floor. Soon the kitchen gleamed, and Anna stood at the stove cooking a real batch of pancakes. She turned them over quietly and Joe and Nehemiah began protesting. Anna grinned and started flipping. Tanzid and Harry yelped as pancakes started flying around the kitchen, but Nehi and Joe laughed and started catching. After a minute, Joe started catching and handing to Nehemiah who didn't feel like jumping and sank into one of the pretty red chairs at the white table.

"Nehi, I didn't tell you why I was straightening up this morning," Anna commented as she sent a pancake flying into a corner and frowned as Joe caught it despite her best efforts.

"I didn't know you needed a reason," Nehemiah commented as he caught the pancake Joe tossed to him.

"Just so I know what to expect, is breakfast often this...exciting?" Harry asked as he sat down across from Nehemiah and instinctively caught the pancake Anna flipped over her brother's head. He took a bite. "Never mind, it can be as exciting as you want if you keep cooking like this."

"Hey Anna, send us a hard one!" Tanzid grinned.

"As I was saying," Anna said as she continued flipping pancakes, "our group's three mornings here–"

"Three mornings!" Nehemiah interrupted. Joe paused in his pancake catching to spin toward him.

"That's Doctor's main cure for beatings and such like," the mute signed. "He knocked you out for a couple of days, to let your body repair itself without the usual annoyances from consciously knowing about it. Disconcerting isn't it?"

"Yes, and while we've been waiting for you," Anna took up again, "we've gotten poor Harry's house rather a mess. So while Daniel and Beau went to go fetch some things–"

"Hey that's right, they aren't here," Nehemiah interrupted again. "And where's Quintus?"

"He's staked a claim on the old shed in back, calls it his workshop and hardly ever comes out," Harry answered, then started laughing heartily as Joe and Tanzid dived for the same pancake, smacked their noses together, and fell on the ground with the pancake on top.

"Pancake two, agents zero!" the doctor cried.

"Anyway, Nehemiah," Anna began again, "Peter and Elizabeth are coming to visit this morning."

"Pete and Lizzy, really? I thought they were going to stay in KAM till their wedding."

"They're married, and have a daughter too," Anna answered. Nehemiah began to count on his fingers, missing his pancake and accidentally letting it hit the doctor in the face. "You needn't count," Anna said as he apologized to the confused doctor, "it's only been six months since we left them, and don't be despicable. She's a dear, and her name's Martha."

"Who's a dear and is named Martha?" Nehemiah asked as he slumped in his chair and picked up the pancake Joe tossed on the table next to him.

"Their daughter. They've been over here a couple of times, but you were still unconscious. Peter went on a raid in the Institute–"

"He did what?" Nehemiah said in surprise and Tanzid paused in his pancake catching to join the conversation.

"I was shocked too, you Christians are a lot tougher than I thought. In two days I find one that can run the Brotherhood's gates taking two blacklisted people with him, and another who goes raiding in the Advancer's Institute."

"Remarkable," Harry commented. "But we aren't 'you Christians' anymore, brother." Anna hit Tanzid in the forehead with a pancake before he could reply, and picked up her conversation again.

"So, Peter was on a raid at the Institute," she started again. "While there he came across a newborn deaf-mute and fell in love with her. He talked it over with Elizabeth, and they went out and got married that night and took the fastest transport here to Story Land so they could speak up for her, and that's their daughter Martha."

"Good for them," Nehemiah mumbled, his mouth full of pancake. Joe beamed at him, then suddenly dived across the room to snatch a pancake before Tanzid could get it.

"She's a month old now, and an absolute dear," Anna added. "She didn't have a sign name, and Pete and Lizzy asked Joe to do it as a sort of godfather thing, and wanted them to get to know each other. So they've been over here a lot. Joe was kind of scared at first, but I think he likes her now. Right Joe?"

"He had better considering the moment that family walks through the door Martha and Joe are inseparable," Harry smiled, his eye on the little mute. Joe let a pancake sail over his head in order to sign his answer.

"Not scared, terrified. I thought I'd break her, but once I found out babies are pretty tough, she's great fun!"

"I don't think I want to know how you found that out!" Nehemiah laughed. "So what did you name her?"

"Blessed Gift," Joe signed. "As a reminder of God's love, her parents love, and her love to them. It's an interlaced gift, though it was a little odd to explain to Rock (my name for P-e-t-e-r, since it was Jesus' name for His P-e-t-e-r), but he took it–" The timer on the stove went off and Anna shoved the pancake flipper into Joe's hands, stopping his signing, and darted over to take her cookies out of the oven. Daniel and Cobeau stepped into the tiled kitchen with their arms full of groceries as the mute took over the pancakes and Anna slipped an oven mitt

over her hand. Daniel grinned at Anna as he dumped his stuff on the counter.

"Cookies in the morning?" he commented. "I'm not sure about your breakfasts."

"They're oatmeal cookies," Anna answered defensively. Daniel didn't bother to answer as he noticed Nehemiah in the chair at the table, and bounded over to hug his little brother and demand to know how he felt. Joe whistled a merry tune while he flipped and Cobeau reached two large arms around him and squeezed.

"You are happy," he rumbled. "Me too." Joe patted him affectionately on the head and signed for him to put him down because the pancakes were burning. Beau dropped him with a thump and yawned a huge, loud yawn. His eyes went hopefully to the stairs, thinking fond thoughts of a nap in the attic dormitory up the three flights. Twelve beds lined the area, and the men had claimed it as their room during their stay at Harry's.

"You have been awfully cheerful lately, Joe," Harry said as he began to get out plates for a more conventional breakfast. "More cheerful than I've seen you in years. What's gotten into you?"

"I retired right before I came here," Joe signed, and decided to leave it at that. But Harry saw his eyes dart happily to Anna and Nehemiah and got a better answer to his question.

"Retired from what?" the doctor asked simply. Joe pretended not to hear, signed he was going to go get Quintus in from his shed, and danced out of the kitchen whistling. Harry watched him go with a thoughtful look, then shrugged and took over the pancakes.

"So are we going exploring the town with Pete and Lizzy after breakfast?" Nehemiah asked as he stood up slowly to help lay out the table.

"No we are not!" Anna said firmly, as Daniel pushed him back in his seat. "You just got off the couch, Nehemiah Hillson, and you are going right back there after you eat. Peter said the same thing, not to let you up yet." Nehemiah started to object, but Anna wouldn't hear it. Nehemiah realized he wouldn't win this battle, and ruefully let the subject drop. Anna had grown up to be a lot like their mother. He wondered how long it would be before his sister would let him up as he filled his plate gratefully.

Nehemiah ate his fill, and a little more, and settled into his chair to enjoy watching the interaction of this strange bunch of brothers gathered around him. Tanzid watched in silence as he ate, observing as if he didn't know what to think of anyone, and wasn't about to make the wrong comment. Nehi would have thought it funny if the agent's quiet fear wasn't so pitiful. Tanzid was the only one quiet there. Daniel and Anna still debated if a cookie could be a valid breakfast food, while Joe inserted ridiculous couplets into their discussion through Beau's booming voice. Harry and Quintus, meanwhile, talked over everyone's heads about internal matters. Humanity's insides, that is, as Quintus originally got his schooling in the medical fields before turning to other branches of science. Nehi chuckled quietly to himself and couldn't blame Tanzid for being confused. They were an odd bunch.

A cheerful bell tinkled through the house, and Joe leapt to his feet, a happy whistle sliding from him. The mute left in a manner that Nehi could only describe as a scamper, and he grinned to himself as he rose slowly. It was good to see Joe relaxed and happy. Daniel's hand landed on Nehemiah's chest and the young man stopped still, swaying under the pressure.

"Where do you think you're going?" Daniel asked, adding a prod with a finger.

"Pete–" Nehi answered, but got no further, as both his siblings shook their heads and pointed at the den. "Really? That's the way it's going to be? I thought I escaped prison!"

"I'll go find a jailor's hat if I need to," Daniel said placidly, and gave another little push toward the den. Nehemiah sighed and shuffled toward the couch again, looking as dejected as he could manage. He could feel the others grinning at his back. He dropped onto the couch with a sigh that was a groan held back,

listened to someone close the door behind him cutting off the cheerful sound of voices, and stared at the ceiling.

This wasn't what he needed. Sure, he didn't feel well. But... he needed distraction more than rest. Each ache and tear carried a nasty memory with it. He didn't want to stare at ceilings and try to keep back the constant push in his head; they turned into fears all too quickly. Fears that were too real in the past, and that made him dread tomorrow. Nehemiah hated the dread. The sick weight in his stomach, the way he couldn't concentrate on anything but the worries that the pain would all come back, the tenseness that wouldn't leave his body, the constriction on his lungs. Nehi forced a breath in, looked away from the blue-painted ceiling and worked silently on getting his mind back away from it again. He couldn't explain it to Anna and Daniel. It was...too personal? Too hard to go into? Just unexplainable? Nehi's jaw clamped down on a sigh and he tried to relax. Alone staring at a ceiling wasn't what he needed right now.

The screen door swung open and Nehi's muscles bunched. Every instinct screamed at him to jerk up and snatch Hope at the unexpected movement. Joe hopped through the door. He caught the fear in Nehi's eye, the quickness of his breathing, and a gentle smile crossed his face that said he knew all about it. He patted Nehi's shoulder and then dropped on the ground to sit beside the couch. A harmonica slid into the mute's hand and he started to send a quiet tune waltzing around the room. Nehemiah sank back, steadily relaxing. After a minute the tenseness left and a smile hovered on his face.

"So what happened to the toad tongue?" Nehi interrupted before Joe could start the next tune. The mute lifted his foot, still encased in his habitual black boot. Three black circles clung to the leather at the ankle, and they looked like leather themselves now.

"It's still there!" Nehi laughed.

"I said it never lets go. Just be glad it picked my ankle and my boot was on. And that most of the smell is gone now," Joe shrugged with a smile. "I borrowed Hope to get rid of the excess." He lifted the harmonica again and Nehi sank back and let him disappear into the music. Two hymns, three reels, and a new song danced around the room, then Joe smiled up at his friend.

"You've been napping," he signed.

"What?"

"You've been napping. The door is thick enough to block out the music. I'm not supposed to be here, they think I've slipped out for a walk and you've been resting like a good invalid. I'll be back when you need me." The mute stood up abruptly and walked out the back door. Nehi lay on the couch, idly humming the last tune. A harsh, blaring bagpipe call shot through the wooden door from the kitchen, and Nehi jerked with a start, his head pounding with the noise. But he laughed and didn't mind the headache. His amusement just increased as he heard Anna, Daniel, and Pete yelling at Joe to put the pipes away, and could picture the innocent confusion plastered over the mute. But behind his laughter hovered a damp note as gratefulness whelmed up inside him. Joe had given him what he needed, and then gotten himself yelled at to pave the way for others to keep the invalid company, all without Nehi's having to explain a word. In his silent way, Joe had just said he understood Nehemiah, and he would never have to soldier through it alone.

The door pushed open and Nehi smiled at the man peeking through the crack.

"Yes, I'm awake," he chuckled. "Hello, Pete. You've been busy since the last time we talked, I hear you have a daughter now." The door shoved open all the way and Peter strolled in.

"Everyone in the neighborhood must be awake after Joe's stunt with the pipes," Peter grumbled as he dropped into a chair across from Nehi's couch. "Caught again? You really don't understand clandestine operations, do you?"

"I only failed one of those tests," Nehi grinned at him. "You crashed the simulator eight times."

"So I can't pilot a hover car in a high-speed chase, and you

give yourself away the minute you're seen by an enemy," Peter shrugged. "Easy fix. You're the get-away man, I'm the infiltrator."

"What's our swag?" Nehi asked,

"Cocktail shrimp. But only the tails," Peter replied without hesitation.

"Because...we grind them into plant food?"

"Poison for those with sea food allergies, only for the most advanced assassins. We'll make a fortune selling it to the right people."

"You have gotten nefarious. Must be your daughter's influence."

"Say, you haven't met her yet! I think Lizzy claimed her back from Anna, just a second." Peter dashed off to find Martha, and Nehi leaned back, a half smile cocked over his face, and his eyes closed. He and Peter had so many of these ridiculous conversations, it made all the world feel right. And with Joe around he didn't have to worry about tomorrow.

# Chapter Thirteen: Rooftop Revival

*"For we are saved by hope..."* Romans 8:24

The walls closed in on Nehemiah.

Anna and Daniel wouldn't let him up. Sometimes when he dozed, in the half-awake state between sleep and consciousness, he would see Abid coming for him, and it took a mental struggle to remember these four square walls were not his master's rooms. Nights were worse. When the darkness closed in, it was Simmons' steps he heard, and his low chuckle that haunted every dreamscape. Nehi tried leaving a light on. But his subconscious somehow still knew the night. The third night, Nehi swallowed what little pride he had left. He woke up strangling in his dreams, soaked in sweat. His hand shot back for his pillow and he slammed it down to hit Joe, where the mute curled on a sleeping bag beside the couch. Joe's tousled blond head came up with a jerk, his hand already slashing at Nehi's throat in a defensive move. The hand froze in midair as green eyes landed on Nehemiah and focused blearily.

"I need air," Nehi hissed, the desperation dripping from it. Joe nodded, still blinking heavily. He slid to the backdoor, did something with the lock, oiled the old hinges, and swung open the door to the backyard. Nehemiah was out, down the steps, and gulping in the balmy night air before the door reached its end swing and started to close again. Joe closed it silently, stepped beside him, motioned briefly to the windows in the house behind them, and began to lead the way through the gate and into an alley. Nehi followed stiffly, aching and weak, but his mind a relieved blank. The world did exist beyond those four den walls.

A salty breeze blew from the bay, and Nehi breathed deep, able to catch his breath for the first time in two days. He was still free. Out here with the open sky he knew it. Joe climbed on a bench, stepped onto a sloping roof of a house that seemed to be half buried in the ground, and began to stroll up it. Nehemiah

followed, a smile beginning to hover over his face as the adventure took hold. Joe reached the top of the roof and stepped off it to the next, a flat two-storied hacienda. From one roof to the next he walked, always higher, piecing together a path like a puzzle. Eight minutes later, the mute dropped to sit cross legged on the top of an eight-story apartment building, and Nehi settled with a stifled groan beside him.

The breeze blew strong up here. Below them lights twinkled everywhere. The little dots of yellow surrounded them, until they ended abruptly in a horseshoe shape at the edge of the bay. The giant ferns and tillandsias moved in the breeze, blocking out a light here, revealing another there, creating a mysterious beauty. The breeze blew into his face and Nehemiah leaned back to stare at the sky, feeling the wind blow away his pent-up claustrophobia and nightmares. Empty, free space closed around him, encapsulated by the brilliant stars scattered over the black sky. He just blinked, his spirit still and easy and happy. *Thank you, Jesus. This is You, in the breeze, in the freedom...*

After a few minutes his gaze wandered idly to Joe. The mute sat beside him, his hands in his lap, his legs crossed. But he sat stiff in the starlight, staring straight ahead at the blackness of the bay. Suddenly the silence didn't seem quite as friendly to Nehi.

"Thanks," he broke it.

"I used to come up here often at nights. I don't think Diamond ever knew," Joe signed. His green eyes flicked to Nehi's. "He was amazing, Knee-High, really wonderful. Sometimes I... Being here, it sometimes..." The mute's hands dropped gently to his lap.

"I dread going back to the Sojourners' House. I'll have to face the familiar rooms without my parents then," Nehi said softly. Joe sighed and nodded. He looked idly up at the stars with his friend.

"I didn't mean to bring that up. But it always breaks open again when I come to visit Doctor, and I thought I would tell you… Well, even though Diamond was the best man I ever met, he never understood. Why I would slip out at night sometimes, why I needed to get away from walls, see the sun or a star that proved I was out. That I was free. It's nice to have someone around who understands."

"Yeah," Nehi said simply, his voice quiet. The two sat silently on the roof. Joe shifted, lending himself as a prop for Nehi. Nehi gratefully accepted the support, leaned against him, and let his mind wander. The balmy breeze brushed them, salty and humid. Black hair and blond stirred and mingled, broke apart, and collided again in the breeze. Nehi pointed at a group of five stars in the rough form of a circle.

"They call that the empty tomb. There's only one that's empty now. But because of that one empty tomb, we'll meet them again, Mom and Dad and Josh. 'Blessed be the God and Father of our Lord Jesus Christ, which according to his abundant mercy hath begotten us again unto a lively hope by the resurrection of Jesus Christ from the dead, to an inheritance incorruptible, and undefiled, and that fadeth not away, reserved in heaven for you, who are kept by the power of God through faith unto salvation ready to be revealed in the last time[5].'"

"It says that?" Joe asked, his signs small in his wonder.

"It does. I wasn't happy about the author having made it all one really long thought, because memorizing it took longer than I liked when I was young. But now I'm so thankful I have that sure knowledge of our solid hope, held for us by God's power and not our own. It would be really hard to live without that hope."

"You can't live without hope," Joe signed. Something in the adamancy of the signs made Nehi pause, waiting for more. A fine blush crept over Joe's face and he looked away. Nehi decided to push; Joe wouldn't have brought the subject up unless a part of him wanted to talk about it.

"I was born into a house that offered me God's truth and

---

[5] 1 Peter 1:3-5

hope from the start," Nehi said, a weight very similar to guilt pressing on him as he looked at the sharp, scarred friend beside him. Why had he been blessed with such a good life, while Joe... "But that's not how it worked for you?"

Joe sat still, his eyes on the sky. Then he spun slowly to face Nehi, his hands lifted, and he began to sign, his face still turned to the stars.

"I was born a dreamer. I hope for better things even when there's no hope to be found. Sometimes it's the only thing that keeps me in this world. Hope, the idea that there must be something better if I can only hold on long enough to find it, has saved my life more times than I can count. A man without hope withers away. That's how we're wired. And there is no hope if what most of the world believes is factual. If there is no Creator, there is no purpose, and that leaves us with no hope. And if there is no hope, there is no life. Why do we hope? That's the question that plagued me about the idea of nothing but random evolutional chance in life, it was what kept me chafing at the idea of there being no ultimate truth. Why do we automatically hope? What was hope that made it so strong?"

"So what did you answer yourself?" Nehemiah asked. He watched his friend's absent expression as he stared at the stars, the smooth slowness of his signs...he saw a new opening in the little mute. Nehi had met the thoughtful dreamer. But never this openly. When this part of the mute showed he always ducked out of sight, embarrassed and shy. Tonight he emerged into the starlight, and he emerged volubly. And somehow Nehi felt this was the last piece to Joe, the final layer under all the others.

"I was in KAM with Diamond, a few months after he had picked me up. Never mind all the circumstances, but an old man gave up his life so I could keep mine. I couldn't sleep that night. There were a lot of nights I couldn't sleep, but this one was more intense. I kept remembering his face as he died, and others that I had seen, and the contrast was killing me. I saw hope and peace in some and terror in others and I couldn't understand the difference and was too tired to try. Too tired of hoping with no reason, too tired of life when I didn't want it. I slipped out before dawn, restless, unable to stay still but with no idea where to go. I ended up kneeling beside the grave Diamond commissioned for the old man, and I stayed there with my thoughts and the open grave in front of me. I couldn't give it a name, couldn't understand it, but hope wouldn't let me drop everything and join that old man in the hole. When dawn came Diamond sat beside me. I don't know how he found me, but there he was, in his pajamas and with that energetic love of his just as bright and painfully hard as ever. He knelt beside me and gave me twenty words. That was all.

"'Do you know why you're here instead of there?' and he pointed from the ground beside me to the black hole of the grave. 'Because Jesus' grave is empty. He is the God of hope.' And he left me there and went and sat down on a bench a few plots away. I finally understood what hope is then and why it's so powerful." Joe stirred and glanced away.

"Good man," Nehemiah murmured, silently thanking God again for Joshua Noble. "What did you understand?" Joe's hands lifted again and he began to sign slowly, as if feeling his way.

"If an abstract is only an abstract in a void of random time, it isn't solid enough to grab onto and pull yourself away from a grave. But that's just what I'd done with hope. Again and again, I had hovered over a grave, held between life and death, and had pulled myself back to life with hope. Hope is a solid thing, a real thing. Hope is a Person. And with that simple, sudden realization, I stood up and walked away from that grave, and sat down on the bench with Diamond." A smile spread over Joe's face, his eyes distant as he saw something beyond Nehemiah's vision. It was an expression of peace and joy, that ran deeper than humor, deeper than happiness, delving into a well that never could run dry. It beautified the mute, turning even his scars into marks of honor, signposts of the way that had led him to the well. He began to sign with great distinctness.

"Jesus Christ is Hope. He is Truth. He is Reason. His grave is empty, death couldn't hold Him and nothing can overcome

Him. He is the living, creating God. And He is real. The moment you realize that everything else falls away, all random existence disappears, and all life takes on meaning and reality and purpose. There is hope because there is God. God is." Joe suddenly shrugged, his vibrant earnestness melting into a shy smile. "I guess I answered more than you asked. But you know, Knee-High..." His frown came back and he looked away. Nehemiah waited a moment. Nothing came from the mute. He shifted one foot and jogged Joe's knee.

"They shouldn't be dead," Joe signed, almost viciously. "Your parents, Diamond, it was betrayal and violence that took them from us so soon. And we shouldn't need to slip out at night to sit up here, it's wrong, all of it's wrong! God is, but we're here, and it's all wrong! I know about Jesus coming in the end, but... I keep trying to make things right, to get the old voices out of my head and...I'm not really a good person, Knee-High even though I keep trying, and I keep fighting to right the world, and..." Joe sighed and his signs slowed. "I'm just tired. Ignore my ramblings. That's not why we slid out, to load you down with more."

"His grave is empty, Joe." Nehi's voice was soft, but the conviction it carried sang over the rooftop, caught by the wind and turned back to the young men. "'But now is Christ risen from the dead...[6]' Yes, sin is still here, with all its nasty consequences, inside us and outside. Mom and Dad and Josh, they aren't here with us and we will always have that hole as long as we are here on earth. But not as long as we live. Coffin nails and dirt aren't going to hold them back. There's more to life. More than death and sin and violence. We have an eternity to see Goodness face to face. And down here, yes we work every day to make the world a little better, and claim more of our own lives away from sin and back for Christ. But we don't do it alone. 'For he must reign, till he hath put all enemies under his feet[7].' His grave is

---

[6] 1 Corinthians 15:20
[7] 1 Corinthians 15:25

empty. Jesus is alive. He didn't just win the war, He's fighting the battles with us still. Mopping up the remaining foes and comforting even in our darkest times. If there's one thing I've realized Abid's rooms taught me, it's that. Jesus is alive, and with us, and the hope that we carry inside us isn't just a feeling. It's a Person. Just like you've felt. And we will live forever and meet Him face to face, and all that together makes every moment vibrate with meaning and expectation. Keep that vision of Who holds us fast and will take us home, Joe. Especially when you're tired, keep the vision of our home burning in front of your eyes."

The mute nodded slowly, his smile creeping back over his face. He saw a wince go over Nehi, and swiveled to lean against his friend again. Nehi slumped against him gratefully. The two stared at the scenery, enjoying the space and freedom. Time ticked on. The breeze blew around them, then died to a whisper, and left altogether. A balmy humidity closed over them like a wet, stifling blanket. The mute stirred, shifting to a position where Nehi could see his signs.

"What did you say to D to get him to take the bomb off?" the mute asked.

"It really wasn't that hard," Nehemiah said, his voice dreamy and his eyes still on the stars. "You have so many layers and masks, after the initial shock of it the UPC was just one more. We finally got through to Daniel that he's never even met you."

"What?"

"You, the one under the layers, the one who's been talking to me tonight." Nehemiah's gaze turned to his friend, an amused smile on his face. "You don't make it easy to find you. But I'm really glad you've let me in, thanks. Anyway, Ann and I finally got Danny to realize he's never met you, and that the UPC thing really wasn't an issue when you think about everything else we know about you too."

Joe sat still, his head tipped so his hair fell over his eyes, a blank veneer over his face. Nehemiah stirred, sitting up and rolling his shoulders slowly.

"Ok, what are you thinking about," he demanded. Joe's hands lifted and he signed, slowly, a little reluctantly.

"I have to leave tomorrow."

"What? Where to?"

"Things are happening this week. I have to get the Bible back. I shouldn't have told you, but this is the most important raid I'll ever make, and you're right about Jesus fighting with us. I need all the prayers you can send." Joe's hands dropped to his lap. Nehi studied him and noted the tired crinkle around the mute's eyes and his frown back on as he stared out at the bay.

"You're headed for a bad patch, aren't you?" he prodded. Joe shrugged. Nehi jabbed a finger into his knee impatiently.

"Ok, yes, it's probably not going to be pleasant. But it shouldn't be too bad if I can get out fast."

"And if you can't? Does anyone know where you're going to be?"

"I'm leaving Glue to keep an eye on you pitiful lot gathered here, you need him," Joe signed, attempting to change the subject with a tease. It didn't work.

"So even Beau isn't going to be there to help get you out of a mess. He's saved your life before, a lot, why aren't you bringing him?"

"That Wolf, Knee-High, he's–" Joe cut his signs off mid-sentence.

"Here," Nehi finished quietly. The mute turned his face away and didn't answer. Which was an answer in itself. A chill ran down Nehi's spine that had nothing to do with the sweat steadily dripping down his back from this humidity.

"Near." Joe signed suddenly. "I didn't sign 'here,' and near isn't the same thing."

"It's awfully close. Can't you just tell us his name?"

"You keep assuming I know!" The mute's lips pressed together and his expression hardened. "Knee-High, presumptions are dangerous. I don't have to know the Wolf's full identity to fight back, I don't have to know who he is without the mask to fight what he does in the mask. Stop presuming!" Nehi let it drop. He wouldn't press a conversation Joe refused to have.

"You're worried and don't want to go, which means it's a bad situation to be in, and you're going alone," Nehi summed up the situation. "Joe, I know you've been trying to play this close, but please. At least tell me where you'll be and promise to get a message through if you get in trouble." Joe sat for a moment contemplating. Then his lips pressed together and he signed quickly, as if he were letting a secret out against his better judgement.

"Sojourners' Way. At least at first," Joe signed. Nehi jerked away, his ears ringing. "But you can't tell anyone, not even Beauty. I thought you two were safe enough, but after the People's Kingdom... Promise me Knee-High, promise you'll tell no one!"

"Only if you promise to get a message to me if you're in trouble." His voice came husky and fast, as if he knew he shouldn't be promising this. "Use the trackers you handed out, set off the alarm and I'll be able to trace you."

"They'll block it."

"But I'll have a moment before they do," Nehi said quickly, his ears still ringing and his aching body feeling weak and worn out. Who were 'they'? What kind of trouble was Joe headed to? And in his own home country! The Way wasn't supposed to be like that! "You promise and I'll promise." Joe hesitated again, his head bowed. Then he looked up, spit on his hand and held it out. A smile cracked over Nehi's wan face as he spit and slapped his palm into his friend's in a time honored covenant. "Promise," Nehi nodded.

"Promise," Joe nodded. "Now let's get you back before I have to get Glue to carry you."

*Harry's Kitchen*

Anna stifled a yawn as she stepped off the stairs and walked down the hall toward the kitchen. Somehow she always woke up before everyone else, even when she wanted to sleep in. Oh well, she would make more cookies for breakfast, just to annoy Daniel.

A lovely smell of melted chocolate and fresh baked sweetness enfolded her as she pushed open the door, and Anna stopped in surprise, blinking in the glare of the kitchen's lights. Joe turned from the oven, an apron wrapped twice around his waist, a pan of fresh cookies in one hand, and a good morning smile on.

"Good morning to you too," Anna murmured, staring at the cookies sliding on a plate to cool. Joe paused to sign at her.

"I bought the dough off a shelf when I went shopping for Doctor yesterday," he confessed.

"In that case they might be edible," Anna grinned at him. "What are you doing up? Or did you never go to bed?" Joe just shrugged. But his eyes didn't meet hers, and stayed that way as Anna started to get her morning cup of tea and Joe finished his cookies. Anna poured water over her leaves and watched the wonderful cloud of brown swirl up. Her hand slid under the saucer and she turned with her cup and leaned against the counter.

"What do you need to tell me, Joe?" she asked. The mute stopped puttering. He stood still in the center of the black and white tiles, his hair spilling over his eyes.

"I won't ask how you know," Joe said, a smile hovering on his lips. Then his smile dropped into seriousness. "Don't cage Knee-High so close, Beauty. It isn't what he needs right now."

"I've noticed you seem to be in with him a lot when I try to keep him down," Anna said. She took a sip of her tea and allowed the delightful, comforting flavor to fill her senses. "Why are you telling me this instead of just giving him what he needs, like you have been doing?"

"I'm leaving this morning for another raid," Joe signed. Anna's eyes went to her cup and she said nothing. But Joe could

watch her processing it, and she didn't like it.

"You don't want to go," Anna stated. Joe's eyes darted away and then back as he looked at her in a little surprise. Anna sat her cup down and met his look. "I'm not going to tell you to stay, because I know you wouldn't listen to me. But I really hope you told Nehi something about what you're doing." Joe just shrugged. He swept a cookie up, tossed it to her, and waved as he turned to the door.

"I want you to come back, Joe."

The words stopped him short in the middle of the doorway. The mute turned slowly, looking at the beautiful young woman standing in the kitchen, her arms crossed, chin lifted, no hint of her usual smile on her face.

"Do what you need to. But be careful. I want you back."

Joe nodded once. A smile twitched over him, pleasure, confusion, a little shyness, it all mixed there for an instant. Then he slipped through the door, and was gone. Anna heaved a sigh and turned back to the tea kettle. She needed a second cup today.

# Chapter Fourteen: Sojourner's Way

*"The wicked in his pride doth persecute the poor: let them be taken in the devices that they have imagined."* Psalm 10:2

Freezing wind whirled and roared, turning Joe's hair into writhing whipcords. They spun around his face, swirling and stinging, but he couldn't feel them. His face was numb. His whole body was numb with the cold. The freezing, spinning, blackness seemed alive; a living menace eating at his mind and slowly ripping his skin off. Solid ground slammed through the soles of his feet out the top of his head. He crashed into the ground and curled around himself. The freezing air cut off with the sharp hiss of the SOLTD sucking into itself. Joe lay in a ball, shivering and gasping, his fingers biting into the soft, wet earth he had brought along from Story Land. Apparently his old SOLTD needed some tweaking to make long journeys comfortable. The wary experience of a lifetime as the hunted sent him staggering up, looking for a place to get out of sight. Someone would have noticed the noise and light of the SOLTD, and the gashed hole he created with his landing. A small tree even lay rooted up, jerked toward the black hole effect.

Joe's eyes ran around the area as he staggered away from the destruction. *There's not much left to destroy,* he decided. The invaders had done their work. His map told him he stood in the farmland of Sojourner's Way. He only saw scorched black earth and ruined buildings. A mound of blackened boards rose into the night and Joe ducked behind them and crouched watching to see what would happen next.

His eyes focused on the dirt and dust lying thick amongst the heaped boards. Joe carefully, slowly pulled the boards apart to create a hole. He slid his SOLTD inside, shoved it harder till he felt it thunk into the dirt, then pulled the boards back in place. Joe's fingers dug into the black dirt and he flung it onto the boards, then blew. He evened the dirt out, rubbed it in, and carefully covered the bright sheen of the copper SOLTD hidden

within.

A murmur drifted to him and Joe froze. People, coming nearer, wondering what had just zipped over their heads, materialized in a pulsing ball, and disappeared again. Most of the voices came from behind him, but some drifted from a pitiful scraggily bunch of pines with fire-blackened trunks standing defiantly together. They were the only trees Joe could see on the horizon. The little copse stood just a few yards in front of Joe as he shivered and tried to get his teeth to stop chattering. The mute slipped his black leather mask over his head and slid his white hands into his pockets, blending into the dirt.

Twelve people trickled out of the trees. They looked as ragged as the copse and less defiant. Joe huddled perfectly still, watching under lowered lids to keep his eyes from glittering in what little light came from the half moon. The last of the group walked past him. Joe stood up, smooth and easy, just behind a tall man with faded, ripped jeans and shirt. The mute's black leather mask slid back in his pocket, but a mask of quiet, nervous fear played over the young man's face. His gate matched the tired, hesitant stride of the others to perfection. He stayed in the group, hanging on the fringes, constantly hunched, and darting scared glances everywhere.

The group of people reached the edge of the small crater created by Joe's landing, meeting up with a larger band of the same ragged, cautious slaves. The two groups stood and stared. No one wanted to risk being the first to speak. A young lady, probably about fourteen Joe guessed, stood in front of him in a tattered, broken dress that had once been a cheerful red. She stared at the little tree lying in the crater, her facial bones sharp and distinct from starvation. She stood fixated on that tree.

"My father planted that," came the whisper. Her voice was musical and sweet, with such a deep sorrow she had no place left for fear.

A new sound invaded the torn up area. Rough, angry voices. They came nearer quickly. The group by the crater quavered, and people began to slink away into the night. Except the girl in the faded red dress. She walked forward, her eyes still on the little tree. Blue uniformed soldiers stomped into view from around a burned out building. Their coats were unbuttoned, their boots mud-stained, and half of them had faces flushed with drink. But even with the lax way they kept themselves in this outpost, Joe recognized the IK. He would always know their kind, no matter what they wore. His eyes darted to the girl in red. She stepped out of the crowd and walked over the torn ground to the tree.

The group around him quivered and began to retreat. Where Joe had been at the back of the crowd, now he stood at the front, as the rest moved in restless fear. The girl in red wrapped her pale, bone-thin hands around the tree's white trunk. The soldiers reached the outer fringes of the group. Fists rammed into faces, bully sticks came down indiscriminately, and one short man slashed a pulsing electric whip into any bare skin he could see. Whimpers, cries, muffled screams, IK laughter, it closed around Joe like one of his nightmares come to life. But he didn't turn and slink off with the others.

The girl in red hefted the tree back in its hole and began to push good black dirt over the roots. The short man's piggy eyes settled on her. His wrist flicked and the four pulsing whip cords shimmered their unnatural white as the current coursed through them, recharging for their next victim. The man tapped one soldier who held a bully stick (an unpleasant IK female) and pointed at the girl in red. The girl carefully patted down the earth, making certain the tree could stay upright on its own. The IK began to stalk closer. The girl sat back on her heels and looked up at the branches swaying gently in the breeze. A half smile twitched over her bruised face. The pulsing cords whipped toward her neck.

A fire-blackened board shot between the white neck and the cords. They wrapped hungrily around the wood, crackling as they burnt deep, deeper with every second they stayed connected. The board jerked hard. The whip's stick snapped out of the IK's hand and into a scarred, thin hand that seemed to

materialize from the darkness. The short soldier staggered, gaping at a small blond man as he stepped into the pulsing white light of the whip. Joe didn't give him time to recover. The board sailed for the man's face, the cords still pulsing as they bit deeper and deeper into the wood. A scream of pure agony rent from the man as it connected. The crackling cords loosened their hold on the board, attaching to the bare skin. Joe jerked the stick and the four cords snapped like living snakes. They splayed over the ground by his feet, pulsing, twitching, looking for the next victim.

For an instant the scene went still. Everyone stared at the blond man who had just dared to interfere with an IK. Joe felt the malevolent murmur of every living soul around him. Even the slaves glared, knowing they would suffer for his moment's insurrection.

A roar of furious anger lifted from the female and she charged the mute, snatching her prod and taser off her belt. Red buttons lit on each belt, as the soldiers alerted their fellow slave-drivers of an insubordinate situation. Hatred turned on the mute with all the cruel fury of years of practice. But Joe also had years of practice in his own unique art of self-defense.

The taser sparked and crackled as it shot out. Joe kicked the girl in red in the shoulder, sending her crashing around the little tree, out of the way. He spun to the side and slammed the whip's stick into a rock jutting from the torn ground. The weapon broke in half with a sharp crack. Two white cords sailed over his head, writhing and whistling, as the other two curved around his body. A stun dart sizzled into ash as it hit the mute's wall of writhing protective cords. The cords moved in ceaseless arches, creating solid white lines in the dark air and illuminating the mute's face in a ghostly light. His scarred features were hard and angry. The youngest IK soldier took a quick step back after a glance at that face. Joe swirled and spun, and the oldest soldier backed away; experience had taught him when it wasn't going to be fun.

The other six advanced, gathering their weaponry. The

female lunged, snarling, her bully stick jabbing out in the same trick Joe had used to foul the whip cords. The white lines dodged and swirled in his hands, crackling and hissing. The woman jerked back with a muffled shriek, her hand sliced and pulsing and her stick lying on the ground. Joe turned with animal fury on the remaining five. The four cords suddenly broke into individual lances of tangible anger as they bit and tore and burned, wielded by one made into an expert on electric whips. The IK fell back, crying and yelping in undignified disorder. The cords followed, driving them into a single mass. Joe's fingers shifted on his right hand. The cords swirled with less intensity for a single second. Then he had his grenade.

Joe jabbed the activation button and flicked the black canister into the middle of the massed IK. A dense gray cloud mushroomed into the dark air. The clamor suddenly stopped. No coughs, no screams, no whimpers. Only sudden, terrifying silence in the midst of that gray. The girl in red stared, propped numbly on her elbow where Joe's kick had sent her beside the little tree. The mute noticed her large eyes were a beautiful, distinctive violet as his hands clamped onto her arms and he jerked her to her feet. He mentally dubbed her Violet, knowing he was unlikely to learn her real name. The ground felt soft, pulling at his feet as Joe dashed over the scorched earth toward the copse of trees. But he didn't duck under their sheltering branches. The slaves had slipped away at the first opportunity, but some of them would have stayed to watch in those trees. Possibly a brave few would be allies. Almost certainly the crowd would club them senseless and turn them over to the IK in the hope of avoiding a little of the usual punishments from their merciless drivers.

Joe veered to the side at the first deep shadow and his hand dove into his bag. A light-weight black cloth sailed over Violet's head and fell to her feet. A slim cord tightened around her waist, holding the cloth in place, as long gloves slid over her arms. The pinching hand on her shoulder jerked, pulling her stumbling deeper into the darkness as she gasped and tried

desperately to see. A thin finger pressed against the cloth over her mouth. Even through the black fabric the cold of that finger bit into her, and she felt it shaking. She swallowed her gasps. Only blackness surrounded her as she stumbled along with this stranger, the cloth catching at her legs. Her feet hit a rise and she clambered up the short incline.

Light bit into her face, a white beam that seemed to seer her eyeballs and go on through the back of her skull. The hand jerked her to the ground and she hit the dirt hard. The hand on her shoulder suddenly became a pair of iron-strong arms wrapped around her and holding her perfectly still. She froze, half in obedience, half in terror. The spotlight swept away. Her eyes pulsed with white sparks, but even through it she could see more than before. Normal yellow lights burned ahead of them, marking the windows of a building. That would be the slavers' house. They called it something else officially, but that's what she knew it as. The arms left, the pinching grip grabbed her hand and jerked, and they started running. It took a moment for her to realize they were headed for the lights.

Violet stopped short, jerking Joe off balance. He turned, a desperate need to get out of sight making him decidedly irritable. The girl stood rigid, riveted on the IK building. Every muscle was tight, her eyes stretched so wide they shown through the fabric, her breath coming in ragged gasps of panic. For the thousandth time Joe cursed his silence. He would have liked to tell her he wasn't one of them. He would have loved to sooth her terror with a single gentle word, something she probably hadn't heard since the disintegration hit. Instead he could only drag her along and pray she could trust him blindly. He wrapped his arm around her waist and began to run again, half carrying the terrified girl. After a few yards Violet's struggles slowed. Joe could feel her eyes on him. He gave her a confident wink and hoped she could see his smile behind his mask.

A spotlight swept toward them with blinding speed. Joe's leg shot out and kicked Violet's feet from her. He slammed them both into the ground. He heard the breath go out of her lungs as they hit the black dirt. Half of him felt glad of it as it meant she would be still, while the other half cursed himself hard as a ruffian. The light swept over the two black lumps on the black earth. Joe slid to his feet, taking the girl with him, and headed for the house. He could see the outline of the backdoor now, a rectangle of yellow light spilling out around the frame. Joe dropped the girl's waist to flick his arm. The black leather flapped back to reveal his array of instruments strapped to his sleeve. Violet's eyes grew wider still as she saw the twenty little bands of high-tech gadgetry running up that arm; things that looked like watches and compasses, a miniature blowtorch, a full set of tiny throwing knives, a band of wire-thin black cord, undefinable bits of metal and springs and gears. Joe focused on the bio scanner. Little green dots moved everywhere (the IK out looking for them) and milling blobs showed him where the slaves huddled waiting till it was over. But none of the dots were here, in the way of his dash for the door. And only three pulsed inside. One of those would be Amran, calibrating the in-struments for the hunt.

Joe started to run. Violet ran beside him this time, he didn't have to drag her. Good. He let go of her arm and cupped his dart gun in his hand. A rectangle of light marked the door, the light seeping through the cracks. It grew large as they rushed it. The door gave a sharp snap as Joe rammed his shoulder into it and spun inside, eyes half closed against the yellow glare. He stepped into his spin and raised his dart gun. Joe's thin form showed for an instant in the doorway of the IK Outworks Mo-bilization room. Three men looked up from their scanners and microphones, gaping as the one they were directing the search for glared at them from behind an elegant black leather mask. Amran stood a little apart from the other two, his hand hover-ing over his toolbox, his height causing his black hair to brush the ceiling. Then Joe's darts found their marks. Three men top-pled silently over their instruments, their eyes rolling back in their heads.

Violet leaned weakly against the wall, gasping and trying to

comprehend what this strange little person was doing. He ignored the two beefiest men, and seemed to be tying wheels on the third fellow's back, a tall one with black wavy hair. Heavy footsteps rang just outside the splintered door. In an instant Violet's eyes fastened on the cracked door as it hung crooked, recognized what that would intimate, and icy horror closed her throat at the knowledge a signal was about to beam out; "Found." But the same terror that closed her throat steeled her muscles. Violet sprang forward and rammed both her hands into the door, palms out. It slammed into something that went, "Whoomph!" and rebounded back to her. A large plank broke and spun crazily, and a sliver of green hat showed through the hole. Violet wrenched the plank off, and smashed it down on the hat, twice. The broken door swung open with a creak. A large soldier stood outside. His eyes rolled back. His knees buckled and he thudded at Violet's feet as she jerked back with a squeak.

The strange, silent young man in black walked past her. He glanced at the fallen man, then up at the panting girl, half a plank raised over her head. An approving smile curved under his mask, she could see it in his eyes. He gave her a thumbs up. Then his dart gun popped as he made sure the soldier stayed down. He jerked his head to say follow and walked out the door. The tall IK rolled behind the man in black, the soldier's feet and hands tied in a bunch that her ally tugged on as a handle. Violet's whole body shook and even with the years of disintegration behind her, she felt she had never been so scared. The young man poked his face back around the broken door. He winked and jerked his chin, telling her to come along. Violet's legs moved, following his orders. She stumbled back into the darkness beyond the door, clutching the plank like a shield.

Joe tossed a black cloth over Amran, grabbed the man's bound arm, and jerked, half carrying him, half wheeling him along the broken dirt. Violet stumbled behind him. He glanced at her plank and smiled again. Joe knew more about her now and didn't feel the need to hold her hand like a child. Shouts rose into the night air around them. The IK had noticed no more orders came over their feeds. They would be converging at the headquarters in seconds. Joe did what he did best and melted into the shadows as he ducked through the desolate land. But it was a very desolate land. Nothing except scorched earth and a few pitiful trees gallantly trying to stay alive through the fires and hacking. Nowhere to stop where they wouldn't be silhouetted against the night sky if that dad-blamed spotlight came back.

Violet recognized it too. Amran's wheels tangled in a turned up root and Joe jerked to a stop, barely managing to keep the man from falling, and blowing hard with the effort. Violet's shoulder rammed into the IK, the wheels hopped, spun, caught on fresh earth, and they were off again, both pushing this time. Joe shot the girl another appreciative glance. This time she had the energy to notice the look swelled within her and gave her strength. Whoever this weird little man was, approval from him in a wild night like this meant something.

"Where can we go?" she murmured, the words low as she worked to keep her voice from shrilling in panic. Joe's hand rose briefly to wave in front of them. "That's not an answer!" Violet shrilled. The small party rolled and stumbled over another rise in the ground, and the lights of Crosstown came in view, three miles away. Joe's finger rose and pointed at the lights.

A blinding beam hit Violet's heels. She flung herself over the rise and lay still on the ground. She pressed her face into her black-gloved arm, but she could feel the light playing over them. It seemed to burn her skin, every inch of her prickled and shook. Then it swept on and the strong hands of the strange little man pulled her upright again. Violet helped jerk Amran back up onto his wheels and they were off, stumbling over the broken, uneven ground toward the town.

It wouldn't do any good to go there. No one would hide them. The IK ruled Crosstown now. But they had nowhere else to go. And she would run as long as she had the strength left.

# Chapter Fifteen: The Tunnels

*"Teach me good judgment and knowledge: for I have believed thy commandments."* Psalm 199:66

Hinges squeaked and Nehi's head snapped around like it had just unhinged. Tanzid stood in the door, a small box tucked under one arm. Nehemiah did his best not to wince at the sudden pounding in his head after that involuntary maneuver and forced his breathing to even out. The agent stepped into the room and headed for the coffee table beside Nehi, his expression betraying nothing of what he thought of the invalid's performance. It had been two days since Joe slipped off. Nehi hadn't been let up, he didn't sleep, his nerves were raw, and his temper volatile and unhappy. Because of that temper, he had been left mostly alone in his backroom prison. Which hadn't improved things. Tanzid hooked a bare toe around a green padded chair's leg, pulled it over, and dropped to sit across from Nehi at the table. The box slid on his lap.

"Chess?" Nehi asked in surprise.

"Chess," Tanzid said evenly. He pulled the box open, slapped the board on the table and began to set up the pieces, riveted by the task. Nehi felt cardboard tap his fingers where they hung listlessly off the couch. He grabbed it and found it was the chess box. Tanzid didn't look up. Nehi leaned over and looked at the box. A compact Grady personal tracker rested inside. Nehemiah gently stirred the PT with his finger; about the size and thinness of a standard greeting card, it was the best thing in tracking. A Grady PT had been known to track a mouse twelve hundred miles away, down to the square inch. And it had the basic functions of most other personal pads programmed in its slim insides. The screen took up most of the front, but when his finger brushed it, a digital keyboard flew into view, glowing an iridescent blue.

"Do you know Joe's code?" Tanzid's voice was low, his eyes focused on the chess board.

"I don't think he has a bone plant. Does he?"

"I found out by accident. A bad accident, actually, the mute nearly got his head chopped off. He was lying there unconscious with his jaw bared to the bone, and I saw it. The numbers were still visible, though it's an older model. I sewed him up while he was still out and never told anyone."

"Is that where he got that whacking huge scar?" Nehi asked in surprise. Tanzid rubbed his chin, embarrassment shining from him.

"I've never been good at field medicine. I always felt a little bad about that," he mumbled, then rushed the conversation on. "Bone plants can be deactivated. But they're usually removed then, so if he still had it, I figured it's worth knowing."

"It is. Thanks. How long have you been watching me?" Nehi asked. Tanzid's white teeth flashed in his dark face as he grinned, and it made him suddenly very likeable.

"It isn't personal, I've been watching everyone. It's a habit. But I have noticed you clutching that tracker like you're terrified to put it down for even a second, ever since Joe left. I figured maybe you'd want to know there's a more certain way, even if you miss his call." Nehi nodded, but his lips pursed. How much dared he ask this man? He knew so little about him.

"I'll be black," Tanzid ordered. "Don't comment, no pun intended." Nehi grinned and propped himself a little higher to look at the board. The pieces were set up with a precision verging on compulsive. He moved a pawn. Tanzid countered in almost a bored way. Three minutes later, Nehi stared at the majority of his pieces lined up neatly in front of Tanzid, and then looked back at his cornered king. He reached out a finger and knocked the king over. Tanzid set up the board again. This time Nehi actually paid attention. It took ten minutes for Tanzid to beat him. Nehi studied him from lowered lids as they both began to set it up again. The muscular, serious agent didn't seem the type to be a compulsive chess player.

"So, Tanzid. Did you always want to be a UPC agent?" he asked. Tanzid's gaze flicked up at him.

"It won't work. I don't get distracted by talking," he said.

"It's worth a try," Nehi grinned at him. "Besides winning chess games, what are you thinking about now?" Tanzid studied him a minute longer. Then he moved his bishop across the board to take Nehi's knight, and obliged.

"Mostly, where do I get a job around here?" Tanzid responded. "Not that I'm not grateful. Harry has been great to let us all mooch off him. I've never had anyone take me in like you people have."

"What have you had?" Nehemiah asked bluntly.

"Making it on my own, I guess," Tanzid shrugged. "My dad was a wandering card sharp who got himself stabbed in the back when I was nine. A good dad, till he wasn't anything but dead matter anymore. I had a sister, and hung around her place in Gaia for a little after Dad died, before her boyfriend decided they were moving and kicked me out. I assume she's still alive somewhere."

"Then what did you do?" Nehi prodded.

"Delivered things, swept walkways, wandered, escorted tourist, explored the Wild Lands, pretended I was tough," Tanzid said, studying the chess board and speaking almost absently.

"So how did you end up in the UPC?"

"Eight years ago I was out wandering near the Prophet's Peace when I ran into the middle of a UPC operation. It looked like fun, and seemed a little more...important than my life then. So I bluffed my way in and helped them blackmail the Wazir into taking the kingdom's claws off of KAM'S throat. I pretended I was an emissary from the Battle Kingdom, backing up KAM in the hope of a looming battle."

"Seriously, you got away with that?"

"Well, the UPC found out pretty quick after the business was over," Tanzid smiled. "But I had been a help. And there was an old guy who happened to be semi-open to new recruits and I shouldered my way into being an agent. You know, I could be lying through my teeth. Just asking someone to talk about themselves isn't really the best way to learn if you can trust them." Nehemiah laughed.

"True enough," he said. "But I made up my mind anyway. Really I decided you're reliable that first night, when you saved my family and Joe vouched for you."

"You're awfully trusting," Tanzid muttered with a that's-likely-to-get-you-killed-fast undertone. Nehi grinned at him again.

"You and Joe have some things in common. Anyway, here's the thing. I can't tell you what I know about Joe's business, mostly because I don't really know anything because he never tells anything. Also because I promised. But he did let out one fact. He said if he gets in trouble this time, all signals will be blocked almost immediately."

"That's why you've been clutching that cube like it's a last defense. You'll only have a second if he gets a signal through."

"Exactly. But what about a bone plant? Is it blocked as fast?"

"No..." Tanzid sat back as he stared at the chess board and pondered. "That was an old model that I saw in the beast – sorry, habits of a lifetime die hard, I mean in Joe. It's probably been in him for ten years or so. Which means it's deep inset; fused to the bone inset."

"Which is why he hasn't had it taken out," Nehi said, and Tanzid nodded. "That kind of corrosion over time interferes with the mechanism, doesn't it?" Nehemiah racked his brains trying to remember the lectures Mickelson had given on these things. And four numbers danced in his head, four numbers that had been shoved into his hand by a converted Muslim in a dark prison. Atif and his little band were out to help Christians, what if they were stationed in Sojourner's Way...

"Yeah, it slows it down, makes it weaker, and sometimes even sends it to a different wavelength." Tanzid spoke slowly, still thinking on it. "That could mean these folks wouldn't even notice it's in him. Could."

"It gives us a chance. A better one than a split second with a tracker. The Grady doesn't show its tracking, does it? I mean,

we could theoretically use it on anyone and it wouldn't put that person in any danger?"

"Right, it's specifically designed to stay off any radars or scanners, and remain silent even to the one you're tracking. Communicates with them only if you want it to. It also makes a pretty good personal pad, the Grady can do most things the Personal Pad's do. It's the latest thing."

"And it gives us a chance. Thanks, Tanzid." The agent's white teeth showed again, but this time it was from lowered lids and a face that looked bashful. Nehi realized that was probably the first time any of them had used his name like a friend, and not just like a label. Nehi suddenly wanted Tanzid to know he was a friend. But first, he might as well test the new gadget with a bit of a challenge. Hope flitted through Nehi as he typed four numbers swiftly into the keyboard and ostensibly studied the chess board. Maybe in God's providence the stiff ex-Muslim and his team would be… A glance down showed the smooth screen alive with a topographical map laid out in grid lines, coordinates in perfect precision, and one pulsing green dot in the center. Rats. Atif's dot pulsed in a completely different spot, nowhere near Sojourner's Way. Oh well. It had been a long shot, and he would have contacted him only in an emergency anyway. Nehi prayed no emergency happened, again, turned his attention to the chess board, and started trying to actually win. A contented sigh slid from Tanzid and a smile crept over his face as he settled in for a good game.

Violet's chest heaved and the sound of her gulping, whistling efforts to drag in air filled her world. Her whole frame shook as she leaned against the fire-scarred wall, the new thatch roof overshadowing her. Her lungs constricted harder and panic closed off what oxygen she managed to drag in after the three mile run. The caterwauling alarm blared everywhere.

It rang through the town, bouncing off ancient stone streets from the last world, and new wooden houses built since the invaders had burnt things to the ground, echoing down from the stone bell tower in the center of town. It used to be the church tower. Now it housed the alarm for the slavers.

They would be here in seconds.

She couldn't really understand how they had made it all the way here still free. Violet's hands trembled uncontrollably as they pressed into the wall to hold herself upright. She knew what happened to those who tried to run and were caught. They had been forced to watch. And then the broken, mutilated slaves were thrown back into the huts with their fellow slaves, to die slowly, or survive, the slavers didn't really care which. Her breath choked her as her mind filled with the terror. If she had anything in her stomach, she would have lost it then.

The strange one in black knelt beside the slaver they had dragged for miles and miles. The wheels were off, somewhere slipped into the black folds of his clothes. She watched in fascination as the black one flicked the leather on his arm to show all those wonderful things he wore, slid a knife off, and sliced the man's bonds. Limbs splayed around them as the slaver went limp. Violet pulled her toes back with a gasp as his arm tumbled over her foot. The black one shot her a glance and she swallowed her noise. He was so quiet. He hadn't made a sound the whole time, it was unnatural.

A tiny bottle came off the black one's wrist, uncapped under the slaver's nose for an instant, and then slid back into its tiny pocket, and the black leather closed so smoothly she couldn't even see a line in the fabric. The slaver twitched. Then he coughed and jerked into a sitting position, hacking and gasping. The black one's arms slid around him, jerked, and slammed him into the side of the building. One strong hand caught Violet's arm, and she squeaked despite herself.

The wall became a door. One moment her feet stumbled over hewn stones, then she scuffled over polished wood, while the dark, frightening shadows gave way to warm yellow

lamplight. A middle-aged couple stared up at them from matching armchairs, their mouths wide open. A ball of bright blue yarn tumbled off the woman's lap and rolled gently into the corner.

"Charles?" the slaver slurred. Violet just had time to feel shock he recognized the couple, and note the black one had removed his gloves and mask somewhere between the street and here. He looked remarkably small and young and unthreatening with his messy blond hair. Then everything shifted to business. The man leapt from his chair and grabbed the slaver by the arm. Without a word he dragged him to a wall, as the woman hustled Violet and the black one after them. The wall became a door. Violet blinked around her, sliding the black fabric from off her head in an automatic way as she followed numbly behind the black one. Her feet moved over dirt now, and they went down, while plain dirt walls closed in. White bulbs dangled off the ceiling and shone dim light around them as they shuffled deeper. A tunnel. She was in a dirt tunnel, winding downward.

"What happened?" Charles, the middle-aged man, muttered from the front of the little band. "Who are these with you?"

"What?" the slaver slurred. Charles came to an abrupt stop. The rest of the party stopped jerkily under one of the cones of glaring white light. The slaver swayed in place. A metal cross suddenly appeared, glinting in the light as it dangled from the black one's hand. Charles stared from it to the black one. So did the woman, her eyes wide and scared as she watched over Violet's shoulder. Fear shone on her face. It echoed in Violet's soul and she felt her heart leapt out to the woman.

"Who are you?" Charles asked. His voice came hoarse and harsh. "What did you do to Amran?" The one in black reached smoothly for his turtleneck collar, every movement deliberate, so the company knew exactly what he was doing. He pulled it down and tipped his head, getting his blond hair out of the way. Violet saw a circle with a "GI" and a line through it tattooed on his neck. She had no idea what it meant. But recognition flashed over Charles. Confusion moved over him, his lips twisting as if a bad smell wafted in. It didn't change the worry wrinkling his round features. "An incomplete? Can...You...Hear...Me?" he almost yelled, every word loud and accentuated by itself, as if he spoke to a half-wit. The black one just nodded, nothing showing on his face about what he thought of the performance.

The woman behind Violet moved. Her hand went to her throat, and she pulled out an identical metal cross to the one that still dangled from the black one's hand. The black one met her steady gaze and gave her a little smile. He nodded at Violet, and she blinked at him, wondering wildly what that meant. The slaver Amran sagged. His knees gave out, and he toppled onto Charles. The middle-aged man struggled to stay upright as the slaver's weight hit him. The black one stepped forward, deftly got Amran situated so he held the man's feet as Charles supported the slaver's shoulders, and began to shuffle forward. Charles staggered, forced on a few steps. Then his feet seemed to make up their mind, and he moved off down the hall. A hand landed on Violet's shoulder as she followed automatically. The girl stifled a shriek and froze.

"There, there, nothing to worry you, dearie," the woman said in such a motherly tone it resonated in the girl's battered heart. Every dear old lady at church, her own sweet mother and grandmother, all of them had used that tone. She had heard it so often before the disintegration, it was simply another part of life then, the sweet love it carried just the way of things. Now it pierced through the years straight into a young woman's tattered soul, and began the long process of draining away the horrors.

Violet sagged into the woman's arms and began to shake with blubbering, wet, sobs.

"It's all right, child," the woman said, two chubby arms wrapping around the girl's shaking shoulders. Violet could hear the woman's voice crack with sorrow in time with her own. "It's all right now. You just tell Nanna all about it. What happened tonight?"

Nehi lay still staring at the ceiling. Night shadows crawled over it, shifting as the trees and blooming bushes in the back-yard moved with a breeze. He shivered and wished for the hundredth time he dared go to sleep. But sleep brought the dreams...

A shadow deeper and bigger than just the night loomed beside him. Nehi started up, his hand darting for Hope where she lay propped against his couch. But the shadow shifted and he could see the silhouette more clearly; fuzzy hair sticking out in every direction, massive shoulders tapering down into a waist twice the size of his own.

"Beau!" he gasped. "What are you doing popping up like a fiend in the night?"

"Friend," the chimera rumbled, a little offended. Nehi's tight features melted into a smile.

"Yes, I'm sorry, I used the wrong word. Definitely friend. What are you doing down here?"

"Pray." The big voice rumbled around him, and Nehi caught himself glancing at the rafters to see if they shook. They didn't.

"What?" he asked.

"Not alone. Pray. Then you remember God's here too, and bigger than the shadows. Bigger than the dreams. When the shadows keep coming, you keep praying." Beau stood immove-able, solid and still, and Nehi just blinked at him for a moment.

"You're right," he said, his voice quiet. "I have been but I... I let myself stop and forget. I'm an idiot, Beau, and an ungrateful one too."

"No. Just get tired sometimes. We all do."

"You don't," Nehi answered, a smile creeping over him again. "Not too tired to remember Christ. You're a solid rock of faith, Beau. Thanks for coming down to remind me."

"Brought these," Beau rumbled, and lifted his hand. Moon-light sparkled on a set of slim silver tools lying on his palm.

"What...?" Nehi blinked.

"Lockpicks. Backdoor locks inside and outside, I know," Beau said. "I can teach." Nehemiah laughed in delight and untangled the blanket from his legs.

"Beau, you're a gift straight from the hand of God!"

# Chapter Sixteen: The Silver-Haired Leader

*"For a bishop must be blameless...But a lover of hospitality, a lover of good men, sober, just, holy, temperate..."* Titus 1:8

W e cannot let him leave alive," Charles stated as they walked. Stated it, Samuel noted, as a fact that had already been decided.

"He knows too much about us, has seen too many faces," Amran added. The door deep in the tunnel appeared in the glaring lights. Charles fidgeted and looked up at the man beside him, into the bright blue eyes under the mop of silver hair. "You're the leader of our branch of the IDP, all of it. I don't like you going in there alone!"

"So you've said. Several times since I got here thirty minutes ago." Samuel smiled at the huge guard standing in front of the iron door, pretending he didn't notice the enormous laser the man held; or the stun gun, truncheon, and electric prod on his belt. Really? He had been trying to get mercy and hospitality through their stubborn heads for two years! "Open it, please."

The guard pulled, the iron door swung ponderously open, and Samuel watched the muscles straining on Gregson's back as he worked. They considered it necessary to keep this person behind that, for the past two and a half days. Who was this silent intruder? The door squealed open. Samuel walked through and nodded back over his shoulder at the huge man. Gregson strained again and the door swung shut with a click. Samuel didn't really notice. His eyes were on the small, scarred figure rising smoothly to his feet in the far corner. The corner with the most shadows. Only his bright blond hair and white skin allowed Samuel to know someone stood there in the blackness. And the someone reached to about his chest, thin and very short.

"Hello. I'm Samuel," the old man decided to start out. "They tell me you can understand, but not speak with them. Even by writing, so they say. I'm the only one in our area who knows your language, so here I am. I had a dear sister once who was a deaf mute and I used to know it as well as my own, so I expect we can get by."

"I know," Joe signed. It took Samuel off guard. But he went on easily, deciding not to show it.

"Good, that's settled. It was very brave of you to go to that girl's rescue like you did," Samuel stated in admiration, to see if this little fellow would brag about it. Joe stood still in his corner and signed nothing. "I don't suppose you have a name?"

"J-o-e," Joe signed. Samuel nodded affably, walked a little farther into the room and lowered himself stiffly into a cross-legged position on the dirt floor. There was nothing but dirt floor in this tiny, stinky room.

"I am sorry about the accommodations. I strongly suggested they not keep you locked up, but it took me two days to get here, and they insisted." Samuel waved at the dirt in front of him in a comradely manner. Joe moved forward obediently and dropped to sit across from him. He moved like a jungle cat, Samuel noted, or a dancer, with every muscle tuned and sleek and under perfect control. The two looked at each other. Samuel decided to stop playing games, ignore the people listening at the door, and just be his normal self. He settled back and stretched his legs out with a little groan. "I'm really much too old for this. My fellow conspirators didn't want me to come in here, especially not alone. But I think you knew that, didn't you? Just like you knew it would have to be me who would come to speak with you?" A little smile lifted Joe's mouth. He appreciated smart.

"The IDP leader sent me because he knew to learn more they would have to get you," Joe signed. Samuel blinked.

"I'm sorry, but did you just say the leader?" he asked. Samuel rushed on, his face flushed. "You've met him? It is a him? We had a letter, about a week ago that Charles from Gaia copied and sent out to the branch leaders, two pages of suggestions about what to do if we never heard from him again. Is the leader

all right, can I count your being here as a mark to disregard that letter?" Joe hesitated, pulling back into himself, the wall that Nehi had run into so often slamming down between them so hard it could almost be felt. Samuel did feel it. His hand went up in apology. "Forgive me, he (whoever he is) obviously doesn't want any of that known. It is enough for me to know the IDP leader is a brother, and a clever one, who has proved himself very competent at this job. You are from the IDP though? Not just carrying one of our crosses to keep from getting shot while you infiltrated?"

"I am a brother," Joe signed, meeting Samuel's bright blue eyes solidly. No, defiantly would be a better term. Deep, deep behind the defiance in those green eyes lurked fear. A sigh slid from Samuel.

"Look, I'm sorry my comrades in arms here are such...well, *idiots* about incompletes and all that, I know it couldn't have been pleasant for you the past two days. Most of them in this section are fairly recent Christians, coming out of the People's Kingdom. I expect you know what that means?"

"I know."

"Yes. I think you know a great deal more than I guess, and definitely more than they think you know. May I ask you a few questions?" Samuel asked, smiling in his friendly way. No, Joe recognized that look, not just friendly because it was his way, but friendly because this man honestly took an interest in those around him; Josh used to show that same interest, watching his fellow men to see how he could help them get closer to Jesus. Joe nodded and waited to see what this stranger would do next.

The next ten minutes passed quickly, as Samuel fired theological questions at the little person across from him, and Joe answered as best he could. This wasn't easy for him, Samuel could tell. The mute had to think hard for most of his questions, as if he had never heard them before. But many in the IDP hadn't even a rudimental knowledge of good theology, Samuel knew from hard won experience. It came from living in countries where one had to sneak to church, and most of the sermons dealt with everyday things, like making it through martyrdom if it came your way. And it was hard enough to get biblical passages passed among Sojourners even in the old days before the disintegration, other kingdoms had no access to the source of correct theology. Without biblical texts to check it, manmade theories ran rampant, even among the Christians. But Joe came up with the right answers, proving he had the right starting point and (if it could be proved) that his heart belonged to Jesus. Usually the mute phrased it in brilliant ways Samuel had never thought about before. At the end of the ten minutes, Samuel smiled again.

"Joe, I do believe you love our Savior very much," he declared. Joe looked away, uncomfortable with the other's openness. "Now, that being out of the way, what did you come here for?" Joe looked at him, his head tilting in a question. Samuel laughed. It burst out of him, a deep, booming noise, and the mute couldn't help but smile as it filled the filthy little room. Samuel silently noticed the laughter lines and natural mischievous twinkle that came into the green eyes with that smile, and felt an instant liking for the young man across from him. But he just answered the question. "Of course you came here on purpose, you weren't driven here for help because you were escaping the IK, as you've let it be understood from the story told by Violet (the young girl with the vivid eyes you rescued)." She actually was a Violet! Joe burst into a laugh, but waved Samuel on again before he could ask about it. "You knew Amran was a spy for the Sojourner's branch of the IDP, knew where he would be, exactly where to take him, and even brought someone along because you wouldn't be able to explain the events of the evening yourself. It was a very ingenious method of infiltrating our underground system, drugging Amran like that so Charles assumed you were with him. All while rescuing a young lady in desperate need of rescue. I have forbidden Amran from returning to his post. Until I know more about this, I'm not going to risk our only spy in the IK being dismembered as a known Christian. Has he been found out?" The twinkle shone strong in

the young man's eyes now. He was a very young man, Samuel noted absently, it could be seen through the scars with that twinkle.

"What else do you know I know?" Joe signed with interest.

"Let's see. You did all that so they would have to send for me. Which is why you've stuck around for the past two days despite the useful items strapped to your arm that would let you walk out of here whenever you want." Joe's head tipped again and Samuel grinned. "I talked with Violet privately before I came down. I am right, aren't I?" Joe studied him for a moment, a little smile playing over him. Then he rolled easily to the side (never quite turning his back on his guest, Samuel noted), dug a hand into the corner, and two metal water bottles rolled out, bumping to a stop as they hit Samuel's foot.

"I've already been out, yesterday. I got thirsty," Joe signed as he straightened up again with his smooth exactness. He swept up the second bottle, cracked it open, and took a sip. Samuel could watch him relaxing, unfolding his bow-taught muscles. Good. Very good.

"You had to go fetch it yourself," Samuel murmured, throwing a dark glance at the door. "I hope they at least fed you?" No response. They hadn't. Samuel cut a grumble short and focused on the mute again. "Well, I'm glad you were able to go raiding. Why are you here?"

"To get to you." He reached into an inner pocket in his soft leather jacket and Samuel could hear the squeak of metal on the door, as the three watchers stuck their weapons through the grill in panic. Joe ignored them as if they weren't there. He pulled a sheet of paper from somewhere, and held it out. Samuel took it and saw a list of names, each one a member of his IDP branch, in a position to spy for the group. "These have been betrayed. Not just found out, but deliberately betrayed. You have a wolf in your flock. That's why I had to give it to you specifically."

"Do you know who?" Samuel asked quickly.

"I wasn't told," Joe answered.

"That's not what I asked," Samuel cut in. The two looked at each other for a moment. Joe had never been caught in a dodge so quickly. This old man was a very smart person. Samuel wondered why this little person had used a dodge that could be caught and hadn't just lied to him. This intriguing little mute was trying to be honest.

"A-m-r-a-n is known to be in the IDP," Joe signed. Not answering the earlier question. Samuel didn't press it, and Joe had never liked someone so much so quickly.

"Thank you for pulling him out for us. I had best get word to these people as soon as possible. Will you come with me?" It wasn't just a polite question, or because Samuel thought he needed his backup, Joe could tell. The old man was curious, but recognized Joe had come for more than just this short talk, and trusted him enough to let him get on with whatever it was. For just a moment Joe longed with everything in him to say yes and walk out with this nice old gent.

"No," he signed.

Samuel wavered. Hesitation and fear had just run past behind Joe's stiff features, he had seen it for an instant. Samuel just nodded, and stood up creakily. Whatever this little person was up to, he would have to trust he knew what he was doing. Joe got to his feet, a smile on his face in admiration for this old fellow who had seen through every mask he tried to put on and seen *him*. No one had ever done that, not like this man. Joe's trust meter, usually buried so deep it took months of close association to lift, shifted a nanometer. Two hands reached out, pulled him into a tight bear hug, squeezed, and then let him go, all in a moment that left Joe a little breathless; and feeling a fuzzy, pleasant warmth.

"Be careful, Joe. We've lost too many people to these invaders. I won't ask if you need help, because I assume you'll tell me if you do. Go with Christ, brother." The white-haired old gent stepped through the heavy iron door, ordered the guard sharply to keep it open and leave the no-longer-prisoner alone, and strode up the tunnel. The giant Gregson followed a little

sheepishly, his big laser bouncing at his side. Joe stood blinking in the stuffy little room, lost in wonder that a man could walk in, talk to him for twenty minutes, give a quick hug, and walk out as a friend. Still on trial and probably just a good actor who would betray him at the first opportunity, of course, not a friend like Nehi or Beau but...still. That hadn't happened to Joe since he was six years old and that little viper of a complete had–

A sizzle came from the hall and Joe's thoughts eclipsed into a spinning ball of sparking white pain. Four wires spun around his neck and four red-hot needles plunged deep through his backbone into his spinal column. Muscles convulsed he didn't even remember he had, till his mind cringed and darkened and his mouth parted in a silent scream. Amran stood in the hall watching as Joe stiffened like a ramrod, sucking air in little gasps, eyes wide with the agony of every muscle pulling against each other. The tall IK stepped forward and leaned down so his mouth was an inch from Joe's ear.

"Now you're not watched, you're 'free' to leave. You are mine now, beast. Freddy wants you." His lithe finger touched a control he held cupped in his hand. Joe twitched, and started to move, stiff, torturously, and completely against his will as his nervous system was taken over by someone else. The mute's eyes dimmed, then the light died as his consciousness spun away. A little smile of amusement slid over Amran, and he manipulated his puppet down the hall.

"You, Nehemiah Hillson," Harry said as he stepped back and draped his stethoscope over his neck, "are officially declared out of my care."

"Really?" Nehi beamed. A full week of enforced rest had slid by, with Anna insisting he stayed down, and only Daniel and Tanzid's company making it bearable. And Beau's tutorial with a lockpick; Nehi slipped out into the dark last night, and spent hours exploring the town and sitting on Joe's building enjoying the freedom. He snuck back in just before dawn and slept like a log for five hours. Today he felt almost like his normal self. And if Harry declared him well, it meant he didn't have to slip out in secret anymore! "Boy am I glad to hear that," he said heartily as he slipped on his shirt again. "Thank you, Harry–"

"Because now you can tell Anna and Daniel my declaration. You're welcome. I'll tell you a secret, Nehi," Harry said, his usually business-like face suddenly breaking into a mischievous grin. "You're not really entirely healed, but we both know you're plenty strong enough to function normally and your siblings won't let you. I'm declaring you well to get them off your back." Nehemiah started laughing and Harry put a finger to his lips, still with the same mischievous look. "Shh, don't tell, I'll lose my reputation as a competent doctor."

"I won't say a word," Nehemiah grinned. "But really I meant thank you for more than that. Thanks for taking us in, all seven of us, and giving us our room and board and medical treatment, and letting Elizabeth and Peter come over all the time, and–" Harry waved a hand at him, interrupting almost irritably.

"Hush now, I won't hear another word. It's good to be grateful, but in this case it's not needed. You came as Christian brothers, and that's enough for me to take you in right there," Harry said as he opened the wooden cabinet beside Nehi's head and began to put his things away. "But you also came with Joe. That's more than enough for me to do everything I can for you."

"You two go a long way back, don't you?" Nehemiah asked, curiosity almost dripping from him.

"Almost as far back as you can with Joe. Joshua headed to me as the only doctor he knew as soon as he rescued him." Harry paused, one hand still on the pills in the cabinet, staring at the wall, his expression distant and sad. "He shouldn't have been alive. I'll never be able to forget how terrified he was of us that first day. And I'll never be able to explain how much I've learned of Jesus' love and the nature of strength and courage

from watching that little mute climb out of his fears into his heavenly Father's lap!" Harry leaned against the metal table beside his patient, and a humorless smile curved over his face.

"He was a little devil when he first came, Nehi."

"Joe?" Nehemiah asked in surprise.

"If he found you wanted something, he would find a way to keep you from it or ruin it for you," Harry nodded, amusement and seriousness mixing on his simple face. "And oh, was he ever able to annoy! Every little thing that really gets under your skin was immediately noted by Joe and used against you. He would disappear too, just because he knew it drove Josh up the wall. I lost more of my favorite surgery instruments during those first months, stolen and just thrown away vindictively by that little mute. And the lies he spun! Josh was arrested twice due to deliberate work from Joe, and nearly executed the second time."

"Joe?" Nehemiah asked again, his incredulity mounting.

"Yes Joe. He had been through a lot, you know, not just physically… Nehi, sometimes it breaks a person to have no one decent to love, and to have everyone you've ever dared to care for rip your heart in pieces. Joe is a fighter, he always has been. And he fought Josh hard, because he was scared to death of anyone coming close to him. But Josh was a stronger fighter than Joe, Nehi, when it came to an internal struggle like that, and ridiculously optimistic. No, not optimistic. Filled to overflowing with a faith that poured out in practical hope. I tried to explain you can't take a broken person and expect them to be healed the next minute, but you couldn't explain something like that to Josh. He refused to let Joe remain a miserable haunted soul."

"He was tough, then? I know so little about Joshua Nobel…" Nehemiah let the words fade, his expression begging for more.

"'Indominable' would be a better word than tough," Harry grinned. "When he showed up at my door he had just come from the solitude of growing up with a religious hermit for a father. I opened the door that fall morning and found a young man with big ears, a gash down his arm dripping blood all over my porch, a ring with a cross prominent in open sight, and a brilliant grin. 'Excuse me, can I get a bandage?'" A chuckle broke from the doctor and he shook his head in incredulity at the memory. "I couldn't let someone as naive about the world as that man out on his own, it would be like throwing a chicken to the wolves. So he camped on my couch for a week, and became the brother I had always wanted, before insisting on heading out to explore again. His reasoning? 'Harry, if I don't learn who's out there, I'll never learn how to help them get to Christ.' Everything he did, Nehi, was laced with that purpose. I've never met anyone as ridiculously one-minded, he never wavered from that one goal of evangelism, it's like it was etched in front of his eyes in burning letters."

"Sounds like a good man to be around," Nehemiah commented.

"Yes, and a trying one sometimes. He came back with a pile of filth, bones, and torn skin, with blazing green eyes. It took three soaking baths to even tell what color hair that mute had. Then there they were, in a house Josh rented down the street from me. Joshua Noble, twenty-three, so open and optimistic his emotions fell out everywhere, and Joe too hurt to trust in anything and burnt out on life at eleven years old." A chuckle burst from the doctor and he shook his head again, staring at his feet crossed on the surgery floor as he leaned against the cabinet. "I'm honestly a little surprised they didn't kill each other. It would have been deliberate with Joe, with Josh it would have been caused from the exhaustion of his never-ending bounciness and determination to see Joe saved. I tried to explain some people couldn't just be put back together after life had broken them so much… But Josh poked and prodded, and hugged and chased, until even Joe's fighting strength began to waver under the onslaught! I still declare it was Josh's persistence that drove that shattered child to Christ. And that's when everything changed. Joe defined (after he became a Christian) is a logical outworking of God's love, still working through old fears."

"How do you mean?" Nehemiah asked quietly.

"Joe grew up in a world that told him he's only here to serve those over him. His first reaction after being saved was to start digging to find out how he was expected to serve this new, good Master of his. 'Love as I have loved,' is what he found. Joe found love was the service expected of him. Jesus love, unchangeable, deep, self-giving. When Josh started the IDP, and Joe realized it needed help to work, he leapt in with both feet and gives everything he is, where he's needed the most. He's made himself the protective wall around the IDP, Nehi, because of that love that refuses to think of self. He acts like a human sea wall, unbending, unbreakable, and battered against every single day. Until the IDP is strong enough to stand against the world on its own, Joe is the self-appointed defender of Jesus' flock. He has to stay outside it in order to defend it, continually prowling around the perimeter, and it's a lonely, thankless job that he's stuck to for years, despite my pleas for him to stop." Harry looked up at Nehemiah, and the young man suddenly realized the doctor hadn't started this conversation by accident.

"There's a reason behind this," Nehi commented. A smile flitted over the doctor's face, and he nodded.

"I'm not just reminiscing because you're curious," Harry answered, staring hard at Nehi. "I'm telling you this because I've seen the way Joe acts around you. He's taken you as a friend, Nehemiah Hillson. It's more than an honor, it's the fruit from a hard won fight by the little mute, a fight that's had serious setbacks and breakdowns. The last friend he really claimed turned him in to the Battle Kingdom, for the money they would pay for a new fighter in their arena. That was four years ago, Nehi, and ever since Joe's gone blank and hard at even the suggestion he should try again. And now he shows up here with you and Anna, and I couldn't be happier.

"Nehi, don't take his friendship lightly. It wasn't easy for him, and I'm sure took sacrifices from you. Be patient. Be persistent. I will be the last to tell you it's easy. But after almost eight years of struggle, I'm just beginning to understand what the extraordinary Joshua Noble knew the instant he saw a pile of filthy, chained bones curled in despair and decided to save a child. Loving someone who needs it does you more good than anything else in the world, and in the end is one of the only things that matters. I never really understood God's unconditional love for me until Josh's death left me Joe, and I stepped out on a shaky limb to save someone who snapped at me for trying."

"He still snapped?" Nehemiah asked softly. A deep sigh welled from the doctor.

"That was the day he came back from burying Josh. Our Noble man had been turned over to the Battle Kingdom as a Christian, and Joe and Beau got there ten minutes too late to save him, just in time to hold his mangled body as he died. Joe had held himself in till he got back, for Beau's sake. On that day, yes, he snapped," Harry nodded, his face lined with grief and his eyes fastened unseeingly on the ground. "And he cursed, and pinched, and even tore. Then when he realized I wouldn't leave, he collapsed in my arms and wept for hours. It was the last vestige of his old nasty self I've ever seen, and I personally think he cried it out and resolved on Josh's grave not to be that person ever again. Though I've never asked, so don't quote me on that. I hope he keeps coming back to my old house because he likes it here, I've tried to let him know my place is his home."

"I haven't seen Joe so relaxed anywhere else. You've succeeded Harry, I believe he thinks of this as more than just a home, I think it's a refuge from the outside storms for him. Thanks for taking him in. It's good to see Joe happy," Nehemiah said, and went on before the doctor could form his surprised pleasure into words. "And thanks for opening the conversation so I *can* tell you thanks. The more I know Joe, the more I find myself thanking God for Joshua Noble and wishing I could tell him the same thing." A wistful smile crept over Harry's face.

"I've never met anyone like him. I miss that man, Nehi. I guess that's one reason Joe and I get along all right, we both spent so long trying to explain to the wide-eyed Josh how to live in the world, we found when he was taken from us we had no

idea ourselves how to live. Unless it's in Josh's exuberant way of loving the lost so much you forget you even exist. Anyway, what Joe needs now, Nehemiah, is someone to be steady beside him, and let him be him; unless he needs chased out of himself, of course."

"With anyone else I'd think that sentence was silly, but with Joe I understand it," Nehemiah smiled.

"Good, and if you could drop a similar word to your remarkable sister–" The door to the surgery opened and interrupted the doctor's comment. Tanzid stepped in, his hand cupped around the tracker Nehi had left in his care. His eyes were bright and his face hard, and Nehemiah and Harry tensed.

# Chapter Seventeen: The Black Raider

*"The steps of a good man are ordered by the LORD: and he delighteth in his way. Though he fall, he shall not be utterly cast down: for the LORD upholdeth him with his hand."*

*Psalm 37:23-24*

Red-hot needles sizzled in every inch of his flesh and bone. As consciousness seeped back into Joe it surprised him not to smell burning meat. Another horrible moment passed, another breath dragged into his lungs, and he woke up enough to know what he felt. The needles that had claimed his nervous system had been removed. His muscles and nerves were slowly coming back under their rightful owner. And oh, oh, did it hurt. Joe lay in a heap, focusing on dragging oxygen into his body.

The terror grew. Every moment his brain focused a little more, and it could only focus on the terror. Old memories collided with the horrible now, and Joe's stomach convulsed with the fear and heaved. He hacked and sputtered, unable to even move his head away from the mess, and for a blessed instant the pain turned everything dark again. But then it all swept back. Hot, strong fingers wrapped around his arm. Someone started to pull. Joe moved over cold tile, helplessly dragged along as his vision sparked and his system seemed to be trying to climb out of an inferno, like a dead man's body reanimated by a demon.

*Jesus.*

The name screamed through his brain like a drop of cold water on the sizzling needles. Joe grabbed at it, clutching it as it evaporated. *Oh, help!* The mute's lips moved in desperate pleas, horror filled gabble instead of coherent prayers. But slowly the words began to sort themselves out. Prayers formed. Repetitive, desperate prayers. And with each word uttered in his silence, Joe felt the calming drip of the Spirit's work. The fear didn't leave. The pain definitely didn't leave. But it all began to grow manageable. Inch by inch, he was given back himself. A

prayer to his ruling, sovereign God always reoriented the world.

Joe let himself drag. He could feel his body coming back to him. His mind was his own. Gradually he invaded the blankness with sensations and analysis. He could see sunshine. Bright, wonderful, hopeful sunshine. Though his head hurt and the brightness almost made him cringe. A moment later he could focus on the tiles. They were black and white marble, not really tiles at all. With infinite care, Joe turned his head. He saw immaculate white walls tastefully adorned with paintings. Very good paintings. Very, very expensive paintings. If they were the real ones and not just prints. Of course they were the originals. He knew who owned this place.

The hand dragging him stopped. Another hand gripped the back of Joe's neck and heaved. Joe caught a glimpse of a man beside him, more paintings, a white ceiling with crystal light fixtures. Then his world became a bubbling torrent of ice water. It poured over his face and head in a stream that stung his skin with its force. Joe jerked back automatically, but the hand on his neck held him under. His burning lungs burnt harder and Joe fought to keep from gasping. In this weakened state, lungs full of water would be the last debilitating straw that broke his own back (never mind some stupid camel).

Anna's face surfaced in his darkening mind. Steam from her teacup curled around her beautiful face as she stared at him. *"I want you to come back."* It echoed in his memory, her sweet voice, every inflection beautiful. He didn't gasp.

The hand jerked back and let go. Joe folded onto the marble, hacking and gagging, his palms pushing against the floor. Oh, it hurt to breathe. It hurt to move. It hurt to be. Out of the corner of one eye he saw a black boot pull back. Joe's hands found the ornate fountain and he heaved himself to his feet, just avoiding the encouragement that had been headed for his ribs. A disdainful sniff came from above him and Joe focused blearily. Amran towered over him. The IK jerked his head toward an open door. Joe's spinning mind focused on the important bits;

sunlight, fresh breeze, menacing figures with weapons. He walked, obeying automatically because bad things happened when you didn't obey. Really, really bad things. But his mind kicked into focus again as he stepped through the door.

A wall made up of French windows stood across from him. An immaculate garden sprawled into the distance out those windows, with bubbling fountains in the midst of brilliant flowers and white marble statues. A patio rested just outside the room, with a portly figure propped in a large whicker lawn chair. Red hair gleamed in the bright sunlight and Joe's heart began to rhythmically speed up. But this was the adrenaline of the game, not just fear. He would have to be very, very clever today if he hoped to get back to Anna. Especially if he hoped to win this war, and not just this battle.

A hand shoved into his back to get him to move, and Joe stumbled forward into the room. For an instant he registered five FFs, all of them staring at him, and a white asymmetrical shelf filled with brick-a-brack; each brick expensive enough it could have fed a family of ten for months, while the bracks couldn't even be given a price. Then his foot caught on the rug. Joe slammed into the white shelf and crashed onto the Persian rug, as brick-a-brack rained down on him and the whole shelf tottered. A statuette of a toga clad woman bounced on his skull and his headache escalated. Strong hands gripped him, at least five, though he was still a little too dim from the statuette to count well. They jerked him to his feet, a fist rammed into his ear. Then came a heave, and he went uncomfortably weightless, fresh air rushing over him in the one way he didn't want it to, as he sailed through it. Joe smashed down on the smooth concrete of the patio, and the sun went off.

A buzzing sounded in his ears. No, it was in his mind. And his ears. Someone spoke near him. Someones, there were several of them out there in the whirling, sparking world beyond his darkened mind. No, it wasn't all dark now. The light slowly came back. And he lay sprawled on something with cushions. Joe stayed limp with his eyes closed and his breathing

unaltered, waiting till strength returned and he could deal with the situation out there. The buzzing formed into voices. Not quite into words yet, not that he could comprehend, but he recognized the voices. One was Nicky. Bad. But not so bad as Simmons. Simmons was dead, yay. The other...corpulent, friendly and false, cheerful with a dangerous note behind it...Freddy. Fat Freddy, the Friendly Frightening Farcical FF. That's what Joe had been terming him in his mind, because it made him smile. Even now it sparked a cord in his humor, and that went a long way to getting his faculties back in order. Joe cracked his eyes partially open.

Freddy sat across from him on the comfortable patio, his fat hands crossed over his belly and his head turned to look at the den. Clinking noises and quiet voices came from there, and Joe knew they were still putting the shelf back to rights. Good. He had a few minutes. Another person stood out here, a thin lady with her hands clasped tight in front of her, stiffened muscles, and lowered eyes that shifted to a new spot every second. Another prisoner, obviously. Joe moved slowly, testing himself. He felt a little surer of his movements now. But underneath the pain, he could feel weakness claiming him. He would have to watch himself today. He stretched with an indolent yawn and leaned back against the comfortable cushions of the chair as he blinked at the company. He didn't go so far as to smile at them, but he kept his manner relaxed and even languid. Everyone paused and looked at him. Joe pretended not to notice and just turned to Freddy, looking him up and down with an easy nonchalance.

"Good afternoon," Freddy smiled, studying Joe as if he were a particularly interesting moth a friend had brought in for inspection. "Are you awake enough to understand me? I have provided a translator for the weird hand motions you beasts tend to make, can you talk through her?" Freddy said waving at the thin, frightened lady.

"What am I doing here?" Joe signed. The woman stuttered it, her voice low and very nice. The clinking noises started up again in the den.

"You do get down to business, don't you," Freddy said with an easy chuckle. "Well, I had a number of reasons for having you...invited. I wanted to meet the one who has been brilliantly and nearly singlehandedly causing us so much annoyance, for one. You can imagine my shock when I found out you were an incomplete. A GI! I didn't think it would be possible. By the way, as of now your antics in that black outfit of yours are over. I accept your offer to retire, little beast. The IDP need have no more fear of Freddy's Friends." Joe blinked and put the two initials together. He started laughing. Freddy's Friends? All this time, those two initials had sparked such dread, and to find out it actually stood for Freddy's Friends! Joe moved his head too sharply and nearly fainted, and it made him stop laughing. But at least he felt better inside now.

"Sorry, please go on," he signed at Freddy. The woman said it for him, her voice still low but strong enough now to interpret the inflections she saw on the mute's expressive face.

"If you say so," Freddy said, with a bit of confusion. He recovered his easy manner quickly. "On to the next point. I have been watching your little band in the hope of discovering more about the treasure the Hillsons hold, or something new about them that might be useful. Oh come now, you needn't look so innocently surprised, little beast. I know you are especially close with the two younger ones. I think you can tell me what I need to know. Why did you say you would be getting their book back soon? Within the week something would happen, you told young Nehemiah. Isn't that right?" Joe sat still, giving no response. Freddy leaned back with a sigh. "My dear little GI, I'm afraid I require an answer. I don't like to mention it, but the more sophisticated drugs will not work on a GI to find out your secrets. I don't think you could use your language while under their influence, so we would have to revert back to the older and nastier ways to get an answer if you don't do it willingly. I lost my best man for that sort of thing a few months back. Actually, I hear you had something to do with that. You remember

Simmons?" He waited and Joe decided he might as well answer that since it was obvious.

"I remember him," Joe signed and the woman said automatically, her eyes wide.

"I have another idea that I might mention before we move on," Freddy said, knowing he had made his point with just that old, dreaded name. "There is an easy way to avoid that sort of unpleasantness. I've been impressed by your work, beast. It's brilliant, honestly, a touch of genius that is still remarkably practical. I could use that genius in my business. I can offer you very good pay. Very good pay. I doubt you can even imagine the kind of life you could have with what I can offer you, little GI. Let me tell you–"

"No," Joe signed, his green eyes hard.

"Now don't be too hasty, you haven't even heard what I'm offering you."

"I know what you're offering. Money bought with the blood of thousands of innocent lives. Have you seen the countries you've sent into disintegration for the sake of your greed? Have you looked into the eyes of the children you've made orphans, the wives you've widowed?" *Gee, I wish he meant it,* Joe thought idly as he kept signing his bold, brave words. *I could use that to get him off guard and get out. But I'd be dead the moment I said yes and told him what he wants.* "Your hands are bloody and I will have nothing to do with you or your tainted goods. Find another dupe."

"Well, you have to admit I tried." Freddy settled his hands on his ample middle and regarded the mute with a businesslike manner. "Why did you run off to get the Bible back this week, GI? What are you planning? Or what do you know?" Joe sat still, his face blank and eyes dim. "The deadline is almost up for the Hillsons. You know that I will do what I promise. That book will be destroyed in a matter of weeks." Freddy pointed to his shelves and looked along his finger. His mouth dropped open. He shot out of his chair, quicker than it looked like anyone with his bulk could, and was at the shelves in a moment, his eyes and hands searching everywhere. *Here we go,* Joe thought, inwardly tensing. Freddy turned on him, no longer even a trace of his friendly mask on his fat face.

"Where's that book, beast?" he snarled. Joe looked at the shelf in innocent surprise.

"You lost it?" he signed with interest, and the woman said, though she stuttered just a little. Freddy moved in front of him, towering menacingly over the mute curled in the chair.

"You banged against those shelves on purpose. I don't know how you did it, but you have taken that book," Freddy said quietly, forcing himself to at least look calm again. "You can't have hidden it far away, you aren't presently capable of that."

"You have no idea what I'm capable of," Joe signed. Staring into those deep green eyes Freddy knew that was right. He stepped away, forcing his easy manner back over his panic.

"Nicky?" Freddy called. Boots thunked onto the patio, and a shadow fell over Joe. He didn't turn to look. "Take our guests down to the cell block, see that this one's thoroughly searched and secured, then come back here. By the way, did you know the little one is your Black Raider you've complained about so much?" Nicky's eyes widened, then narrowed at the mute. *Great,* Joe thought. *Just what I needed with my headache, thanks a lot Fred.* Guards stepped up beside Joe, eyes hard and watchful, surrounding his chair. Joe kept his face blank and emotionless as he looked up and met Nicky's glare. Nicky's hand landed on his hair, lifted, and tossed him into the den. Joe landed with a heavy crunch. A boot shot out and thudded into his stomach, sending him sliding a foot across the den floor, into another boot that landed on his spine.

"Nicky," Freddy's voice drifted lazily from the bright porch. The man looked up, his face still shining with hatred and his fist pulled back, ready to slam down a blow on the wheezing mute curled on the floor. "I do want to talk to him again later. Keep it in mind, will you, and don't entirely kill him off." A low, bestial growl came from Nicky. But the words had an effect. They dragged Joe to his feet and shoved him into a march. His head

spun and his vision fuzzed. People marched beside him, towering over him with a menacing glint in their eyes, and hands just twitching in anticipation. Joe felt his throat closing, sweat pouring down him, his mind slipping away into the terror again.

*"I want you to come back."*

The words spun through him, and Joe grabbed at them. He kept them pulsing in Anna's beautiful voice. He had to keep his head clear. Keep the terror behind its wall. He had to make it back. If he could get out quick, he would be fine.

Joe let his eyes close for a blessed minute of rest, feeling where he walked. He was so tired. The marble pounded under his feet. Nicky's hands bit and pinched into his arms, shoving him along. A laser butt rammed into his rib cage, and Joe rebounded to the side, into another laser butt on his other ribs. He forced himself to walk steady, and the malicious pounding stopped. Joe flexed his fingers. He would have an instant. That was all. The marble under his feet changed into squeaky wooden floors. Joe cracked his eyes open. The light came dim and dusty, from an older part of the headquarters. A barracks room, he noted automatically as his eye landed on the bunks, playing cards, dirty holograms, and half-clad people lounging around the place. A silver door stood open at the end of the room, and a black cavity yawned beyond it. That blackness seemed to be sucking at him, pulling him toward itself by some other force than just Nicky's biting, bruising grip. If he once went into the dark, he would never come out again. He had to get out fast. Now.

Joe's hand shot up and into his inner pocket, breaking Nicky's grip by the sudden, unexpected strength of his movement. Amran had stripped Joe's jacket off, because Samuel Thomas had carelessly mentioned all the lovely gadgets he had. But there were more pockets to search on Joe than there are mice in a corn field. The scarred hands were a blur as they jerked back out filled with little black canisters. The black cylinders shot out, scattering around the room like hail. Wherever they landed, a gray smoke rose up in a silent, billowing cloud.

In two seconds the room filled with the smoke. The looming menace of Nicky fell away beside him. No coughing filled the room, no gasps or shouts. Just gentle thudding as FFs collapsed, folding over in silent, glazed sleep.

Joe's hand shot to the left, wrapping round a Brunhiem rifle as its owner tumbled gently to the ground, leaving it in the mute's grasp. He had located and analyzed all the weapons near him, and this one suited his needs best. Lighter weight than most, well-charged, and reliable. The mute slid backward, feeling his way, stepping over bodies and around overturned furniture. An image of the thin interpreter came unbidden to his mind, but he shut it out. He couldn't save everyone. Only God could do that, and he wasn't God. *Lord, somehow get her out safe!* One of the dirty holograms flickered in the gray gloom and Joe averted his eyes, feeling for the wall. His fingers touched stucco. He raised them quickly to exactly four feet up, then ran them in a straight line toward the rectangle of sickly white light marking the door out of this place. A slight tinkle of metal hitting metal sounded. He lifted the key ring off its hook, trotted through the white rectangle out of the room, closed the door with a click, glanced at the key ring and saw which one belonged to that type of lock, and slid it in. A satisfying click sounded.

Joe slumped against the wall, the Brunhiem's stock landing on the ground as the gun seemed so heavy. He slid two fingers in his mouth and pulled the clear air filter from his throat, gagging, relief flooding him at having it out. It hadn't been fun to wear that for days, waiting for this moment. Joe leaned there, breathing hard, feeling like his legs and arms were noodles, and moving would take more than he had in him. Harry was right. He needed to stop, to let his body have a year or so to recover itself. But not now. Joe only allowed himself a few seconds of indulgence in the weakness and pain. After a few breaths and a scattered, begging prayer, he forced himself up, slid the Brunhiem over his shoulder, drew in a breath, and stood tall.

Now. Where would Freddy stash the SOLTDs? Somewhere

near his fat form. Joe began to move back toward the marbled halls. He didn't put his black gloves and mask on, and felt naked and exposed without them. No deep shadows played through the sunlit hallways, and no real out-of-the-way corners to duck into with the open layout... Oh Lord Jesus, help him make it through!

*"I want you to come back."*

It would take a miracle to make that happen.

Joe had been unable to ferret out even a hint about what to expect at these headquarters. Bright sunlight, open white rooms, and about two hundred FFs were not what he had hoped for. He didn't even know what region of the world he was in. Joe hoisted the Brunhiem's strap higher over his shoulder, and strode off the wood into the marble halls. His head stayed up, his face hard and unconcerned, his boots striking the marble in a soldier's march. His only chance lay in brazen confidence, to pretend like he belonged here with such aptitude others believed it.

A group of three female FFs turned into his hall, their rifles resting easy against their sides, chatting as they went. Joe glanced at them in an uninterested way and kept walking. They didn't notice him. He turned into three more halls, winding his way back toward the den, knowing Freddy would live somewhere close to all that expensive brick-a-brack. Freddy had nearly as many trust issues as Joe; the cost of dealing with crooks and the lawless. The number of agents grew thicker. He almost waded through them as he moved, and tried desperately to formulate a plan for what to do if asked his business. But no one did ask him. Everyone shoved by, busy with their own little world, and didn't care about someone marching with obvious purpose. This couldn't last. Good luck like this never lasted. A gray metal door loomed up on his right, and Joe glanced in, wondering if it was the door to a safe, and if he had found the SOLTDs.

"Hey you!" someone shouted from inside a cloud of white steam billowing on the other side of the door. Joe pulled back, but the voice yelled again, louder. He couldn't have attention drawn to him. Joe reluctantly looked back through the door. The steam dissipated and a man in a white chef's apron came in sight. He beckoned impatiently for Joe. "One of you soldier boys be of use for once," the cook said irritably. Joe stepped inside, drawn partially by the order, but mostly by the odors. His stomach growled like a fiend. He hadn't been able to eat with that air filter stuffed in his throat. A silver tray shoved into his arms and Joe staggered at the weight. Coffee, fresh bread, bacon and mushrooms and eggs, the scents wafted around him in a heavenly wonder of delight and Joe went giddy with more than his migraine. "The boss is in his room stewing, you take it to him this morning," the cook ordered, and propelled Joe back through the door into the bright hallway.

The mute trotted down the hall through the people, spotted a tiny door, and paused. He carefully knocked the salt cellar over on the tray. A bad-tempered frown cut over his face for the benefit of anyone watching, and he balanced the tray on one bent knee as he reached over to right the salt and swipe the spilt stuff onto the floor. His hand paused at the door on his way off the tray. The door popped open a crack. A broom closet. With excellent rubber insulation on the door frame. A smile twitched over Joe's face as he readjusted the tray and waited for two soldiers to march past him. They walked by without a glance, Joe slipped in, closed the door, slid a rag over the bottom crack, flipped on the light, plopped on the ground, and happily tucked in to Freddy's breakfast. It was very good. Joe didn't know a master chef's cooking from average canned food, really, all he knew was that it tasted great and he really needed it. After about three minutes, Joe sat back with a little sigh. He had to get moving. Half the bread loaf lay on the plate, but he couldn't spare more time. The omelet was gone. Joe took the rest of the mocha with him (steaming, dark espresso swirling with foam and ribbons of liquid chocolate). He slid smoothly out of the closet, and began to march again. His head felt better. Actually, everything felt better after a decent meal. Especially

his soul; the terror shrunk and shriveled into fear, hope soared in him, and everything would be all right. This coffee really helped.

Joe walked on, silently thanking God for the small mercy of a breakfast shoved into his hands, and searching for his way out. Two more turns, and he saw what he needed. Freddy even had the door helpfully labeled, "SOLTD of the Earth." Har har, hilarious. Joe's steps slowed and he sidled by at a creep, savoring his coffee and using it as an excuse to move slowly, analyzing what he saw.

A locked hemlin 200 safe. It worked by DNA from only previously authorized people, and would gas anyone who tampered with it. Joe had heard speculation on how to crack a hemlin 200, but no one had actually done it to his knowledge. Well, done it and lived. Ten guards in the room, five on guard, five off, so that they never really tired. And a room made of glass. Everyone who walked through this busy hallway saw everything going on in that room. There weren't even any curtains to draw. Joe walked on, silently speculating on his chances.

No, that place offered no chance. He had no gadgets, no tricks up his sleeves, no allies to cause a disturbance. So. A SOLTD was out. He had only one option then; gather his prize, slip through the garden, and pray like a fiend he wasn't in the desert wild lands. Or the ones between the People's Kingdom and Gaia. Or...well, any wild lands, really. Alone on his own two feet and practically unarmed, he was in trouble. But Joe would rather take his chances out there with the beasts than in here with the humans. He quickened his pace and began to wind his way toward the outside, as best as he could guess.

His time was running out. Joe eyed a large window set in the wall on his left, sunlight streaming through it. He had gotten away with locking himself in a closet, maybe he could get away with slipping out a window.

A sharp metallic screech cut through the hallway, vibrating in his brain and setting his headache off again. Not an alarm, but something vastly large, metal scraping against metal. It drifted in through the walls from outside. The light changed, beginning to dim. As if a curtain were being drawn over the building. Joe leapt to the window. So did four other people in the busy hallway, and the mute couldn't get close enough to jump through the panes into the freedom of the fresh air. Then he looked out.

His heartbeat paused in hopeless horror.

Two vast half circles of metal rose from the ground, forming a dome over the whole complex. From his window Joe could see them both, rising like two halves of a walnut shell, empty gray discs drawing closer together with each second of the unbearable screech. They stretched over the manicured gardens, over the complex of interconnected buildings, over at least two acers of ground. Vast gray giants rising out of the earth. The sunlight grew dimmer by the second. He watched the blackness drawing over the brilliant flowers and tinkling fountains in the garden. A huge metal curtain shutting out the sun. Shutting out all chances of freedom.

He was too late.

Freddy knew the Black Raider prowled through his headquarters, and he had ordered emergency security. The two metal discs clanged together with a sickening force that shook the ground under Joe's boots.

Artificial white light spread in the hallway. Florescent bulbs set in the elegant crenellations between the ceiling and wall hummed as they warmed to their work. The garden glared back at him, as black as pitch. Only for a moment. Then spotlights flicked on, and began to sweep methodically. Picking out every bush, every fountain, even every flower. Joe turned away from the window and began to walk steadily back where he had come. Around him people huddled in groups murmuring and staring out the darkened windows. Joe walked on until he came to the broom closet again. He waited until two women on the custodial staff walked by him, their heads close as they murmured about the morning's happenings. Then everyone in the hall was in front of him for an instant, and Joe slipped into the

closet, twisted his pick in the lock, shoved the rag over the crack, and flipped on the light.

The mute fell against one wall and slid to the ground, his knees buckling. Every part of him trembled. This was how he died. So many situations, he had made it out alive again and again and again...why now?! Why when dealing with the most important thing he had ever done! His hands clamped on his head and Joe folded into himself, his knees coming up as his head dropped. Not even a crack of light could get through the thick, immense metal casing closing him in. He couldn't slip through a hole. He had no way of knowing how deep the discs still sank into the earth, but it had to be far enough he couldn't tunnel out. Even if he could reach the SOLTDs through some miracle, they would just slam him into the top of the metal casing and smash him like an insect. The only way that metal bowl would open is if the FFs found Joe. No, the mute realized, the trembling turning to violent shakes. Only when they caught him, and he lay firmly, inexorably, hopelessly in the clutches of Freddy's Friends.

Joe sat and shook, his eyes focusing unseeingly on a mop across from him, his arms snaking around his knees. During some of the long, lonely nights on the road he had lain awake and hoped, even prayed, pleadingly, that his end would be easier than what he faced now. Joe hiccoughed in terror, dry sobs beginning to spill from him, and a rocking motion starting. Every faculty he comprehended worked desperately, trying to think up a scheme. His gadgets and clever tricks were stripped from him. He sat alone. Nowhere to run, not from this enclosed, dark, metal bowl. The FFs had everyone here entered into their system, and every kind of scanner imaginable for an intruder not in their system; biotracers, cardiac amplifiers, DNA scenters, even the old-fashioned reliable bloodhounds. He might, with extreme help from Providence and incredible luck, be able to avoid them for half an hour. But that was it. Then Nicky would drag him through that dark door.

*"I want you to come back."*

A wet sobbing breath sounded in the closet, and Joe's face lifted so he could swipe a hand over his nose. Yeah, that wasn't happening anymore. No chance of making it back to Anna. Or good old Beau, or Doctor, or Nehi.

*"There's more to life, Joe. More than death and sin and violence. We have an eternity to see Goodness face to face."* Nehi's voice clanged through his mind like a bell, overshadowing the terror and despair shutting him down. Joe stopped rocking. He stared at the mop, focusing on the individual strands in each little twist of material. *"Jesus is alive. He didn't just win the war, He's fighting the battles with us still. Mopping up the remaining foes and comforting even in our darkest times."* Jesus was here, with him right now. Always. So he was going to die, slowly and painfully. But then…but then. Then came the face of Goodness. A shaky breath rattled into the mute. The terror quieted. Hope slipped back into him, the only kind that couldn't be taken away. He drew in another breath, deeper and steadier. No one could take Jesus from him. And he knew his end, his real final home. *Home.* Keep the vision. He had to keep the goal always burning in front of his eyes. Nehi knew what a man needed in the darkest moments, God bless him.

Nehi… Joe's shaking hand slid into his shirt and came out again with a little black tracker. It was inert until he pushed it on. No one could block it, or trace it, until he pushed that button. Should he? Others besides Nehi had this number to trace, he had tossed one to Ariel to start a conversation… And it would worry them all for no reason. Anna would fret and cry for him without any purpose to it, and poor old faithful Beau! No one could do anything. But he had promised.

Joe's thumb hit the button. A red light flashed on the box for a second, began a second flash, and then cut off. Blocked already. And that meant Nicky had a trace on his current position. Joe tossed the box into the corner, tucked the remains of the bread into one pocket with the lingering unthinking instinct of a starved child, slid the steak knife off the tray into his hand, twisted his wire in the lock again, and slid into the hallway.

His very last game of cat-and-mouse. Joe's chin lifted and his eyes steeled. He would play it well. Maybe he could even keep it up for a full hour. That would annoy Freddy, Joe thought with a grim smile, and turned his steps toward the blackened garden, his hand fingering his mask. Part of him hoped Anna didn't cry too long for him, for her sake. Part of him hoped she cried for him occasionally for the rest of her life, just for the comfort of thinking someone down here might remember him. Joe slid his mask on, twisted out a window into the blackness of the garden, and began the dodging maneuvers of what was left of his life. At least he had been given one last really good meal.

# Chapter Eighteen: The Head of the Snake

*"Lord, how long wilt thou look on? rescue my soul from their destructions..."* Psalm 35:17

Tanzid, where's Quintus? We need his SOLTD." Nehi said as he jumped off the exam table. His bare feet slapped the doctor's tiled floor and sounded very loud in the still room.

"Hm. I know I just declared you whole–" Harry started, a little hesitantly. Nehi's palm rammed into his chest.

"That tracker going off means Joe's in trouble out there, on his own! I am not letting him die alone," the young man snapped, his intensity vibrating in the small room.

"We need things," Tanzid said.

"What?"

"We need things. There's no way to know what we're going into, but we know it will be bad. We need equipment. I know a man, it will only take a few hours–"

"Joe doesn't have hours!" Nehi shouted.

"He's just going to have to hold on," Tanzid said. He stood immoveable, like a piece of ebony rock. But just before Nehi yelled in his face (idiotic things about his not caring) he took a second look. The agent's hands were closed into fists, and the one holding the tracker was white-knuckled. He did care. Nehi forced in a breath and nodded.

"Go, get us what we need," he ordered. "Just one hour, Tanzid."

"There's money in the drawer on the left side of the sink," Harry added in his quick efficiency. Tanzid bolted out of the room, tossing the tracker at Nehi's head. The young man caught it as the door filled with people. Daniel, Anna, Beau, and Quintus spilled into the room, curious about the sudden excitement, and bored enough to be nosy. Nehemiah ignored them, staring at the tracker. Tanzid had saved the coordinates. Nehi blinked at the numbers, a dull humming filling his head. He had seen almost the same set on his Grady tracker earlier this week. The

room filled with questions about the expression on Nehi's face. The young man waved the others at Harry, shoved past them, and pushed through the back door. Balmy sunshine spread over him, enclosing him in flower-scented warmth, but Nehi hardly noticed. He leapt down the stairs and dropped on the ornate iron bench under the blooming lilacs. The slim Grady tracker felt very cold in his hands as he pulled it out. His fingers flew over the keyboard, and Atif's tracker appeared in the same position. Nehi blew out a breath and a prayer filled with confused thanks and pleas, and pushed his thumb down on the communication button.

"Don't freak out, Atif, it's Nehemiah, the person you tackled an Esteemed One for back in the Prophet's Peace," he said, as evenly as he could, and took his thumb off. Five seconds ticked by in silence, and Nehi prayed.

"What do you need?" Atif's grim voice drifted over the tracker. Another breath of relief blew from Nehi.

"That friend of mine, the one with the Wazir's white card that you threw in the cell? He's in trouble, and he's somewhere about a half a mile in front of you." Nehi brought his thumb off the button again and waited. This time the silence stayed for fifteen interminable seconds. A howl of anguish came from inside the house; Cobeau had learned the news.

"I think, Nehemiah, his trouble may be deeper than even you know," Atif finally responded. Great. That wasn't much help.

"Look, my team and I are coming for him, but we can't get away immediately. He needs someone to buy him time. I know it's a lot to ask, but he's a brother, and he's doing important things for the kingdom, and... and I really need the help."

"You do not have to plead with me." Atif sounded stiff, almost offended. "My men are already gearing up. We will do what we can. Are you able to form an extraction plan? I do not have one."

"Yes. We can get you out, we'll be there in one hour."

"Agreed."

"He has a bone plant. It's older than yours, and my trace on it is spotty, but maybe you can use it."

"The numbers." The tone came curt, as if he was done talking. Nehi reported them awkwardly, feeling like a boy talking to a grown-up. No response came. He waited. The seconds ticked into a minute. Nehi's knuckles grew white as he gripped the bench.

"Nehemiah," Atif's voice cut over the gadget. The first name sounded stiff, like a title or even an insult.

"Yes," Nehi burst out.

"Your friend bears a slaver's bone plant, and we need the key. Can you offer us a simple, five letter word a cruel soul would program, something that might get us in?"

An accidental slip of a sentence on a moonlit grassy plain outside of Kallipolis, as an almost stranger opened up a fraction to comfort Nehi's nightmares; the name of the man who had used a child as a tool for two years; disgusted abhorrence at a teasing name after a concert. It all flew into his mind, and he knew.

"Music," Nehi said, his stomach flipping. "Try music." Again silence filled his world, and Nehi felt sick. To take something that comforted and brought joy, and that a child was a genius at, and twist it till even the word became hated! Joe had been through so much, he wasn't going to die out there alone, it wasn't happening!

"We have him."

"Thank you, Atif."

"I need no thanks," Atif muttered, anger in the words.

"God go with you, brother," Nehi said, ignoring the other's bad-tempered grimness.

"One hour." The screen went suddenly blank, as Atif ended the conversation. Nehi leapt from his bench and ran for the door inside. He had bought them time.

*The Black Statuette*

The ground gave under his boots, soft and yielding. Good stuff for running, and Joe used it. He darted and weaved through the black garden, dodging searchlights and the seeking laser beams. If any had been watching him, with his black clothes and elegant swift movements, they would have thought it an intricate war-dance from some past civilization. But Joe was very good at what he did, and no one saw him. A part of his mind registered a dangerous weakness clung to him, and he couldn't force himself to keep this up much longer. But he banished the thought to a corner and kept moving. A half an hour slid by, and he had nearly made it around the headquarters.

A sharp white circle of light swept toward him, and Joe spun to the side, vaulting backward over a red scenter beam. He landed softly on his toes and darted off again, dodging and spinning. The white searchlights swept over two wicker chairs on a lovely little patio, and Joe changed his course to reach it. A little thrill of surprise went through him as he saw where his random movements had taken him. Apparently something in him hadn't been randomizing. Something deep in him brought him here; something still clinging to hope.

*You always have been a dreamer,* Joe told himself, a sad little smile twisting under his mask. He rolled under a netting of red laser beams and vaulted to the side to avoid another search light. Rough wicker rammed into his back and his shaking hand darted under the chair. His searching fingers found the fabric of the chair bottom. Shock fairly shone from his green eyes. Joe's belly hit the tile and his arm shoved farther under the chair, scrabbling, running all along the fabric. It wasn't here. It wasn't here! Out of the corner of one eye he caught a shimmer of brilliant white light. Joe's other hand latched onto the top of the chair and he jerked himself over it, tumbling down the soft cushions. He kept rolling, sliding deftly under the little patio table.

Something squeaked on his left. Joe froze and his gloved fingers dug into the grout between the tiles as his heartbeat banged. A white circle of light swept up from the left, and Joe

just caught a glimpse of a pair of scuffed, worn pumps pulling clumsily away from the light. He knew those shoes. His hurting heartbeat skipped for two beats as his lungs expanded enough to get another breath in. Joe summersaulted between two circling white lights. He banged against a pair of legs, and a sharp gasp came as someone tumbled down on top of him, in a tangle of skinny arms and legs. Something hard and square hit his temple, and relief spun through him as his mind cringed at the blow. Joe's arms shot up, gripped the figure around the waist, and threw himself backward to tug them both out of the line of a set of red scenter beams sweeping toward them. The mute's right hand cupped his lock pick, and his shoulder had hardly brushed the glass of the sliding doors before he shoved them open and drew his person inside. He could feel her shaking.

"I saw you hide it. I'm a Sojourner. I thought since I was forgotten–" she started, in a soft, trembling voice. Joe's gloved hand shot up and he stuck a finger to her lips. He felt them close tight and he sought through the darkness for her hands. This room was riddled with security, any noise would be noticed. Her hands went limp in his gloved fingers. Very good. The mute began to form words with her hands, each movement swift and deliberate, practiced a thousand times.

"You have the book?" he asked. Her hands rotated, taking his.

"Yes," she signed in the blackness with Joe's hands, clumsily, unused to using the language in the dark. "Everyone else was watching the Fat One run for the shelves. But I saw you slip it from your shirt and stick it to the bottom of the chair. How?"

The white searchlights played over the patio outside. They were thickening, converging there. He could dodge the searchlights, but the scanners and bio tracers were steadily pinpointing him, faster every second he stayed in one place.

"An adhesive patch on my back, had an instant to get it stuck."

The white light of the circular beams shone through the glass, and the two began to be able to see each other. The lady interpreter looked disheveled and terrified, her hair frizzed till it stuck out all over her head and her clothes stained, ripped, and rumpled. She clutched an ancient book under her arm. Faded designs stamped its worn leather, and Joe felt his breath catch again tonight, at the beauty and wonder of the object in front of him.

God's own words to His people. His heart, their purpose, so many wonders, so many truths...

She began to lessen her hold on it. The beautiful, wonderful book stretched out toward him. He could see the light glinting off the intricate metal clasp holding it closed, the hundreds of pages, each one etched with so many words written by God Himself... Joe longed to touch it, to cradle it in his arms and feel the comfort and joy of holding the real, actual Bible, even for just an instant. His arm shot out and pushed it back at her.

"Get it out," he signed. "Make for the edge of the dome, at the crack where the two halves meet." The lights thickened outside. He could see her expression clearly. Horror and incredulity shone from her as she stared at the little black form in front of her, tears beginning to glitter in her eyes.

"You come too?" she signed, her hands shaking. Joe shook his head. The lights were gathering thicker and faster, sweeping everywhere outside the room. A dog's deep bay sounded through the dark air.

"Go, quick."

"I can't!" Her hands almost wailed it in her agitation.

"They are looking for me. I can pull them off, and no one will notice you."

"That's not what I mean!" Her hands cut vicious, shaking lines through the whitening room. "I mean, I'm just a sign language teacher, and I'm terrified to fight this war on my own. But I can't leave you, not to them! I can't, I can't leave you to–" A gentle, black gloved hand rested on hers, stopping her outpour. Under the elegant black mask, a smile showed beyond the sadness in those pretty green eyes.

"It's ok. Jesus holds me." A slip of paper shoved into her

palm. "Take the book to here, give it only to that person." Then Mariah Perry felt his firm grip push her gently from the room, into the only shadow left on the porch. She watched in numbed horror as the lithe black figure dashed from the room, away from her. He went directly through the lights.

Pandemonium broke out. Alarms blared, dogs yowled, people shouted. Somewhere glass shattered, as the lights swept off, colliding with each other, shifting in and out, till a bright pillar of white light pooled over the garden, smaller lights zinging around it like gnats on the outskirts of their swarm. A small black shadow danced in the middle of the light. Distantly, Mariah heard a whistled hymn drifting from the center of the uproar. It rose defiant and beautiful, soaring above the clamor into a realm that couldn't be seen.

The song cut off mid verse.

A stifled sob ripped from Mariah Perry. She turned away from the lights and began to run, deeper into the darkness. It engulfed her, and she felt each step with the heavy book clutched to her chest, into that inky blackness and away from that young man with the pretty green eyes, that she ran farther into a darkness of soul.

"Any change today, Naqi?" Atif asked. The dry dust of the wasteland swirled up around him and Atif suppressed a cough as he lifted his glasses and focused again on the circle of luscious garden green, a quarter mile from them.

"Nothing, boss," Naqi said, hating to report it. Atif only nodded. But one hand ran absently over the back of his neck and the lines tightened on his grim face. A month they had waited out here. A month, and still no way to pull down the head of this snake! It was a vast animal with a thousand poisonous stings, and there were few options for hacking off the head.

"We could try another foray inside," Taban suggested, not

very enthusiastically.

"You are still coughing from the dart in your lung from the last one," Naqi objected.

"I still say tunneling," suggested Shareef, his brightness clashing with the gloom of the rest of the team. "The network of tunnels running under the building is where the interesting things happen, that's where Naqi is even baffled. It's a rat's den of evil down there, I can feel it. If we could just get in something's bound to turn up!"

"And how do you suggest we get through the metal bowl encasing that rat's den?" Naqi asked, his thin voice annoyed. "A huge metal screen, you have seen it on my equipment. It is titanium, lead, and steel, of a very impressive make, and it runs under the whole of the tunnel systems!"

"Above ground we couldn't even approach the way in without dying," Otar growled. Silence fell as the swirling dust rose with the sun. Taban coughed, a wet sound in the dry air.

"We could go raiding somewhere else," Taban suggested hopefully. "We were able to do some real good in the Sojourner chaos when the Southern slaves attempted a revolt."

"And you got to fight a full contingent and enjoyed it so much you want to do it again," Naqi commented.

"We were able to do some good," Taban repeated, his voice quiet as he stared at the techy. Naqi looked away.

"And while we were gone," Atif said, standing stiff and staring at the complex, "this snake pulled twenty-four of our brothers and sisters into its vile maw while Otar, on watch here alone, was helpless. According to Naqi's scanners, only fourteen left again." Silence fell around them.

"Even here we have managed to do some good," Shareef put in, still trying to be bright. "We were able to warn the Story Land IDP before these FFs struck. That annoyed our snake."

"In a month, all we have done is annoy," Taban sneered. "Oh yes, we are doing wonderful things here." Silence fell again. It dragged through the morning. The team gradually scattered, going about various little chores in the arid land, and then drew

back together behind the silent, staring Atif. The boss stood with his glasses sweeping the complex of buildings. No one ventured a comment while they gathered lunch. Atif didn't come and join the others. Shareef sighed and walked up next to him. The supplier hated having to coax and cajole Atif into taking care of himself. But the boss had a total lack of concern where it came to his own good. The dust began to resettle around Shareef's boots, and he tried to think of an argument that would make his boss eat at least one decent meal today. Shareef opened his mouth, but it was Atif's voice that broke the silence.

"The fat one is on the patio," the boss reported. "A frightened woman is there too, just standing. As if they wait for someone." Atif drew the glasses down, blinking as if undecided if he had actually seen what he thought. He lifted them again quickly. The rest of the team clambered up and stepped to his side. Shareef snapped his telescopic goggles over his eyes and waited the two seconds as they adjusted the focus. There. He could see even the grout between the elegant tiles. There was the woman, and the fat one, as reported. And just outside the double glass doors, a small hubbub centered around a small black-clad form being manhandled off the tiles. A very limp, small, blond-headed figure. As he watched, the small one was plucked from the ground and flung into the only empty chair.

"Is that..." Taban murmured, letting the question hang.

"It can't be the same little black-clad guy we tried to rescue before," Naqi said incredulously.

"We never saw his face, so who knows?" Shareef murmured.

"No, I meant the one who came with that Nehemiah into Tariq's prison," Taban said. Silence tingled around them. It always did at the mention of Nehemiah. All but Taban had been drawn into this group by the tortured slave in Abid's rooms. "Can you get us sound, Naqi?"

"Not unless you want them pinpointing us and the entire base converging on our heads," Naqi said. Atif ignored the chatter. He stood watching the interaction between the fat one and the small one. The captive spoke with the mute's language, just as Nehemiah's friend had. It was him. A familiar burning passed along the back of Atif's neck, just at the name. Why had he helped, for so long, to hold down a boy while he screamed and fought, how could he still live... Atif forced a breath through the familiar heat rushing through him and focused outside himself again. It hurt too much to look inward. Atif was an expert by now at avoiding himself.

The fat one pointed inside the glass. His fat quivered with alarm and he dashed off to see something through the doors. The small one bent down and shot back up again. Whatever that strange enactment meant, it changed the scene.

Everything on the patio became menacing. Stances, hand motions, facial expressions, everything reeked of hatred and threat. The mute had finally broken the polite veneer off the fat one, and Atif respected the little man for it. And for his bravery, as he sat calm and steady amidst the outpour. The hateful Nicky converged on the mute and forced the captive inside. Atif lowered his glasses as the party disappeared into the hallways and rooms blocked so efficiently from every gadget they had. His face creased with his frown, and his mind whirled, looking for a way in. Atif had been waiting for a hole in the FFs tight defense. But now they were needed, urgently. The boss stepped backward, away from the group of men, and moved a few paces off, his mind buzzing as he formed plan after plan and rejected them. But from each rejected plan he kept a tiny piece that made sense. The minutes ticked on, dust swirling around them, laden with enough detritus of the past world's destruction that it interfered with the FFs scanners and kept the little team from being spotted.

The dust shook. It shot up, then down, in an unnatural pattern. The ground under his boots quivered. He looked down, watching the dust and pebbles move and vibrate, feeling something shaking through the soles of his boots.

"Whoa," Shareef muttered.

"Golly-gee," Naqi breathed.

"Boss?" Taban called. Atif looked up. At the edges of the

green circle of garden, gray metal rose out of the earth. It came up like two vast shields, moving impossibly fast for such giants. Higher and higher they shot up into the air, curving over the green and the blocky buildings. It was the shield that rested under the earth, blocking the rat's den from any tunneling effort. Now it rose into the air to prevent any escape from inside that place. He watched the shadows from these vast giants stretch farther every millisecond, as if they were a monster swallowing the complex.

His jawbone vibrated, pulsing with an uncomfortable current. A hundred enemies who might have found his numbers flew through the warrior's mind and for an instant he forgot to breathe.

"Don't freak out, Atif, it's Nehemiah, the person you tackled an Esteemed One for back in the Prophet's Peace." The voice coursed through his bone to his ear, and Atif breathed out in a tight gasp. He took another step farther from his men, one hand going automatically to the side of his face as the uncomfortable vibration went on.

"What do you need?" His answer to Nehemiah came curt, almost sharp. It was hard to speak to the young man without his conscience tearing him open with nearly physical pain, even after two years had passed. Nehemiah started to answer, but Atif only half listened. He could guess what he wanted. He shot a glance at Naqi. The tech man whipped his PP into his hand, and his fingers flew along the gadget. The two great halves clicked into one another, a horrible grinding of metal rolled over the land, then silence fell with deadly completeness. Even the sound from the complex was swallowed by that vast metal dome glinting in the desert sun.

"Whoa," Shareef said again.

"I think, Nehemiah, his trouble may be deeper even than you know," Atif commented dryly.

"There's so much going on right now that I haven't seen in this place," Naqi murmured. Atif's arm shot out, pointing at the team's gear. There was a concentrated rush at the equipment.

Atif spun and strode to his tech man.

"Track a plant, 52890," Atif barked. An eyebrow rose as Naqi whipped out a second gadget, working one with each hand.

"That's not like our plants," Naqi murmured.

"What is different?" Atif prodded, one hand poised near his jaw.

"Ours are for soldiers, or high-tech civilian businessmen. They're voluntary." Naqi pointed at his PP screen. "These five numbers are older, but they're more than that. It's a slaver's tool."

"What?" Atif asked.

"I've seen them at Tariq's, he had a couple of the fellows program one, for a favorite woman from his harem who kept slipping away. It's not designed for communication. Well, not two-way communication, not the normal kind where you actually hold a conversation. It's used to tell the location of the bearer, can be used for orders, and can also transmit an electrical current from the lowest spark to killing levels. This type isn't voluntary, and it doesn't come out."

"Why would it transmit electric... Oh," Shareef said, and his voice died away.

"Exactly," Naqi nodded, "and that can be used to set a radius for the slave, an invisible cage if you will."

"Well?" Atif demanded. "Can you track it?"

"It is a personal tool. It has a code encrypted on it, you have to know the key to get in, to keep just anybody from being able to control the bearer. If you mess around with the plant without the key you might end up killing the person wearing it. The key is always five letters, usually something simple. Tariq told the fellows something that made them blush and grimace, and he gets that grin of his, you know–"

"I know," Atif interrupted, and then clarified. "It is the tool of a cruel man, used to victimize and control, and you need a key to get in." Naqi nodded, his fingers flying over his second gadget. Atif touched his jaw again.

"Your friend bears a slaver's bone plant, and we need the key. Can you offer us a simple, five letter word a cruel soul would program, something that might get us in?" Atif kept his hand on his jaw, waiting. He could hear birdsong through the plant, and the rustling of large leaves. *Story Land,* his brain identified automatically.

"Music," Nehemiah said. There was a tight, disgusted sound to the word. "Try music."

Atif reported, and watched his man. Naqi stared at his gadget, then his brow cleared, he nodded, and went back to his PP. Atif strode away, speaking softly. He cut the call short and spun to face his men. Naqi interrupted before he could say anything.

"I don't know who this guy is, boss," Naqi said, the green light from his PP screen lighting up the young man's skinny face, "but he wasn't always an esteemed bearer of the Wazir's white card. You need to be careful with him."

"Why?" Taban demanded.

"Because he got away alive from whoever put that in him," Naqi said flatly. "I did a little research once, curious about the second kind of bone plants. No one gets away alive once the slaver plant is set in the bone."

"No one?"

"No one. I mean, you can run. But through that little piece of gadgetry, you can be tracked, and you can be immobilized, so every time you try to get up and move again, you're sent back writhing to the ground, till you just lay there and wait to be picked up. Or you're killed by the current. Usually the slaver programs it to automatically kill if they die first. I read of one case where–" Naqi looked up, his face working, shook his head, and went back to his gadget. "Just be careful with him. Whoever he is, he's tougher than anyone has a right to be, and is probably smarter than any of you."

"Thank you for that vote of confidence," Taban commented.

"Well, it's not like you can work a havershome 24, Taban, or even know–"

"Enough, Naqi," Atif interrupted, knowing nerves were strung tight and banter now was liable to become fighting insults. He pointed at the gray dome rising over the horizon. "Can you tap in?" Atif asked. The tech man's fingers slid and jabbed furiously for another five seconds. Then he blew out a breath and his speed slowed a fraction, his eyes never lifting from the screen.

"I cracked it. I'm in. But it will take everything I have to move those giants, and even with everything I'm not certain I can actually open them," Naqi reported.

"Once open, could you keep them open?" Atif asked.

"Yes." Naqi rattled off a series of statements no one understood. The rest of the team ignored the technicalities spouting from the young man, the "yes" was all they needed. Naqi's voice died away. Everyone looked at Atif, almost holding their breaths. The boss stood straight and grim, not a trace of doubt on his face; obviously he had a plan, a good one that would work. Inside, Atif felt the old failure and break burning a hole deeper in his soul. He wouldn't stand by and watch another brother be tortured, it would not happen while he lived! His brain ached as he furiously searched for a way to get the dome to open just enough to let them in. He didn't let it show in the firm look he swept over his men.

"We're going in. But not like last time."

Strong fingers darted from the shadows by the door and latched onto Nehemiah's shoulder as he barreled in from the garden. His feet tripped over each other as he was jerked aside, into the small shadowed alcove created by the open back door.

"Tell me again exactly what Joe said about the IDP wolf," Daniel demanded.

"Now?" Nehi gaped.

"What if it's the doctor?"

"Look Dan, I know you don't like trusting people, but right now–" Nehi began, but a palm in his chest shoved him backward. His back rammed into the wall and his mouth slammed shut as his cuts woke up.

"Right now you're about to run off and leave Anna here," Daniel growled. A cold wave of indecision ran through Nehi. But even as his "protective brother" woke up to its full inside him, his reason told him Anna was capable of handling herself. Daniel didn't give him the chance to say it. His palm still pressed into Nehi's chest. "Tell me again exactly what Joe told you before he left."

"He didn't really tell me anything," Nehi said, one hand going to his forehead and starting to rub it. "He signed that he was leaving Beau, and when I pressed him, he mentioned the Wolf, and then cut it off. I said the Wolf was here, to see his reaction. Joe told me no, not here, near, and there was a difference."

"'Near' doesn't necessarily negate 'here.'"

"Or it could mean 'near' as in we know them, we're close, friends with whoever this is." A cold wave slid through him at the thought. "Joe insists he doesn't know the Wolf's name."

"That's one point where I'm starting to believe the little mute. If he did he would have just shot the guy in the head years ago and been done with it." Daniel's hand pulled away from his little brother and he stood still, biting his lip. "Darn it! I don't like it, Nehi, I don't like any of it!"

"I'm going after Joe," Nehi said, determination in every syllable.

"I know! And Anna's staying here, I know that too, because I'm not letting her run off on this madcap errand and losing both of you at once." Daniel sighed. His brown eyes flicked up from the floor and locked onto Nehi's. "I'm letting you go alone."

"What?"

"You go bring Joe back, do whatever you have to. I know you'll do a good job, Nehi, and he needs you like he never has before. You'll have Tanzid and Cobeau... Just be careful, ok? I'll have to stay here and make sure Harold Pablo doesn't backstab our sister." He shrugged, some of his intensity melting into a sardonic smile. "Maybe we'll trap a wolf while you're gone."

# Chapter Nineteen: Tug of an Arrow

*"Blessed be the Lord my strength, which teacheth my hands to war, and my fingers to fight."* Psalm 144:1

"Can we slow down a little?" Naqi panted, his voice vibrating as he jogged behind Otar.

"No," Atif said. Atif and his men ran over the dry ground, Taban and Shareef behind the others, spraying water in a steady stream to keep the dust cloud down. Their movements were clumsy, choppy, awkwardly running in the dark with heavy material pulled over the team. The FFs used radar as the main sweeper for outside their headquarters. Anti-radar paint splayed over the material in a desert camo-pattern. The heavy sheet made running clumsy, but it deflected the seeking radar beams and no one complained. Otar kept running, hefting the cloaking lens a little higher. It was heavy; three metal sheets, each one almost as tall as Otar, and covered with a host of fractals and lenses. If someone glanced at it the cloaking mechanism shifted the line of vision, and they saw only more of the empty landscape.

In Atif's pocket, Naqi's arrow tracker pulsed consistently every second, always tugging gently forward and down. Naqi had it linked to the mute's bone plant. The little gadget pulsed and tugged, longing to reach the source drawing on it. Atif could find their man easily, so long as the arrow stayed true.

"No slowing?" Naqi panted.

"No," Atif ordered, priming his Healy laser as he ran beside his techy. He had two, a matching set, and they were rarely out of his reach. The team moved in the dark, but each had a military contact in the right eye. Rocks and dust, the bulk of the other's bodies, each shift of a piece of equipment, everything under the material showed up in eerie green luminescence. Atif's showed the world outside the material too. His was the master device. At each new yard his team's coordinates flashed in front of his eye, while the outside world shimmered green and ominous through his contact. Defensible positions, possible threats, moving bodies (from a fly by Otar's ear to a swallow flapping overhead), each small rock in their way, it all flashed past his vision in a constant stream as he ran. Labels, warnings, information piled on information. Atif kept one hand on Otar's large shoulder and focused on their destination, ignoring the rest.

The gray dome loomed over them, nearer with each pounding step through this dusty land. It towered over the landscape, becoming the horizon. No sound but their own movements and the slight wind stirred around them. Shareef had the urge to burst into a marching song. But even he knew it wasn't the time. Boots rose and fell. Dust spurted up, water caught it and the dust sank again. Sweat trickled down Otar and he shifted the hulking cloaking lens in his bulging arms. Atif's mind would not be still. It kept rushing over all the possibilities of failure in this run. There were so many ways they could die!

A sharp crack broke the still air. Atif's eye ran up the gray bubble blotting out the horizon. The line running along the dome became a black tear, then a gaping hole, then the gray dome was once more two halves of metal instead of a single entity. Otar's steady run stumbled, and stopped, as he wondered what the noise meant. Atif drove a hand into his back, forcing him on. They had to get there now, while chaos still reigned. Their only window lay in the twenty minutes it would take for the security system to reset to normal. They had to slide in under its nose in those few minutes. And it would begin when that dome opened. The gray metal shimmered and shone in the bright sunlight, and Atif tried not to wince as his contact mimicked the outer world, and he watched the vast shields pulling apart. His hand shot into Otar's back again, and the team picked it up to a race. They dashed over the ground, Taban and Shareef hardly able to keep the billowing dust cloud down.

The splitting halves loomed closer, the screech of metal almost unbearable. A sliver of garden green could be seen through the lowest portion, where the two hinged together.

The crack grew wider still, a hand could have shoved through it, as the two halves dropped, screeching and rumbling in protest. The steady thudding of their boots and quiet hiss of water pumps became invaded by other living noises. Movement, shouts, dogs' bays, even a woman's laughter, drifted out of the sinking dome into the sunlight. The ground shook under their boots and Shareef stumbled. Atif caught his jacket and jerked him upright, and suddenly they were there. Otar slammed the cloaking lens in the dust, just where the crack was widening enough to allow a human entrance, and they shrugged the anti-radar material off; it would be too easily seen by the naked eye, this close to people. Time for the cloaking lens to do its work.

Something thunked into the lens, a female voice squeaked, and a thump sounded on the ground just on the other side. Atif spun around their lens, his Healys sweeping the area.

A frizzy haired, thin, terrified woman lay in the dirt blinking owlishly at the sun. As he spotted her, she tucked something hurriedly behind her back. The woman stumbled into a crouch, one hand held out in a pitiful, begging defensive gesture, as she scuttled around the other side of the lens. Taban's strong brown arm grabbed her shoulder, and jerked. Atif spun back around the cloaking lens. The frizzy-haired one crouched on the ground, her lips pressed together, both hands behind her, and two pretty brown eyes staring up at them in wonder and fear.

"You didn't see us, did you?" Shareef whispered loudly, grinning like a boy. She shook her head and a bewildered little twitching smile answered him.

"Are you one of them?" Taban growled. His teeth showed, but not in a smile. She shook her head, as she pulled back farther against the lens. They all recognized her from the scene on the porch, and knew the answer to his question. But somehow he felt it had to be asked. Taban liked things properly laid out.

"I am a Sojourner," the woman said, her voice soft and beautiful.

"Good, stay here. Naqi, keep her alive," Atif ordered, and

waved the rest of the team forward. He spun around the cloaking lens and darted past the dropping shield. There was more crack than shield now. But a heavy shadow still fell over the garden from where the highest peak of the shield blocked the sun. Atif kept in the shadow, running on the fringe of the blackness. Shouts and orders rang around the complex of buildings. Dogs bayed nearer the patio. The gardens were alive with people. Atif swept the area, adjusting his mind to notice only one thing from his contact. Strobing in his eye flashed the defensible positions. One caught in his mind as the rest skimmed past. An artificial hill rose gently in the corner of this immaculate garden, red with waving hollyhocks. Four patrolling guards jogged toward it as they swept the grounds. Atif veered from the shadows, sprinting hunched and trusting to his camo and the chaos. The guard at the rear, a thick, handsome young man, looked up and focused directly on him. His laser jerked up, but he was too slow at his job. Atif's Healy warmed in his hand, and the man dropped lifeless with a dull thud. His companions spun, lasers coming off their shoulders, beginning to tense and sweep the area. But then Taban reached them. None had the chance to raise a shout.

Otar scooped two of the guards from the stained grass and jogged behind the hill, where Atif crouched over his fallen guard. The boss stripped the man of his black tactical uniform. Shareef and Taban turned, selected the closest to their own sizes, and began to do the same. Atif tossed the clothes at Otar, glared at him when his agent almost stood up to dress, and then went back to the guard in front of him as Otar dropped sheepishly back on the grass where he stayed hidden by the hill.

Atif slipped his hand in his pocket and brought out a thin rectangle of metal; it looked like an identification card. His thumb pressed the side as he held the card over the guard prone on the grass in front of him. A gentle beep and a blue arrow flashed, pointing at the man's hand. Atif picked up the limp hand, cradling it in his own and studying it. The other three stared at him, beginning to understand. Fear started to claw up

their throats as they realized how close to disaster they ran. Their timing had to be perfect. A small white scar stood out on the man's palm. Atif slid the corner of his metal card under the skin, and pressed again on the button. It flashed red twice, then blue, and another small beep sounded. The card came up, a tiny chip attached to the corner. Atif held out his hand to Otar. The big man stuck his right hand in his boss's without hesitation. But a frown plastered over his face as he watched the chip slide under his skin.

"The security must already be resetting. The first scan is always a sweeping check to locate their operatives," Shareef murmured, voicing the other's complaint. "They will find our bone plants! We will be pinpointed, identified, surrounded, and immobilized in minutes. While our plants are in, adding one of their chips is not going to save us from–" Atif slapped a clear, fishing-line-thin wire onto Shareef's jaw bone. The supplier grunted and reeled, his hand coming up automatically as the wire hissed its way through his skin to his bone. Atif caught his arm and held it down, drawing Shareef's head close, almost forcing their eyes to meet. After a moment his blue eyes focused on Atif's steady ones. Shareef's breathing evened out, and he stopped swaying.

"A warning would have been nice," he muttered, his voice husky. Atif flipped his card at the supplier.

"Get outfitted, set the first distraction," the boss ordered. Atif's dark eyes settled on the hill. The bombs were only to be used in case of an emergency. Hopefully they wouldn't need them, but if they did... "Shareef, set two distractions. If we need it out here, we want it big." He held the wire out to Otar. While he extracted the chip and set the first of the bombs he had carried in, Shareef kept an eye on his teammates. Otar didn't hesitate to slap the wire to his jaw. He gasped and folded over slowly, his hands splaying over the grass as it wormed its way in and deactivated the bone plant. Taban grunted and his eyes crossed when his wire went in. Atif only paled. His features never even changed their hard lines. Shareef tossed the card to

Taban and ran a hand over the laser he had acquired from the guard. It was a Krackmen, excellent, a weapon this nice needed liberated from these people. Atif glanced at his men to be sure they were ready, and waited for Taban to tuck the last of his two dozen armaments into his new uniform. He nodded once, swung to his feet, and trotted around the hill.

In a moment, four men jogged through the gardens in perfectly drilled double time. The arrow in Atif's pocket tugged persistently to the left, and always down. Atif watched for the right entrance. For a guard to be in an unauthorized position spelled questions, and questions meant exposure. They ran, over the manicured grass, onto the gravel walkway snaking like a mote around the buildings, and stepped into the cool artificial air of a square brick building. Atif chose one on the perimeter. It seemed likely security would run a check of the outer edges. He slowed to a march, his black army boots thudding into the marble tiles. There were so many people in this hall. So many people everywhere.

A stab of pain shot through Atif's palm, as the chip jumped. A surge of energy, not his own, swept through him and his eyes narrowed as his ears hummed and popped. He spun on his heel and held up a palm. His men were already stopped, reeling and staring glassy eyed. They had to look tough and in charge if they wished to win today. He would keep up the appearance for them. One hand went to his ear, as if he were listening to a receiver. The security sweeper finished locating the available operatives and syncing them into the system, and Atif's men blinked back into focus. He waved them forward, picking it up to a trot, his gaze sweeping the hall for a place to duck out of sight. People were everywhere, and so much sun and openness! Atif appreciated the layout from a security standpoint. This design definitely made it hard for an enemy to slip in undetected.

Atif took the first turning left, shoving open a plain metal door. He stepped off marble onto wooden slats. A middle-aged officer with an eye patch blocked the simple, windowless hallway, one hand holding a clipboard and his single eye glaring

like an angry eagle. The man held a scanner in his other hand. He would have already used that on them, while Atif pushed into the hall. Thank God for the palm chips.

"Squad number!" he barked.

"Five, Sir," Atif reported, ripping off a smart salute and hoping a Squad Five existed in this place.

"Identification," snarled the officer. Atif's fist shot into the man's soler plexus. He moved so fast, all Shareef saw was a blur, then the officer bending double, trying to cough and breathe at the same time. Atif's knee cracked into his chin, the single eye rolled up, and the man collapsed. A quick shove with his boot, and Atif sent him rolling to the side of the hall. He pointed at a stack of orange crates, and Otar quickly shifted the crates to cover their victim, as Shareef whipped out a set of leather cuffs and a gag. Atif decided not to ask where the supplier had slipped those in his uniform, or what else he had, and just held out his hand for the second distraction. Shareef handed him the explosives and the timing mechanism. Atif knelt in the corner and began to set it as Taban stood watch and the officer was neutralized.

"How long after an operative sweep would you make a body sweep?" Atif asked his fighter as he finished with the bomb.

"It would be the last precaution. Fifteen minutes," Taban answered immediately. Atif nodded. That meant he could allow his team ten minutes of safety before the bodies in the garden and here were found and chaos broke loose looking for them. Shareef and Otar swung back into line, and the team started to run. The arrow tugged forward and down, and it grew stronger, the tugging more frantic; they neared their man. Atif gripped a support beam holding up the hallway corner and swung around it. He slammed into something gray and yielding that went, "Oof," and he rebounded back into Shareef. One blink, and Atif registered sixteen FF agents, all in various states of off duty relaxation, and all staring at them. A massive metal door, with nothing but blackness showing through the glass pane in the center, rested in the wall opposite him. A man to the left of Atif raised a hand toward his jaw to report a squad of unrecognized men in an unauthorized position.

Both Atif's Healys went up. Unlike Nehemiah, he had never bothered to learn the art of creasing an enemy and leaving them senseless. His strength lay in making sure they didn't make a sound to alert more enemies; ever again. The compact lasers whined, their red dots lighting the barracks room as they appeared in enemies like lethal fireflies. Taban swung beside him, and in nine seconds they were done. Atif let his lasers drop to hang from their shoulder straps, steaming as they recharged, and trotted forward, stepping over the mess and ignoring the stench. They had eight minutes of safety to get this done.

A bio scanner held the door locked fast against them. Atif swung to the side and waved for Shareef to use one of his magical gadgets to deal with the situation. The supplier shrugged and looked helplessly at his boss, a fine blush covering his face. Taban clicked in annoyance, shouldered him aside, and slapped a finger on the scanner. Atif and Shareef looked away, swallowing and not really wanting to notice more. It was enough to know it wasn't Taban's finger. A click sounded in the still room, and the door cracked open. Taban shoved it farther open and stepped through into the blackness, his laser sweeping the area. Shareef slid in after him, as Atif spun toward the thick Otar and handed him a third bomb.

"Set this to collapse these stairs. Keep the door open, and our exit clear," the boss ordered. He spun on his heel and stepped through, leaving all trace of sunlight behind him.

The smell hit him first. It was blood, and dirt, and refuse, and decay, the scent of black despair. His contact picked out the area for him in its eerie green glow. A small entry room, with a flight of steps winding down into the earth. Atif's grim face hardened, but his feet sped up. Something in him, from the experiences he had known in his short life, told him if they were caught down here they would never see the sunlight again. They had to get their man and get out. His boots flew down the wooden stairs, passing Shareef and Taban as the two crept,

trying to see what lay below. The arrow jerked and tugged, so strong he could see it bulging in his pocket.

Sounds began to invade the close, stinking air. Chains clinking, jibes and evil laughter, unmistakable hissing as instruments primed and heated for their work. Atif's heartbeat began to hammer in his chest. He had avoided *that* part of Tariq's prison, everyone but the most vilely cruel did. Yet contamination had been unavoidable, and he knew what he heard. But the instruments primed. Maybe, if the Lord felt gracious, they had made it in time. The last two turns of the stairs blurred in his vision as he flew off the wood onto the packed dirt of the rat's den. Dim, dirty, yellow light flickered from hanging bulbs tacked to the ceiling, snaking off through the oval tunnels.

But Atif hardly noticed the area. He focused on one room to his right, where bright white light streamed through a reinforced window set in a metal wall. The white light mixed with laughter that acted like alcohol on a mad-drunk's brain when it hit Atif. He could feel the boiling starting in him, the pent-up fury that always rested just under the surface. Anger at the evil of man, anger at particular evil men he had met. But mostly anger at himself. He could do more. He had to do more, to make it right! In that single glance Atif registered the high-priority cell, the door already locked down. He focused on the large, reinforced window.

Atif wore two rings on each hand. They were large, and ornate, with a diamond set in the center of each. Shareef once commented on them, as the rest of his boss's outfits were remarkably austere, even depressing and shabby hidden under his sweeping black greatcoat. Taban gave his cat-like laugh and Atif hadn't responded. The two fighters knew a heavy ring is only a weapon disguised.

The diamonds smashed into the glass, biting through the pane and creating enough weakness a single blow was enough. Glass shattered, shards scattering into the room in a piercing hail. Atif rolled through the flying glass, his Healys already whining their deadly song. He vaguely registered two other forms fly through behind him, but the anger boiled strong, and focused on the five forms gathered around the metal table. Six seconds, as the enemy dodged and yelped, and all five splayed on the ground. What was left of them. Only then Atif realized one had been a woman. None were faces he recognized.

"Atif," Shareef said. His voice came quiet and urgent, the sound of a man standing on a viper waiting for it to strike. Atif swung toward his agent. In an instant his anger chilled into cold fear. Shareef stood as still as stone. A red tracer beam played on his chest. Just over his heart. Atif's vision shot along the red line to its source.

In the deepest shadows under the table, two green eyes shone behind a ruby pistol. His clothes were ripped and tattered, and his skin was little better. Atif's contact picked out the marks left by leather cuffs on his ankles and wrists, and on each a smoking burn where a laser had shorn through chain and flesh to gain his freedom. One ankle twisted unnaturally. The face and shoulders were broken with electric whip cuts, the skin with deep tears that could only have come from dogs' jaws, the worst shining with positively-charged chitosan gel to stop the hemorrhaging and keep him alive. At least God had been gracious, and the instruments hadn't begun their work.

But those green eyes... They were unnaturally bright, shining with the fear and pain and the incredible strength of the man under the table. To have taken that much, and still react in six seconds, burning himself free with a snatched laser, and holding it steady... Naqi's warning rang through Atif's mind and the chill ran deeper. He understood now. And Shareef was about to die. Atif dropped slowly to his hands and knees, smoothly, wishing he knew how to make it gentle. The green eyes flicked, focusing on him with an intensity that took Atif's breath away. But the red tracer never wavered from Shareef's heart.

"Nehemiah sent us," Atif murmured. He couldn't make it comforting. His voice could not comfort. "We are here to get you out. Not to hurt you. Let us help." The green eyes just stared

back at him. It was impossible to tell if this little person had enough sense left in his shredded body to even understand him. He should be lying somewhere mostly insensible. But here he was. Stinking of burnt flesh and blood and vomit, staring from out of the shadows. Ready to kill and run. "Lay down the pistol. We are not your enemies. We have only seven minutes to get you out. Put the laser down." The red line did not waver. Atif's contact zoomed in on one filthy finger, beginning to close on the trigger sensor. The trigger registered to heat, if that finger got near, the pistol would fire, and Shareef would die. Atif's hand rose to his neck and pulled. A soft tinkling of metal filled the still room as a folk-art Healy laser shifted and morphed into an IDP cross. The metal cross dangled from its chain, glinting in the artificial light spilling down in that horrible room. Three seconds ticked by. They could hear the painful wheezing gasps from under the table.

"Please," Atif said, as close to begging as he had ever gotten. "I promised Nehemiah I would get you out."

The finger hovering over the trigger button shook. The burnt hand dropped, and the clatter of the pistol hitting the ground shattered the quiet. Shareef sucked in a noisy breath and his shoulders sagged. Atif dove under the table, his strong arms slid around the torn figure and he gathered him like a child. The small, light body felt like a child. As he pulled back out and rose to his feet, Atif could feel the tense trembling in this little person. He still clutched the pistol in his broken hand. Trust went only to a point. Atif reminded himself to do nothing that could be interpreted as a threat, vaulted out the broken window, and took off up the stairs at a run. He slowed fractionally, and Taban darted past, taking point. Atif blinked as he ran, and the constant stream of information shivered in front of his eye, then the contact flashed his teams' coordinates in a swift file. Otar moved above them, pacing and free. All went well. Too well?

The figure in his arms stirred. Atif felt two fingers on the side of his neck and tensed despite himself. The fingers started to tap. After three taps, he realized the mute spoke to him in Morse. The end of the stairs came in sight and Atif only half paid attention, his mind running along all they had to do to get back to Naqi undetected. Then he comprehended the words this small man tapped out.

"FF expected rescue."

Naqi watched the frizzy-haired woman from lowered lids, as he pretended to work with his tools. In reality, he had every gadget set up, and plugged into the joint of this vast shield. His only task was to keep the thing open. And so long as no hitch in the plan came, that meant he did nothing, because it would stay open on its own. The woman's eyes suddenly flicked down and latched onto his. Naqi coughed and began to study the sky, a nonchalant whistle sliding from him. When he dared to look back, she still sat watching him, and in the middle of her confusion he thought he could see amusement. He took heart, and offered a smile. She swallowed and spoke, in her soft voice that sounded to Naqi like the perfect fit of a neutron to an atom.

"So…when he said, 'Keep her alive,' did he mean, 'I want her alive to question later,' or, 'Protect her'?"

"I don't know. With the boss, it could have been either," Naqi said truthfully.

"Oh." She looked at the dirt, studying it with sudden fascination.

"Let's say it was the second one," Naqi grinned, "I like that one better." Half a smile twitched over her face as a polite answer, but she offered nothing else. The sounds of the busy complex took over, shouts and dogs baying, and the rush of restarting generators. An unconscious, nervous little whistle slid from between Naqi's teeth. He went back to pretending to be busy with his gadgets and she kept studying the dirt. Five minutes later, she spoke again.

"Are you…" she asked, her voice soft, hesitating. Her eyes strayed to the IDP emblem dangling from the chain around his neck; it still lay in its hidden form (a PP screen open to a grid), but she could recognize the workmanship.

"Single?" Naqi broke in before she could finish. "I am." She blinked at him, a smile beginning as amusement caught her.

"But I–" she started, and Naqi interrupted again.

"You are too, right?"

"No, I–"

"Really?" he asked, mournfulness dripping from the single word. Her smile stretched into a laugh. Confused and hesitant, and mixed with worry, but still a laugh.

"Yes, I am single," she corrected, her eyes twinkling, "but that's not the point."

"Maybe it is to someone…nearby."

"Look, are you Christian?" she asked, in her best I'm-really-serious-about-this teacher voice.

"Yes! We have a lot in common, don't we?"

"Shut up!"

Naqi pulled back, looking like a puppy who just got shouted at. She took a breath and corrected herself.

"I didn't mean that, not really. But this is important, more important," she went on quickly, forestalling him as his mouth opened to interject a comment, "than what you want to talk about." She hesitated another moment, studying the weird wispy man. Then her hands came out from behind her back. An ancient, leather-bound, beautiful Bible rested in those pretty hands. A huge family edition, the leather tooled into intricate designs, and the yellowed paper thick and edged with faded, flecked gold, the cover held closed by a swirled clasp. Naqi's jaw dropped onto his chest and he vaguely registered he was ogling the book like an idiot.

"I thought it might fit in your black bag," she said, and he heard her through the sudden ringing in his ears. "I think we should get it out of sight."

The boards squeaked under his heavy boots as Otar paced the barracks room. He patrolled and waited, his fingers running up and down the Krackmen laser dwarfed by his huge person. Footsteps rang from behind him and Otar spun toward the door to the rat's den, the laser springing up.

"Too slow, you would be dead now," Taban commented as he trotted out. He headed toward the window in the room, checking the situation. Shareef and Atif trotted right behind him, and Otar breathed again.

"No trouble, boss," he reported. Atif didn't seem to listen. The boss stopped and stood still, clutching the bloodstained ragged figure they had retrieved. Atif wasn't listening. They knew about the rescue? How could they have known? Surely if it was known, Atif and his men would have been stopped by now! He looked down at the small figure in his arms. The green eyes stared back. The hand slid from Atif's neck and slowly, painfully turned toward the boss. In the midst of the dog bites and filth, a small neat cut could be seen in the center of the palm.

"Card," Atif snapped at Shareef. The supplier swung around to him, the card already in his hand. He held it to the mute's palm, the gadget flashed red twice, then its blue, and came away with a chip. A receiver. Someone had heard everything said around the mute, and knew his position now. Shareef flung the chip at the pile of bodies, his expression one of triumph and disdain; he considered it finished, the single trick of the enemy puerile and already counteracted.

"Run," Atif growled. He spun toward the window as Taban shoved it open. A low curse sounded from the fighter.

"A patrol is passing, there are too many outside," he reported. Atif swung to the hallway they had entered by and began to run, steadily and cautiously. Taban passed him, his hands on his laser. Cold, trembling fingers touched the side of

Atif's neck again.

"Lady," the mute tapped.

"Thin, wild-haired, Sojourner?" Atif murmured, glancing down. The green eyes were focused on his and a soft nod told him he had guessed the word's meaning correctly. "She is with my man outside, waiting." The eyes closed for a moment and Atif felt the little man draw in a shuddering breath. Then the fingers started to tap again.

"FF waiting," the mute tapped. Waiting? What were they waiting for? Wait, why hadn't there been any trouble for Otar if these people knew about the rescue? It would have been easiest to catch the interlopers (since they were known to be coming) when they went to get the prisoner. A squad of men should have appeared, overpowered Otar, and waited for the others to come out with the mute. Why hadn't they? Another thing, the top brass hadn't been in the cell, gloating over the prisoner. It had been dupes there, expendables. Taban pushed through the metal door back into the bright, populated, marble-tiled hall, and Atif kept on his heels, thinking furiously. Around him custodial workers shrunk to the sides of the hall as they gaped, ordinary FFs turned their heads to stare sullenly at them, fellow security looked away as if pretending they didn't see the four men, and Atif silently wondered if he had picked the wrong uniforms. Taban trotted on, surreptitiously glancing out each window and door they came to. The fighter's lips pursed. His tanned finger began to tap his palm and Atif felt his bone chip vibrating in code.

"Outside each exit," Taban told him. Someone waited outside each exit they passed, the gardens were alive with operatives. And if Atif let Taban or Otar take them out and ran for it, in these populated halls it would be known immediately and they would be tagged for what they were, spies and enemies. A group of four guards turned around the corner, wearing the same uniforms as the team's stolen ones. For an instant, Atif saw the leader's eyes land on Taban. In the same instant, the man looked away. As if pretending the team didn't exist. In a flash Atif understood.

They were known as spies. Something (besides the filthy figure in his arms) told these people as clearly as if "Spies" were stamped on the team's foreheads. But the FFs in this hall had orders to do nothing. While Atif and his men were inside, the FFs knew they had the team pinned down, easy to capture, and there were people carefully placed at each exit to keep them inside. Because the FFs were waiting. But not for Atif and his team, they were waiting for the real rescue.

This evil snake wanted Nehemiah.

*Watch for*

# Ravens Rebirth

*final book of the epic!*

# Appendices

# *903*

*March 234:* Born in KAM, marked as GI, "adopted" by the Incomplete Keepers of the People's Kingdom.

*April 238:* Successfully ran from the IK Station.

*August 238:* Picked up by Geego Thomle's slaver caravan.

*January 239:* Sold to Bart Meilson as a pet for his ninth birthday present.

*February 240:* Acquired by the Advancers of KAM for testing.

*March 241:* Bought by Jarl Furt, the Music Maker, traveling musician and cat burglar.

*April 243:* Upon the death of Furt, able to slip off into the streets of Hurn in the Kingdom of the Wise.

*The cellar window cracked open. Freezing wind whistled through it, wet snow swirling in mini blizzards, twisting and coating the dusty boxes nearest the window. A small form slid through the crack. The window snapped shut. Closing the wind outside. The boy stole forward, shuffling on numb feet toward the furnace pouring heat into the house above.*

*The massive metal furnace presided over the cellar like a fat lord over his tenants. The boy held shaking blue hands toward the heat. His face was discolored from the cold, gaunt and pale. Fresh scars stood out on that pale skin. Easily visible through the rags clinging to him in wet clumps. But a smile stood on his face as the heat poured into him and the wind raged on the other side of the window. Scarred hands and feet turned slowly back to their natural color. The tingling even stopped. A thankful sigh slid from him; the cold would not claim his life. Not tonight at least.*

*The boy's bloated belly made a noise and his face tightened. He turned toward the dusty boxes piled around him to get his mind off his hunger, lifting flaps and peering into the interior. What did normal people keep in boxes inside their homes? So much stuff! Did people really own this much? What did they do with it all? Could he own things now?*

*He lifted a box lid and a silent laugh slid from him in his delight. His boney hands slid into the box and came out with piles of clothes, almost his size.*

*A few minutes later he pranced across the room, a pair of shorts pulled over pants, a sweater and shirt hanging off his stick-thin body, a cap perched sideways on his head, and a twinkle in his green eyes.*

*The hinges on the door leading into the house squeaked.*

*The boy dodged for the furnace, crouching behind it, his twinkle gone.*

*Soft thumping steps came down the wooden stairs, and his face crinkled in confusion. Those footsteps didn't sound right... He leaned cautiously out, letting himself glimpse the room, his face flushed with the heat from the furnace.*

*A big yellow dog padded into the room and headed for the old rug in front of the furnace. Her tail waggled happily. And a whole chicken dangled from her mouth. The boy spun around the furnace, his eyes bright. He held his hand out gently, clucking at the dog. The animal froze for a moment, cocking her head at the boy. Then the tail waggled again and she padded forward, head dropping and ears going back, asking to be scratched. One of the boy's hands obligingly scratched behind a silky yellow ear. The other dove for the chicken.*

*Twenty minutes later Joe lay in a happy tangle with the yellow dog. They splayed over the rug, the chicken carcass scattered around them, the furnace warm and bright, their bellies full. A long sigh slid from Joe, his eyes closed as his head lay on the silky yellow fur. He couldn't remember ever feeling full. To have no hunger at all clawing inside him. It was a wonderful, dreamlike sensation.*

*The door to the street opened and closed, up there in the house. The dog's head lifted, her ears perking. Joe sat up, letting her leave. A wet tongue clipped his face, and the boy laughed silently, then the dog bounded up the stairs and disappeared through the crack to the door.*

*Joe stirred the pile of chicken bones into a shape that spoke only of a dog having eaten it, and stood up. His eyes went to the cracked door. He could hear voices now. Happy voices, children and grownups... He let his curiosity win. Joe stole silently up the stairs. He laid on the top step, peering*

*through the crack under the door, listening to the family on the other side.*

*The father had just come home from his job in the Underground Market. The three children tackling him, begging for presents. The mother sweeping in, pushing them all to the kitchen. He lay still, entranced. Listening to the clatter of dishes, the hum of normal conversations, siblings squabbling, parents scolding about table manners. As they finished, he was close enough to see how much wasn't finished. How much went in the trash under the kitchen sink. How much would later go into the bin half buried in snow in the alley outside that cellar window.*

*Bedtime, with tears and laughter and changing one set of clothes for another. Even doing something with teeth, for some unearthly reason. The daughter's room lay within sight of Joe's crack. He lay still, watching wide-eyed as the father pulled the covers over the three-year-old. Listening in wonder as the mother's voice spun a lullaby of love and peace around the child.*

*A whole new world opened in front of his eyes. It slid neatly into holes in his soul, and he just barely began to understand what he longed for.*

**June 244:** *Captured by Gretta Netters, Purveyor of Inferior Peoples.*

*Nanna cackled, and Joe writhed inside. He couldn't outside. Nothing could move, everything dead to his commands. He lay in the alley, paralyzed, limp and helpless. She had poisoned his cup. Tears sprung into his eyes, his mind unable to shut out the words she had spoken to him again and again this past month, after he had slipped away from The Family's basement into the spring; too lonely to watch anymore. Too lonely to be there, but always on the outside.*

*"I'll watch out for you." "I'll be your friend." "There's nothing to fear from old Nanna." "Trust me." She said them so often. And he had wanted so badly to believe it.*

*The thump of heavy boots landed on the ground and he saw her. Gretta Netters, striding up the alley, her sinewy form moving with grace and utter ruthlessness. The woman slaver, hated and feared by all the tenants of the back allies.*

His eyes closed, the salt tears stinging as he lay still and help-less beside old Nanna's dancing feet.

**September 244:** *Sold to Valus, pawn shop owner in Kallipolis, for odd-jobbing, renting out, and venting anger.*

**February 245:** *Freedom purchased and home established by Joshua Noble.*

**October 246:** *Rescued the chimera Cobeau in the People's Kingdom.*

**November 248:** *Joshua Noble betrayed and slaughtered in the arena of the Battle Kingdom.*

**December 250:** *Met Nehemiah and Anna Hillson.*

# Chimeras

Calla stood in the shadow by the door as the last of the Shadow Fangs slipped out. The sack of coins slung over Bristle's back shifted and a single "clink" drifted into the air. Calla's eyes narrowed and Bristle's gaze darted to him, shame and a little fear wrinkling his calico face as he ducked his head. The pack leader said nothing. His eyes darted to the sign posted on the building as he pushed the massive lead door closed with one foot. Why did the Kingdom of the Wise label their treasury? It made no sense to Calla. Couldn't they smell the gold? It seeped into the air for blocks around the building to the Shadow Fangs, and none of them needed the sign.

The door clicked shut. Tomorrow the five dead guards inside and the absent gold would be noticed. Tonight, nothing looked out of the ordinary. Calla stole toward his pack, waiting for him under the shadow of a great willow. The fronds shifted in the breeze, playing a tune of their own into the darkness. The smell of his pack surrounded Calla and a lump caught in his throat. But Ydara's scent overhung it all and filled his head.

Bristle loaded the last of the sacks into the hoverer, the coins silent and still. Cobeau flung the tarp over the eighteen sacks and tucked it in with quick precision. Heard pushed the stick forward, and she rushed off into the night in a cloud of white steam, disappearing in seconds. She would take the load back to the People's Kingdom, as their instructions commanded.

The pack looked at Calla. They knew what came next. To melt into the shadows, slip away into the wild lands and stow away on a transport. This would be the eighth time the pack had done it. Sometimes it meant dead Riders, those of the transport line who found the pack huddled in their corner. But usually they made it through unnoticed.

Tonight Calla stared back at them. He didn't give the order. Ydara's hand slid into his, and hackles rose around the pack. This felt different. Something wasn't right here.

"We two don't go back," Calla rumbled. Eight pairs of eyes blinked at him. Cobeau felt his stomach drop into his large feet. He

slumped against the willow's trunk, his head hanging. "The rest of you, back, report, obey. But we stay."

"Why?" Bristle barked, agitation pouring off him. "Why now?"

"We are away," Calla answered. His hand moved, resting on Ydara's belly. "And we have new life." Cobeau's dark eyes rose, fastening on his sister-in-law. New life. His mind flew to his earliest days. To watching his mother torn from her pups, screaming and scratching, the prods firing doing nothing to stop her frantic attempts to get back to them. He had never seen her again. His mind shifted to the littermates he hadn't thought of in years, who had died, one by one through the training, with no mother to lick the wounds or weep over their dead fur. Now only four were left. He. Calla. Heala. And Hemsfer. A shudder ran through Cobeau, a ripple of anger on his face at the memory of the name, the memory of the hatred Hemsfer had for Calla. Cobeau stared into the dark around them, his brain moving in its slow, methodical, loyal way.

Hemsfer would come for them. And he would find them, despite Calla's skill.

The others melted away. In ones and twos, awkward yips and whines their only goodbyes. Calla and Ydara stood still, hand in hand under the willow. Only Cobeau still stayed.

"Go, brother," Calla rumbled.

For the first time in their lives, Cobeau squared his shoulders and defied his brother's orders. Black hair bristled as he stared at him, waiting for a response, an answer to his challenge. Calla's hair rippled with a snarl as instinct told him to take down a challenger. But his eyes met the deep brown wells of his brother's anguished look, and Ydara took a better hold on his arm. Calla's shoulders slumped. His eyes dropped and he turned into the darkness of the park. Ydara kept her hand in his as they moved off. But she looked over her shoulder as they slid into the night, and a smile shifted her blond hair and blunt nose. All for Cobeau. A sweet thank you for the support, an understanding that he cared, and loved the new life that grew.

Cobeau followed them into the night.

He never realized he was running. To him, it meant protection of his pack. Loyalty to his own. They would need him, he knew. Especially when the time came, and pups yipped and howled in hunger.

If they lived that long.

As they slipped off into the wild lands Hemsfer's hate filled face seemed to leer behind every dark shadow the moon's light picked out.

> Report: Chimera Trainer Carl Handberg to Whom It May Concern.
> Operation Dark Horse is reported as successful. The total sum of the rescued items are enclosed in the accompanying note. The pack Shadow Fangs has returned in safety.
> One small item, three missing packmembers, is being taken care of as I write.

The stars faded as Cobeau lay on his back, watching the sky. The wild lands sang around him. Birds began to wake to the morning. Clouds skittered away with the dawn's light. A smile crept over the chimera as he watched and listened. His face was thin and sallow after months surviving on what they could scrounge, constantly battling off infections from the wounds gained in hunting and defending from the other hunters. But today he felt only happiness. He could see every dawn here. Not covered by the soot and smoke of the stations, or even the great dark trees of the People's Kingdom. Here the new dawn came like laughter from the Living One. None of the chimeras had a name for the Creator. The People's Kingdom did not allow conversations about Him. But the chimeras all knew of Him. Cobeau loved the sensation of knowing He lived and held, and the chimera loved Him back for it. Out here, it felt like He spoke in every new sunrise. As if His breath rode the wind, calling Cobeau to rise too.

Cobeau gained his feet silently. Ydara and Calla lay a few yards

away, nestled together. Her belly looked swollen and large. Cobeau could see a pup moving, shifting the skin under her stained tunic. He wondered again how many curled there, waiting to see the sun. It would be soon now.

The birds stopped singing.

Cobeau's ears twitched and his nostrils flared. In one bound he was beside his brother, tapping Calla awake as he studied the area.

Calla rose like a monster of the night. Every hair bristling, his hand clutching the iron post he had found and used to bring down hundreds of monsters out here. His eyes flicked to his brother, questioning. Cobeau's huge shoulders rose in a quick shrug. But every flicker of skin, every movement of muscle, showed his tension as he turned in a slow circle. Looking for the reason the birds stopped singing. The reason he could not smell the reason.

Something was very wrong.

The woods around them filled with chimeras.

Teeth bared, they stalked out of the woods, tasers and stunners flickering with their unnatural sparks in the early dawn light. Calla and Cobeau turned back to back, slowly circling around Ydara as she stared with silent, tired eyes. They all knew the pack. The BloodLusts. Once put on someone's track, they never stopped until they dragged their victims back to their masters. Scars marred every face, ugly slashes where no hair grew. Some came as war wounds. Most came from their pack leader, from being in his way when his angry moods took him.

Hemsfer stole from the woods into Calla's clearing. Triumph twisted his red face, twitching and burning in his eyes. Behind him Heala slunk, beaten and cowed, her eyes flicking constantly between Hemsfer and his three prey.

Behind the chimeras the green of the soldiers began to peek through the foliage. Many were here. Cobeau's eyes ran around the circle. Surrounded. His eyes darted to the dart guns in the soldier's hands, the stunners held by the chimeras. They had no chance of escape. No chance of death.

A snarl rippled his face and he lunged for Hemsfer's throat.

# Lasers and Gadgets

In the early days of research, the main problems with using lasers as a weapon were the source of energy and the heat emitted by the process. It takes so much power to create a weaponized laser, the apparatus used to excite the atoms was too heavy for even a tank to carry, and handheld weapons were out of the question. Also, most of a laser's energy burns off as heat, before the laser light becomes strong enough to be useful. One more problem with the practicality of lasers was atmospheric interference. A high concentration of dust or water in the air might tamper with a laser's accuracy, bending the beam, or causing it to reflect off the atmospheric conditions.

The first two problems were finally solved by the Pylum battery. A man named Ralph Pylum, in the year 20 of the Book Base Age, discovered a battery powered by heat. It is the perfect solution for a laser weapon energy source. The Pylum battery requires an initial charge, which it uses to start the lasing process in a weapon. The laser passes through its chosen medium and begins to bounce between a complicated series of mirrors, increasing the atoms' excitement and thus the power of the laser. This is called priming. Some take more time than others to reach a weaponized level of energy, it depends on many factors, including the size of the battery and the medium chosen. But as it primes, the laser is giving off wave after wave of heat. The Pylum battery absorbs it and uses the energy. This creates a weapon which basically powers itself. If allowed to sit unused for some time the battery loses its charge and needs a "jump start" of external heat to start the lasing process. But if kept in proper order, a Pylum battery laser will provide its own energy indefinitely.

Atmospheric conditions are still an issue with some lasers, throwing off the accuracy. The lens of a laser (what the beam is finally sent through, after the energy has climbed to useful levels) as well as the lasing medium affect the accuracy. It is possible for the beams to be reflected back, or even scattered. This kind of reflection would be too weak to cause much damage, unless they landed in a person's fragile eyes. Because of this danger lasers are never to be fired without safety-dyed goggles.

## Blaster

A solid state laser employing alexandrite (an artificially grown crystal of crysoberyl), the blaster carries two Pylum batteries for maximum power. The weapon is capable of felling a wall with a prolonged shot, and can decimate enemies at a range of two miles. It is necessarily a large weapon, and most do not like it because of the weight, size, and priming time. But those who want a devastating weapon that is technically still handheld are enamored with the blaster.

Priming: 8 seconds
Health Length Without Charging: 5 weeks
Weight: 27.4 pounds
Accuracy: Excellent

## Brunhiem

The laser of choice for the Sojourner Guards, the Brunhiem is a compact liquid fiber laser. The lasing medium is optical fibers, coiled to pack more power into a weapon that is smaller, lighter, and more easily maneuverable than most of its contemporaries. The Brunhiem employs three separate packets of carefully coiled optical fibers. The packets each have access to the Pylum battery, a relatively small affair for a laser. Because of the smaller size, the Pylum does not consume all the heat created by the lasing process, and so is surrounded by a liquid coolant, running through tubes wrapped around the battery. The separate beams from the three packets combine in the reflective chamber as the weapon primes.

Priming: 3 seconds
Health Length Without Charging: 2 weeks
Weight: 9.27 pounds
Accuracy: Excellent

## Compton

A revolutionary weapon, the Compton laser is the first to utilize dark energy and matter as an energy source. Two balls of carefully fashioned Z shielding are bound next to each other in a copper fitting. Inside one is a ball of dark matter, inside the other dark energy; they are small enough as to be almost trace amounts. But when activated, a "window" is cracked between the two. Dark matter and dark energy excite each other when combined, and create what science currently sees as an inexhaustible source of energy. The gun then utilizes Compton scattering between the two balls to harvest gamma rays. The rays are fired through a crystal lens fashioned after the Krackmens' excellent design. Gamma rays are invisible to the human eye, and so most Compton guns are sold with specially dyed goggles to allow the shooter to see where his rays land. Currently thought inexhaustible, nearly unbreakable, and as small as a Ruby laser (though considerably heavier), a Compton is viewed as the best weapons breakthrough since the Pylum battery.

Priming: 0 seconds
Health Length Without Charging: Unknown
Weight: 9.4 pounds
Accuracy: Very Exceptional

## Healy

Termed by some a variation of a Brunhiem, the Healy laser is a liquid fiber laser, with the battery wrapped in liquid coolant, as the heat from the lasing process is not fully consumed by the Pylum. It contains four chambers of optical fibers. With the smaller size, and the four chambers placed directly against the Pylum battery, the priming time is excessively short, and the energy impressive especially with being emitted almost immediately.

Priming: 1.5 seconds
Health Length Without Charging: 2 weeks
Weight: 9.47 pounds
Accuracy: Excellent

## Krackmen

The Krackmen is a prepossessing weapon with its intricately crafted red carbon stock. It is a dye laser utilizing rhodamine, and the accuracy is legendary, though the priming time is a serious

drawback to the weapon.
Priming: 7 seconds
Health Length Without Charging: 1 week
Weight: 15.9 pounds
Accuracy: Exceptional

## Luttle

A dye laser, the luttle uses a gain medium of organic dye that can be switched out according to the type of beam desired. It is a fairly small, light rifle, designed to be adaptable to the particular skills and preferences of a shooter. Often the choice for young learners, as the dye can be adapted to less dangerous options. Some object to the luttle on the grounds the aiming mechanism is not as advanced as others, such as the Krackmen, but many prefer it for the size and flexibility.
Priming: 3 seconds
Health Length Without Charging: 3 weeks
Weight: 7.2 pounds
Accuracy: Moderate

## Ruby

A mass market weapon, the Ruby is a solid-state laser found in most kingdoms during the Book Base Age. It employs a synthetic ruby rod as a medium and is prized for its small size. Because of the single-handed size, the battery is necessarily smaller, making the power less effective. It creates a lethal laser shot, but only at a range of up to six feet. A popular choice for personal defense, but not optimal as an army weapon.
Priming: 4 seconds
Health Length Without Charging: 5 days
Weight: 6.3 pounds
Accuracy: Average

## PUDRE Dark Ray

The Pulsating Ultrasonic Dark Ray Emitter, or PUDRE, came

on the market ten years after the invention of the first Compton laser pistol. Observing the interaction between the dark matter and dark energy, the inventor of the PUDRE foresaw a different use than the laser; through careful experimentation he discovered how to form a localized, directed black hole effect. The ray beams a concentrated black hole, sucking anything it hits into the devastating dark force. It is capable of twisting steel and titanium, breaking diamond glass, generally wrecking anything it hits. The distance and concentration of the beam can be adjusted, its range being between six yards to twelve yards.

**Speed of Light Transportation Device - SOLTD**

A foray into new technology during the mid-200s of the Book Age, the SOLTD utilizes dark matter and dark energy to form what the inventor, Quintus Leeman, terms a space-warp bubble. Originally he was searching for a method of time travel, and speculated on the possibility of creating a time-warp bubble by the use of the black hole. Through careful experimentation he discovered there is a calm at the center of the massive force caused by mixing dark matter and energy, and it is possible to be enclosed safely in the midst of the swirling mass of a black hole by intentionally causing it. The bioelectricity of living beings is "felt out" by the black hole as it forms, and it molds itself around it. The SOLTD makes it possible to move large amounts of living things at the speed of light, if there is no break in the chain of bioelectricity within the center of the hole.

The inventor admits it was an accident that set him in history as the first SOLTD traveler. During an experiment his assistant entered, opening the specially-reinforced door. The black hole currently formed in his lab sensed a small source of other dark matter and energy and the inventor found himself displaced, suddenly in the Kingdom of the Wise quite literally crashing in on the inventor of the PUDRE, as Hyram Grange completed his work on that gadget. Leeman did not travel through time as he had originally hoped, instead he found he had moved kingdoms with almost no time involved. He was quick to see the possibilities of the SOLTD as a transportation device.

The method of programming the direction of travel took him two years to perfect, and to this day only those specially licensed to build the SOLTDs are allowed to know the intricacies of the method involved. We do know it employs small bits of dark matter and dark energy, attracted to particular places through the peculiarities of the earth's magnetism. The smaller pieces are carefully introduced to the larger pieces contained in each individual SOLTD's Z shielding balls. Through this they come to "know" each other, thus eliminating the possibility of multiple SOLTDs detecting the same pieces of matter and energy and intersecting.

The SOLTD changed the course of the Book Age, allowing those kingdoms and peoples who first attained proficiency in the gadget to gain a solid foothold over those slower to acknowledge the incredible usefulness of being able to "zap" people anywhere on the planet. To this day it marks a turning point in the technologies of mankind.

# Kingdom's Worldview

## The People's Kingdom

**Book Base**

*The Communist Manifesto*

Karl, Marx, and Engels, Fredrick. *The Communist Manifesto.* Penguin Classics; 1st edition, 2002.

**Government Structure:**

*"The history of all hitherto existing society is the history of class struggles." Pg. 1*

*"In short, the Communists everywhere support every revolutionary movement against the existing social and political order of things." Pg. 39*

The People's Kingdom exists in cycles of revolution. It is a land where all classes are to be hunted out and extinguished, leaving one glorious society where all are equal in status and ownership.

But someone still has to decide what industries the kingdom focuses on, how things are divided, deal with interactions with outside kingdoms, etc. Those who make the decisions for the kingdom are known as the Brotherhood, and they are to be a voice for the people.

But that is only the beginning of the story.

*"...their mission is to destroy all previous securities for, and insurances of, individual property." Pg. 14*

*"Capital is, therefore, not a personal, it is a social power.*

*"When, therefore, capital is converted into common property, into the property of all members of society, personal property is not thereby transformed into social property. It is only the social character of the property that is changed. It loses its class character." Pg. 19*

All income generated within the People's Kingdom goes immediately into the State fund, and is distributed to the general citizenry from there.

Not much excess income is generated, as the kingdom sits on boggy forests in the southern half where agriculture is difficult. The eastern half of the kingdom has rocky, arid flat land where industries do better than agriculture. Particularly mining, and refining of certain chemicals and specialized ore from the mines. Other distinctive means of income are not encouraged (see Art and Music). But enough funds come in from the agricultural work, factories, and mining that there are funds to be used by the citizenry.

The difficulty comes with dividing it.

*"We by no means intend to abolish this personal appropriation of the products of labour, an appropriation that is made for the maintenance and reproduction of human life, and that leaves no surplus wherewith to command the labours of others... In bourgeoisie society, living labour is but a means to increase accumulated labour. In Communist society, accumulated labour is but a means to widen, to enrich, to promote the existence of the labourer." Pg. 19*

The people never have more than the bare minimum of existence. Most citizens do not go hungry in stomach capacity. But they subsist on the cheapest and plainest of foodstuffs and never have excess for the good things which can be seen in the Tourist Quarter of the capital city, designed as an opulent front for visitors from other kingdoms. The work hours in the People's Kingdom are long (being a useful worker is highly valued within the kingdom). But the return for the work is miniscule.

Hunger can be defined in more ways than whether a belly is filled. A classless society where all is held in common and all are brothers sounds beautiful. But the people who actually work ten hour days yet gain just enough to live on, and know this will not change, are rarely satisfied with fine sayings. Discontentment runs as rampant as hunger throughout the People's Kingdom. And discontent in a land where revolution is held up as the inevitable goal of the workers automatically breeds a dangerous situation for anyone in a leadership role.

The Brotherhood inevitably end up augmenting their own danger by having access to the things their fellow citizens do not. Occasionally in the pages of history you will find a member of the

Brotherhood who lives strictly on the minimum pay the ordinary citizens get, and does not favor his own family above any other citizen. But the vast majority of those who are in the Brotherhood end by allowing higher living to creep into their lives. Things such as finer clothes, "to create the correct impression with outside dignitaries." Losing their gauntness as their larders stay full, "to have the means on hand to entertain visitors to a leader of our grand kingdom." Often their family units stay closer together than the majority of citizens (see Social Structure). There have even been several instances in the history of the People's Kingdom of a new boarding school opening in Paradise (the capital city) solely to accommodate the children of the Brotherhood.

The rest of the citizens see these instances and realize a class has arisen among what is supposed to be the one classless society in the world. Murmurs become shouts. In one afternoon, the Brotherhood and all their families are wiped out in a shower of blood and riotous laughter.

A new Brotherhood rises, usually from the leaders of the revolution with the blood still wet on their boots. But the new Brotherhood realizes after a few weeks that the eyes of their fellow workers (tired, hungry eyes, subsisting but never fully satisfied) turn to them.

And thus the cycle of the People's Kingdom goes on.

It is unlikely a Brotherhood would last more than a month without the precautions which have arisen within the kingdom. The end of the *Manifesto* offers a numbered list of what must happen for a country to become a Communist Utopia. (Pgs. 24-25)

*"1. Expropriation of property in land and application of all rents of land to public purposes.*

*2. A heavy progressive tax.*

*3. Abolition of all right of inheritance.*

*4. Confiscation of the property of all emigrants and rebels.*

*5. Centralization of credit in the hands of the State, by means of a national bank with State capital and an exclusive monopoly.*

*6. Centralization of transport in the hands of the State.*

*7. Extension of factories and instruments of production owned by the State; the bringing into cultivation of*

*wastelands, and the improvement of the soil generally in accordance with a common plan.*
*8. Equal liability of all to labour. Establishment of industrial armies, especially for agriculture.*
*9. Combination of agriculture with industry, promotion of the gradual elimination of the contradictions between town and countryside.*
*10. Free education for all children in public schools. Abolition of children's factory labour in its present form. Combination of education with industrial production, &c., &c."*

Numbers 4 and 8 are of especial importance to the Brotherhood. Any who murmur too loud are easily declared rebels. All their property, even that of bare existence, immediately becomes the property of the State. Next, these rebels have the liability (the responsibility), to work. But the Brotherhood set in place a system of State Permits; a person has to be in possession of a permit to be able to work. No one arrested or even under suspicion as a rebel may be granted a permit. All employment opportunities are strictly controlled by the State. Those who murmur too loud, or have even a slight suspicion of murmuring against their leaders, find themselves shoved out of society, into a hopeless cold place where gaining a single meal in a day becomes an impossible task. The slums of Paradise are known as the Traitor's Quarter, where people not allowed to work for their food die slowly and inexorably of pure and brutal want.

In order to see to the rebels (whose numbers grow in accordance with the number of years the same Brotherhood has been in power), the second half of number 8 on the list is employed in its full. The People's Kingdom has a large standing army, paid exclusively by the State. (Which translates in practicality to "paid by the Brotherhood.") Those discontent who speak up against the fattening of the Brotherhood as their fellow citizens remain lean quickly find a blue-coated solider at their door. A bonus is offered to anyone (soldier or citizen) who brings in a rebel, and little proof is required.

Fear runs beside the long work hours and unsatisfied bellies.

But despite the fear, despite the solitude created by the discouragement of family structures (see Social Structure), despite the listening devices and eager eyes of the soldiers, the citizens of the people kingdom still hear one word revolving in their minds. *Revolution.* Each generation or two a revolt comes, the Brotherhood is slaughtered, and a new regime begins.

Sometimes work hours are reduced, and twice in the history of the kingdom wage labor prices rose. But there is always a hunger for the good things seen in the few stores in the Opulent Quarter of the capital city. Favors can be garnered from the Brotherhood depending on those in power, and thus the fat of the land enjoyed.

But the general citizens have found gaining pay only "*for the maintenance and reproduction of human life*" in return for the heavy labors they pour into their kingdom does not satisfy.

**Incompletes and Chimeras**

*"'Undoubtedly,' it will be said... 'There are, besides, eternal truths, such as Freedom, Justice, etc., that are common to all states of society. But Communism abolishes eternal truths, it abolishes all religion, and all morality, instead of constituting them on a new basis...' The Communist revolution is the most radical rupture with traditional property relations; no wonder that its development involves the most radical rupture with traditional ideas." Pg. 24-25*

The People's Kingdom have leave to make their own moralities and justice, according to their needs. And their needs are many. Living is a constant struggle in the People's Kingdom. For those of the agricultural world striving to convince the bad ground to give its fruit, there is constant pressure to increase their yields, and the harvest is immediately taken by the Brotherhood. They work to make food, and never have more than a wheat gruel and occasional haunch of ham. For those who work steadily in the mines, refineries, and towns, they never gain more than their bare existence and live in constant fear of their neighbor's prying eyes and the patrolling army.

But the mines and refineries are the worst. There the normal troubles of the People's Kingdom exist. But added to them is the course ground which will not hold a proper brace, and allows cave-ins on a regular basis. Hundreds die every year. The

refineries produce chemicals noxious in their very basic makeup. Safety equipment is provided, but it is rare the Brotherhood has the funds for the upkeep of that equipment. Sickness develops in the hundreds, often fatal, and always debilitating. And if a person is debilitated and can no longer work, they find himself either wasting without decent care or (depending on the ruthlessness of the current Brotherhood's interpretation of the *Manifesto*) executed as no longer useful to the State.

During the first hundred years of the People's Kingdom, revolutions most often began in the mines and refineries.

The Brotherhood slowly began to allow their citizens to drift away from the harsh conditions there to the slight improvements of the cities and agricultural districts. But the main income of the People's Kingdom comes from the mining operations, and what is created in the refineries from those operations.

Then KAM declared the chimeras and incompletes non-humans. The Brotherhood immediately pricked up its ears. Here lay a source of labor that would not have the right to revolution, or even to complain of the long hours and bad conditions. These laborers would not even require minimum payment. It took a mere ten years to convert the mines and refineries into "stations," the labor wholly provided by those considered non-humans. Those without a voice to raise in complaint, and without a right to cry out at the horrors of the working conditions.

The army increased in number as the stations grew, whole detachments organized to keep the slave labor in line. Chimeras became the coveted workers, especially in the mines where physical strength was required more than intelligence. Soon the chimeras became trained even to help their fellow slaves stay in line with the People's Kingdom's goals, and the Brotherhood was content.

The general citizens do not approach the stations, and never try to learn what happens there. They consider their own lives hard enough, and do not take the effort to bother with those who are not even human.

## Art and Music

*"Modern industry has converted the little workshop of the patriarchal master into the great factory of the industrial capitalist." Pg. 10*

*"The various interests and conditions of life within the ranks of the proletariat are more and more equalized, in proportion as machinery obliterates all distinctions of labour and nearly everywhere reduces wages to the same low level." Pg. 12*

*"The middle estates, the small manufacturer, the shopkeeper, the artisan, the peasants, all these fight against the bourgeoisie, to save from extinction their existence as fractions of the middle class. They are therefore not revolutionary, but conservative. Nay more, they are reactionary, for they try to roll back the wheel of history." Pg. 13*

People with unique skills do not fit the mold of the *Manifesto's* dictums. All are supposed to be equal. Exercising a particular talent makes a person unique in a kingdom that exults the people as one whole. Someone with their own artisan shop and exceptional skills stands out from the rest of the citizenry, and that is not encouraged. And the State strictly controls all means of production, including any form of buying and selling. An artisan cannot sell their wares within the kingdom.

Art will happen in some form whether with official approval or not. Street art appears regularly, in the forms of natural chalks brought from the eastern region. No official declaration has been made on the habit, and sometimes the perpetrators are even encouraged to stray into Tourist Quarter and leave their work. Any art that strays into political areas, however, is quickly cracked down on. Therefore portraits are rarely seen, as the gaunt and angry faces of the people can easily be interpreted as a political statement, and many messages may be read in the portrait of a statesman. Most are still life or landscapes, exceptionally well done.

Music too, will happen. There are "traditional" tunes heard all over the kingdom, and they are greatly enjoyed by the people. Usually hardy, fast paced working songs to aid with the day's labor. But for the same reason portraits are rarely seen,

instrumentals are preferred within the People's Kingdom. Lyrics can be too easily interpreted with hidden meanings, meant or not, and suspicion of traitorous activity can become lethal in an instant. The exception comes when a revolution occurs; each one garners its great anthem and becomes the "song of the people" until the next revolution makes it a traitorous act to recall the lyrics.

## Science and Advancements

*"The bourgeoisie cannot exist without constantly revolutionizing the instruments of production, and thereby the relations of production, and with them the whole relations of society." Pg. 12*

*"And that union, to attain which the burghers of the Middle Ages, with their miserable highways, required centuries, the modern proletarians, thanks to railways, achieve in a few years." Pg. 12*

The *Manifesto* is not clear on its thoughts about scientific advancements. In one sense it seems as if the factories that created the proletariat are a terrible thing. But in other statements, it sounds as if the proletariat cannot be what it is without those same factories. Historically, the People's Kingdom has seen the refineries and other equipment updated with new technology as it has the funds to do so. But because of the lack of good agricultural areas within the kingdom, the limited natural resources, and the discouragement of unique companies or the development of any unique skills, there is a lack of excess money within the kingdom. It is rare they have the funds to update, and most of the equipment is outmoded.

The statement about the railways on page 12 (seen above) is clearly a good thing, however. And number 6 on the list is a statement about the State being in charge of transport lines, and that is also clearly seen as a good thing. The roadways of the People's Kingdom are kept very well, and signaling technology updated regularly.

## Army

*"National differences and antagonisms between peoples are daily more and more vanishing, owing to the development of the bourgeois... The supremacy of the proletariat will cause them to vanish still faster." Pg. 23*

*"The working men have no country. We cannot take from them what they have not got. Since the proletariat must first of all acquire political supremacy, must rise to be the national class, must constitute itself the nation, it is, so far, itself national, though not in the bourgeois sense of the word." Pg. 23*

*"Law, morality, religion, are to him so many bourgeois prejudices, behind which lurk in ambush just as many bourgeois interests." Pg. 14*

*"In one word, for exploitation, veiled by religious and political illusions, it [the bourgeois] has substituted, naked, shameless, direct, brutal exploitation." Pg. 5*

There is a strong sense of holding together as a nation within the People's Kingdom; the people *are* the nation. This thinking stems mainly from the Brotherhood's careful cultivation, however, and they find it necessary to watch their borders and limit access to the transport lines, or they lose too many citizens. It is also necessary to keep a constant watch for revolutionaries. All this requires a host of people to accomplish. It requires an army.

The army is an integral part of the People's Kingdom. The detachments assigned as Chimera Keepers and Incomplete Keepers keep the stations running to gain the main source of income for the kingdom. Outside the stations there is a constant patrol of blue coated soldiers to help search out traitors and keep the populace under control. One visitor once commented, "There is a soldier at every streetcorner. I swear every time I turned around I saw another one." One reason for this abundance of soldiery is the job itself is better than most in the kingdom. It offers a few coins more than the average job, and less suspicion attaches to a soldier on patrol than to a simple citizen.

The lack of suspicion is a trifle incongruous, however, as every revolt sees the army either standing back and watching who wins, or leaping heartily in to sweep away the current Brotherhood. It

is rare the army itself changes, no matter who runs the Brother-hood.

One constant duty of the soldiers of the People's Kingdom is to hunt out the religious. Religion is a bourgeois notion, and is not tolerated within the borders of the People's Kingdom. It sets one group of people apart from the rest, creating artificial "brothers" that are separate from the general citizens, a unique band, and it does not comply with the ideals of the *Manifesto*. It is a strange fact that no matter how many underground churches are found and stamped out, more seem to sprout within their borders.

It is rare the soldiers of the People's Kingdom go on the offensive and actively attack another kingdom. The Brotherhood usually has too much to focus on within their kingdom to bother with outside trouble.

### Social Structure

*"The bourgeoisie has subjected the country to the rule of towns. It has created enormous cities, has greatly increased the urban population as compared with the rural, and has thus rescued a considerable part of the population from the idiocy of rural life." Pg. 7*

*"9. Combination of agriculture with industry, promotion of the gradual elimination of the contradictions between town and countryside." Pg. 25*

It is unclear whether the *Manifesto* approves or disapproves of cities. The People's Kingdom has created a very distinctive agricultural area within their kingdom, and thousands of their citizens drain the bogs, till the soil, and carefully harvest what they can. It is usually enough to feed the kingdom, which is a distinct accomplishment considering the state of the soil when they began. But there is still a distinction between town and countryside within the kingdom.

Only one major city rests within the borders, however, and that is Paradise, the capital of the People's Kingdom. It is massive, filled with the flotsam of the citizens. Those who have avoided the agricultural districts, the army, or the mines and refineries find their place working amongst the industrial section of Paradise. Great factories turn out cheap goods that are exported to the rest of the world for a decent profit. Next to it sits the Boarding Quarter, where apartment houses are stacked crazily high, filled to overflowing with the factory workers. Then there is the Opulent Quarter where the Brotherhood, those they favor, and outside visitors rest. A few middle class areas straggle in between these, until, right in the center of the town, lies the rotting heart of Paradise. The Traitor's Quarter. Slums filled with those under suspicion, failed revolutionaries, people denied work visas by a whim of someone in power. Where people die in the streets everyday, in sight of the jobs and food they need to survive.

*"10. Free education for all children in public schools. Abolition of children's factory labour in its present form. Combination of education with industrial production, &c., &c."*

*"But, you will say, we destroy the most hallowed of relations, when we replace home education by social... The Communists have not invented the intervention of society in education; they do but seek to alter the character of that intervention..." Pg. 22*

*"But you communists would introduce community of women, screams the whole bourgeoisie in chorus...He has not even a suspicion that the real point aimed at is to do away with the status of women as mere instruments of production." Pg. 22*

*"Abolition of the family! Even the most radical flare up at this infamous proposal of the Communists... The bourgeois clap-trap about the family and education about the hallowed co-relation of parent and child, becomes all the more disgusting, the more, by the actions of Modern Industry, all family ties among the proletarians are rent asunder, and their children transformed into simple articles of commerce and instruments of labour." Pg. 21-22*

The *Manifesto* has a section in which it addresses the objections made against the practical application of its philosophical ideas. The authors are very careful never to state the objections are actually a correct interpretation of the Communist ideals. But they also never state they are not. This leads one to assume the quotes above (and others in the section) are actually held as tenants of the Communists. It is a historical fact that the People's

Kingdom treats the ideas found in this section as the correct way for a Communist State to operate.

Traditional families are not encouraged. Marriages do happen, and the couples usually stay married throughout their lifetimes. There is not a "community of women" as the objection fretted over, but neither are there many marriages. Women and men are encouraged to act as if everyone in the kingdom is their sister or brother, or rather (as such a philosophy plays out in reality) as independent workers making their own way through life. Children do come, in the natural state of things. Most do come in the context of marriages, to the credit of the People's Kingdom. But the children spend most of their time in the public boarding schools, and do not come to know their parents well.

The boarding schools provide decent education, and a solid basis for the type of future work a child seems most suited for. They are a combination of strict education, trade school, and social engineering. "Fitting the mold" is highly stressed in the boarding schools, and children come out proper Communists, slipping into their proper places within the kingdom. Any who may not fit the mold either come out pretending very well, or they "remain for another year," as the school officials put it.

---

# Story Land

### Book Base

*Ducky's Big Pond,* Vlanderbelt, Vera, Ducky's Big Pond. Illustrated by Laura Moler, Penguin Random House, 3466.

### Government Structure

*"I will go for a walk today. Perhaps I will find something to do." (Pg. 1)*

Let me tell you a story. There once was a man named Jarrod Talum. As he traveled along the coastline, he came to realize that people understood things differently according to their own experiences and interpretation of the world. And why not? Why should there be one thing that's true for everyone, instead of each individual having their own truths? The more he spoke to people, the more he realized that none of them really understood what he meant. This confirmed his theory that truth could only be grasped by the individual, and that it changes from person to person.

It was about this time *Ducky's Big Pond* came into Talum's hands. He flipped through the book and enjoyed the bright illustrations. Gradually he came to see the small duck's journey to find something to do as an allegorical expression of life. We are all, according to Talum, on a journey to find something to do. And the answer comes differently for each of us. Each individual sees life through their own lens. Sharing viewpoints, or "truth" as most of the world call it, is practically impossible. Even the duck in the book came under Talum's own interpretation. When the duck said, "Quack, quack," to the cat did he mean, "Chase me," or "Please look at the blue sky." The cat heard, "Chase me," but Talum heard, "Look at the blue sky." Both were true according to the different individuals who heard it.

Talum settled along the coast. Gradually others settled around him, those who either agreed with his assumption that truth changes according to each person's perception, and those who simply preferred the tropical flowers and unrestrictive kingdom.

It didn't form into an actual kingdom until a woman named Beria approached Talum with a desperate plea for help to recover her three-year-old son from her husband-turned-nasty. Talum turned to his best friend, a man named Greg. History has lost his last name, it seems everyone knew him as Greg. They also knew him for being just and brave. He listened to Beria, immediately declared that interpretation went only so far as the single individual, when it invaded other individual's lives to their hurt, intervention became necessary. He formed a posse and restored Beria's son to his mother in less than an hour.

For most, that day marks the formal creation of Story Land. Of course there are some who interpret it as other days, that is in the nature of the kingdom. But for most, Story Land formed the day the one law came into being: If one individual's interpretation causes harm to another individual, there is just cause to intervene. Of course there are thousands of interpretations of that one law,

but in the history of the kingdom we find people who are willing to draw a line and step in: those are the people keeping the kingdom functioning as a kingdom. Because of their work, social interactions are possible within Story Land. They gradually became known as the Social Workers, and they have a strict hierarchy and long work hours.

Those who term themselves in charge of Story Land, the government, change frequently. When anyone can extrapolate their own meaning from the kingdom's book, anyone can claim their own form of leadership. Usually the overthrows come by employing mercenaries from outside and the seedier elements within the kingdom. (A kingdom with only one law naturally caters to those who prefer not to follow laws.) But after the dust clears and a new form of governing comes into play, the SW is still there, and still keeps the kingdom's general structure.

## Incompletes and Chimeras

*"'What's your name?' Ducky asked the frog. But the frog just stared." (Pg. 20)*

Once there was a governor named Janet Grange. She admired KAM very much, and declared incompletes and chimeras not wholly human, and therefore not entitled to full rights. But one day she was overthrown by the Neil Family. The Neils, like the other governors of Story Land, took this portion of the book, and the strong leaning toward individualism throughout the kingdom, and choose to see incompletes and chimeras as the same as anyone else.

## Art and Music

*"When the leaf fell from the tree, it danced. Ducky watched as it swirled and spun. 'It needs music to dance to,' thought Ducky. She began to sing." (Pg. 11)*

Let me tell you about Ben Carson. Here is a man who loves music. Ben Carson lived in Story Land in the year 100 of the Book Base Age. It seemed a very significant number to him, and somehow needed marked and celebrated. His interpretation for marking the 100th year turned into the Seal Annual Music Festival, so named after his favorite animal (at that time abundant in great herds on the beaches of Story Land). Let me tell you of another individual, Ben's wife Henrietta Carson. Thanks to Henrietta's exceptional organizational and promotional skills, the SAMF quickly became a worldwide sensation. Any band stamped with the label, "SAMF Champion," can be assured of their future popularity.

Naturally, as the home of the SAMF, musicians and artists abound within the kingdom. Most of them also appreciate the "anything goes" attitude of Story Land, and settle happily within the borders.

## Science and Advancements

*"Ducky waddled on, leaving the frog, and the cat, and the leaf. The pond seemed to stretch out forever in front of her. 'Maybe it does go on forever! How do I find out?' she wondered." (Pg. 21)*

Violeta Yin loved science. She grew up longing for nothing so much as to be a scientist and help the people around her by finding new things. Story Land welcomed her ambitions, and others like her, and she enjoyed a long career in the Neil Science Hall. Some of her interpretation of the world, however, other kingdoms find it hard to agree with. Violeta loved the color violet. She loved it so much, she placed violet dye in her permanent contacts, and thereafter declared the world could only be observed in shades of purple. Another time, she published a widely read paper stating popcorn balls were overgrown atoms humans felt compelled to create, because of outside influence from the stars.

There are many similar storylines of scientists within Story Land. If a scientist has a desire for worldwide recognition, emigration to KAM or the Sojourners is the most often sought course.

## Army

*"The dog ran at Ducky, and his teeth looked very sharp. Ducky fluttered her wings and landed gently in the pond. The dog slid to a stop at the edge and stared at her. 'There you war hound,' Ducky quacked as she paddled, 'you will not eat me today.'" (Pg. 13)*

Once a Story Land governor named Wilt Umtern chose to see the world in red. The export fees had been high that season, the

coffers of the kingdom full. He used it to outfit a great army, and marched off to war. They overthrew two kingdoms before Umtern met his death at the hands of a Battle Kingdom spear, and the army dispersed with their kits.

During his lifetime Wilt Umtern expressed a great loneliness, because no one in the past or present of his kingdom seemed to adhere to his truth. It is a kindness he did not know the future. The coming governors, like those in the past, looked at the dog section of the book, and their own personal stories, and decided being the attacker is not wisdom.

There was another man named Vergal the Vicious, Wazir of the Prophet's Peace, who saw overrunning new kingdoms as his main truth. The year 92 of the BB Age saw his black army ranged against the Story Land border. The citizens decided they did not like the idea of Vergal the Vicious, and raided a local munitions plant. Vergal the Vicious was forced into retreat with only a quarter of his army left alive.

## Social Structure

*"And so Ducky arrived back at her nest. She fluffed the downy feathers and settled in for a rest, suddenly very tired. 'I suppose "having an adventure" was what I did to-day,' she said to herself. 'But I am glad I'm home.'" (Pg. 22)*

There are some interpretations which state Talum lived on the verge of insanity, and just happened on good friends and good luck. Other interpretations place him as one of the smartest leaders in history, who used a philosophy to his advantage. Whichever story you choose, Story Land sits on the best coastland for trading known to the Book Base Age. The import and export fees are usually kept low, which facilitates a great deal of movement back and forth. The busy port creates revenue for the kingdom, and lots of jobs. The high turn-around of governments combined with the heavy emphasis on individual stories fosters factories with almost no government regulations, and medium to low tax rates.

Like Frank and Myra Yeals, makers of personalized bone plants, most of the people of story land enjoy prosperity. This allows them leisure to enjoy each other, and find time to foster the things they love. Architects find a great deal of work around the country, as the citizens enjoy expressing their personal stories through their building styles.

It would take much too long to tell all the stories of the living styles, work ethics, school tactics, and religious preferences of Story Land. Just so long as no serious harm comes to someone against their will, anything is allowed. Some things are quite un-popular, such as holding to a truth that tells others their stories are untrue, or believing there is only actually one truth which ought to be applied to everyone. Usually any who do hold to view-points of that nature (completely at odds with the basic Story Land premise) merely face extreme peer pressure and dislike from their fellow citizens. But there are times the dislike becomes hatred. The lack of laws and government oversight tends to foster a criminal element in Story Land, which are always for hire: those holding fast to the belief there is only one real truth sometimes find their neighbors' hatred flare into violent action against them.

But on the whole, the social structure of Story Land can be summed up in the words, "eclectic and individualistic."

# *Recipe*
## Cinnamon Rolls

Dough:
1 ½ cups milk
2 tsp yeast
½ cup sugar
6 tbs butter
1 egg
1 tsp salt
4 ¼ cups flour

Heat milk until it is warm, but not boiling. Pour into a mixing bowl. Add yeast, sugar, and butter, and beat until butter is mostly melted. Add the egg and beat just until smooth. Beat in three cups of flour. Change to the bread dough hook, if using an electric mixer. Add the rest of the flour slowly, and knead until smooth. Let rise until doubled.

Grease a 13x9 baking dish. Punch the dough down, turn onto a lightly oiled counter, and use a rolling pin to shape into a rectangle, about a ½ inch thick. Now you're ready for the:

Filling:
1 cup brown sugar
2 ½ tbs cinnamon
½ cup butter, softened
 Optional fillers;
½ cup pecans
½ chocolate chips

Spread the softened butter over the rectangle of dough, coating it liberally as close to the edges as you can get. Sprinkle the remaining ingredients evenly over the butter.

Roll the rectangle tightly but carefully, from the long side. When finished, turn so the seem is against a cutting board. Slice into about two inch circles (depends on how thick you want your cinnamon rolls) and arrange in the buttered baking dish. It's ok to squish them together.

Bake them at 375 until golden brown, about twenty-five minutes. (Or, you can refrigerate overnight before baking, and put them in first thing in the morning for hot, fresh rolls for breakfast.)

While they are in the oven, move on to the:

Icing:
½ cup butter, softened
1 ½ cups powdered sugar
4 oz cream cheese, softened
1 tsp vanilla

Beat all ingredients together until smooth. Spread over warm cinnamon rolls, and enjoy!

# Sign Language Alphabet

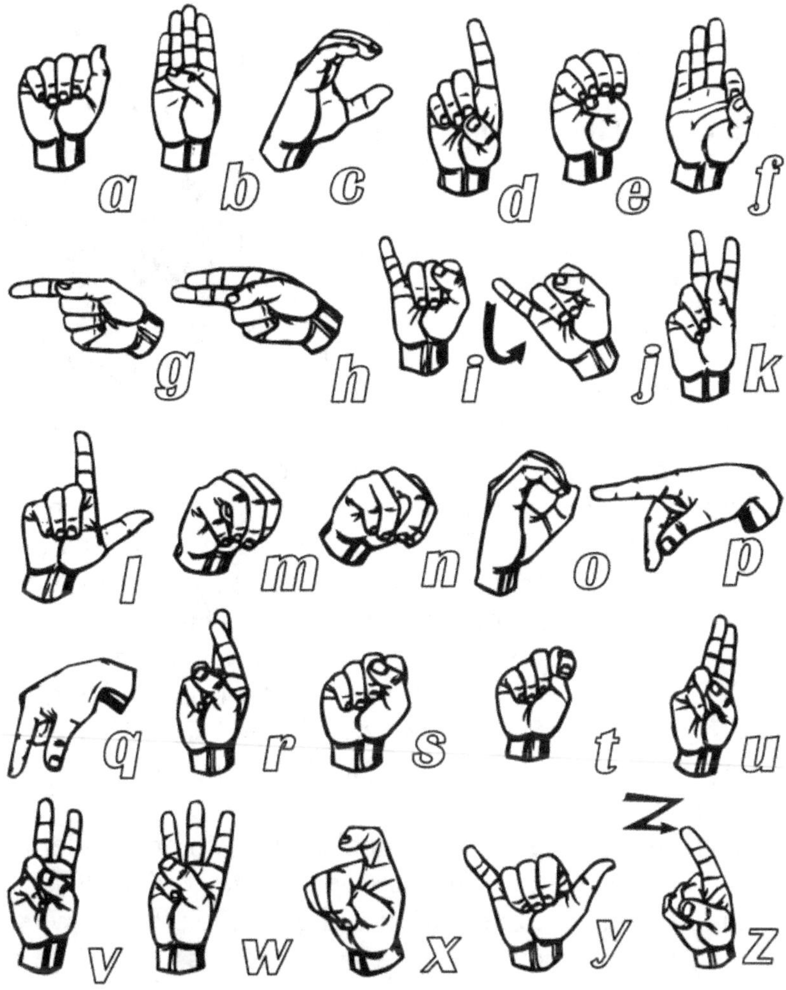

a    b    c    d    e    f

g    h    i    j    k

l    m    n    o    p

q    r    s    t    u

v    w    x    y    z

# Author Bio

Catherine Gruben Smith lives in the middle of Texas, which she begrudgingly admits is probably better than a magical tower. She grew up mostly in a dusty town in the southern New Mexican desert and will always carry the quirks. (Yes, New Mexico is a part of the United States, and no, she was not a missionary, and yes, you can drink the water.) It is her delight and privilege to be a housewife, mother, and an Earl Gray  connoisseur. Another of her constant activities is trying to keep her dogs from terrorizing the house and neighborhood with their determination to be always underfoot and hungry. (The work of a dog lover is never done.) She has always been fascinated by the written word, philosophical reasoning, and good stories of bravery and honor. When not writing, reading, chasing children or dogs, Catherine can be found board-gaming, baking, hiking, or possibly broad sword fighting with her older brother. If you want a fuller explanation of Catherine, go and read Psalm 30. The heart and purpose of her life can be found there, especially in the last two verses.

Catherine prays reading her books will help her readers find the urge to get up off the couch and serve. The Lord of all life calls us to the battlefield, to mop up the enemy after He has won the war. Don't sit on the side-lines. We have the tools to fix this broken world.

**Where to find more information, or contact Catherine:**
catherinegrubensmith.com
catherinegrubensmith@gmail.com
posttenebrasluxbooks.com

*Ravens Raid*

Books by Catherine Gruben Smith

**Sojourners:**
*Ravens Ruins*
*Ravens Rescue*
*Ravens Return*
*Ravens Refuge*
*Ravens Raid*
*Ravens Rebirth*

**Dreaded King Saga:**
*A Son Rises*
*Reign Falls*
*Knight Duty*
*Heir Raising*
*Splitting Heirs*
**Knight Jobs Series:**
*Wail of the Wyrm*

**Parabaloni:**
*The Parabaloni*
*The Slingshot Effect*
*As the Eagle Flies*
*Solitaire*
*Adele Angst*
*Blind Leader*
*Gathering Shadows*
*Black Out*

**Faerytales of Deweot:**
*How to Unmake a Dragon*
*Faery Wings and Pirate Things*

www.ingramcontent.com/pod-product-compliance
Lightning Source LLC
Chambersburg PA
CBHW060524260626
47161CB00003B/754